SALT MAGIC

HOPE LARSON ✳ REBECCA MOCK

MARGARET FERGUSON BOOKS
HOLIDAY HOUSE · NEW YORK

Margaret Ferguson Books
Text copyright © 2021 by Hope Larson
Illustrations copyright © 2021 by Rebecca Mock
Printed and bound in June 2021 at C&C Offset, Shenzhen, China.
The artwork was drawn digitally with charcoal-style and ink wash-style brushes for the
line art, and watercolor-style brush for the colors.
www.holidayhouse.com
First Edition
1 3 5 7 9 10 8 6 4 2
Library of Congress Cataloging-in-Publication Data
Names: Larson, Hope, author. | Mock, Rebecca, illustrator.
Title: Salt magic / by Hope Larson ; illustrated by Rebecca Mock.
Description: First edition. | New York : Margaret Ferguson Books, [2021]
Audience: Ages 10 to 14. | Audience: Grades 7–9. | Summary:
Twelve-year-old Vonceil Taggart, willing to risk everything to set
things right, leaves her family's Oklahoma farm in 1919 seeking the salt
witch who cast a spell that turned their spring to saltwater.
Identifiers: LCCN 2020036302 | ISBN 9780823446209 (hardcover)
Subjects: LCSH: Graphic novels. | CYAC: Graphic novels. | Adventure and
adventurers—Fiction. | Witches—Fiction. | Blessing and
cursing—Fiction. | Farm life—Oklahoma—Fiction.
Oklahoma—History—20th century—Fiction.
Classification: LCC PZ7.7.L37 Sal 2021 | DDC 741.5/973—dc23
LC record available at https://lccn.loc.gov/2020036302

ISBN: 978-0-8234-4620-9 (hardcover)
ISBN: 978-0-8234-5050-3 (paperback)

For P.J.H. —H.L.

For Kate, Lauren, Susan, Christina, Taylor,
K, Laurel, and Amy —R.M.

CONTENTS

Chapter One: Homecoming   7

Chapter Two: Old Dell   25

Chapter Three: The Lady in White   37

Chapter Four: Salt Water   53

Chapter Five: A Sacrificial Pawn   73

Chapter Six: The Lady of Sere   89

Chapter Seven: Scavengers   123

Chapter Eight: Rocky Candy   141

Chapter Nine: Hospitality   153

Chapter Ten: The Magic of Tears   173

Chapter Eleven: An Uninvited Guest   201

Chapter Twelve: About Time   221

Epilogue   227

Chapter One
Homecoming

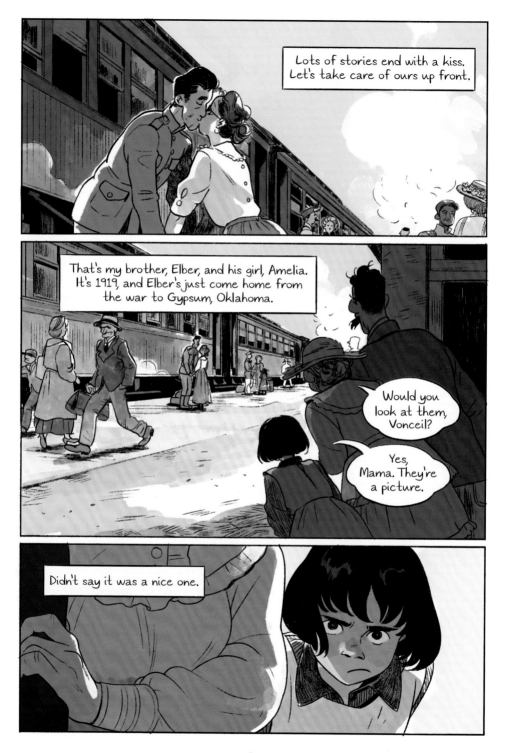

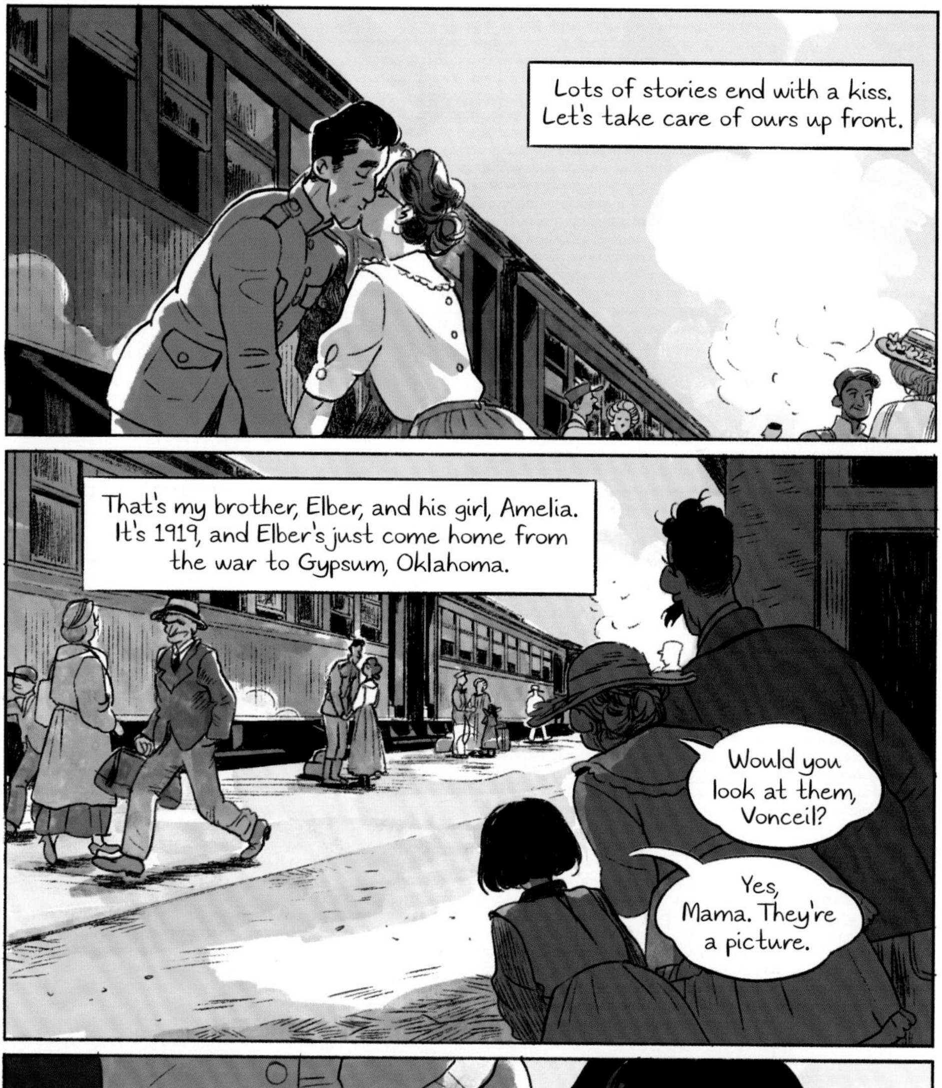
Lots of stories end with a kiss. Let's take care of ours up front.
That's my brother, Elber, and his girl, Amelia. It's 1919, and Elber's just come home from the war to Gypsum, Oklahoma.
Would you look at them, Vonceil?
Yes, Mama. They're a picture.
Didn't say it was a nice one.

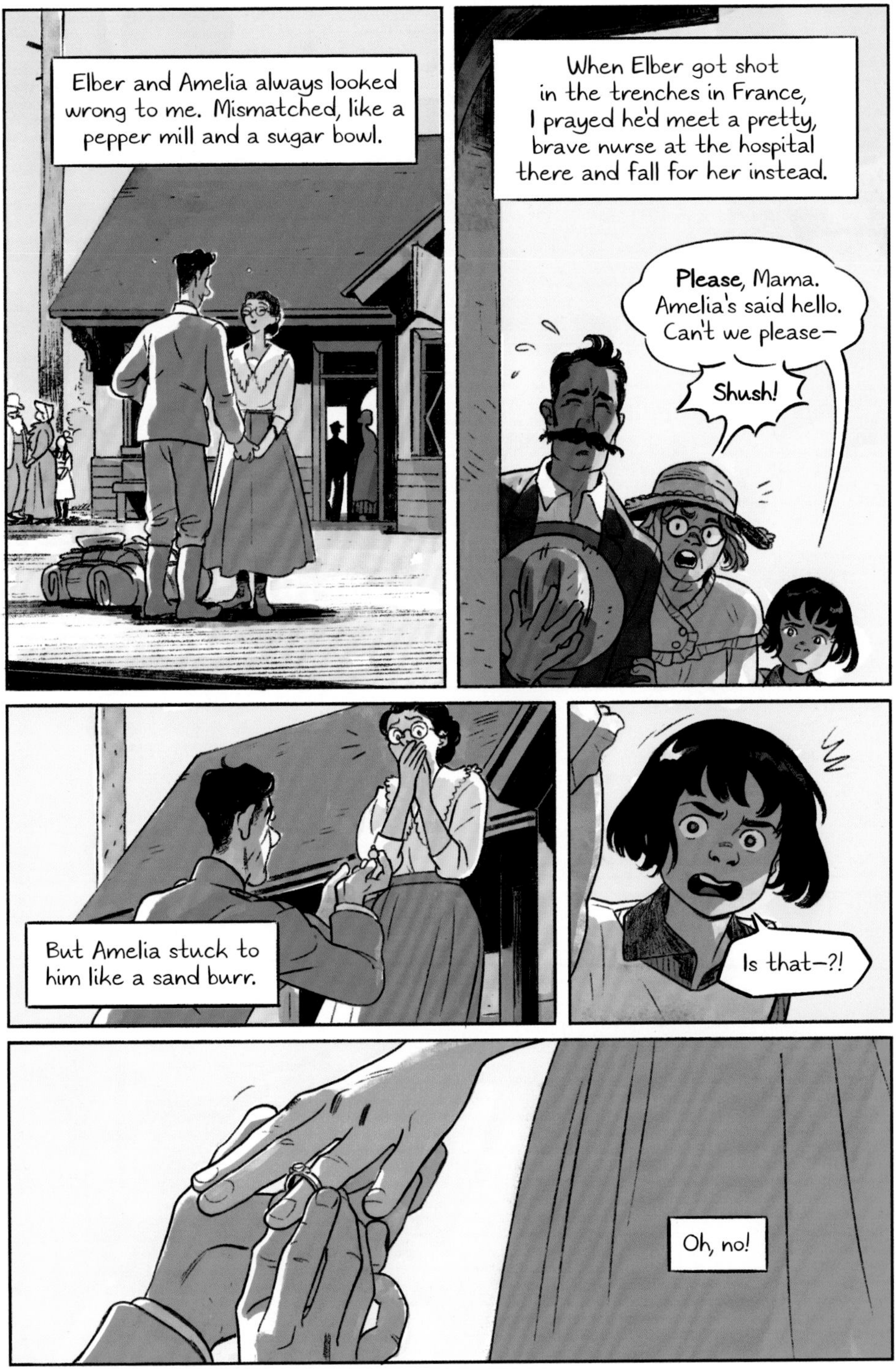
Elber and Amelia always looked wrong to me. Mismatched, like a pepper mill and a sugar bowl.
When Elber got shot in the trenches in France, I prayed he'd meet a pretty, brave nurse at the hospital there and fall for her instead.
Please, Mama. Amelia's said hello. Can't we please—
Shush!
But Amelia stuck to him like a sand burr.
Is that—?!
Oh, no!

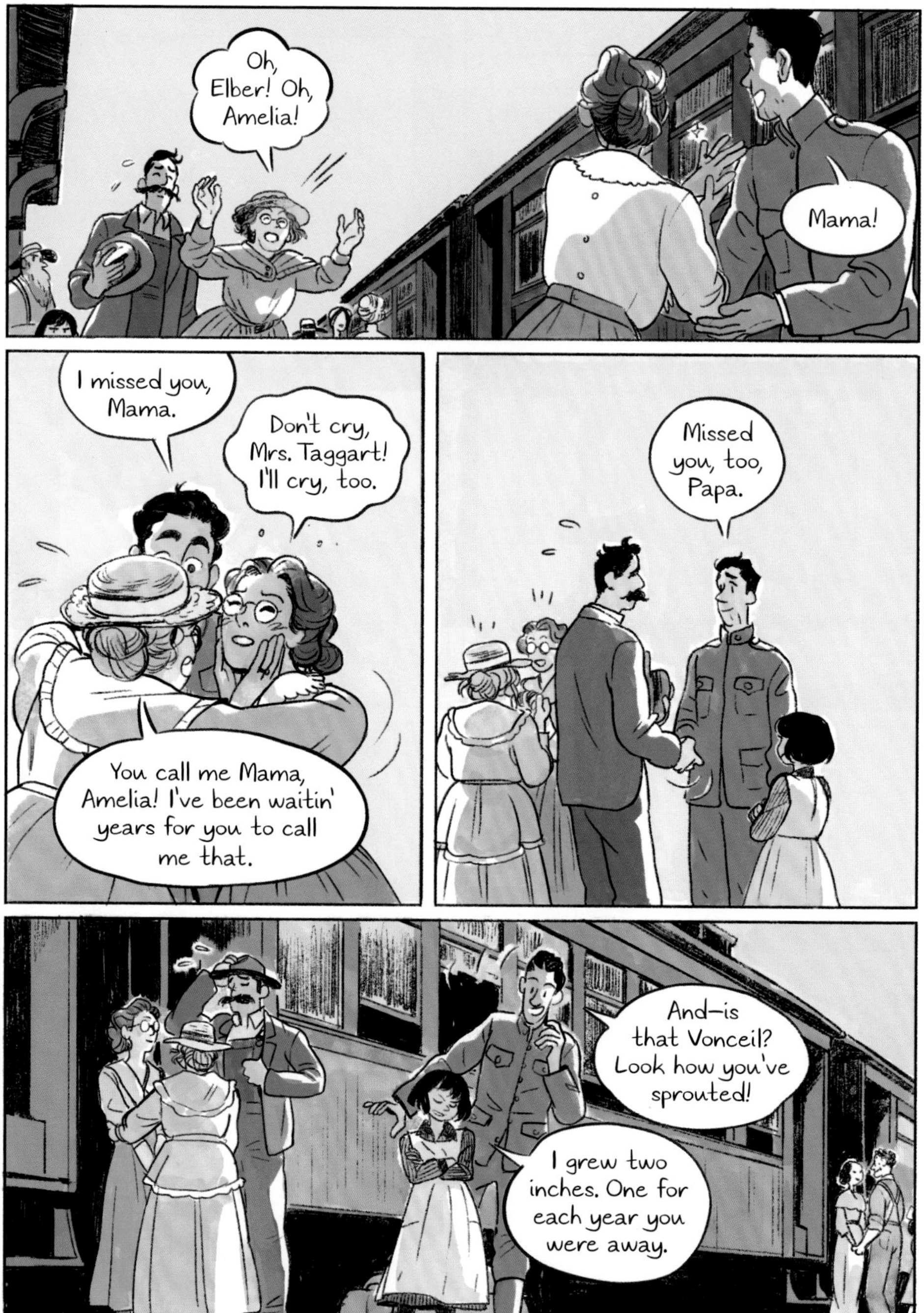
Oh, Elber! Oh, Amelia!
Mama!
I missed you, Mama.
Don't cry, Mrs. Taggart! I'll cry, too.
You call me Mama, Amelia! I've been waitin' years for you to call me that.
Missed you, too, Papa.
And—is that Vonceil? Look how you've sprouted!
I grew two inches. One for each year you were away.

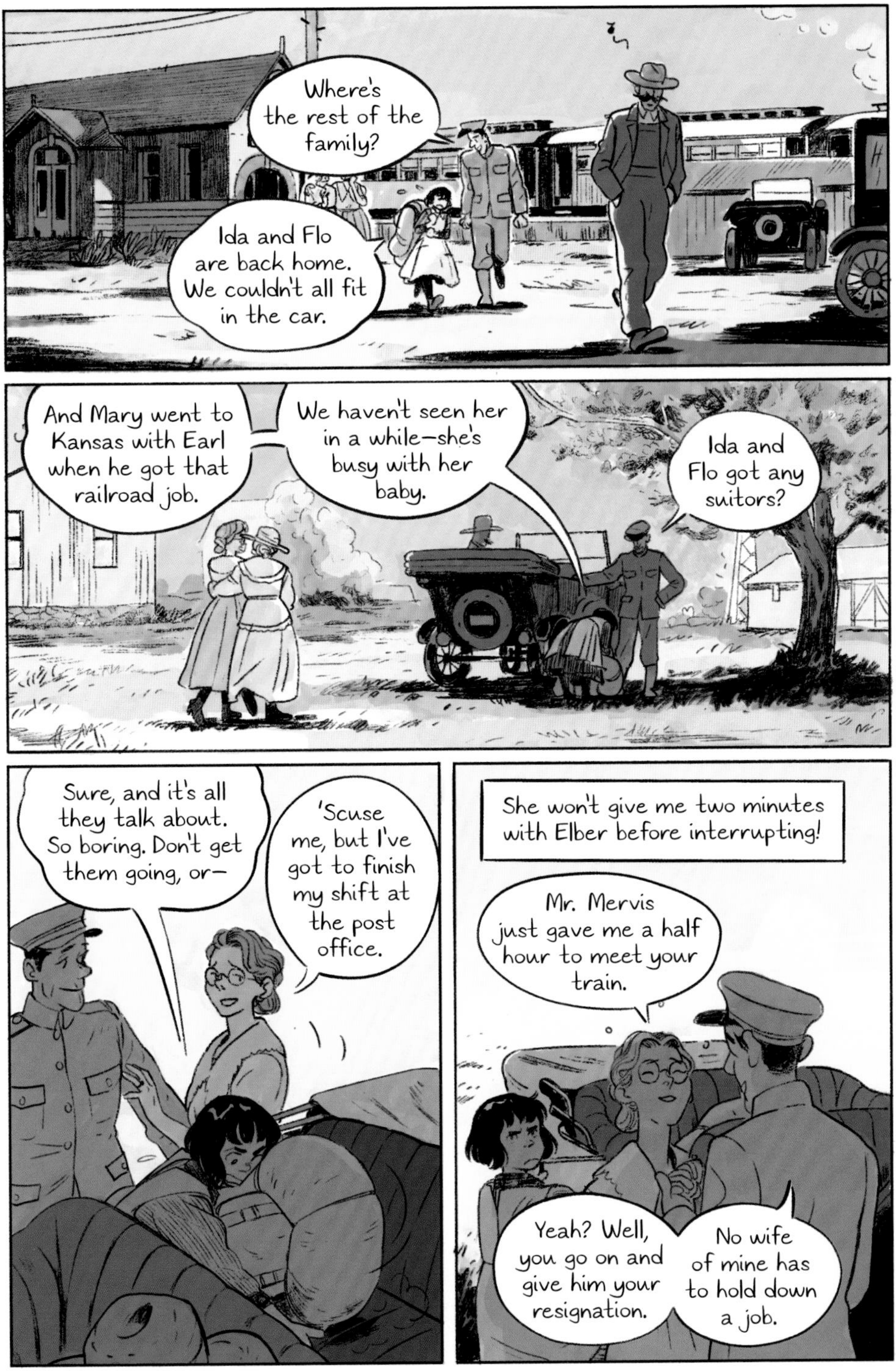
Where's the rest of the family?
Ida and Flo are back home. We couldn't all fit in the car.
And Mary went to Kansas with Earl when he got that railroad job.
We haven't seen her in a while—she's busy with her baby.
Ida and Flo got any suitors?
Sure, and it's all they talk about. So boring. Don't get them going, or—
'Scuse me, but I've got to finish my shift at the post office.
She won't give me two minutes with Elber before interrupting!
Mr. Mervis just gave me a half hour to meet your train.
Yeah? Well, you go on and give him your resignation.
No wife of mine has to hold down a job.

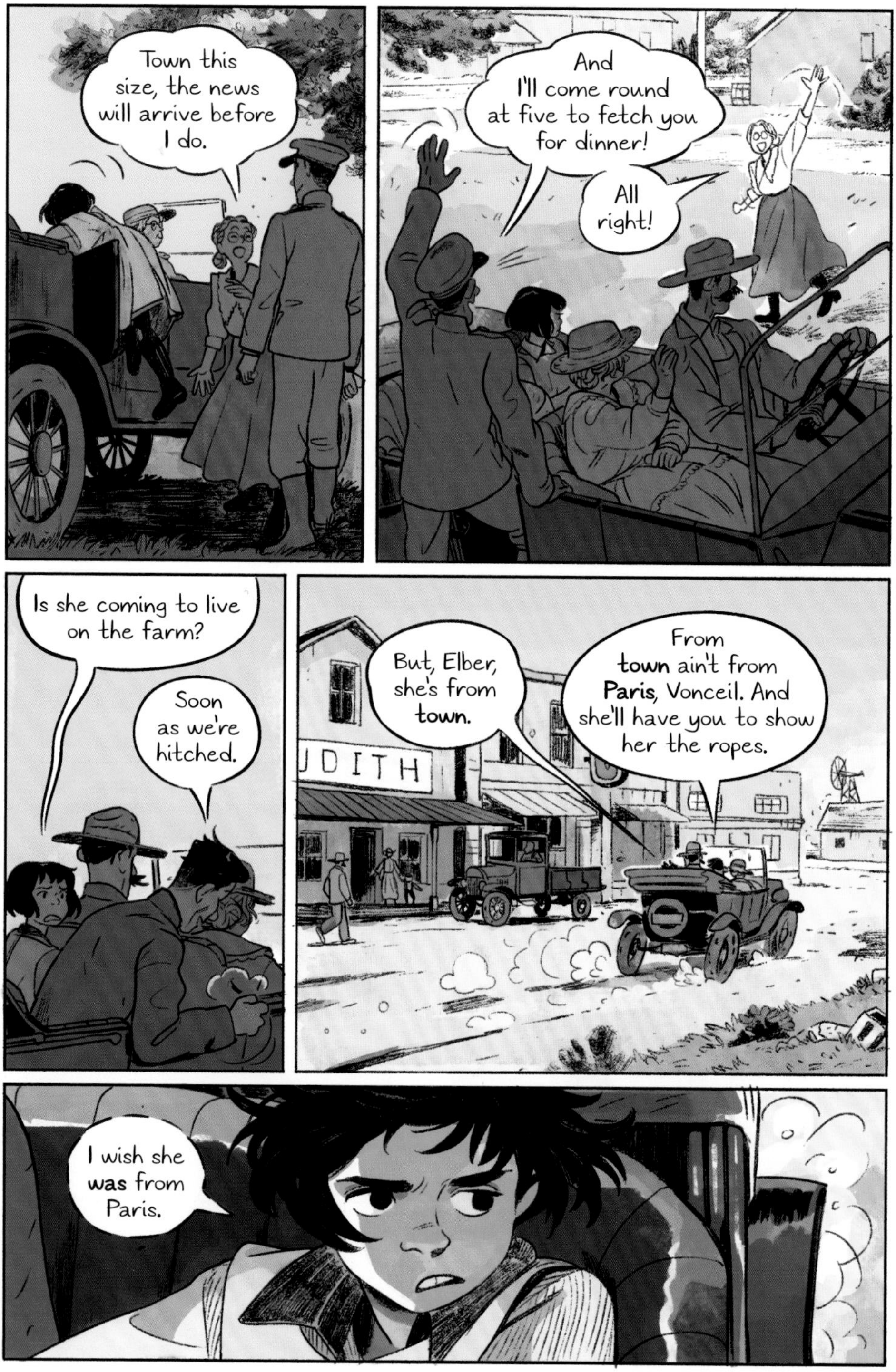
Town this size, the news will arrive before I do.
And I'll come round at five to fetch you for dinner!
All right!
Is she coming to live on the farm?
Soon as we're hitched.
But, Elber, she's from **town.**
From **town** ain't from **Paris**, Vonceil. And she'll have you to show her the ropes.
I wish she **was** from Paris.

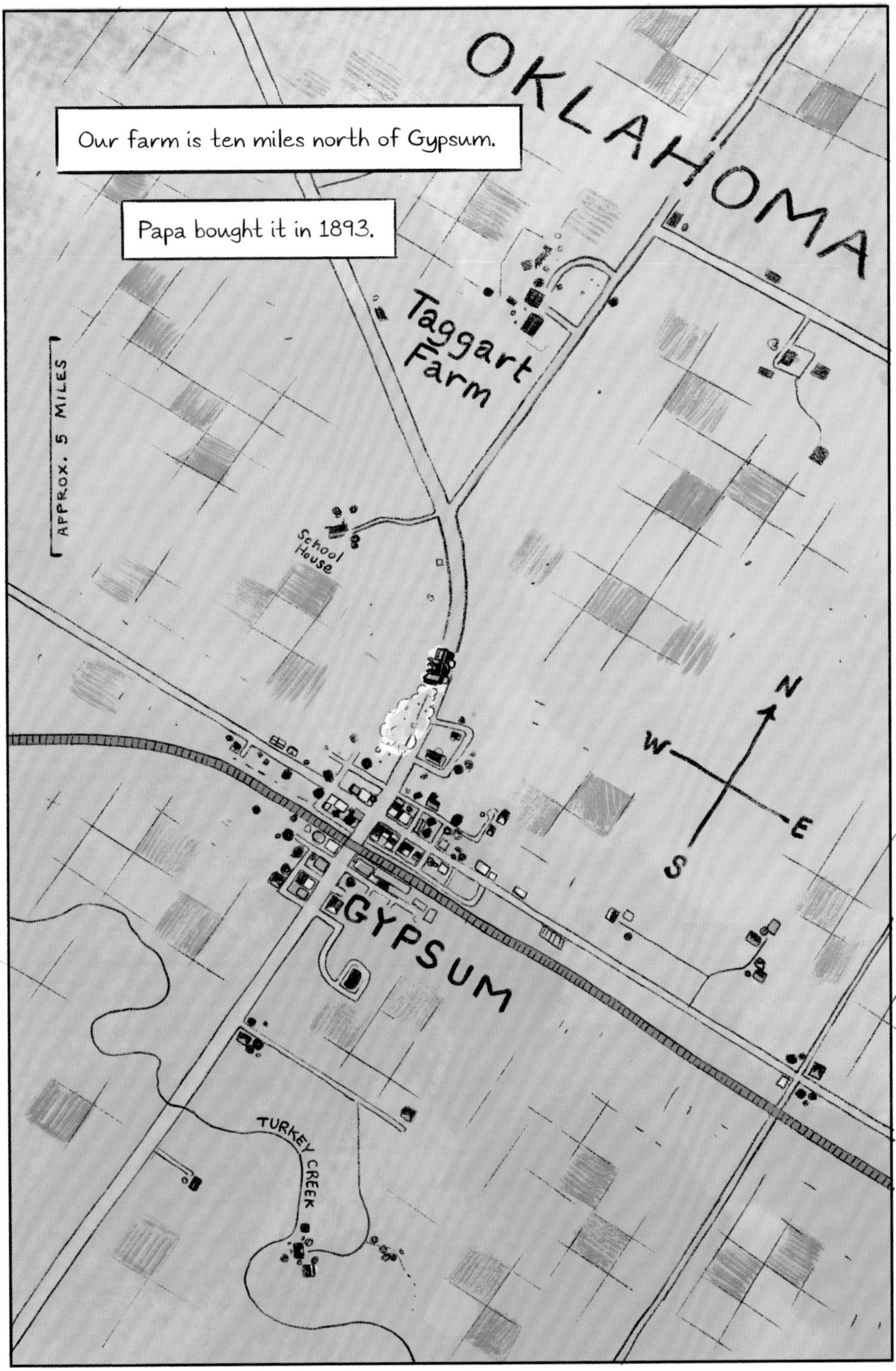
Our farm is ten miles north of Gypsum.
Papa bought it in 1893.
OKLAHOMA
Taggart Farm
APPROX. 5 MILES
School House
N
W
E
S
GYPSUM
TURKEY CREEK

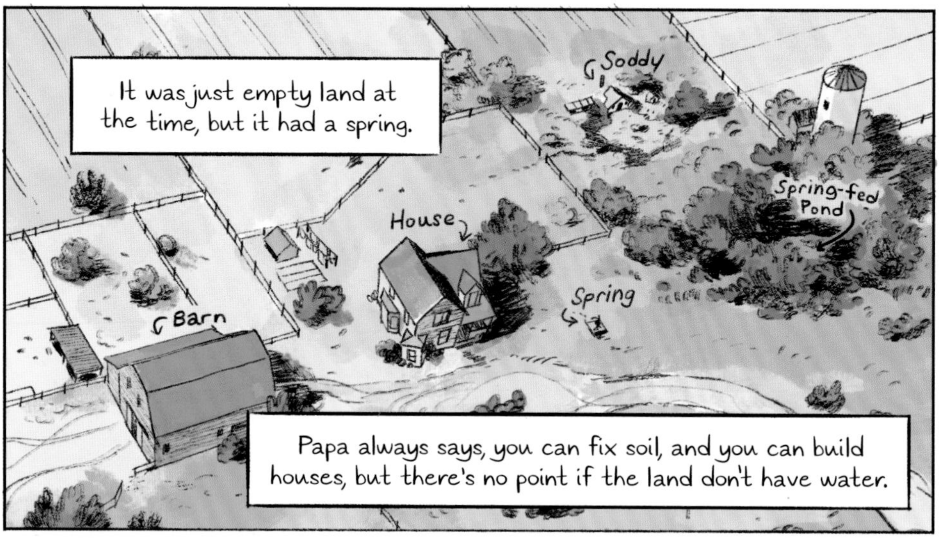
It was just empty land at the time, but it had a spring.
Soddy
Spring-fed Pond
House
Spring
Barn
Papa always says, you can fix soil, and you can build houses, but there's no point if the land don't have water.

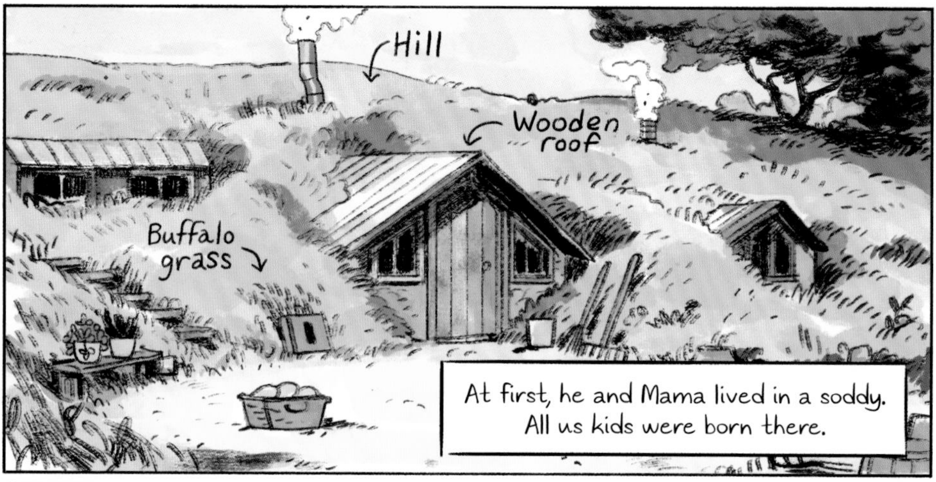
Hill
Wooden roof
Buffalo grass
At first, he and Mama lived in a soddy. All us kids were born there.

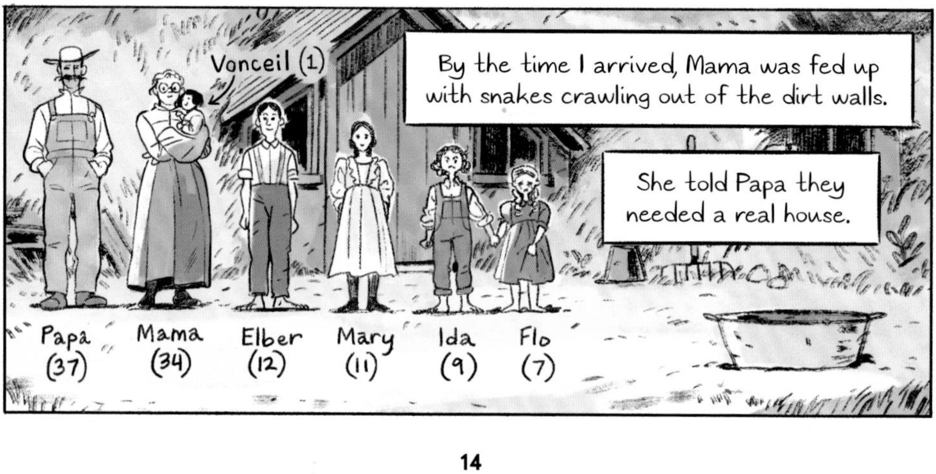
Vonceil (1)
By the time I arrived, Mama was fed up with snakes crawling out of the dirt walls.
She told Papa they needed a real house.
Papa (37)
Mama (34)
Elber (12)
Mary (11)
Ida (9)
Flo (7)

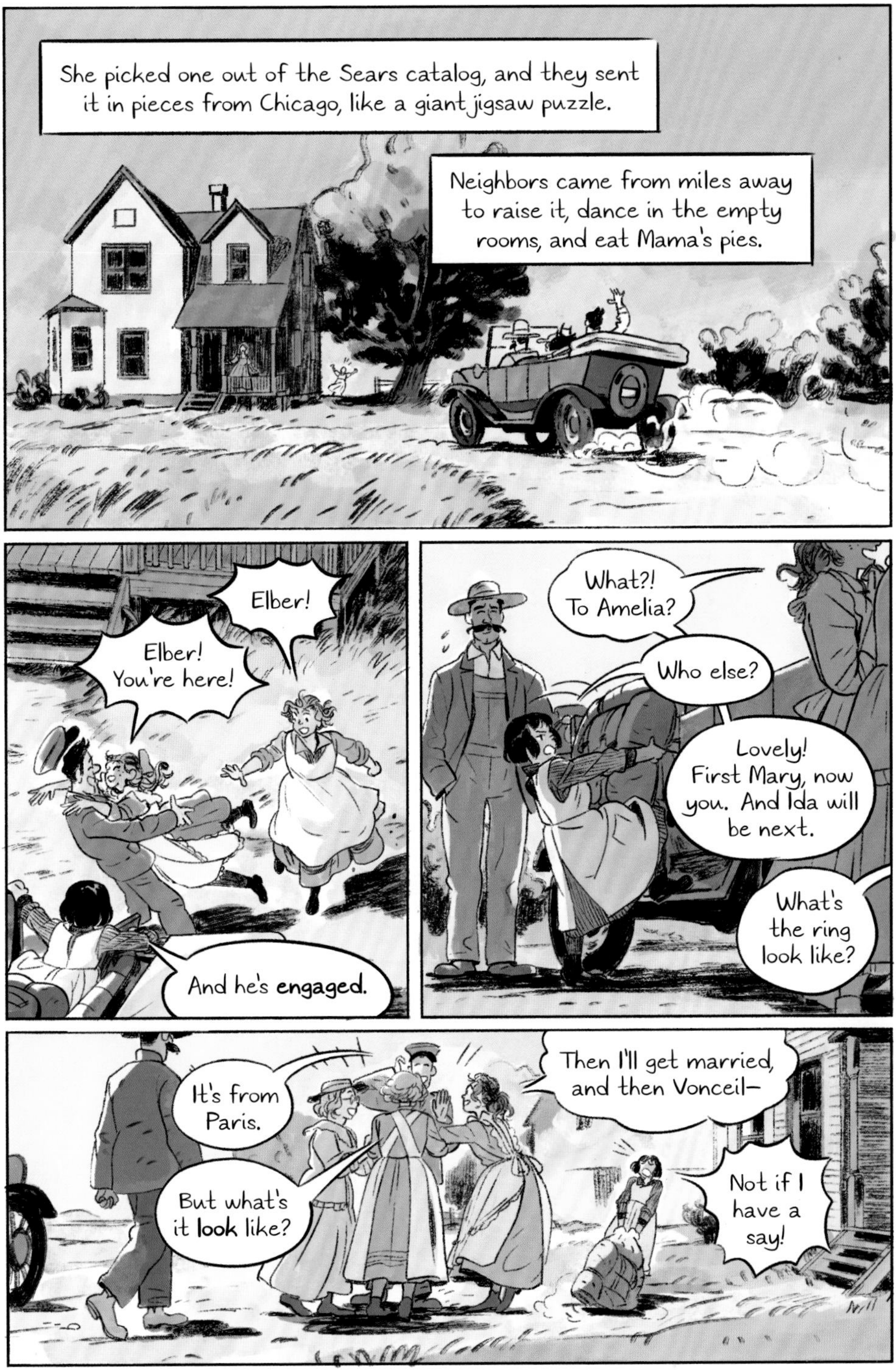

She picked one out of the Sears catalog, and they sent it in pieces from Chicago, like a giant jigsaw puzzle.
Neighbors came from miles away to raise it, dance in the empty rooms, and eat Mama's pies.
Elber!
Elber! You're here!
And he's **engaged**.
What?! To Amelia?
Who else?
Lovely! First Mary, now you. And Ida will be next.
What's the ring look like?
It's from Paris.
But what's it **look** like?
Then I'll get married, and then Vonceil—
Not if I have a say!

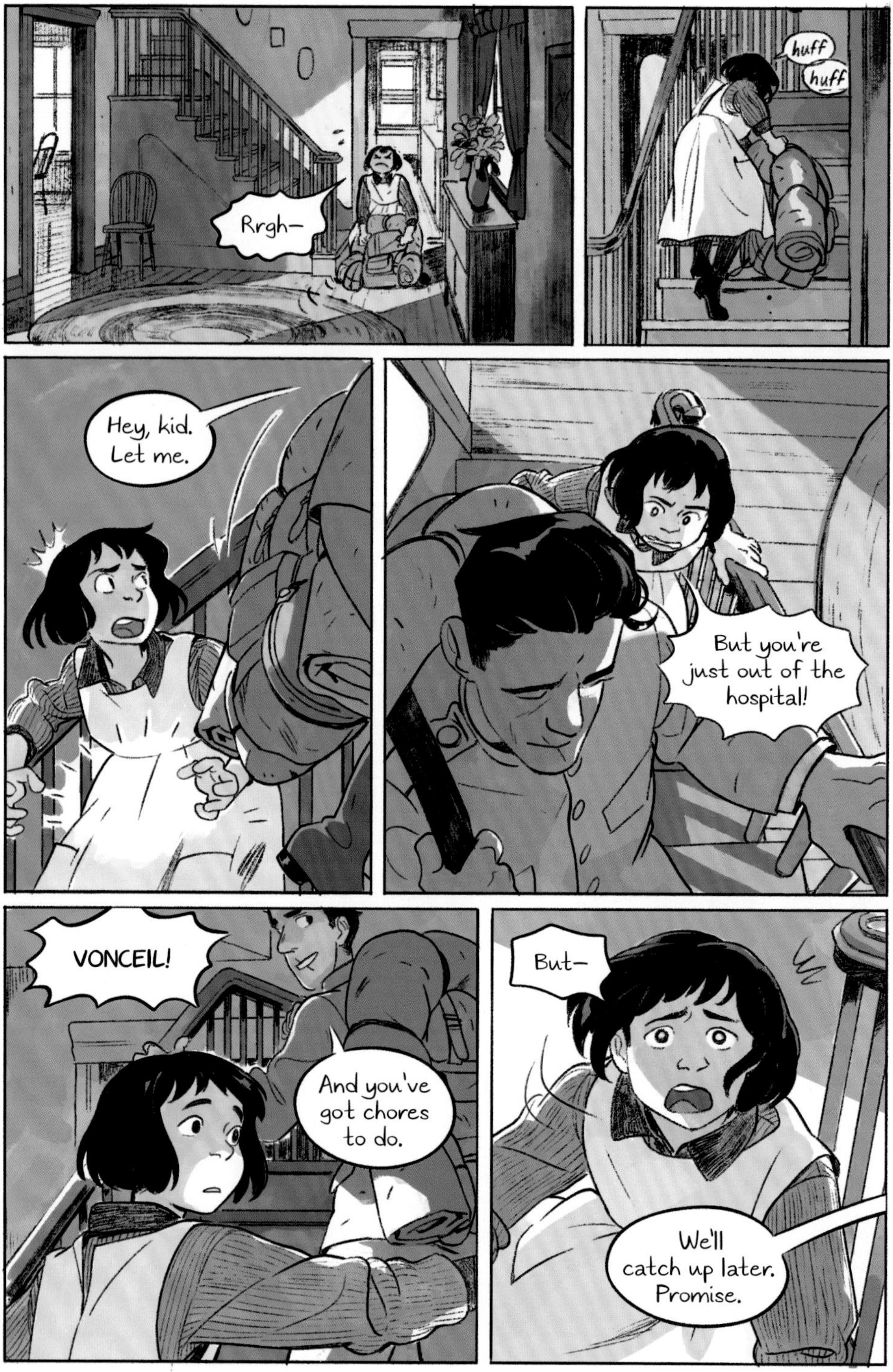
Rrgh–
huff
huff
Hey, kid.
Let me.
But you're
just out of the
hospital!
VONCEIL!
And you've
got chores
to do.
But–
We'll
catch up later.
Promise.

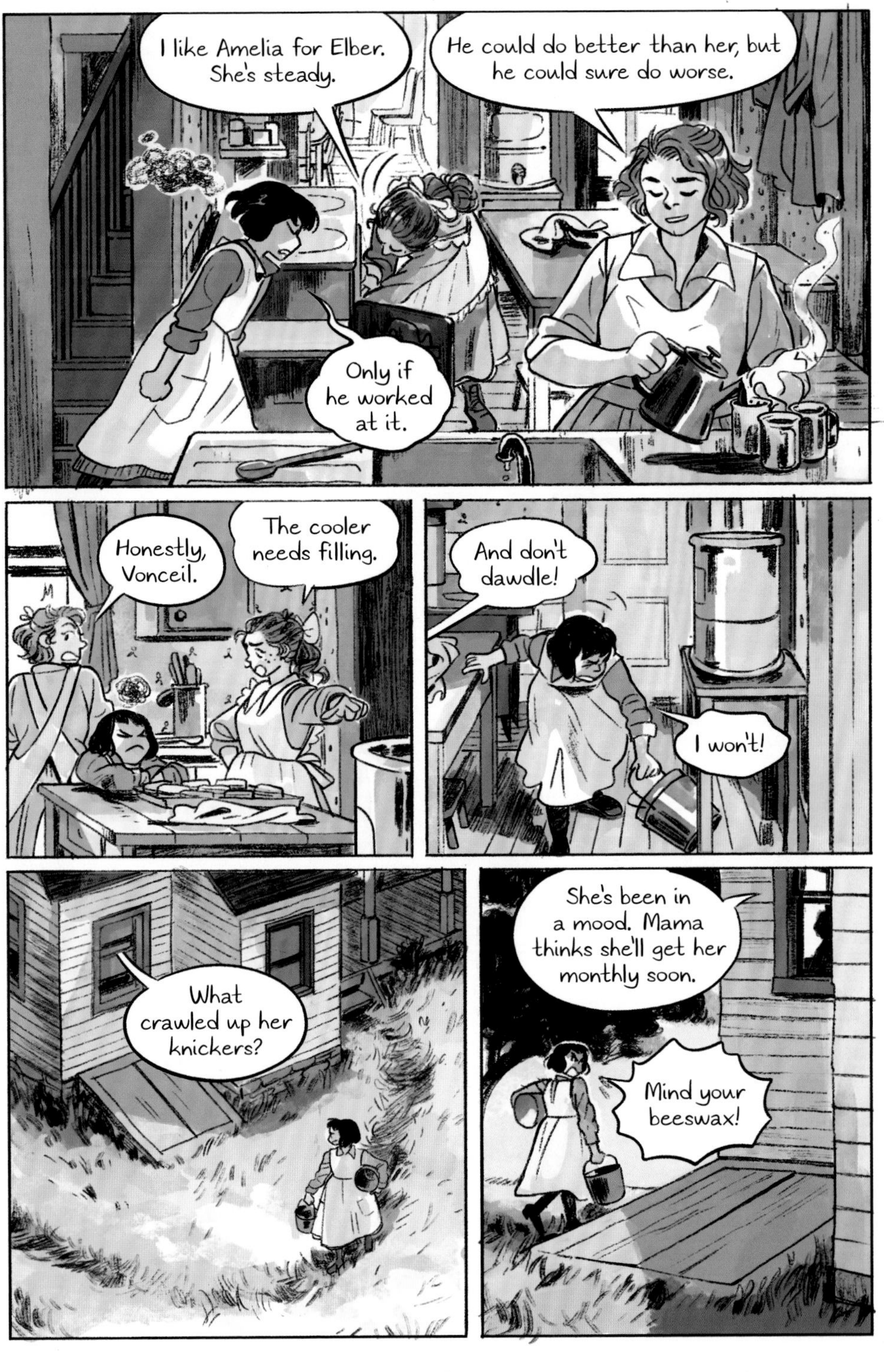
I like Amelia for Elber. She's steady.
He could do better than her, but he could sure do worse.
Only if he worked at it.
Honestly, Vonceil.
The cooler needs filling.
And don't dawdle!
I won't!
What crawled up her knickers?
She's been in a mood. Mama thinks she'll get her monthly soon.
Mind your beeswax!

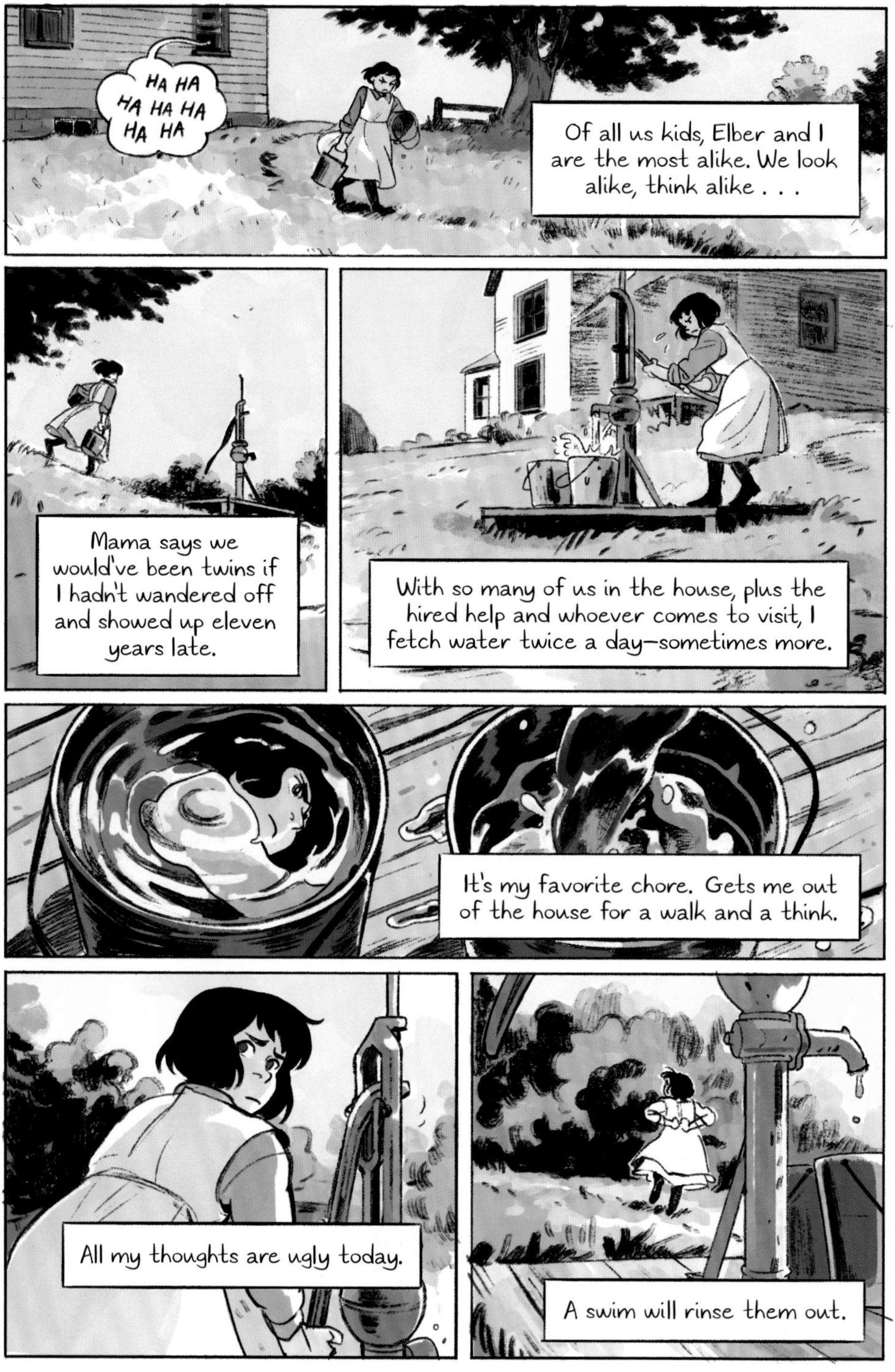
HA HA HA HA HA HA HA
Of all us kids, Elber and I are the most alike. We look alike, think alike . . .
Mama says we would've been twins if I hadn't wandered off and showed up eleven years late.
With so many of us in the house, plus the hired help and whoever comes to visit, I fetch water twice a day—sometimes more.
It's my favorite chore. Gets me out of the house for a walk and a think.
All my thoughts are ugly today.
A swim will rinse them out.

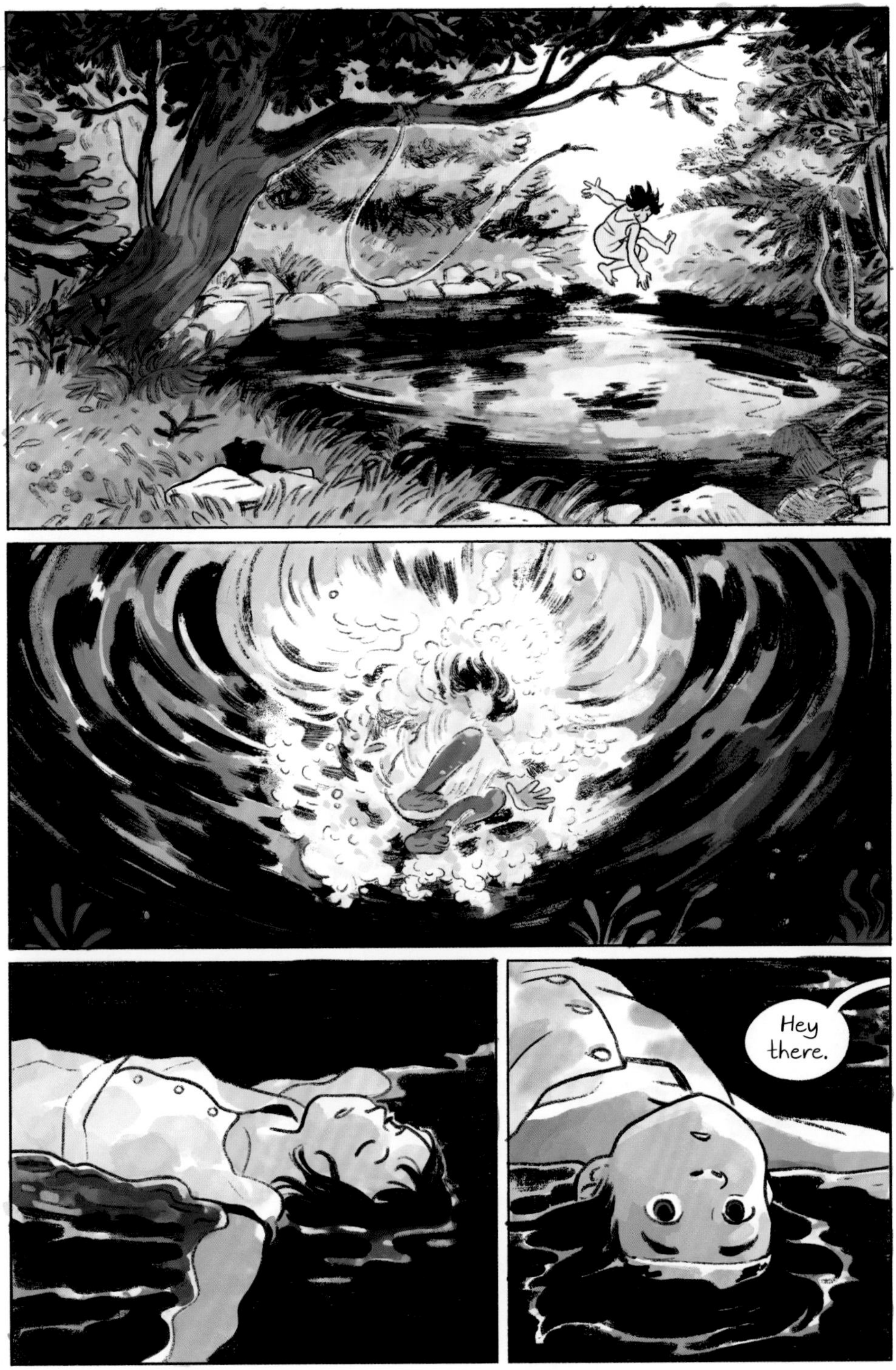
Hey there.

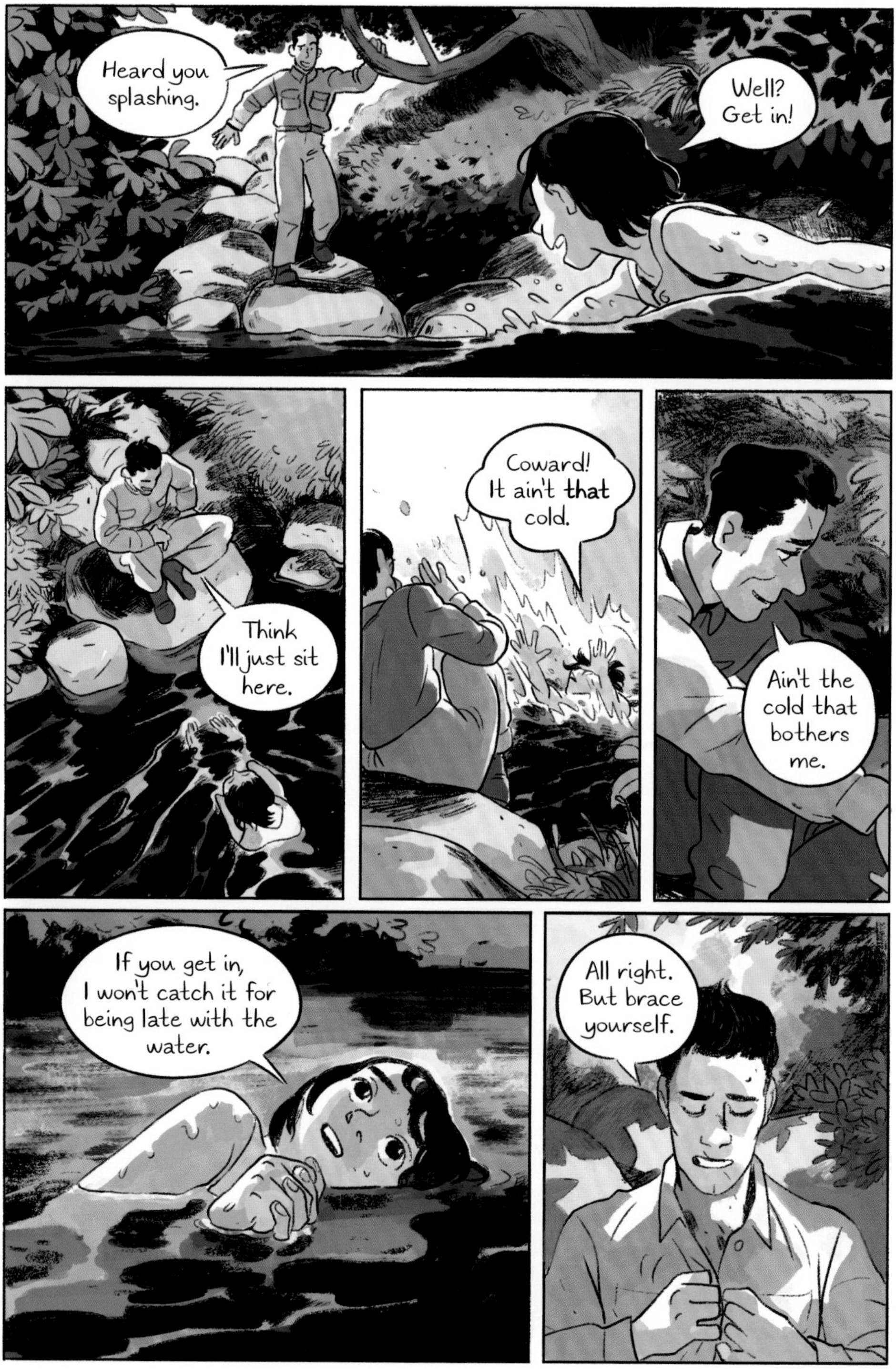
Heard you splashing.
Well? Get in!
Think I'll just sit here.
Coward! It ain't **that** cold.
Ain't the cold that bothers me.
If you get in, I won't catch it for being late with the water.
All right. But brace yourself.

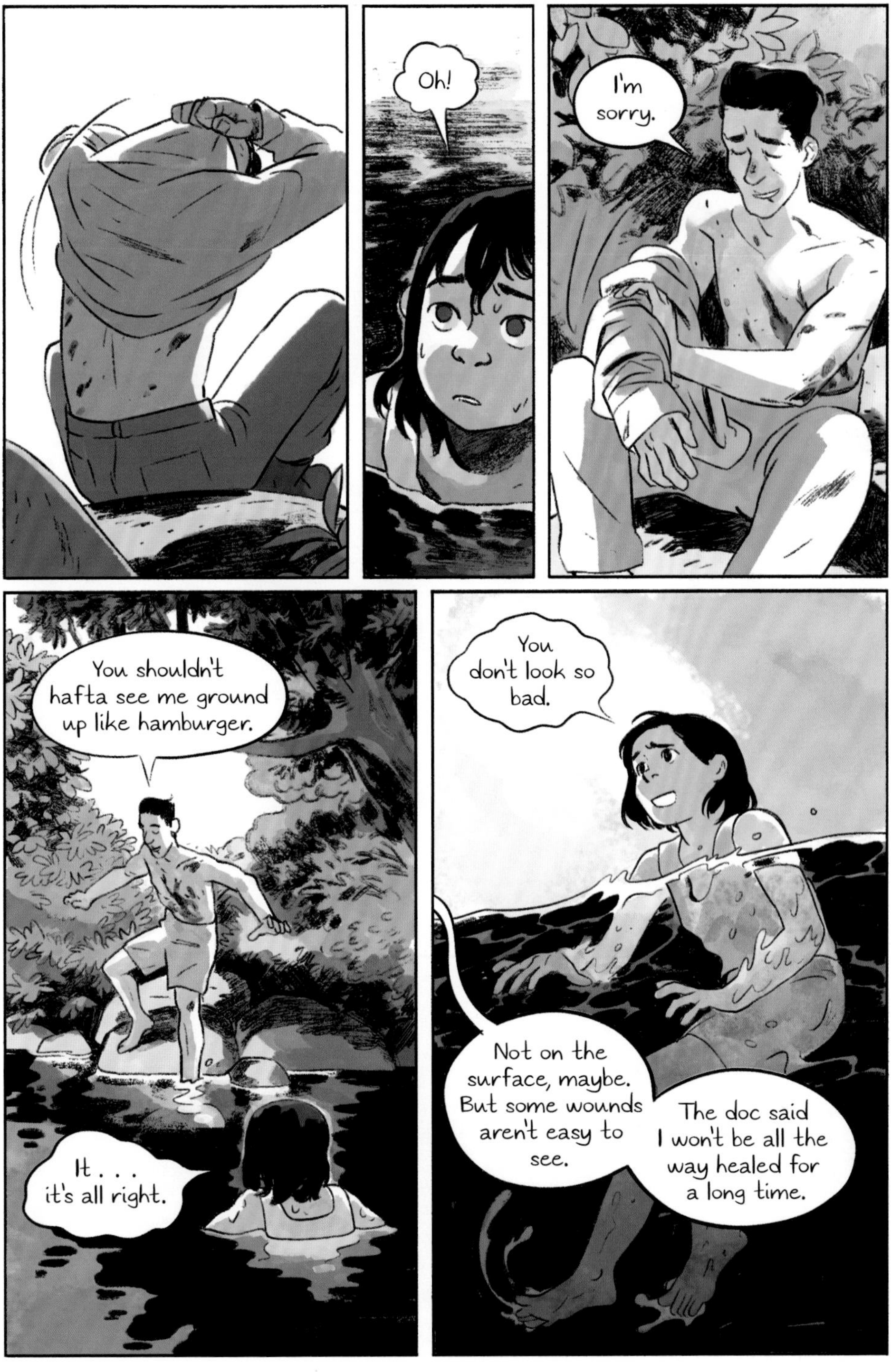
Oh!
I'm sorry.
You shouldn't hafta see me ground up like hamburger.
It . . . it's all right.
You don't look so bad.
Not on the surface, maybe. But some wounds aren't easy to see.
The doc said I won't be all the way healed for a long time.

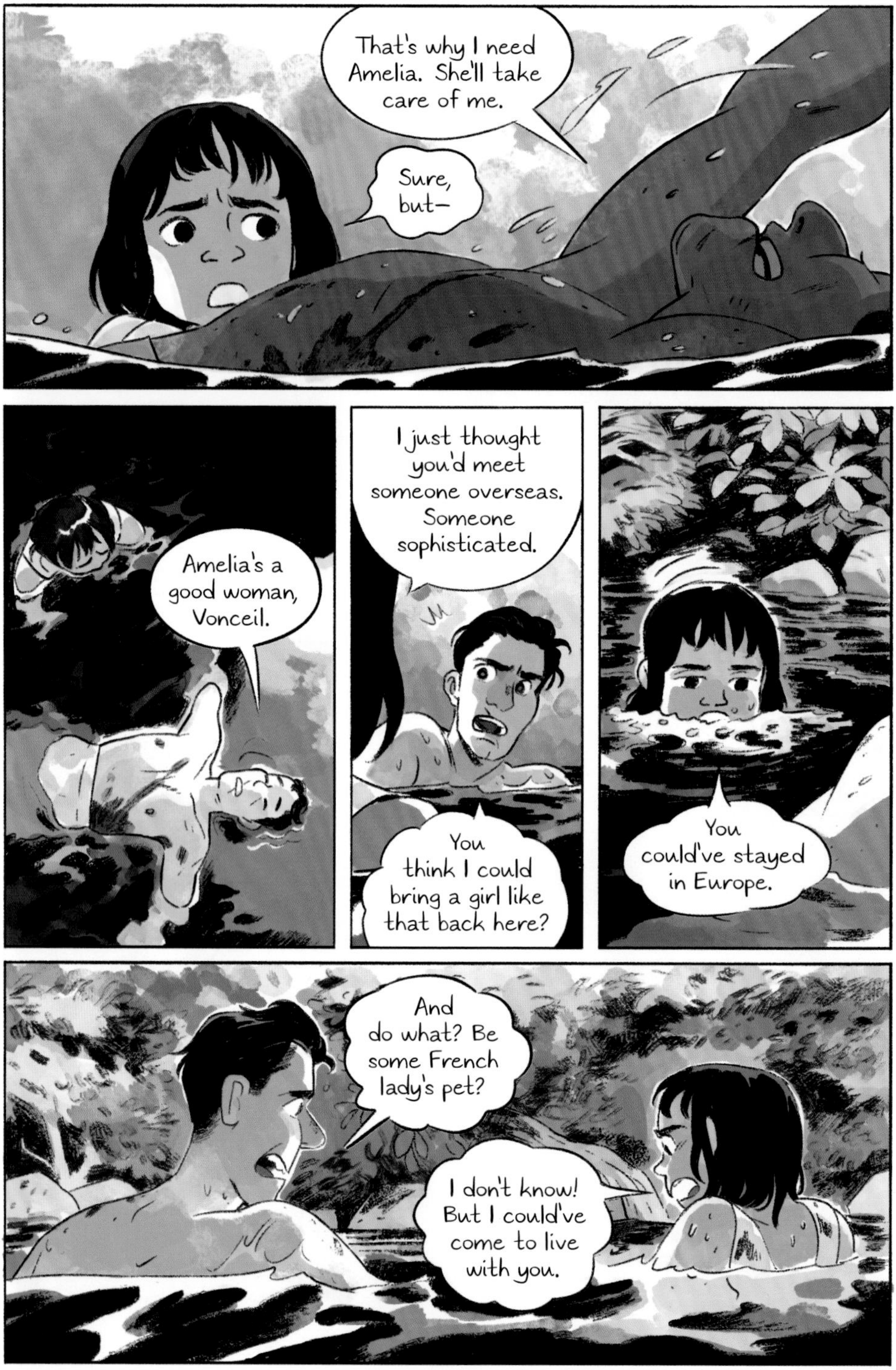
That's why I need Amelia. She'll take care of me.
Sure, but—
Amelia's a good woman, Vonceil.
I just thought you'd meet someone overseas. Someone sophisticated.
You think I could bring a girl like that back here?
You could've stayed in Europe.
And do what? Be some French lady's pet?
I don't know! But I could've come to live with you.

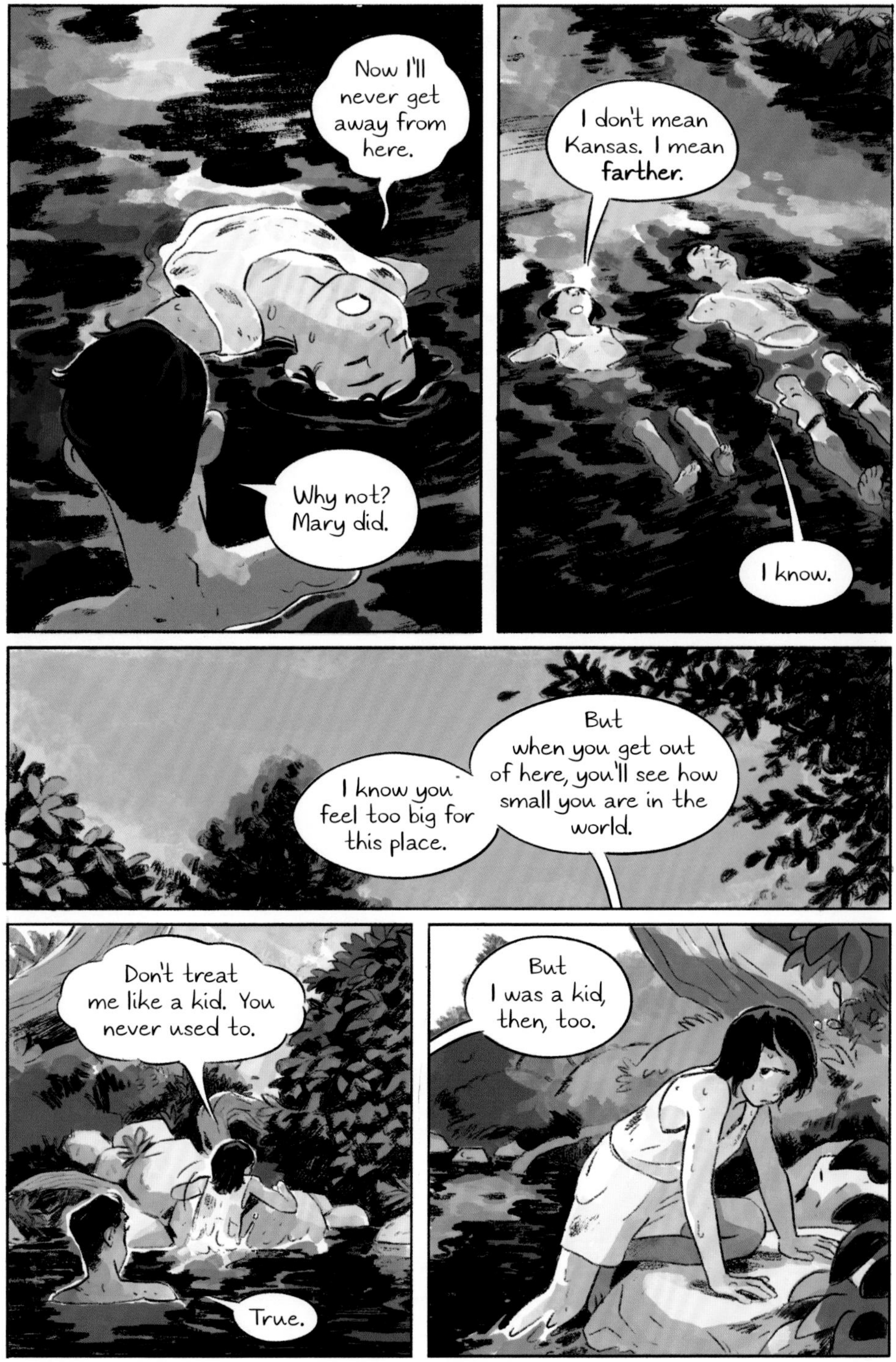
Now I'll never get away from here.
Why not? Mary did.
I don't mean Kansas. I mean **farther.**
I know.
I know you feel too big for this place.
But when you get out of here, you'll see how small you are in the world.
Don't treat me like a kid. You never used to.
True.
But I was a kid, then, too.

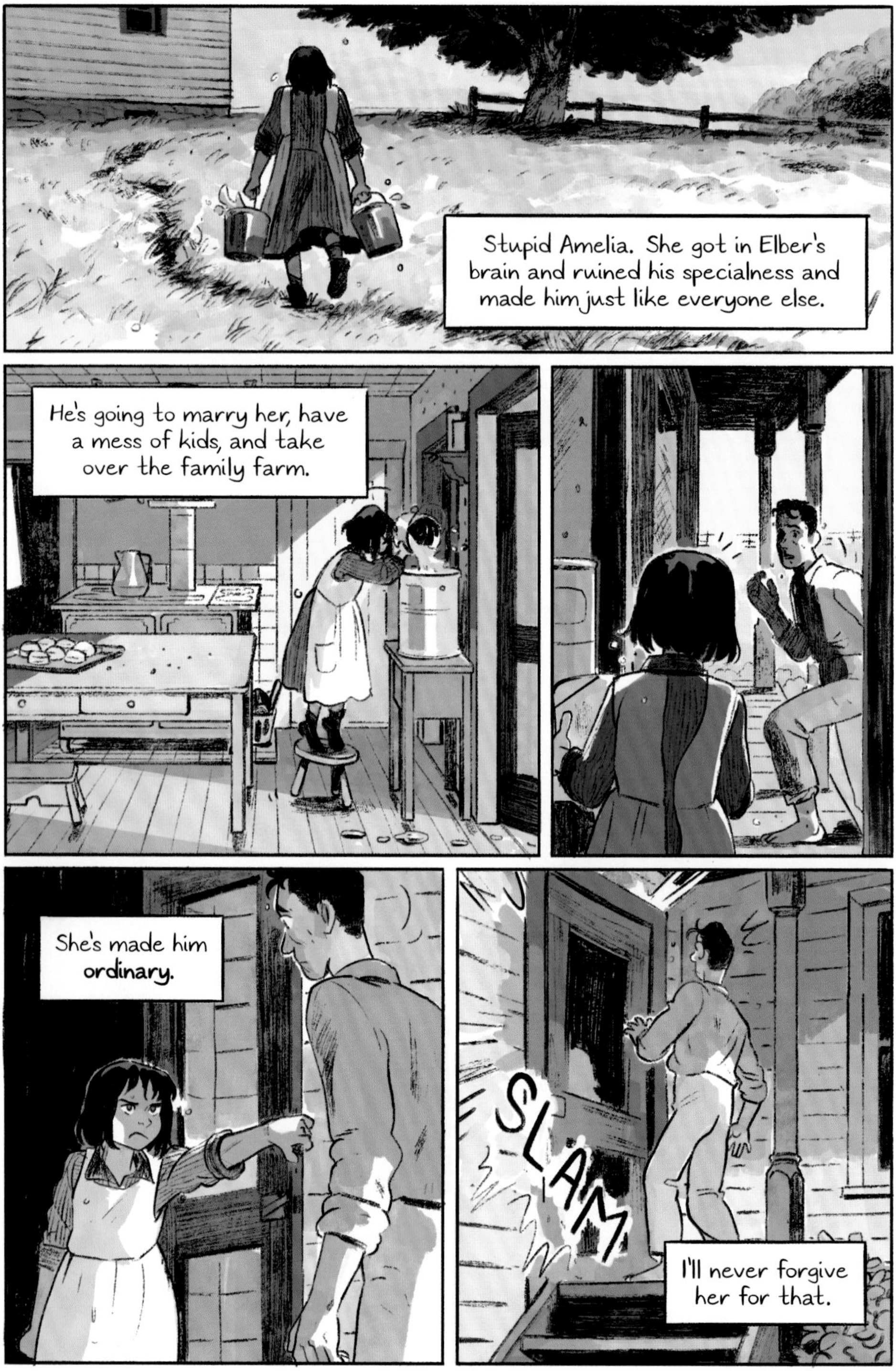
Stupid Amelia. She got in Elber's brain and ruined his specialness and made him just like everyone else.
He's going to marry her, have a mess of kids, and take over the family farm.
She's made him **ordinary.**
SLAM
I'll never forgive her for that.

Chapter Two

Old Dell

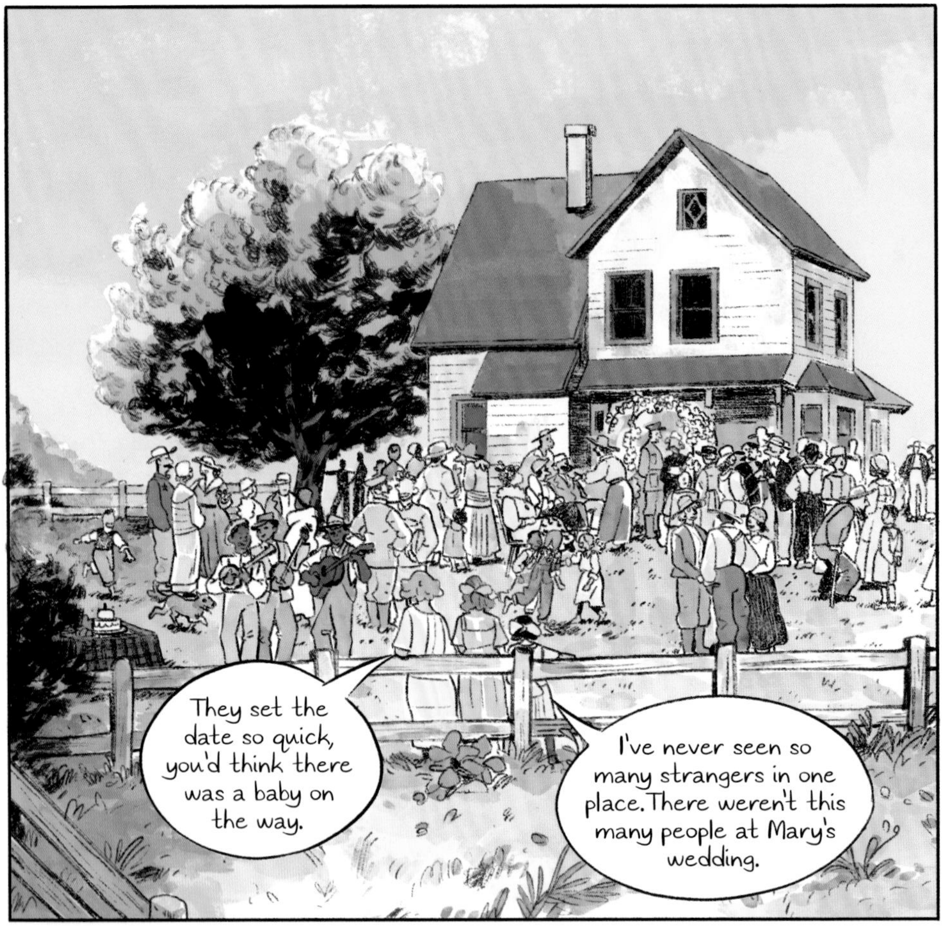
They set the date so quick, you'd think there was a baby on the way.
I've never seen so many strangers in one place. There weren't this many people at Mary's wedding.

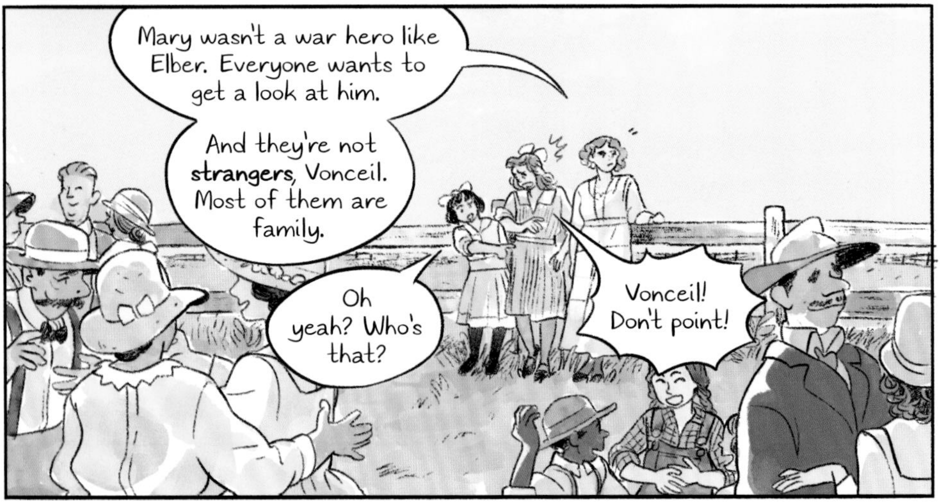
Mary wasn't a war hero like Elber. Everyone wants to get a look at him.
And they're not **strangers**, Vonceil. Most of them are family.
Oh yeah? Who's that?
Vonceil! Don't point!

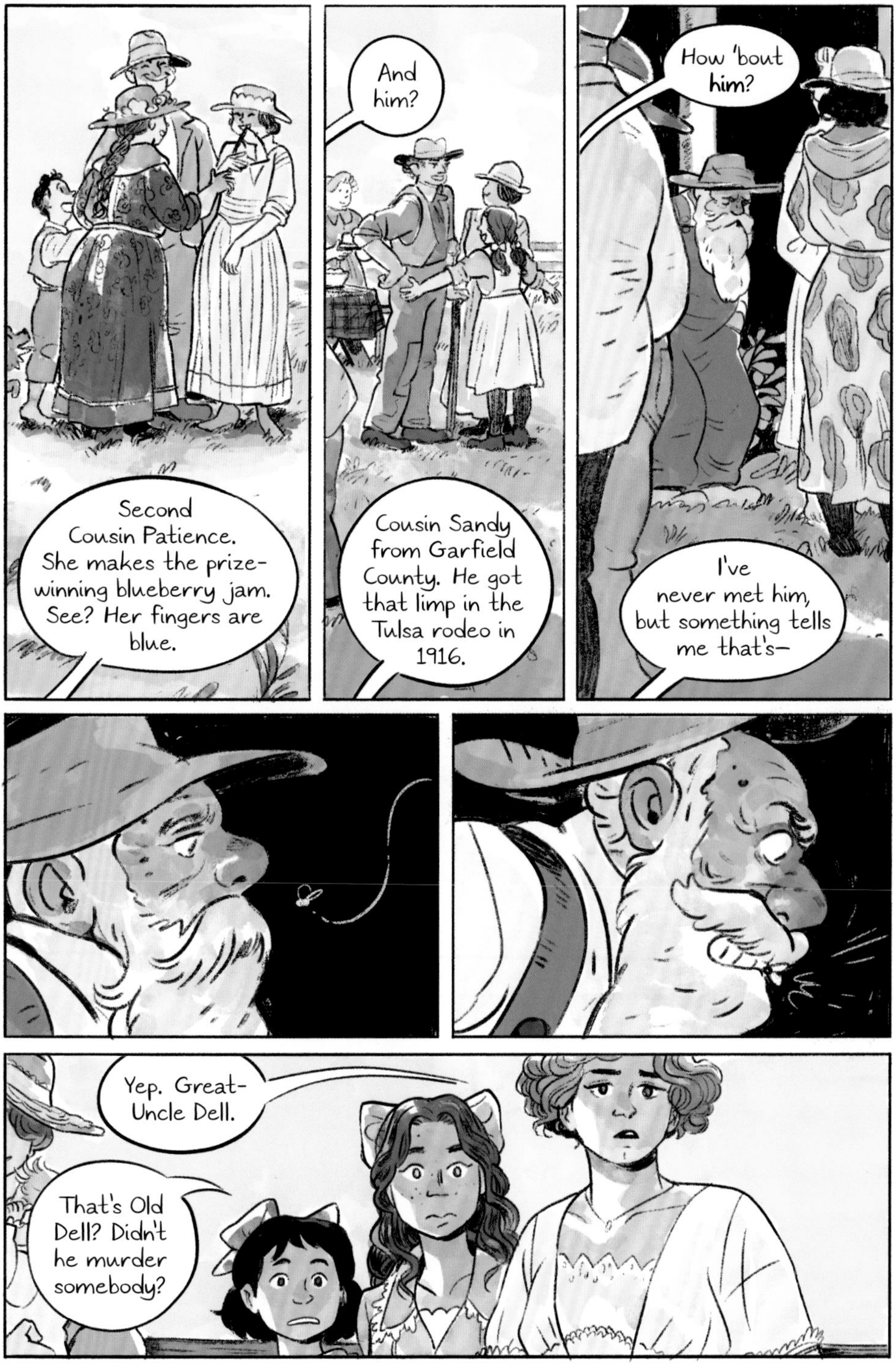
Second Cousin Patience. She makes the prize-winning blueberry jam. See? Her fingers are blue.
And him?
Cousin Sandy from Garfield County. He got that limp in the Tulsa rodeo in 1916.
How 'bout **him**?
I've never met him, but something tells me that's—
Yep. Great-Uncle Dell.
That's Old Dell? Didn't he murder somebody?

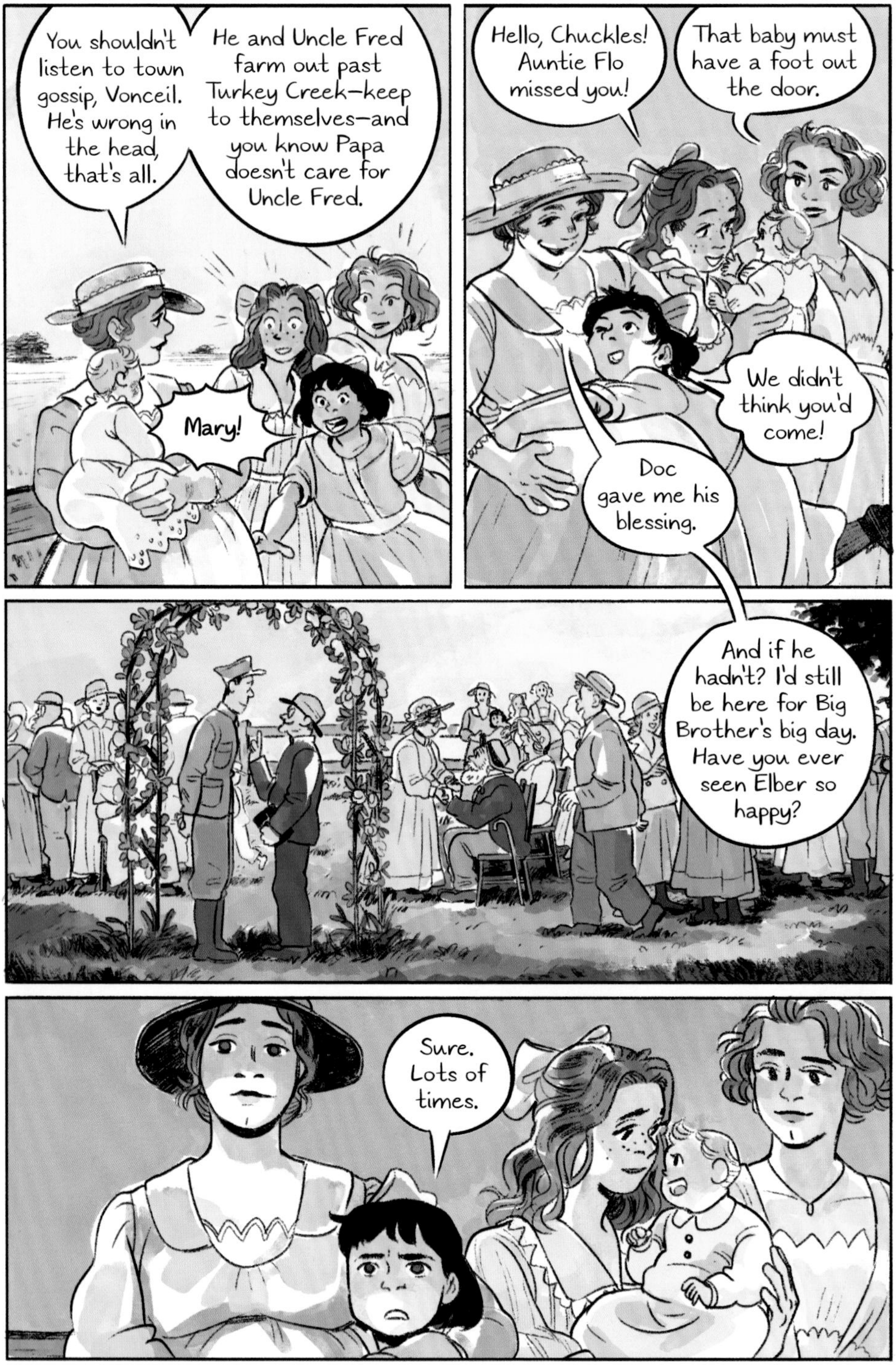
You shouldn't listen to town gossip, Vonceil. He's wrong in the head, that's all.
He and Uncle Fred farm out past Turkey Creek—keep to themselves—and you know Papa doesn't care for Uncle Fred.
Mary!
Hello, Chuckles! Auntie Flo missed you!
That baby must have a foot out the door.
We didn't think you'd come!
Doc gave me his blessing.
And if he hadn't? I'd still be here for Big Brother's big day. Have you ever seen Elber so happy?
Sure. Lots of times.

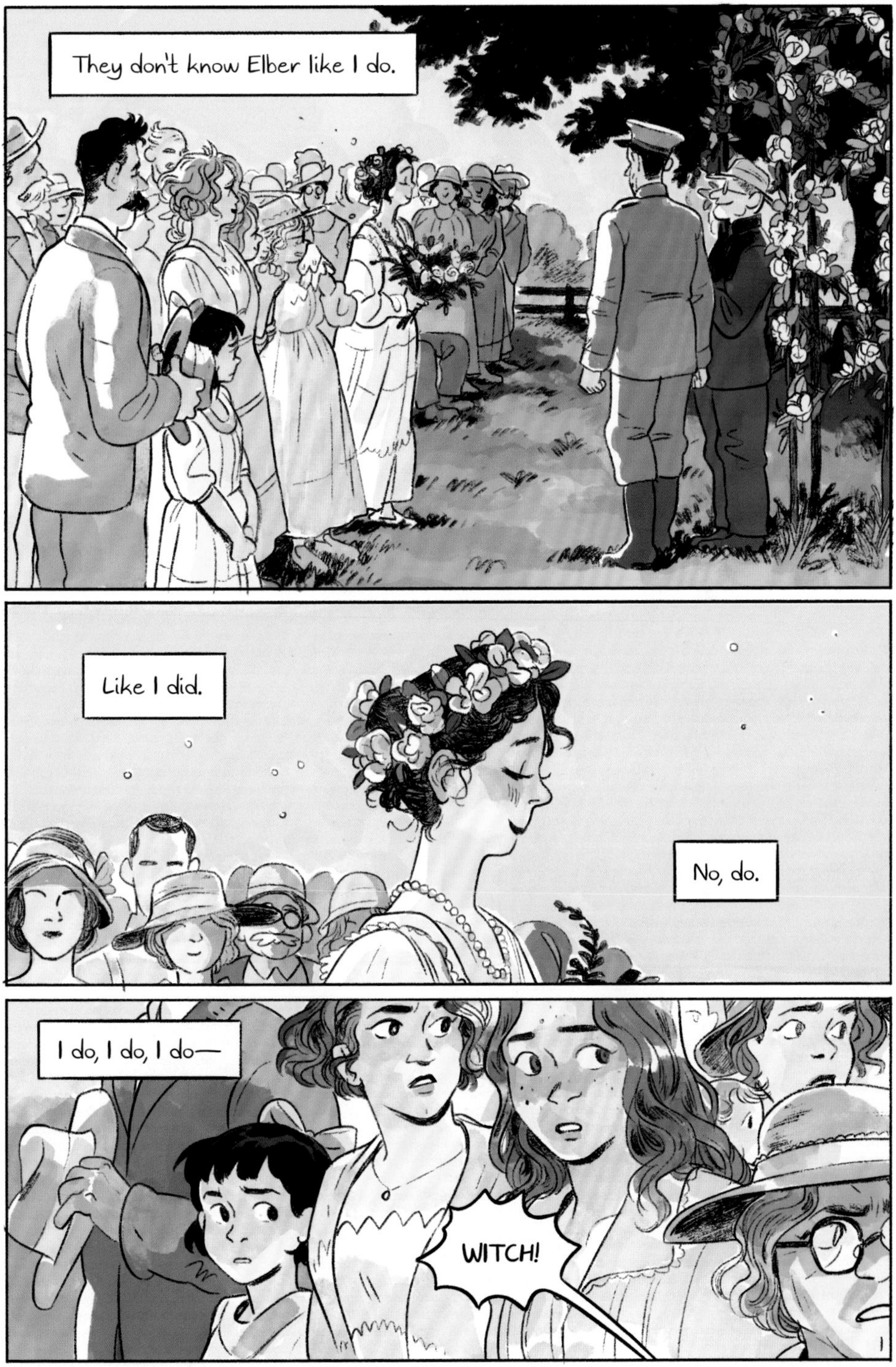
They don't know Elber like I do.
Like I did.
No, do.
I do, I do, I do—
WITCH!

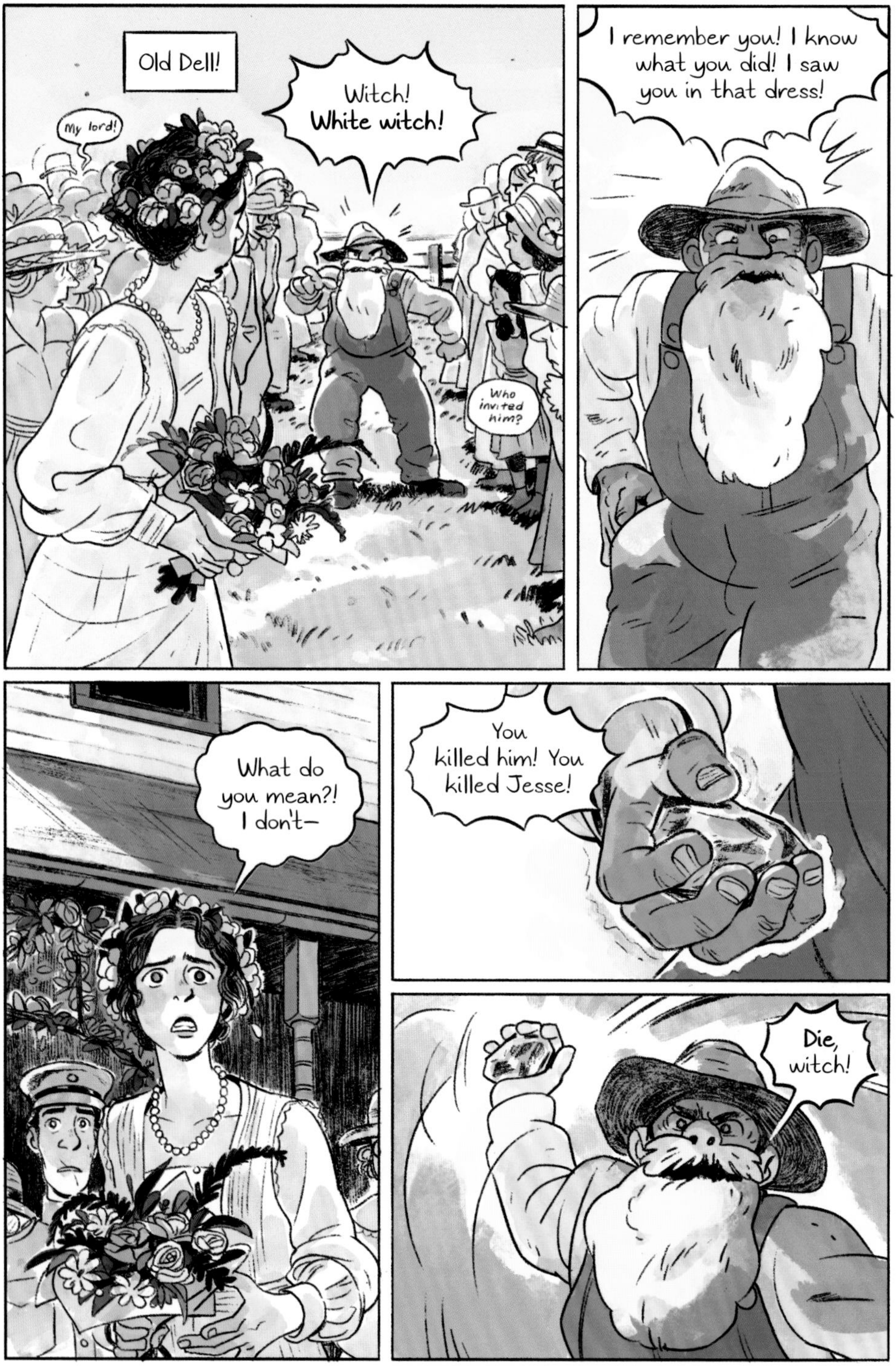
Old Dell!
My lord!
Witch! White witch!
Who invited him?
I remember you! I know what you did! I saw you in that dress!
What do you mean?! I don't—
You killed him! You killed Jesse!
Die, witch!

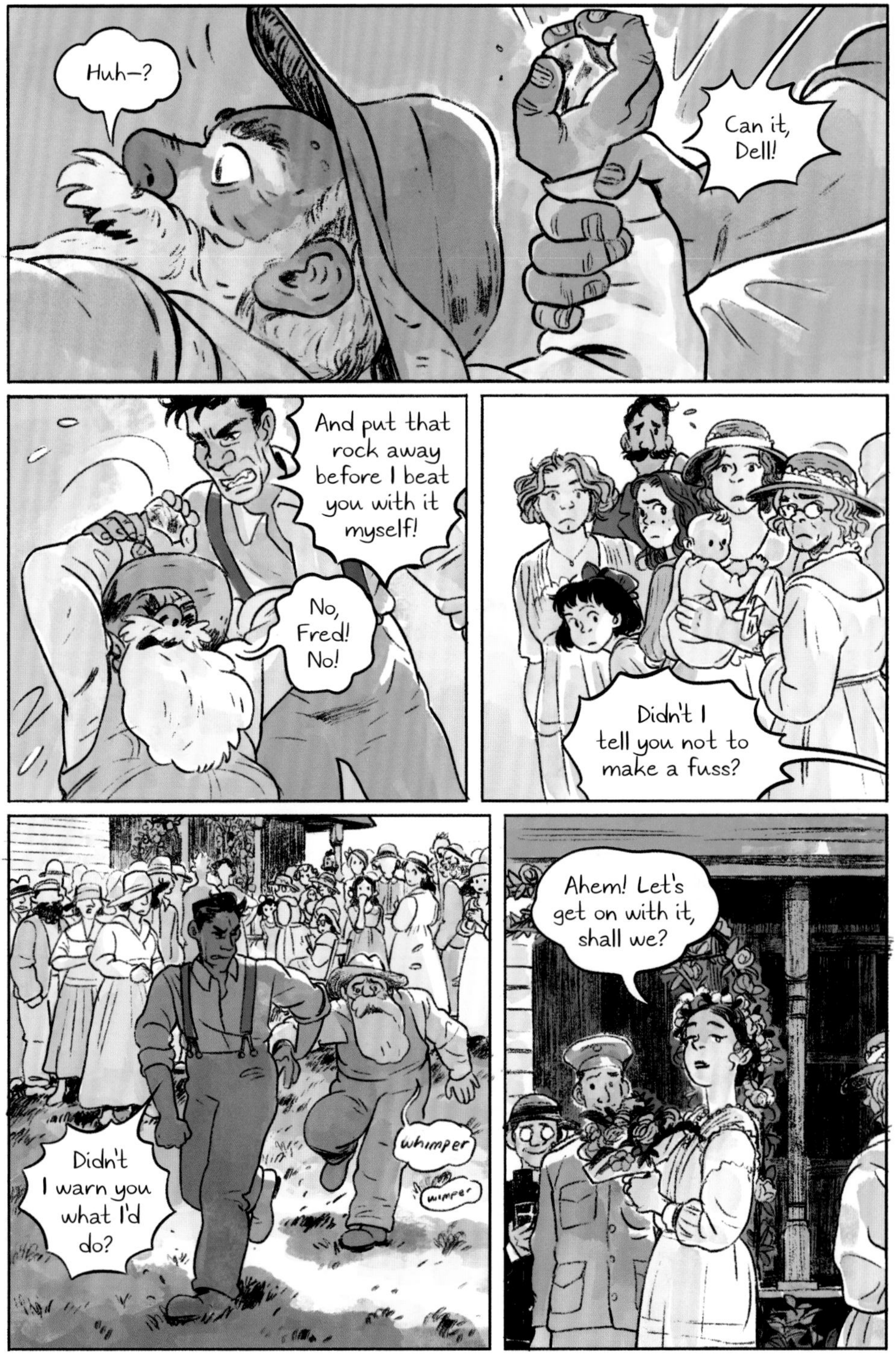
Huh—?
Can it, Dell!
And put that rock away before I beat you with it myself!
No, Fred! No!
Didn't I tell you not to make a fuss?
Didn't I warn you what I'd do?
whimper
whimper
Ahem! Let's get on with it, shall we?

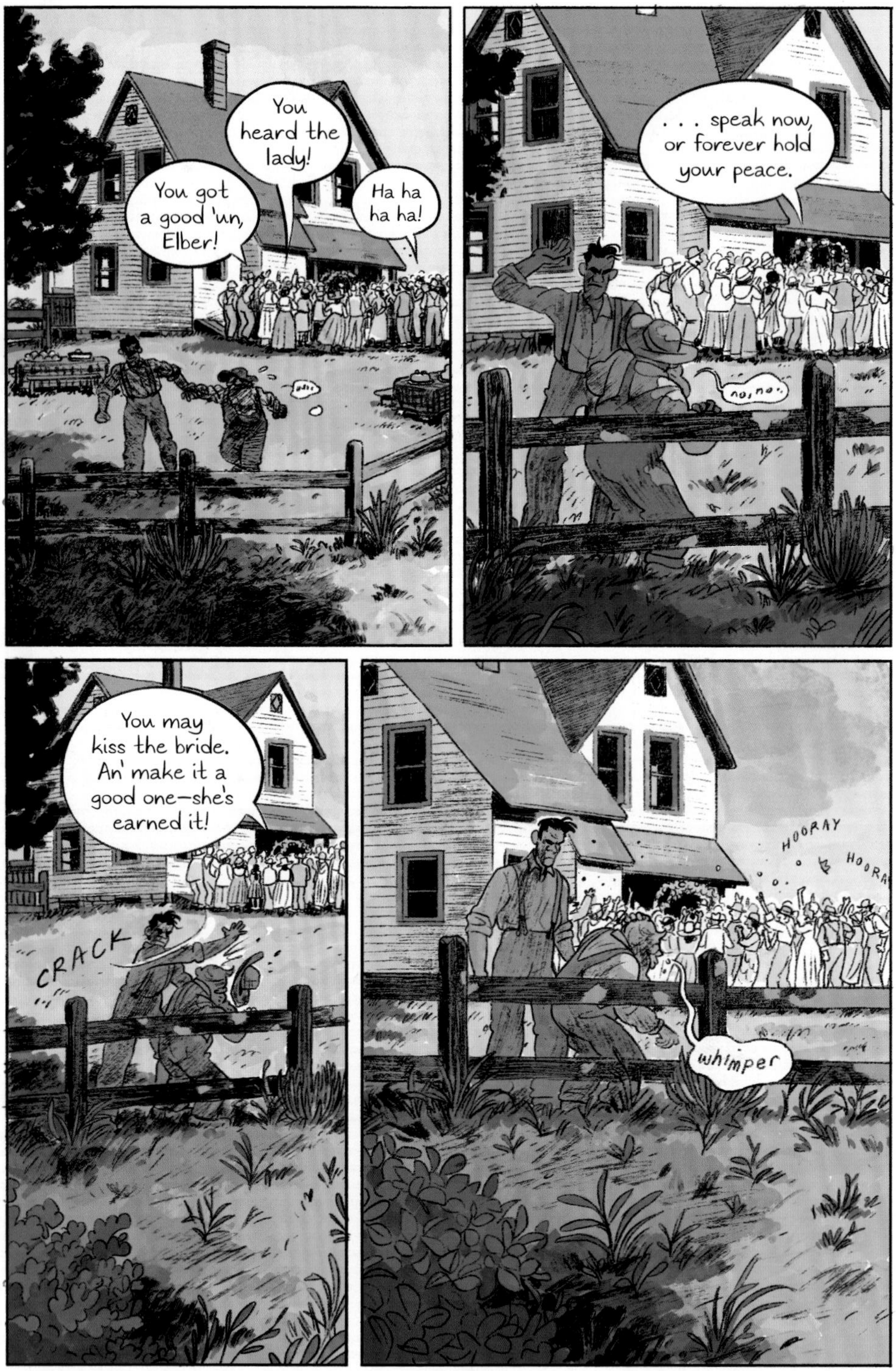
You got a good 'un, Elber!
You heard the lady!
Ha ha ha ha!
. . . speak now, or forever hold your peace.
no, no..
You may kiss the bride. An' make it a good one—she's earned it!
CRACK
HOORAY
HOORA
whimper

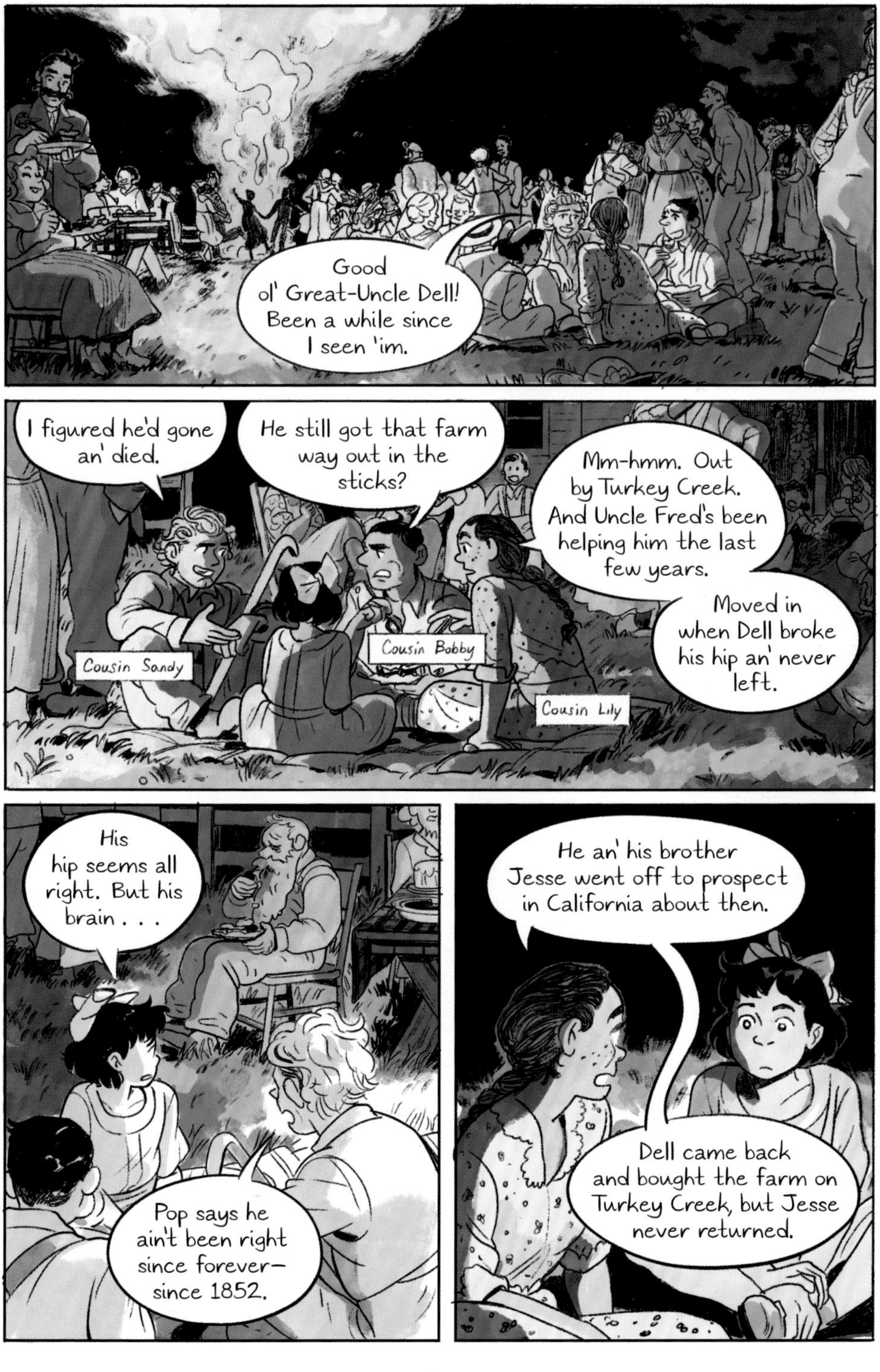
Good ol' Great-Uncle Dell! Been a while since I seen 'im.
I figured he'd gone an' died.
He still got that farm way out in the sticks?
Mm-hmm. Out by Turkey Creek. And Uncle Fred's been helping him the last few years.
Moved in when Dell broke his hip an' never left.
Cousin Sandy
Cousin Bobby
Cousin Lily
His hip seems all right. But his brain . . .
Pop says he ain't been right since forever—since 1852.
He an' his brother Jesse went off to prospect in California about then.
Dell came back and bought the farm on Turkey Creek, but Jesse never returned.

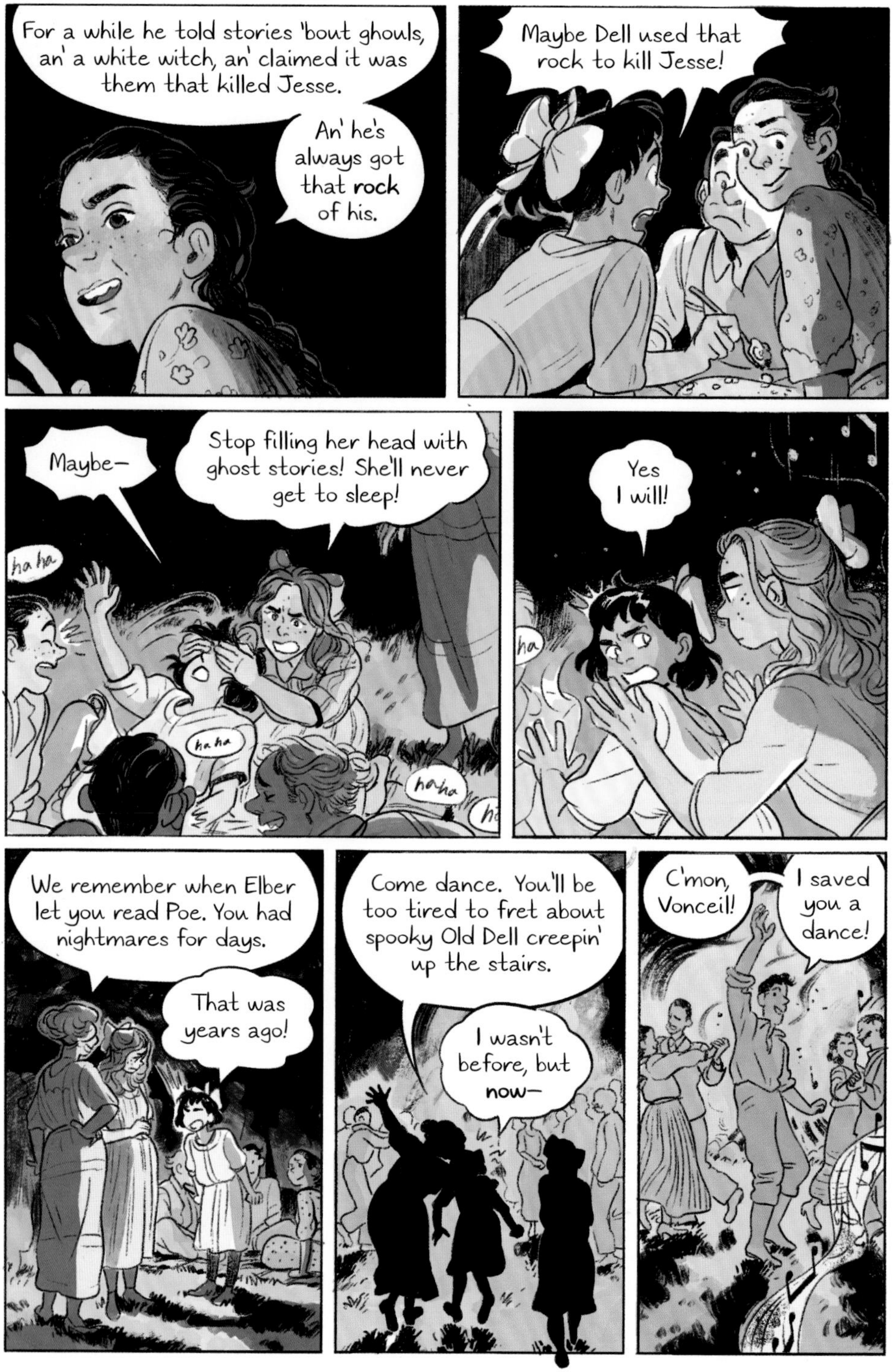

For a while he told stories 'bout ghouls, an' a white witch, an' claimed it was them that killed Jesse.
An' he's always got that **rock** of his.
Maybe Dell used that rock to kill Jesse!
Maybe—
Stop filling her head with ghost stories! She'll never get to sleep!
ha ha
ha ha
haha
Yes I will!
ha
We remember when Elber let you read Poe. You had nightmares for days.
That was years ago!
Come dance. You'll be too tired to fret about spooky Old Dell creepin' up the stairs.
I wasn't before, but **now**—
C'mon, Vonceil!
I saved you a dance!

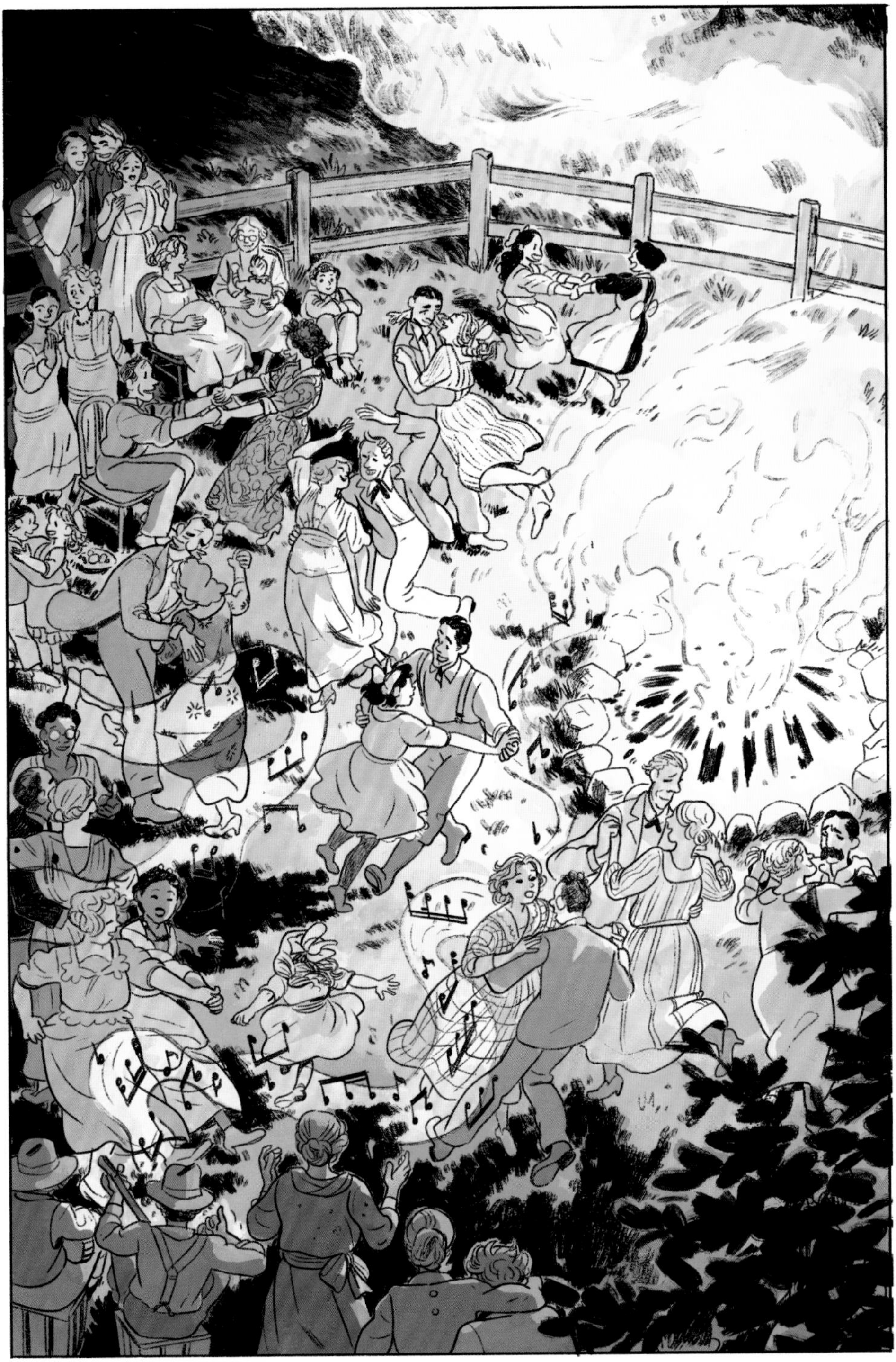

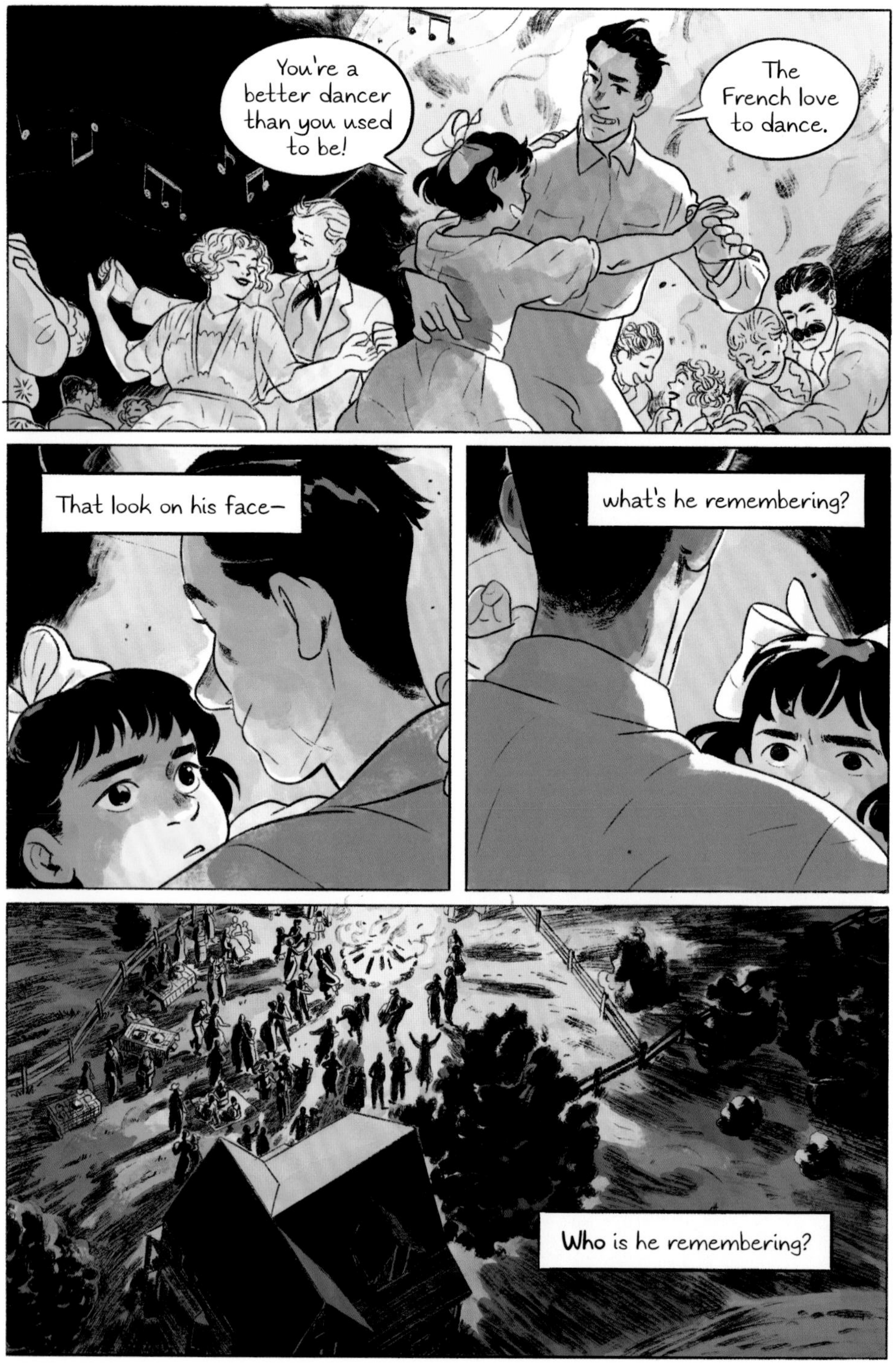
You're a better dancer than you used to be!
The French love to dance.
That look on his face—
what's he remembering?
Who is he remembering?

Chapter Three

The Lady in White

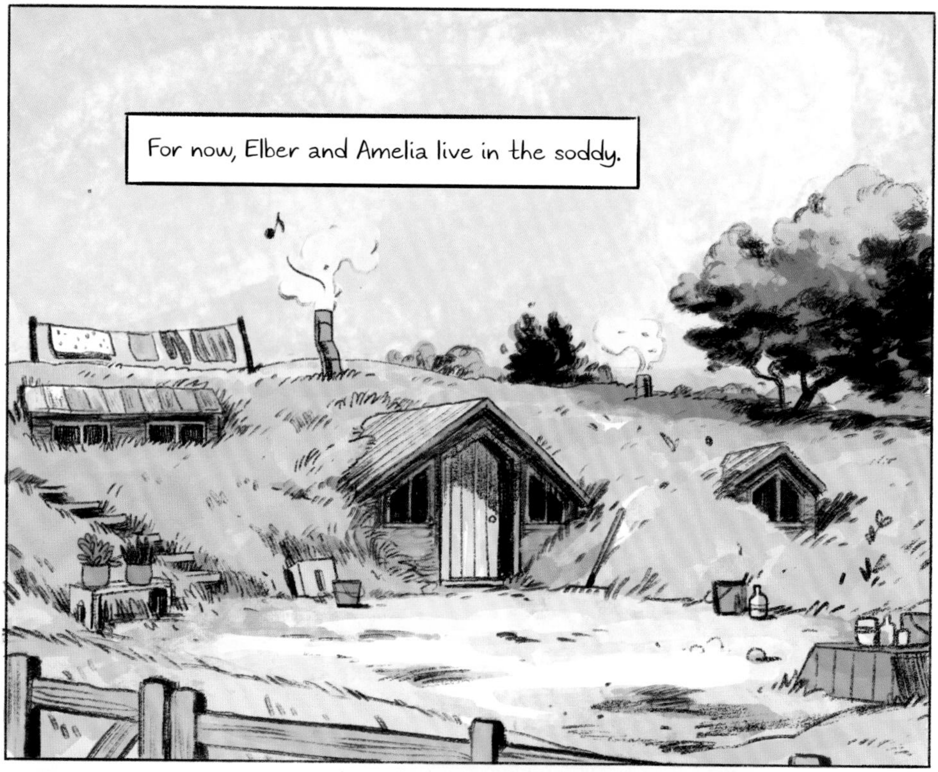
For now, Elber and Amelia live in the soddy.

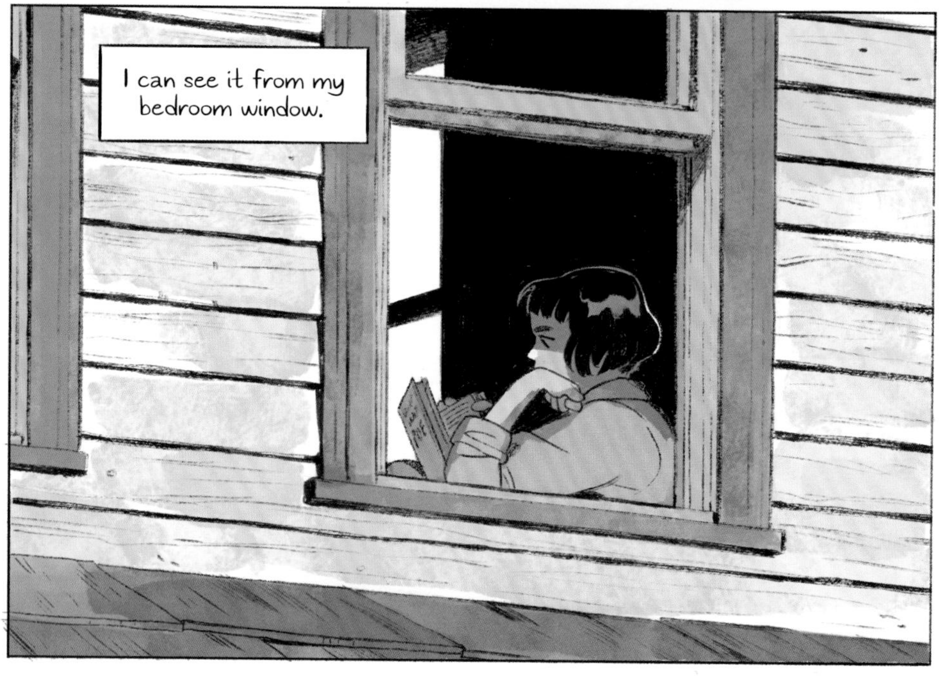
I can see it from my bedroom window.

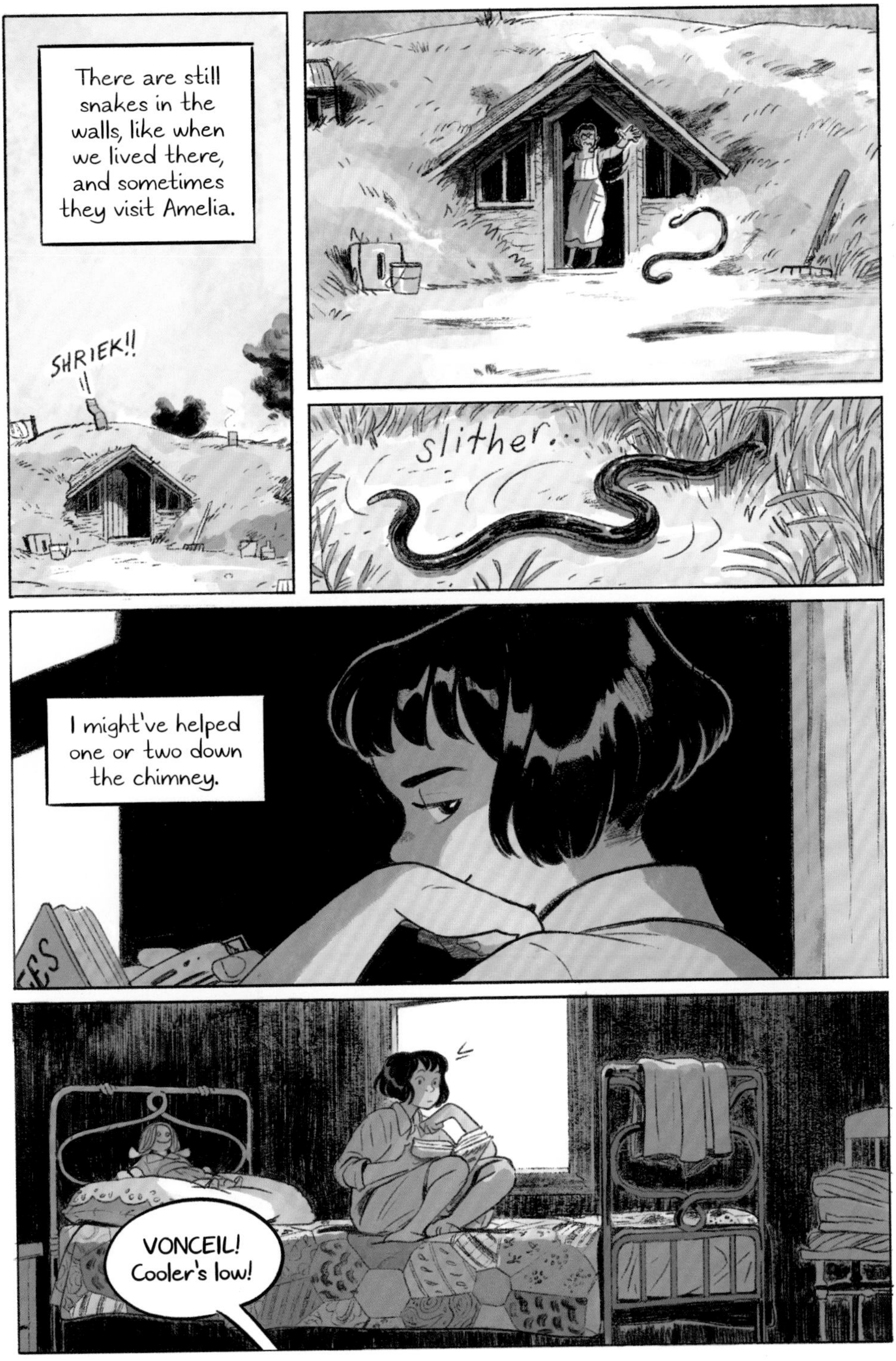
There are still snakes in the walls, like when we lived there, and sometimes they visit Amelia.
SHRIEK!!
slither...
I might've helped one or two down the chimney.
VONCEIL! Cooler's low!

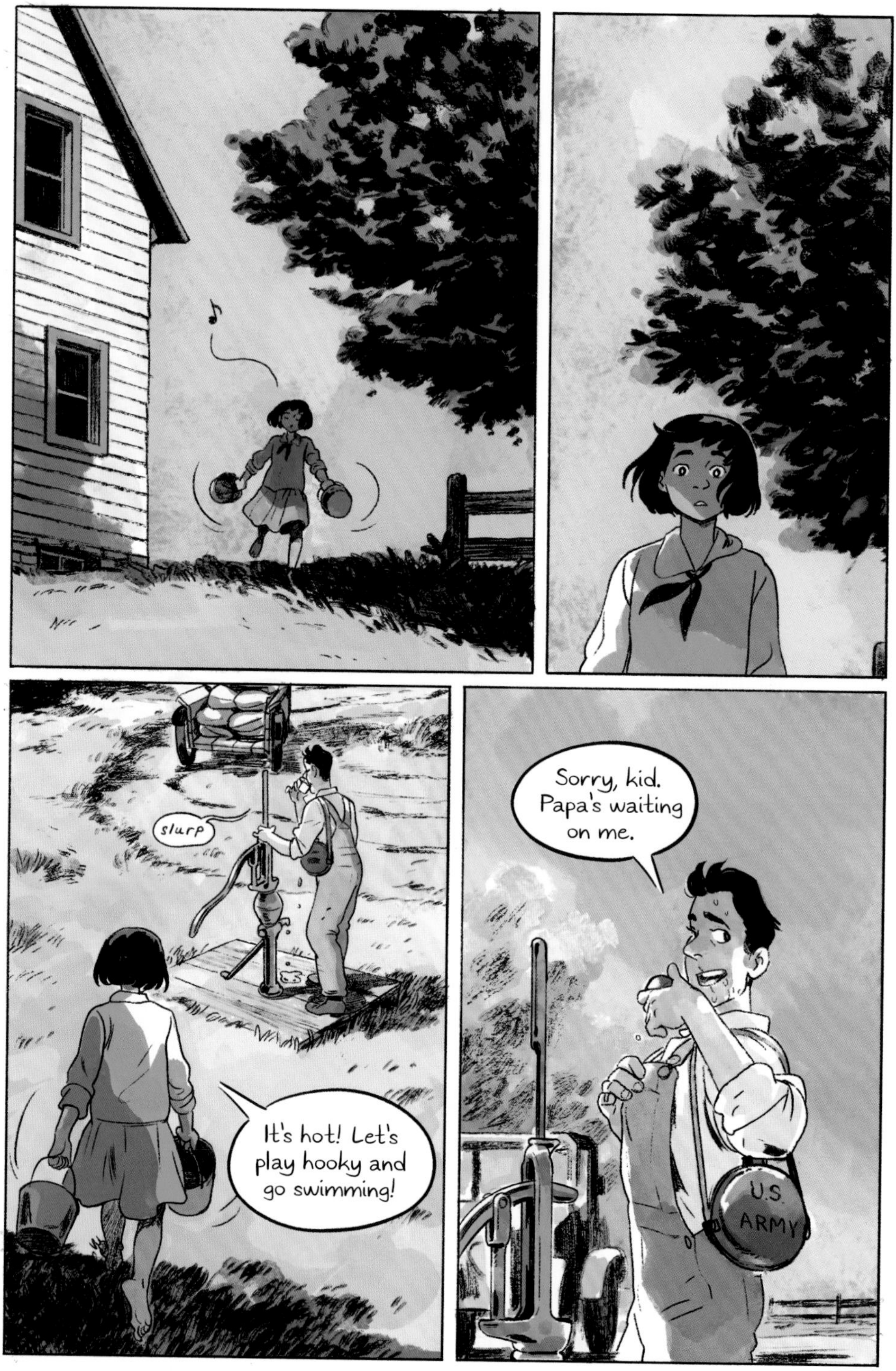
slurp
It's hot! Let's play hooky and go swimming!
Sorry, kid. Papa's waiting on me.
U.S. ARMY

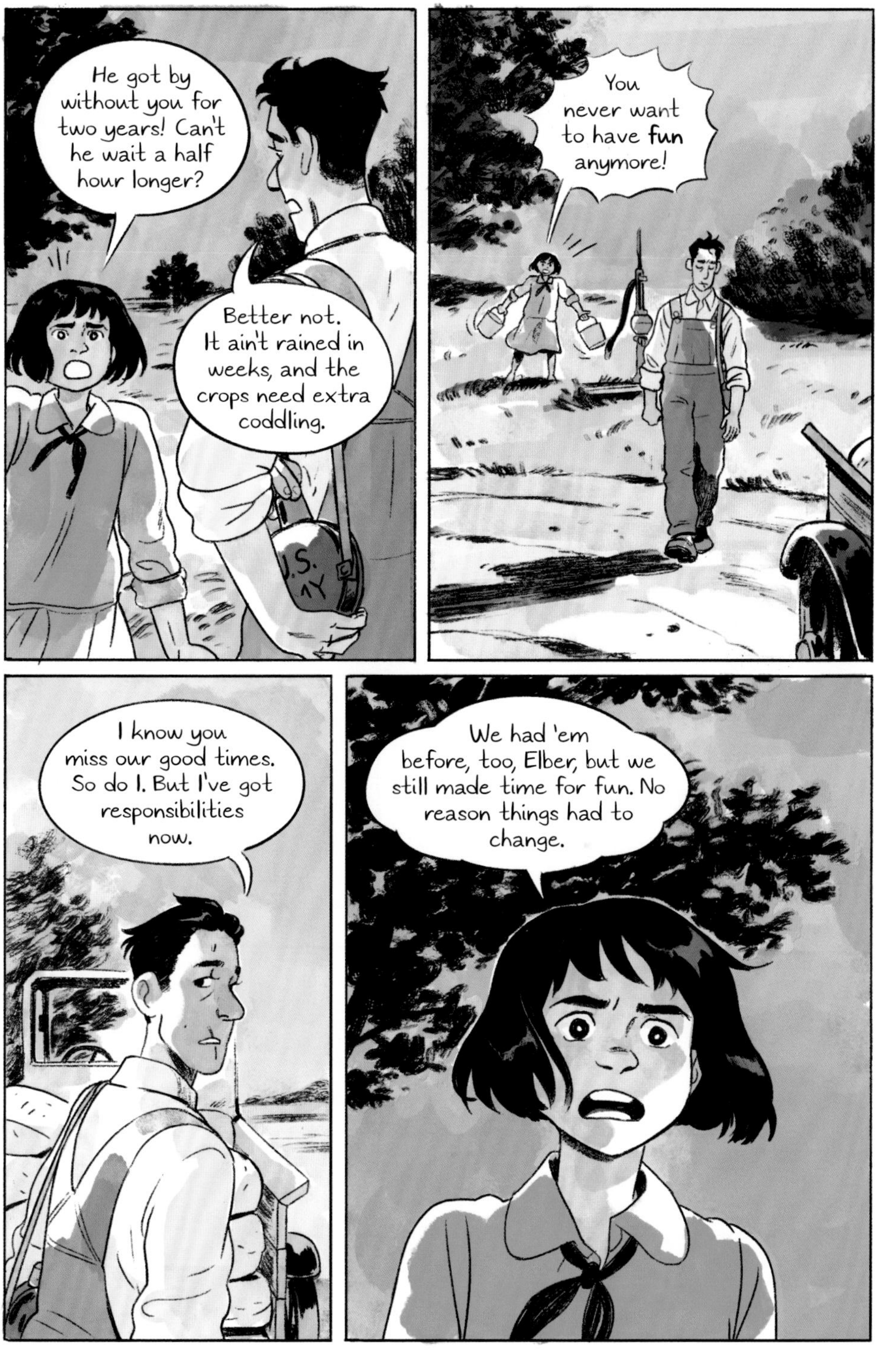
He got by without you for two years! Can't he wait a half hour longer?
Better not. It ain't rained in weeks, and the crops need extra coddling.
U.S.
You never want to have **fun** anymore!
I know you miss our good times. So do I. But I've got responsibilities now.
We had 'em before, too, Elber, but we still made time for fun. No reason things had to change.

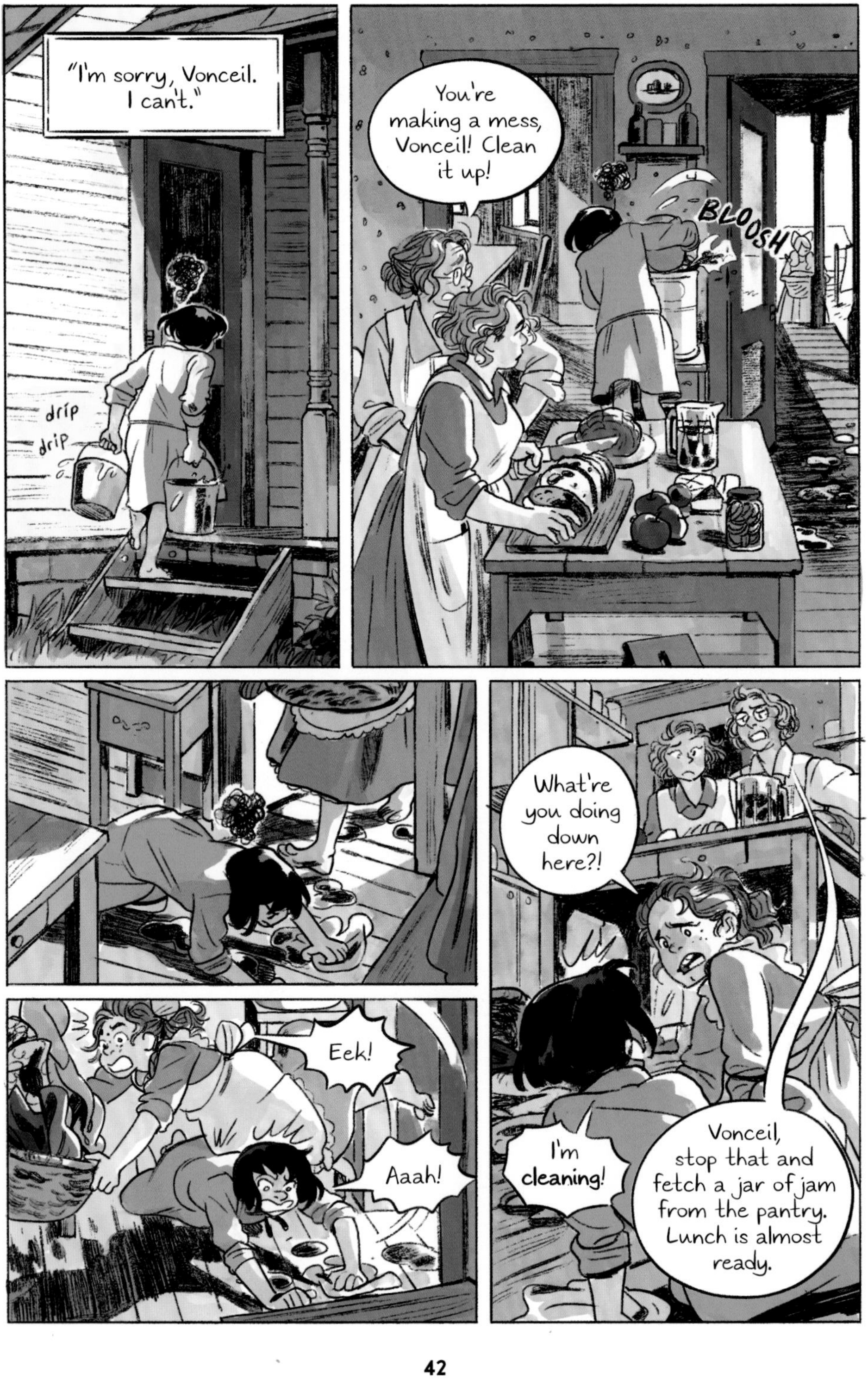
"I'm sorry, Vonceil. I can't."
drip
drip
You're making a mess, Vonceil! Clean it up!
BLOOSH
What're you doing down here?!
Eek!
Aaah!
I'm **cleaning**!
Vonceil, stop that and fetch a jar of jam from the pantry. Lunch is almost ready.

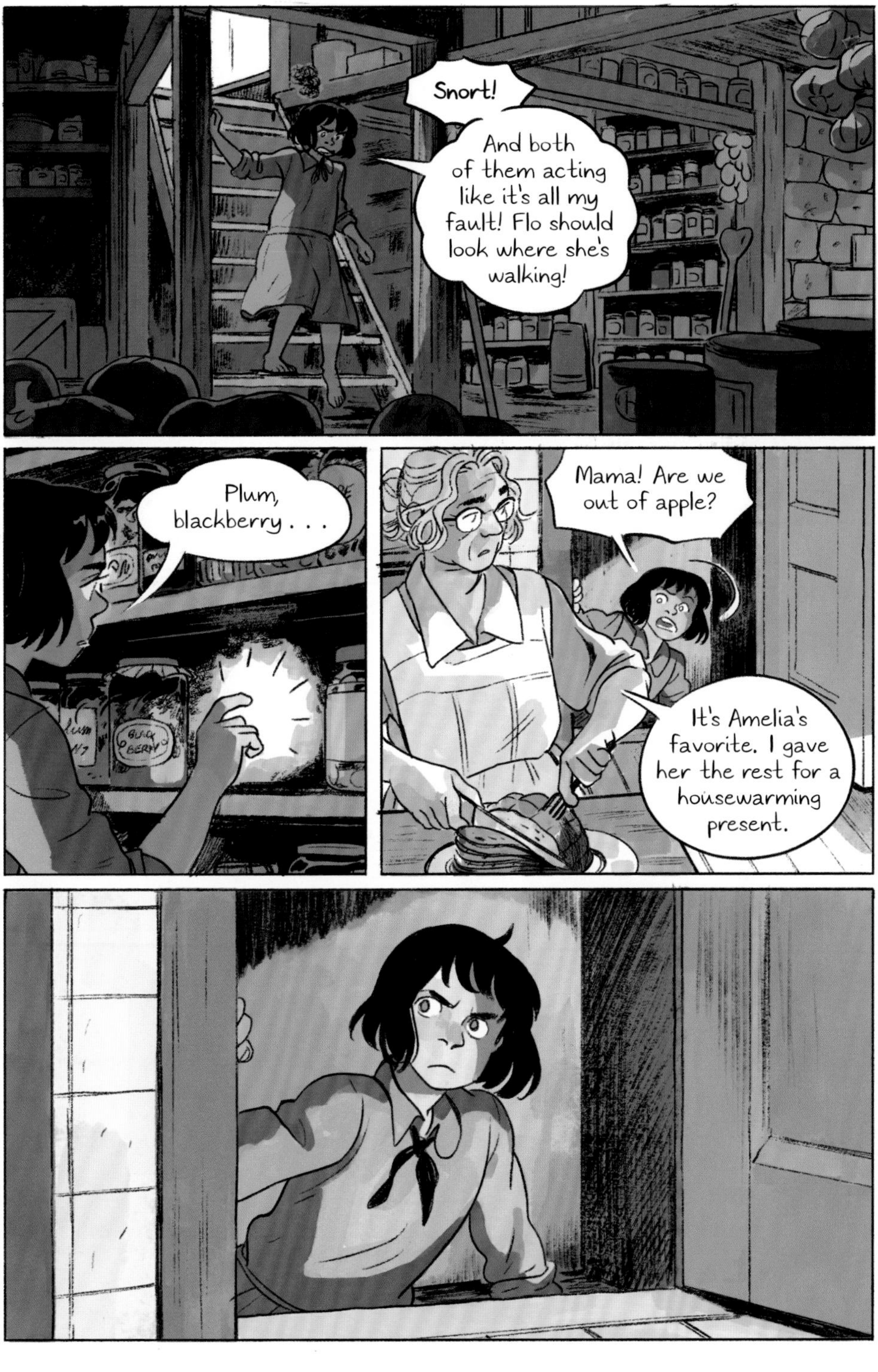
Snort!
And both of them acting like it's all my fault! Flo should look where she's walking!
Plum, blackberry . . .
Mama! Are we out of apple?
It's Amelia's favorite. I gave her the rest for a housewarming present.

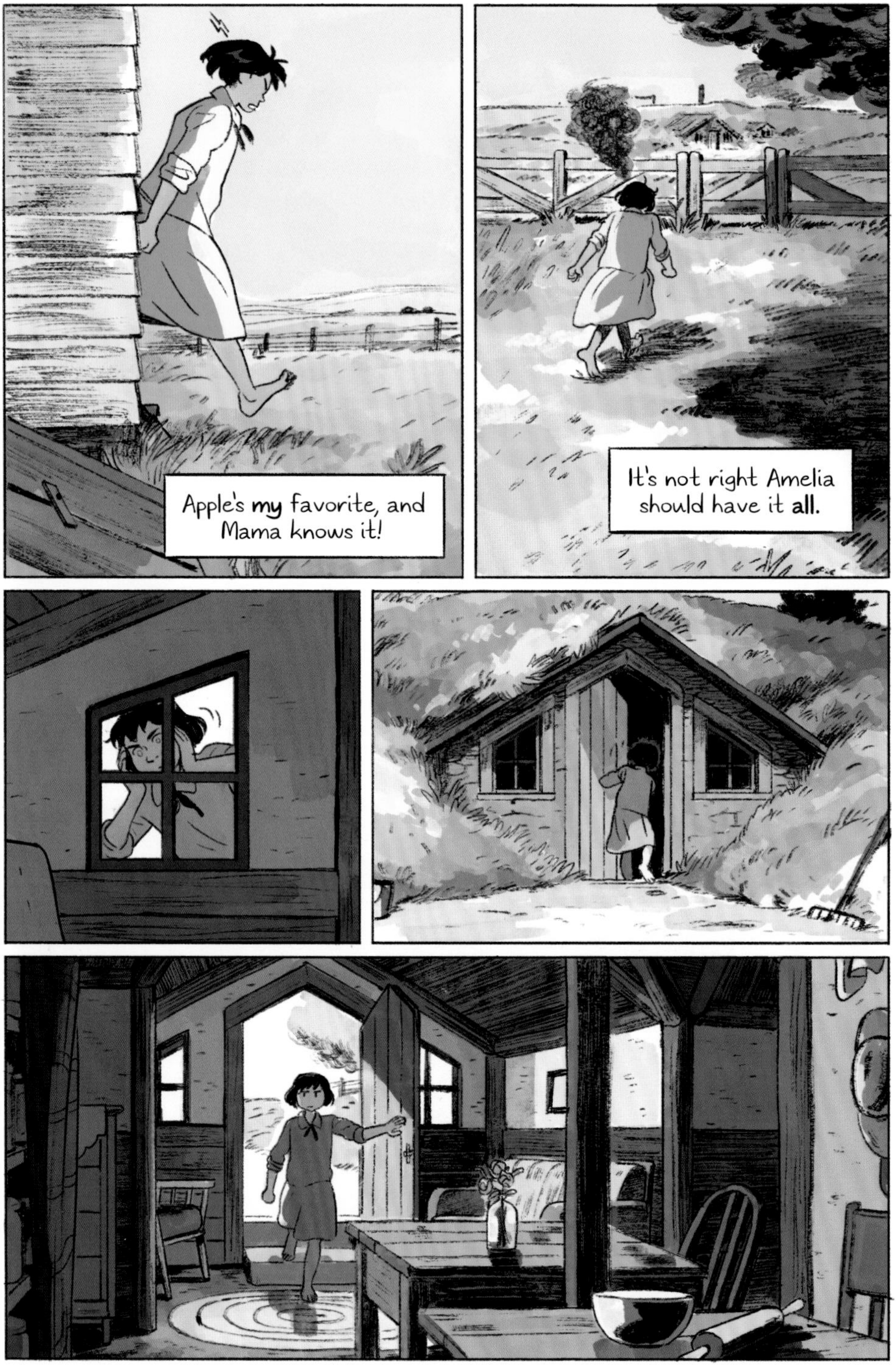
Apple's **my** favorite, and Mama knows it!
It's not right Amelia should have it **all.**

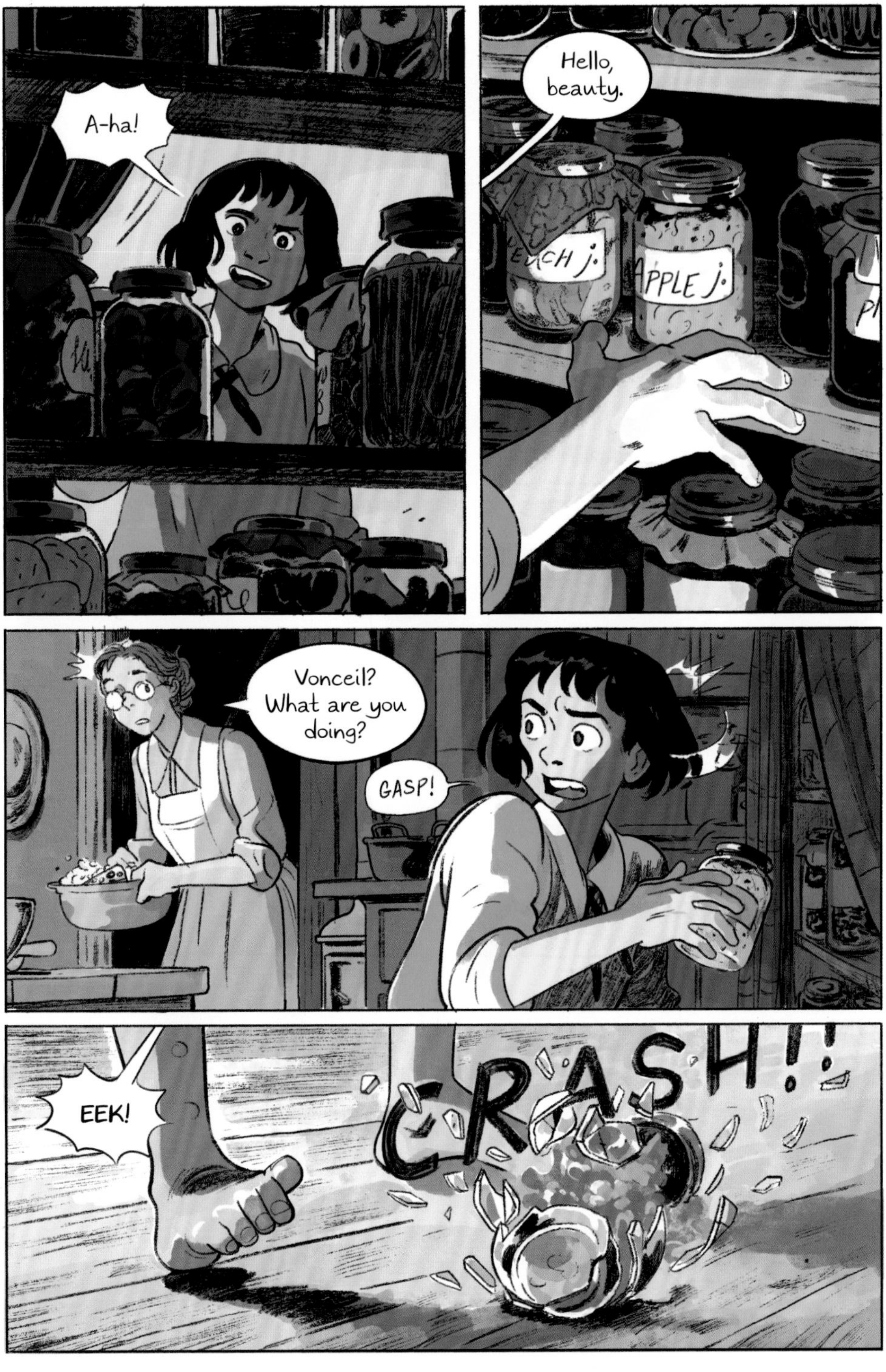
A-ha!
Hello, beauty.
PEACH j.
APPLE j.
Vonceil? What are you doing?
GASP!
EEK!
CRASH!!

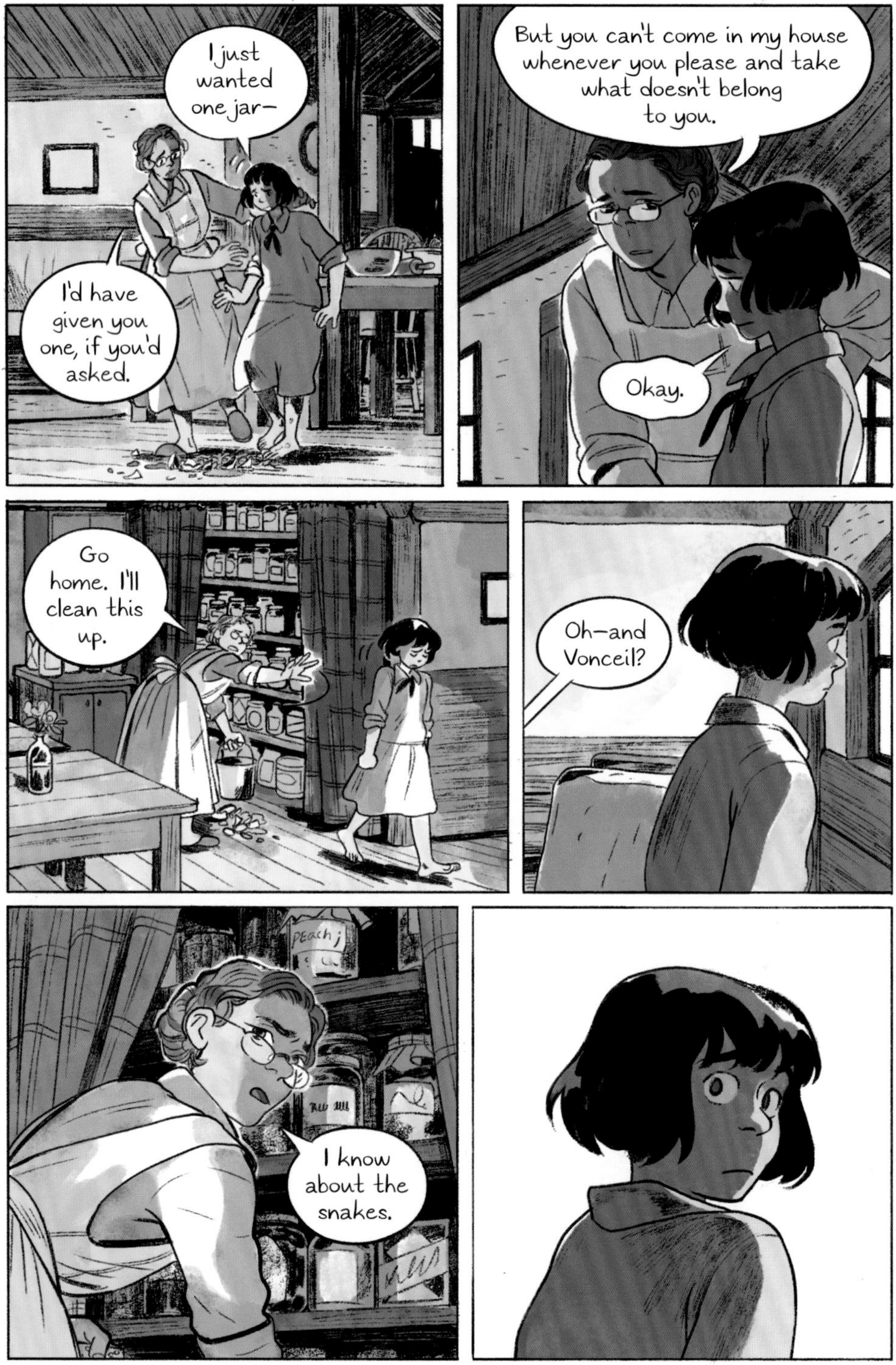
I just wanted one jar—
I'd have given you one, if you'd asked.
But you can't come in my house whenever you please and take what doesn't belong to you.
Okay.
Go home. I'll clean this up.
Oh—and Vonceil?
I know about the snakes.

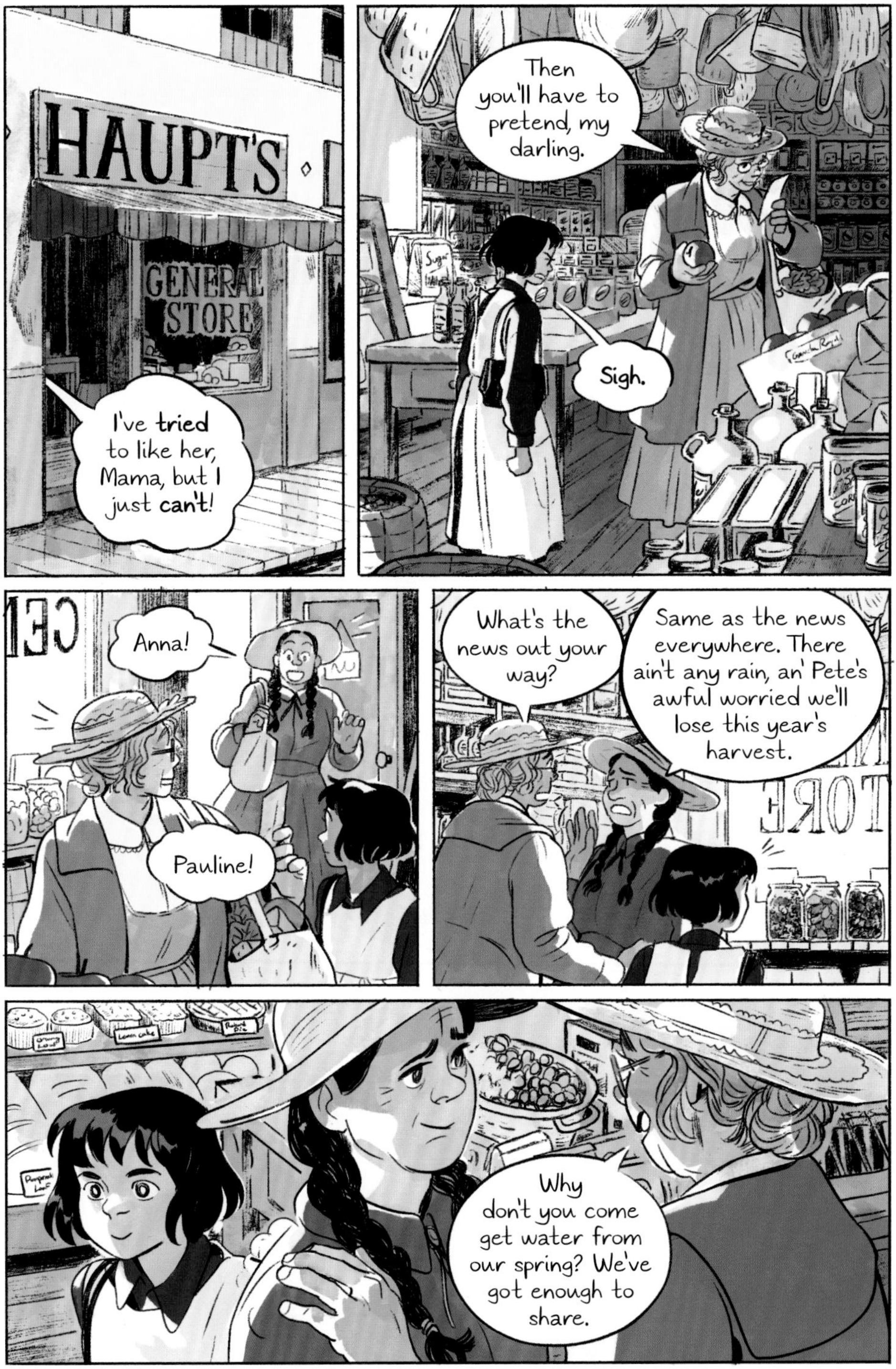
HAUPT'S
GENERAL STORE
I've tried to like her, Mama, but I just can't!
Then you'll have to pretend, my darling.
Sigh.
Sugar
Anna!
Pauline!
What's the news out your way?
Same as the news everywhere. There ain't any rain, an' Pete's awful worried we'll lose this year's harvest.
Lemon cake
Why don't you come get water from our spring? We've got enough to share.

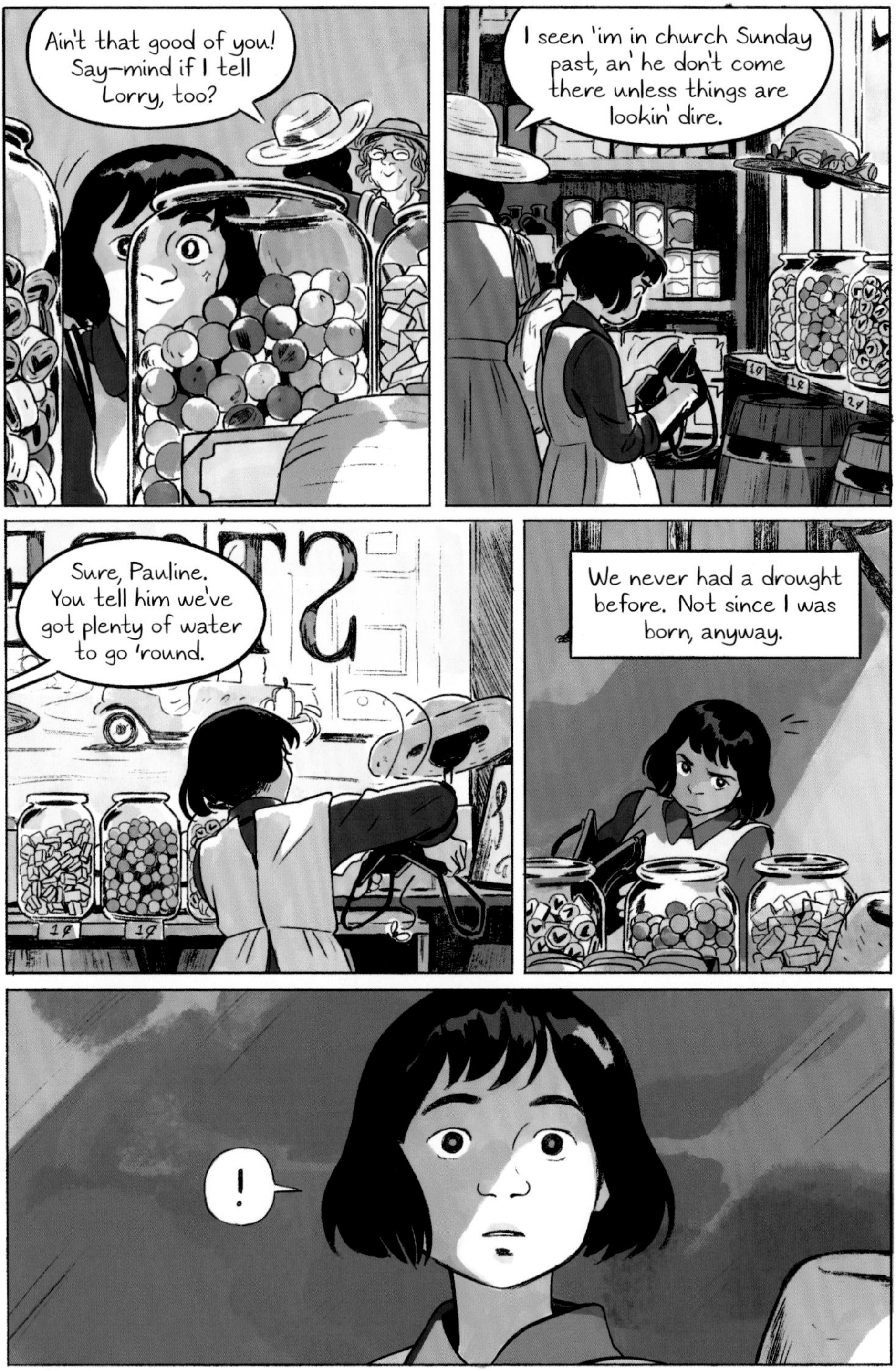
Ain't that good of you! Say—mind if I tell Lorry, too?
I seen 'im in church Sunday past, an' he don't come there unless things are lookin' dire.
Sure, Pauline. You tell him we've got plenty of water to go 'round.
We never had a drought before. Not since I was born, anyway.
!

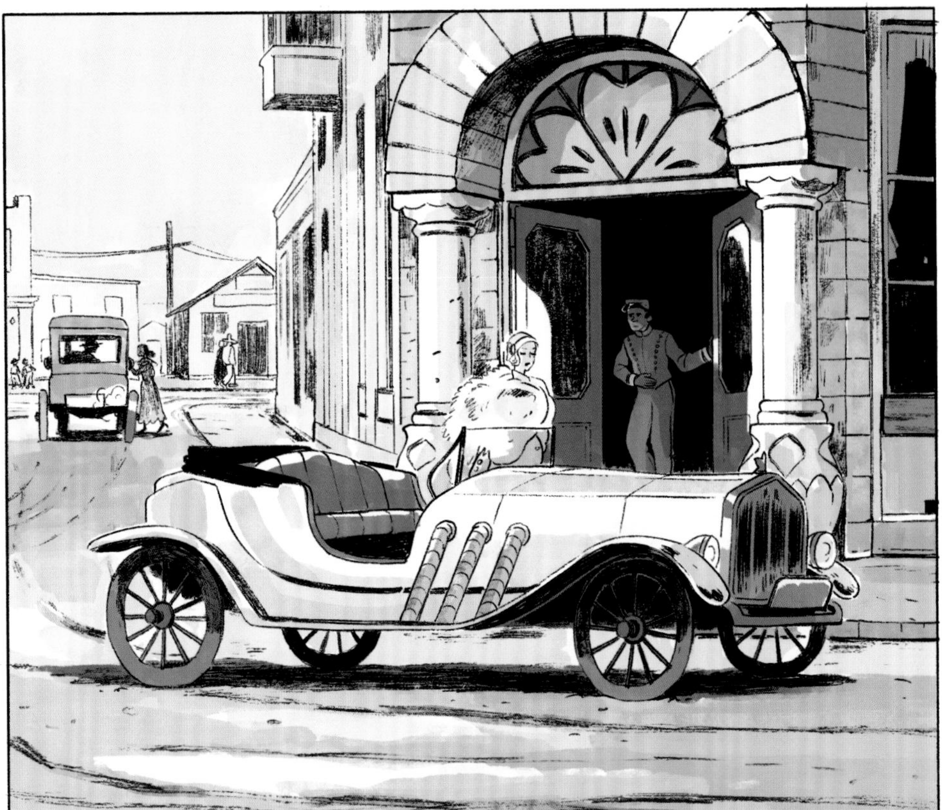

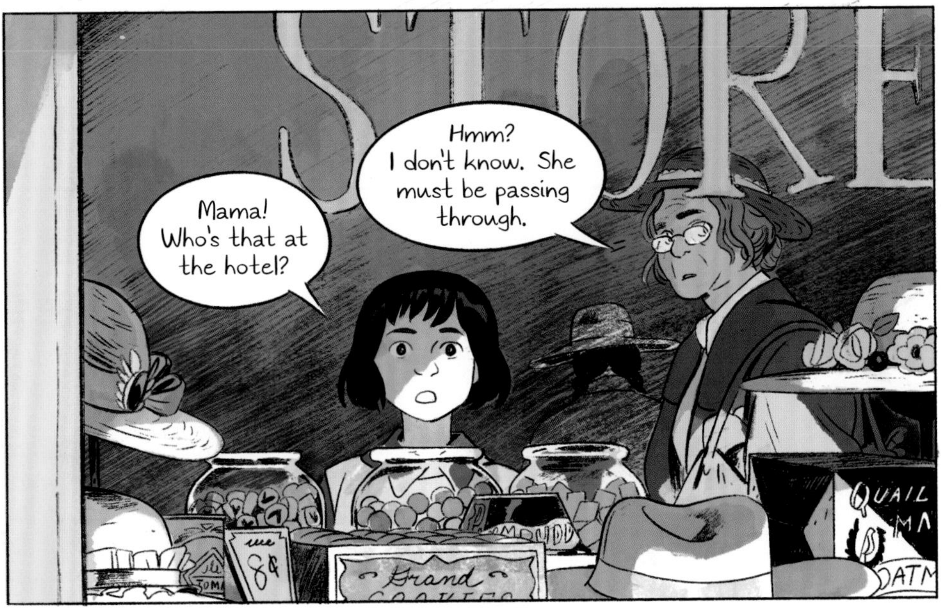
Mama! Who's that at the hotel?
Hmm? I don't know. She must be passing through.
Grand

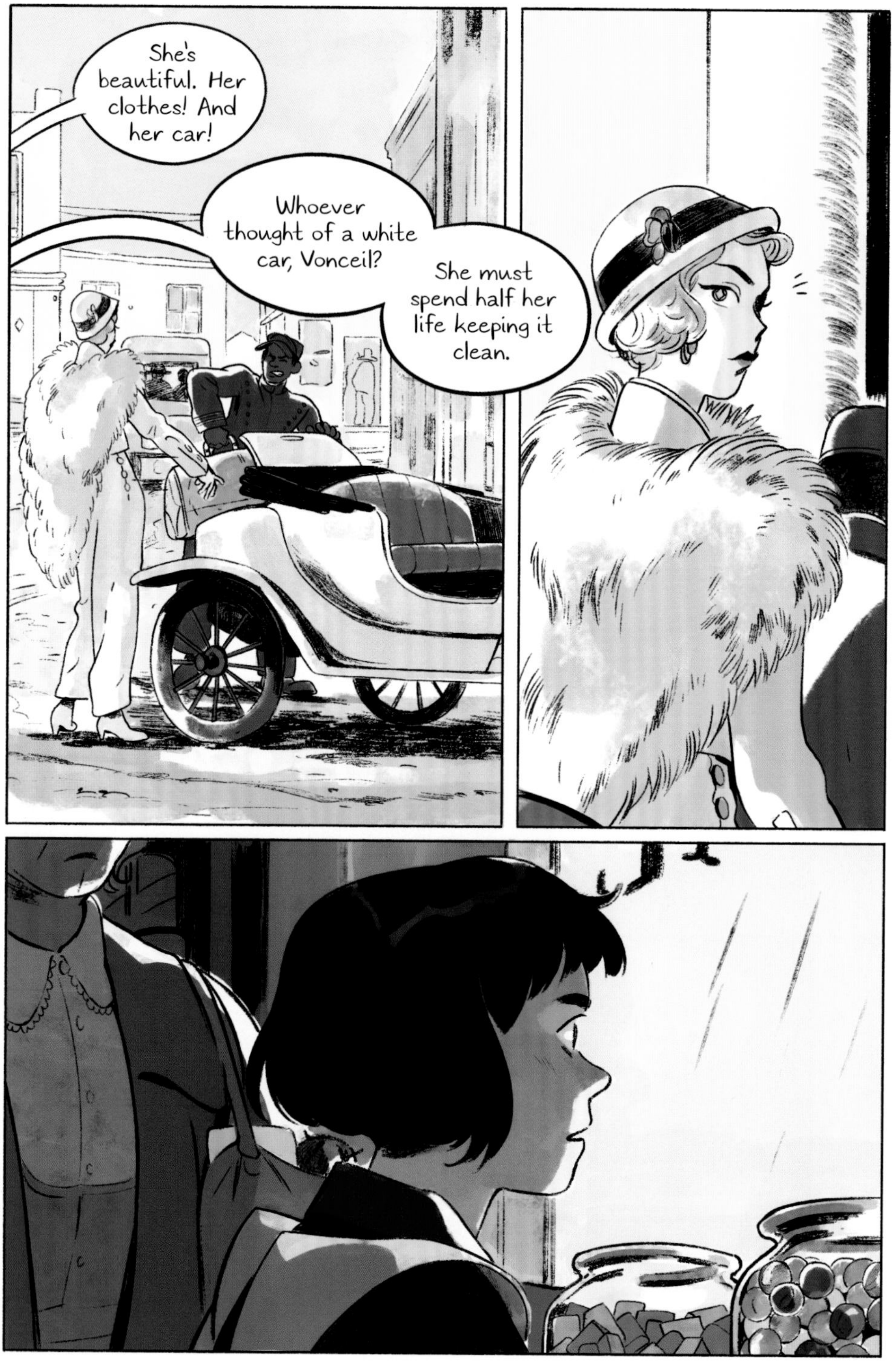
She's beautiful. Her clothes! And her car!
Whoever thought of a white car, Vonceil?
She must spend half her life keeping it clean.

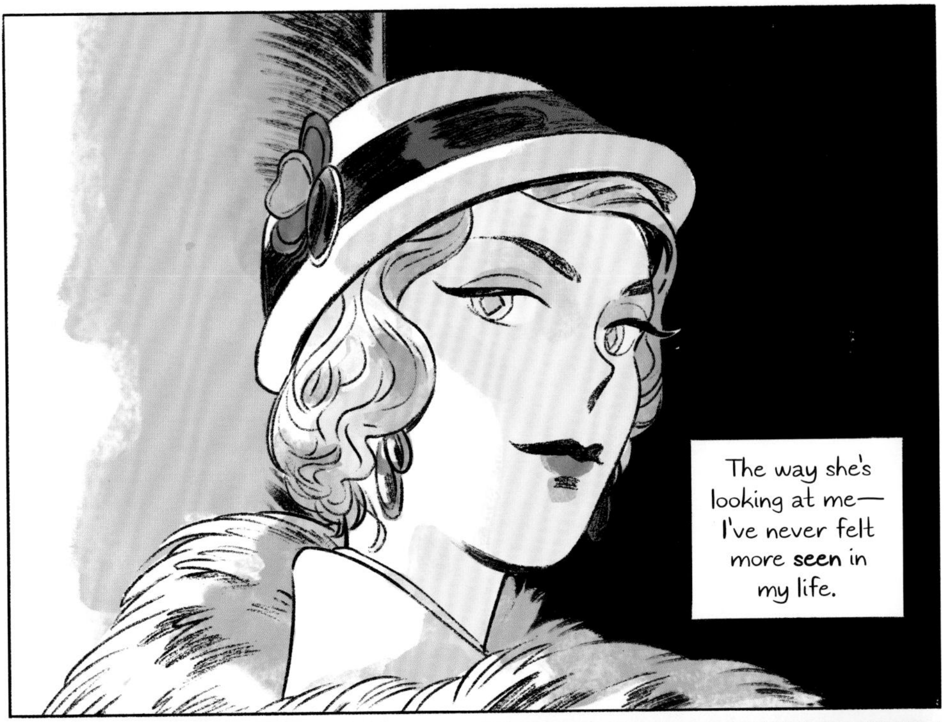
The way she's looking at me—I've never felt more **seen** in my life.

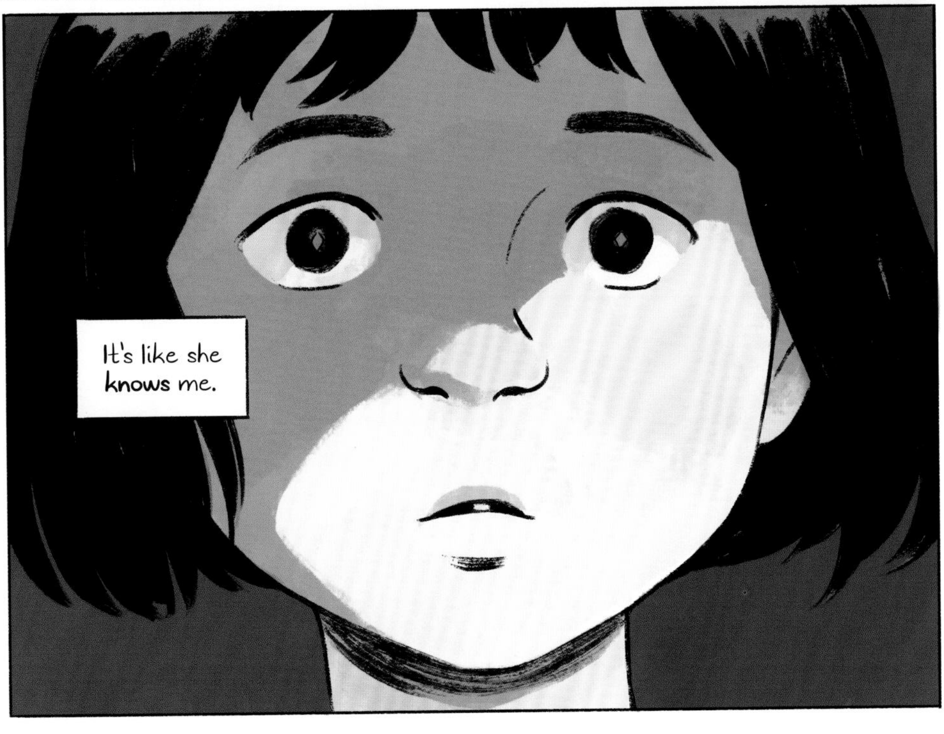
It's like she **knows** me.

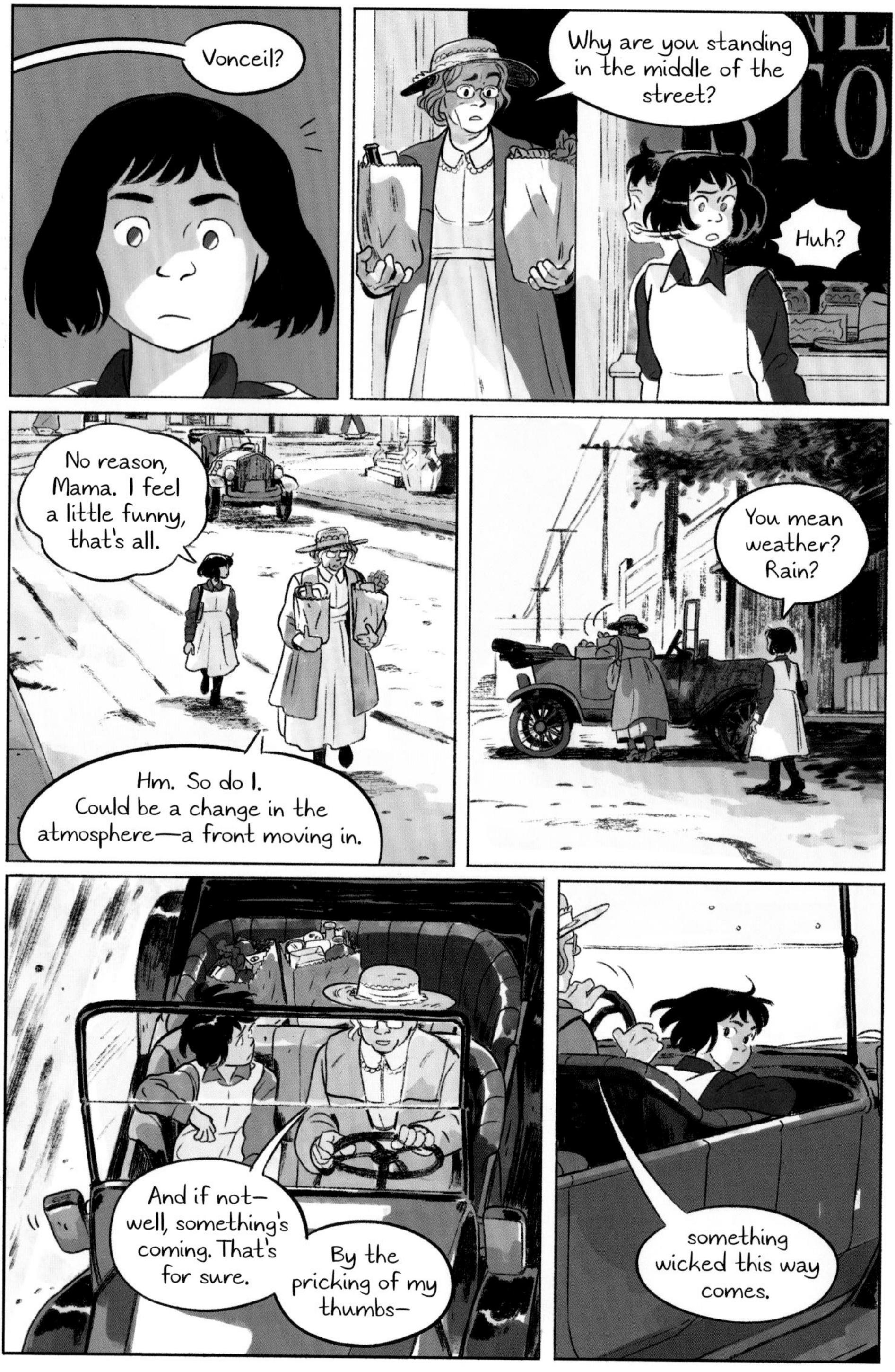

Vonceil?
Why are you standing in the middle of the street?
Huh?
No reason, Mama. I feel a little funny, that's all.
Hm. So do I. Could be a change in the atmosphere—a front moving in.
You mean weather? Rain?
And if not— well, something's coming. That's for sure.
By the pricking of my thumbs—
something wicked this way comes.

Chapter Four

Salt Water

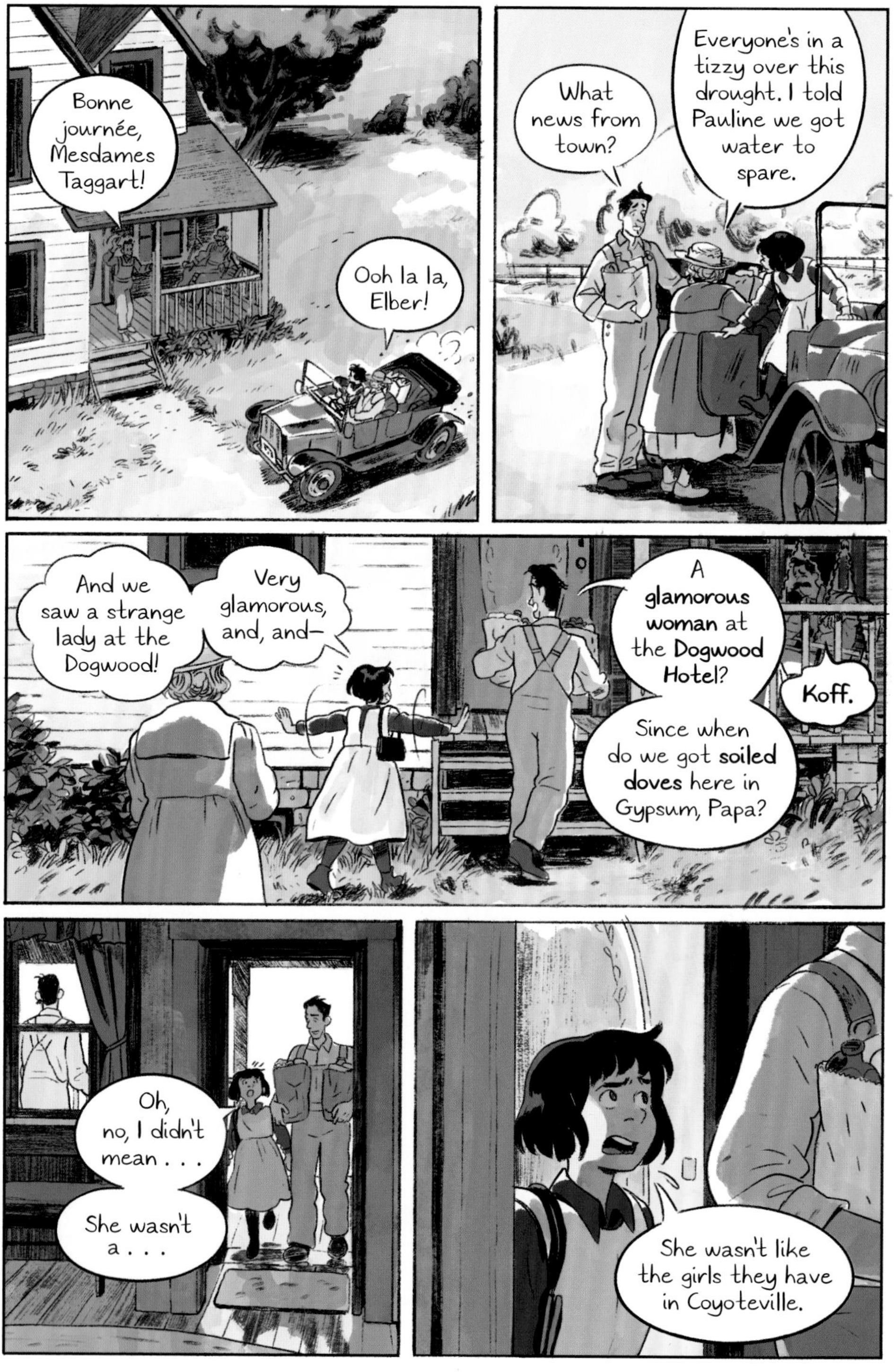
Bonne journée, Mesdames Taggart!
Ooh la la, Elber!
What news from town?
Everyone's in a tizzy over this drought. I told Pauline we got water to spare.
And we saw a strange lady at the Dogwood!
Very glamorous, and, and–
A **glamorous woman** at the **Dogwood Hotel**?
Since when do we got **soiled doves** here in Gypsum, Papa?
Koff.
Oh, no, I didn't mean . . .
She wasn't a . . .
She wasn't like the girls they have in Coyoteville.

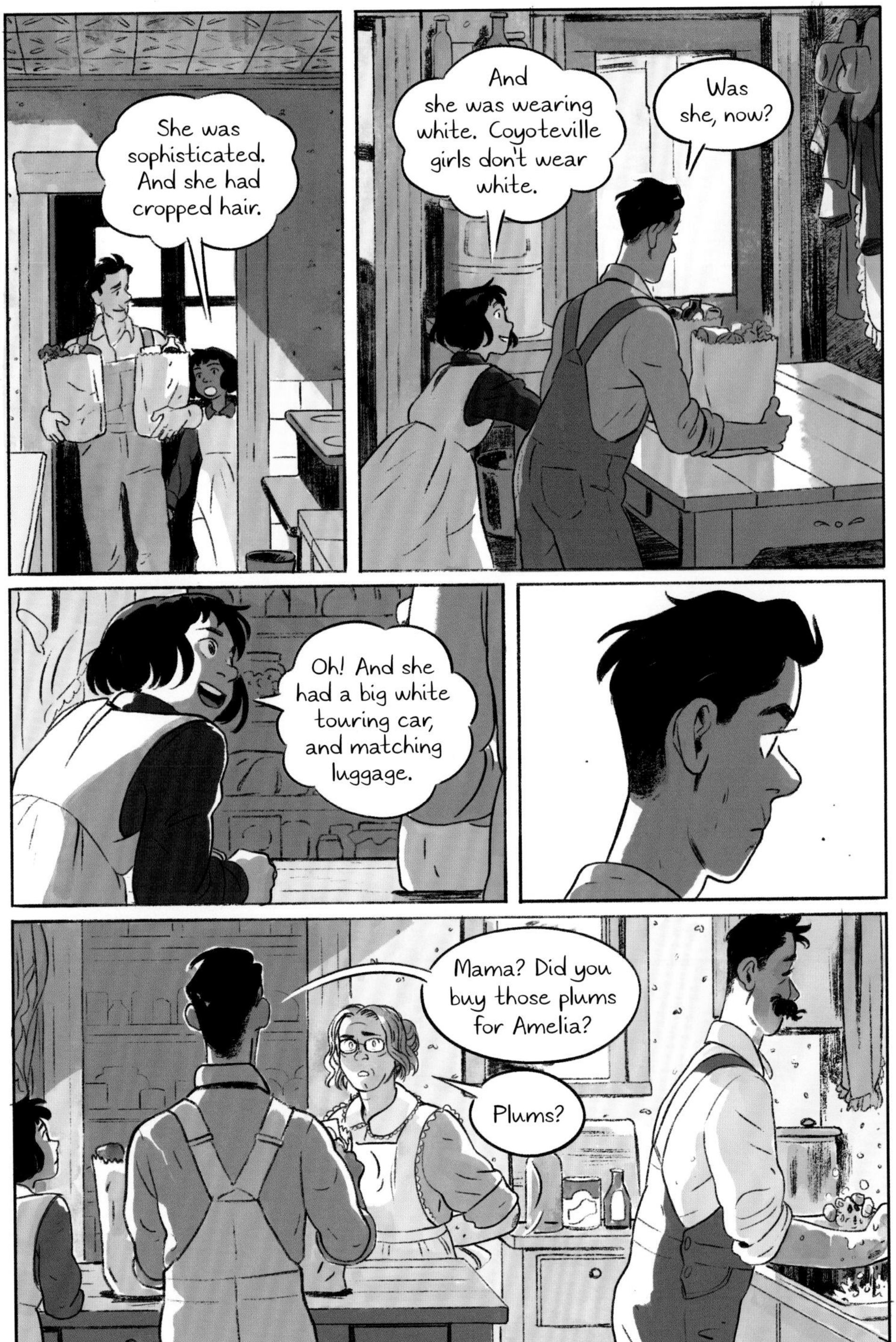
She was sophisticated. And she had cropped hair.
And she was wearing white. Coyoteville girls don't wear white.
Was she, now?
Oh! And she had a big white touring car, and matching luggage.
Mama? Did you buy those plums for Amelia?
Plums?

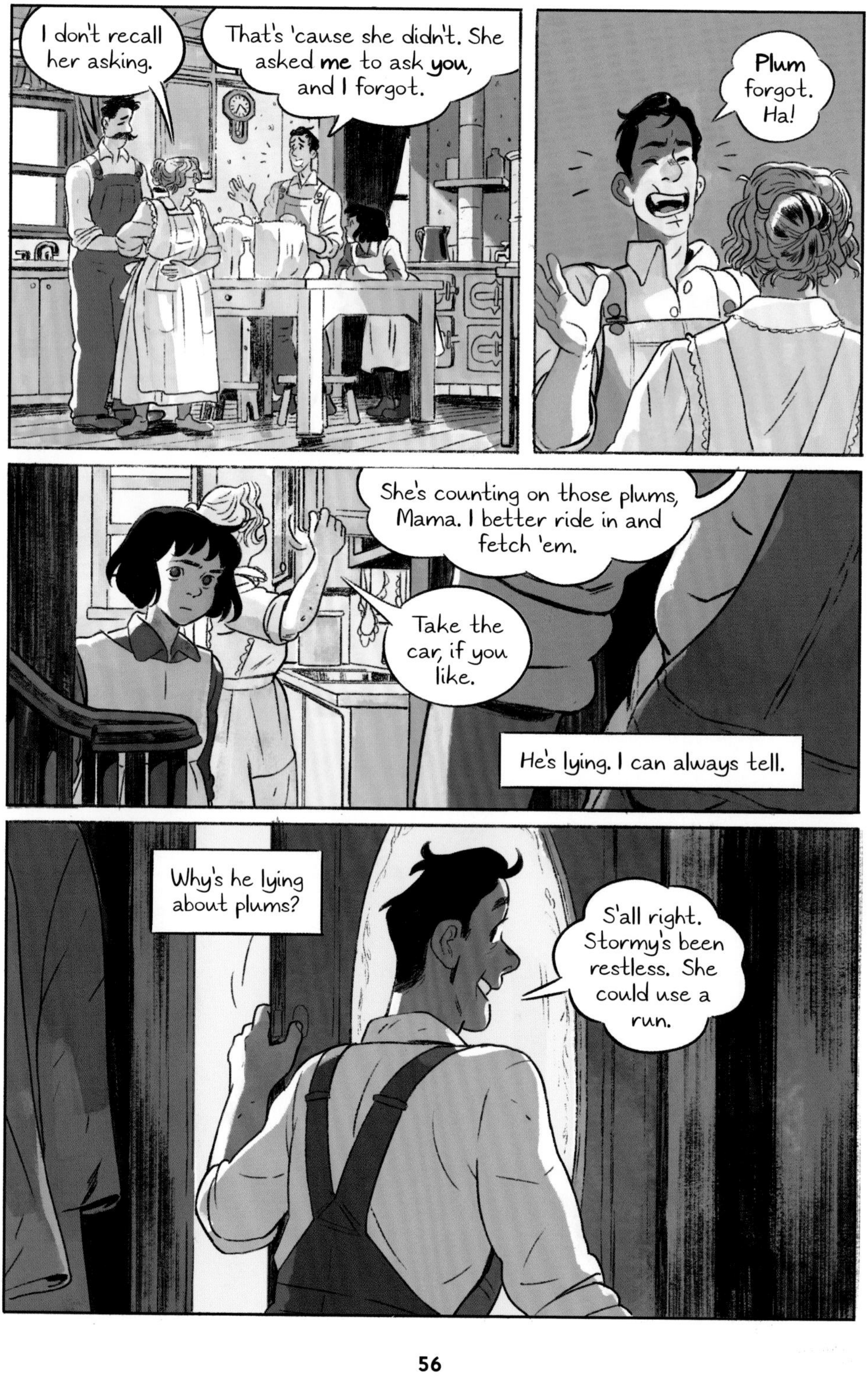
I don't recall her asking.
That's 'cause she didn't. She asked **me** to ask **you**, and I forgot.
Plum forgot. Ha!
She's counting on those plums, Mama. I better ride in and fetch 'em.
Take the car, if you like.
He's lying. I can always tell.
Why's he lying about plums?
S'all right. Stormy's been restless. She could use a run.

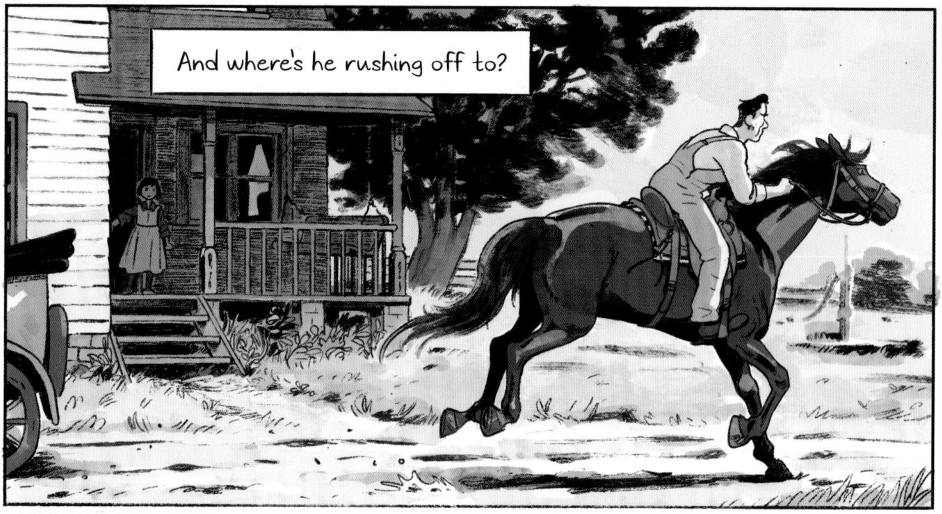
And where's he rushing off to?

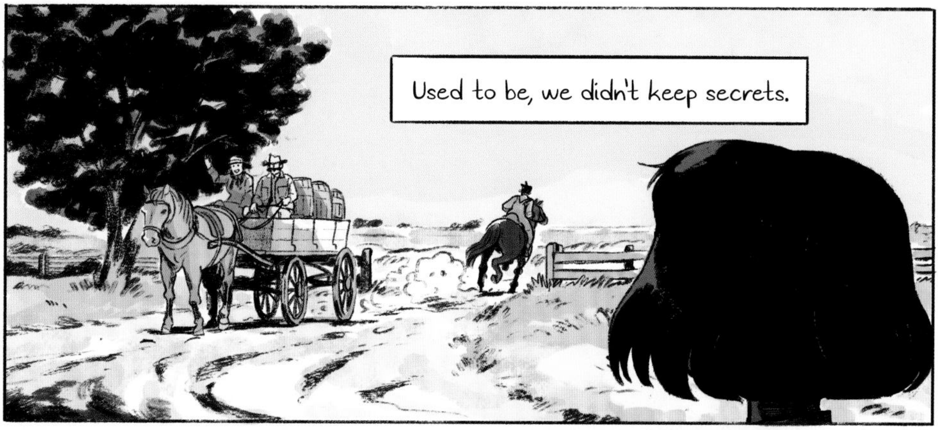
Used to be, we didn't keep secrets.

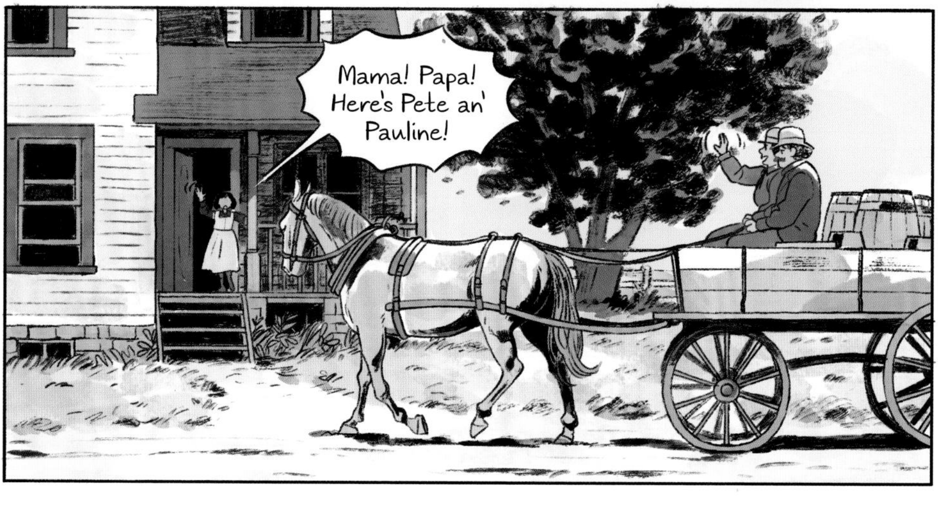
Mama! Papa! Here's Pete an' Pauline!

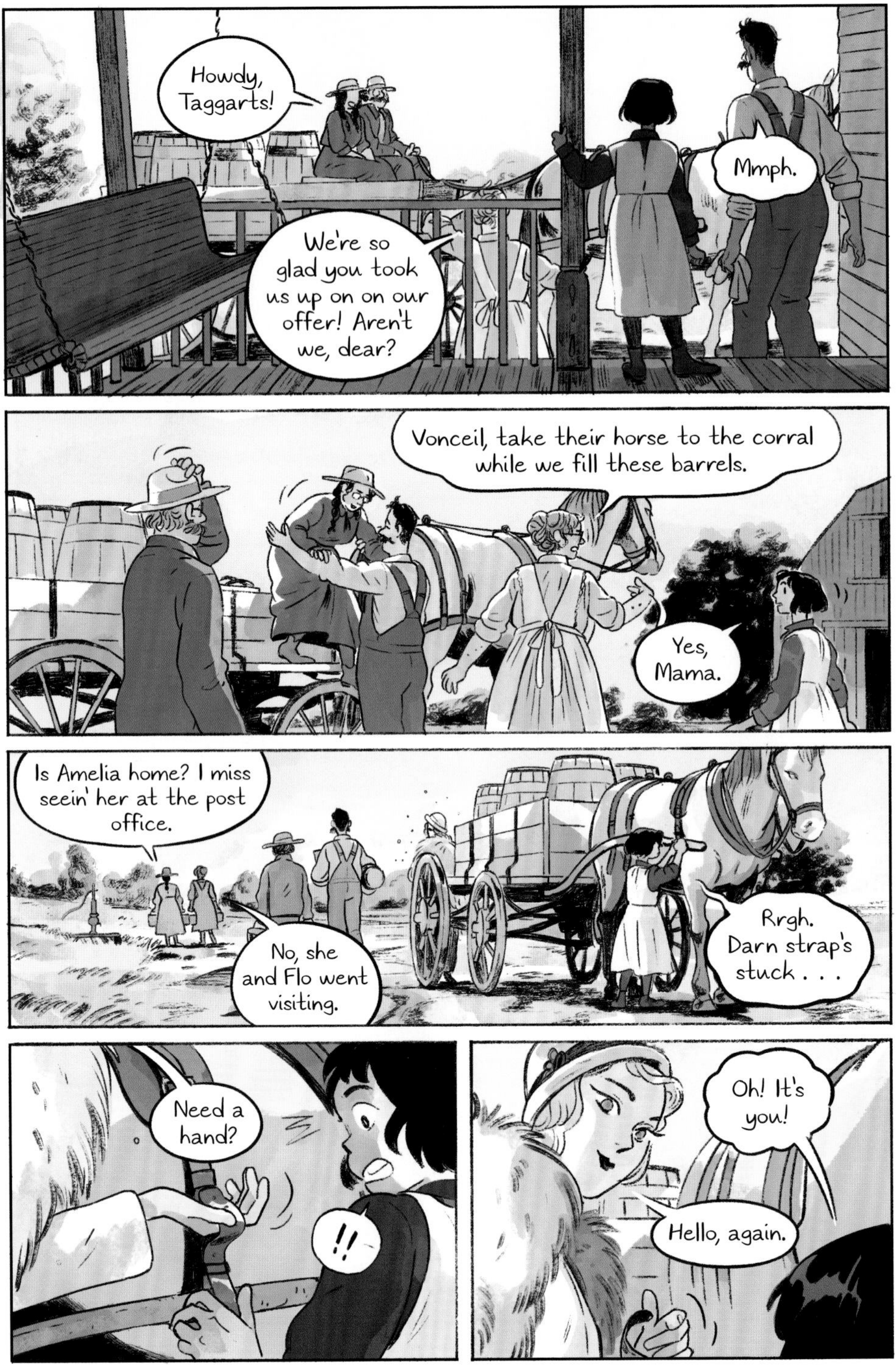
Howdy, Taggarts!
Mmph.
We're so glad you took us up on on our offer! Aren't we, dear?
Vonceil, take their horse to the corral while we fill these barrels.
Yes, Mama.
Is Amelia home? I miss seein' her at the post office.
No, she and Flo went visiting.
Rrgh. Darn strap's stuck . . .
Need a hand?
!!
Oh! It's you!
Hello, again.

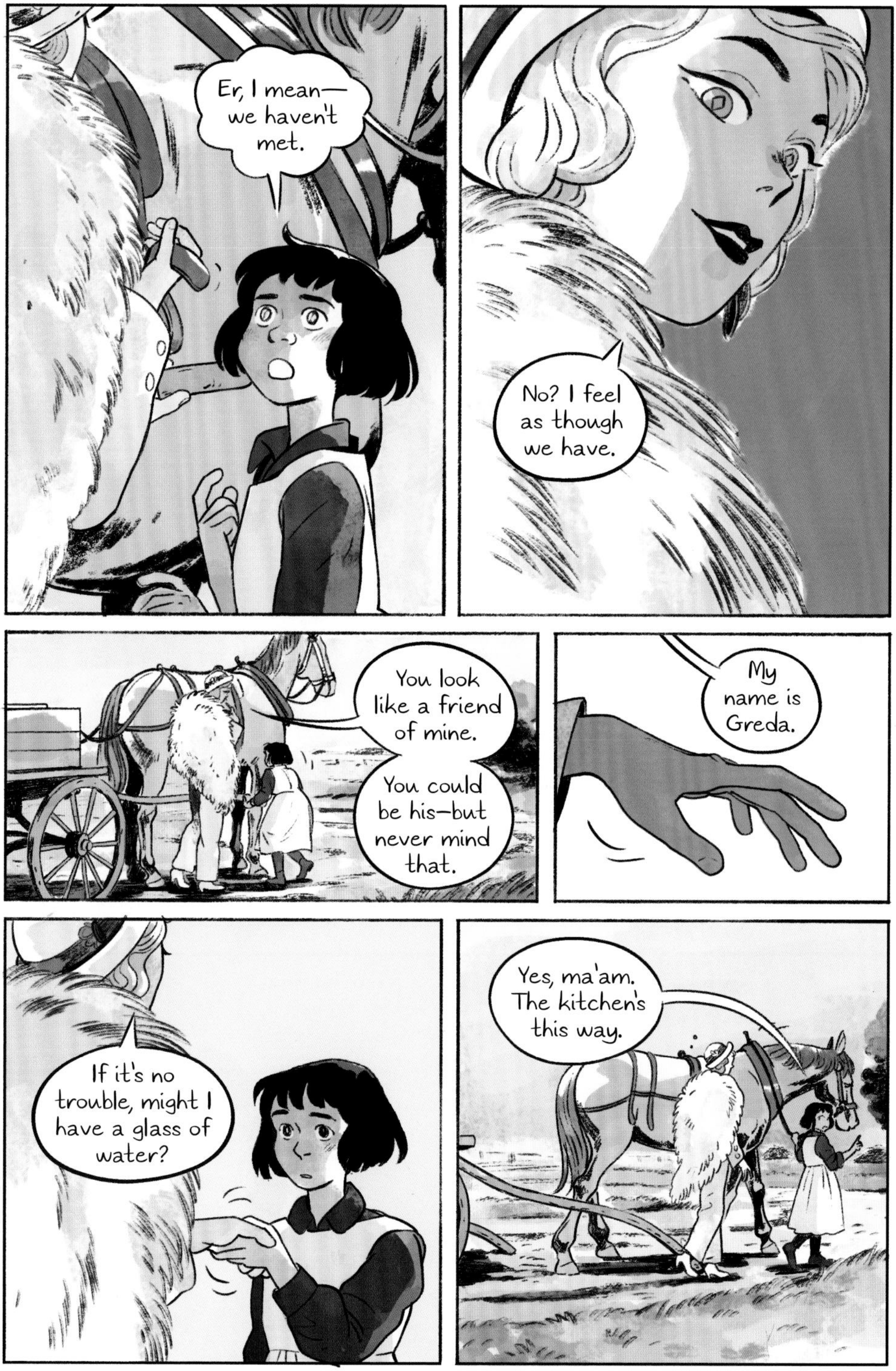

Er, I mean—we haven't met.
No? I feel as though we have.
You look like a friend of mine.
You could be his—but never mind that.
My name is Greda.
If it's no trouble, might I have a glass of water?
Yes, ma'am. The kitchen's this way.

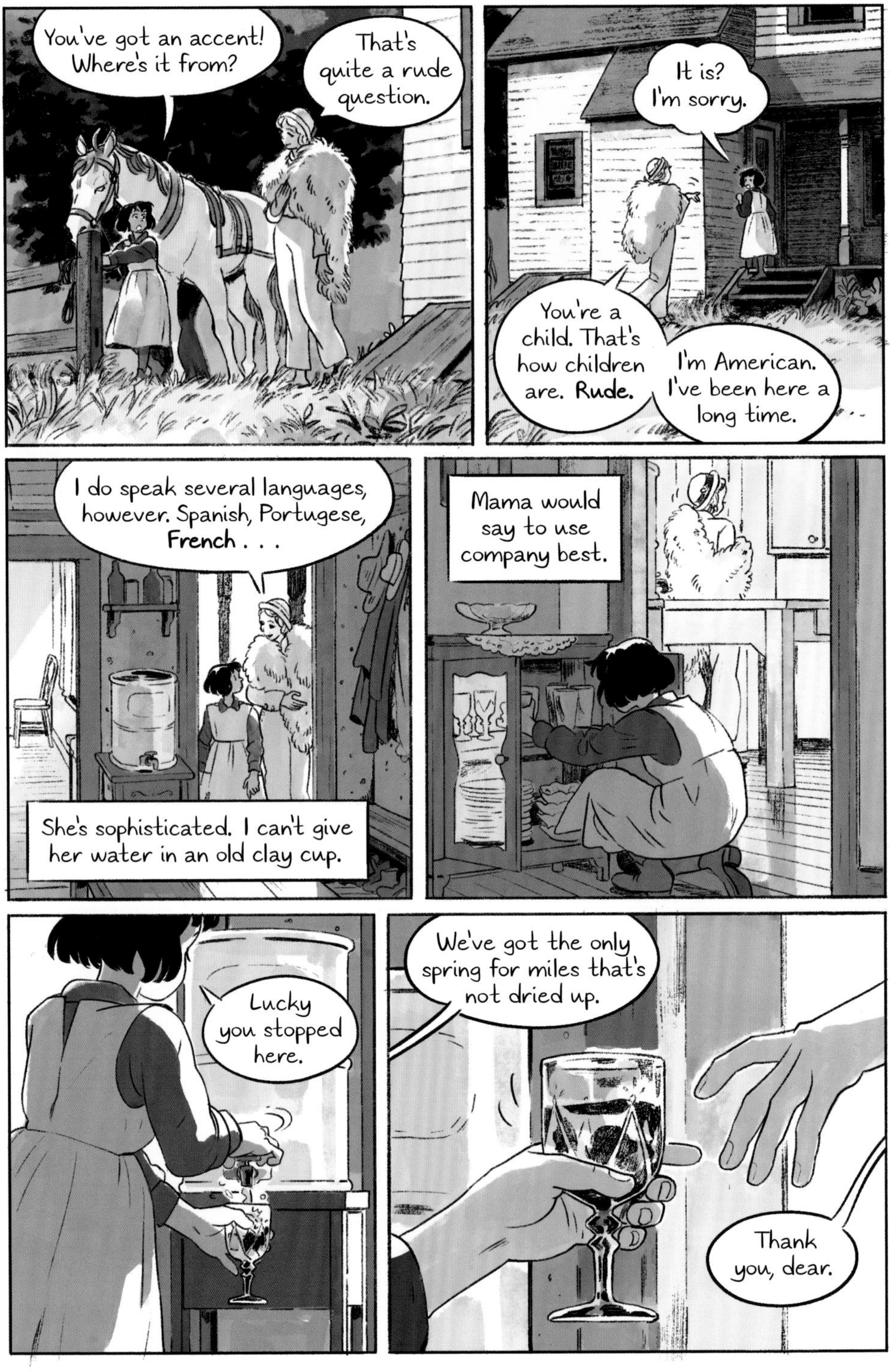
You've got an accent! Where's it from?
That's quite a rude question.
It is? I'm sorry.
You're a child. That's how children are. **Rude.**
I'm American. I've been here a long time.
I do speak several languages, however. Spanish, Portugese, **French** . . .
She's sophisticated. I can't give her water in an old clay cup.
Mama would say to use company best.
Lucky you stopped here.
We've got the only spring for miles that's not dried up.
Thank you, dear.

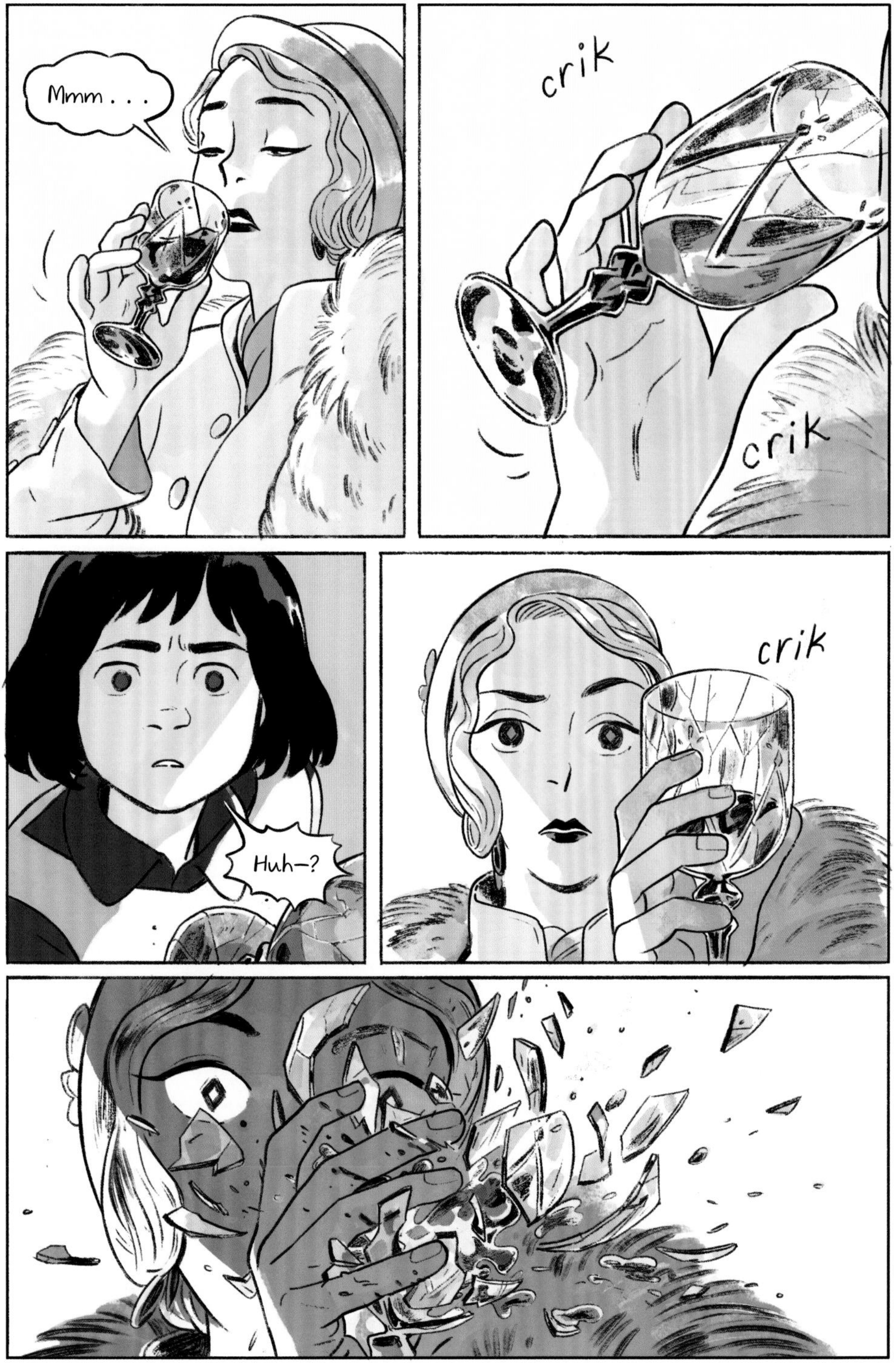
Mmm . . .
crik
crik
Huh–?
crik

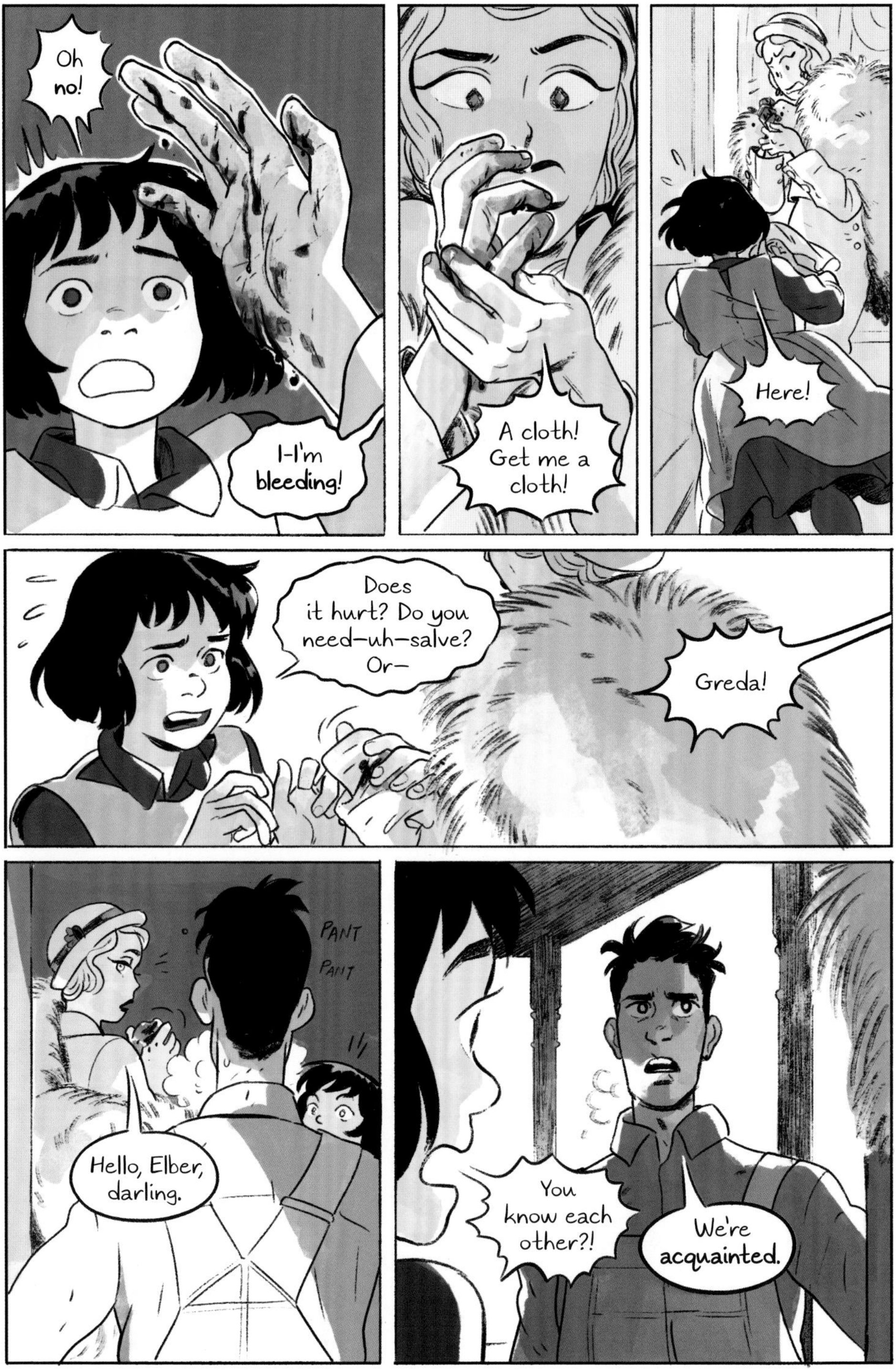
Oh no!
I-I'm bleeding!
A cloth! Get me a cloth!
Here!
Does it hurt? Do you need—uh—salve? Or—
Greda!
PANT
PANT
Hello, Elber, darling.
You know each other?!
We're acquainted.

68

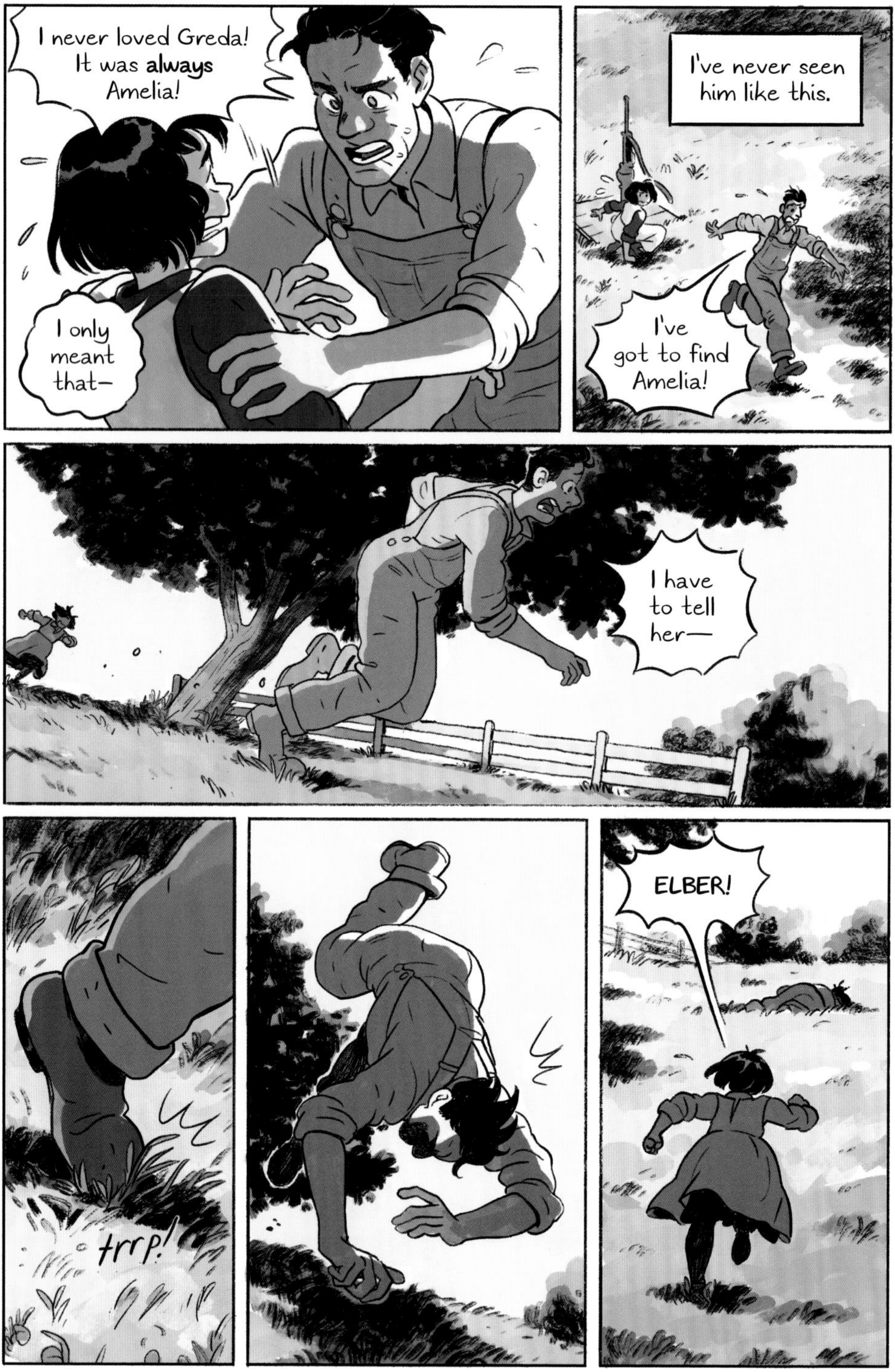

I never loved Greda! It was **always** Amelia!
I only meant that—
I've never seen him like this.
I've got to find Amelia!
I have to tell her—
trrp!
ELBER!

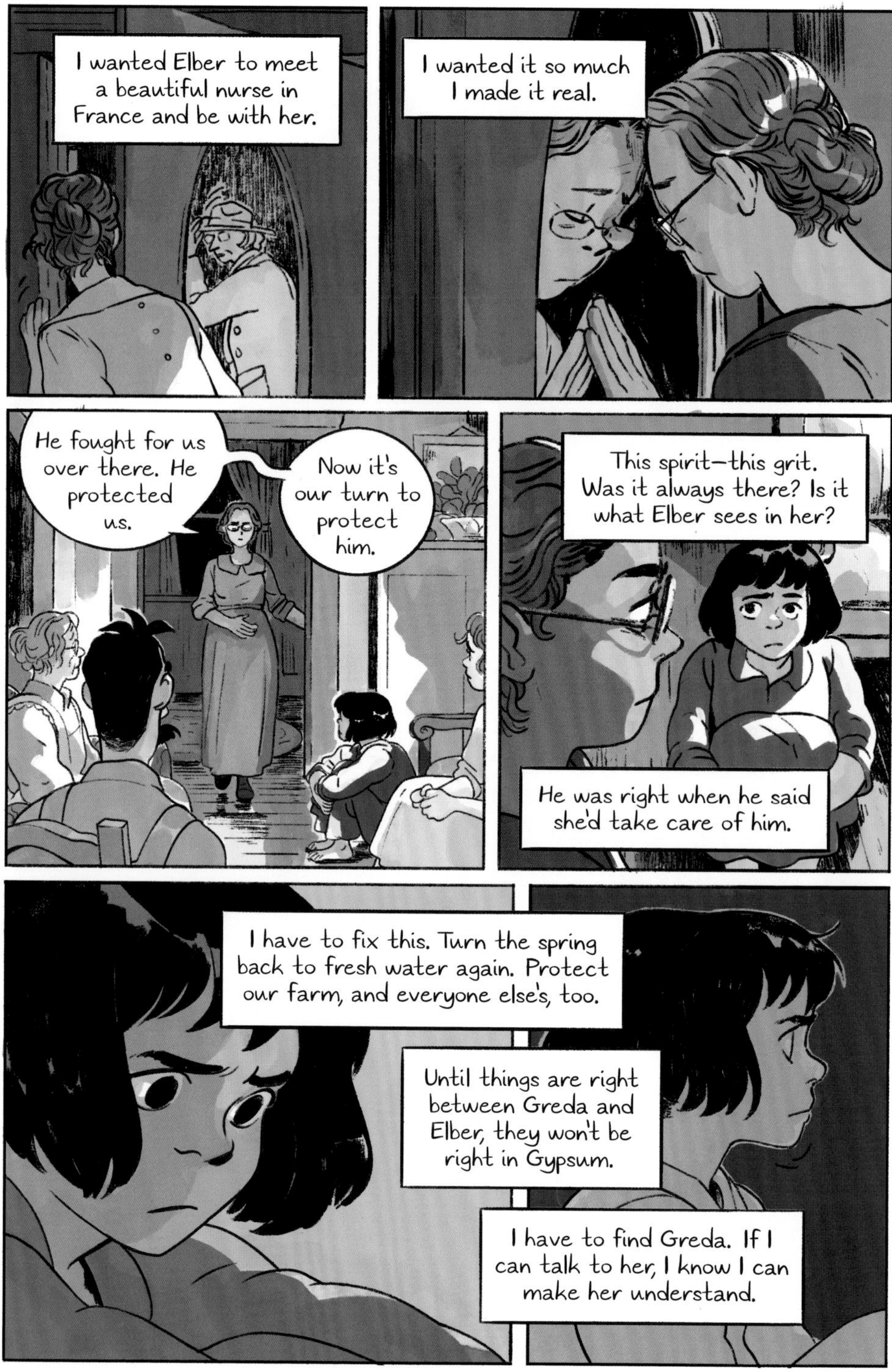
I wanted Elber to meet a beautiful nurse in France and be with her.
I wanted it so much I made it real.
He fought for us over there. He protected us.
Now it's our turn to protect him.
This spirit—this grit. Was it always there? Is it what Elber sees in her?
He was right when he said she'd take care of him.
I have to fix this. Turn the spring back to fresh water again. Protect our farm, and everyone else's, too.
Until things are right between Greda and Elber, they won't be right in Gypsum.
I have to find Greda. If I can talk to her, I know I can make her understand.

Chapter Five

A Sacrificial Pawn

Dear Mama, Papa, Elber, Flo, Ida, and Amelia,

When you wake up, I'll be gone.

There's fresh water in the cooler—

Would you believe me if I said it was a curse? It is, and I've gone to undo it. I'll be back quick as I can.

but when you draw more from the spring, you'll find it's turned salty.

Sorry to wake you, Stormy girl.

Don't worry about me. Worry about Elber. Very truly, Vonceil

Can't believe I'm doing this.

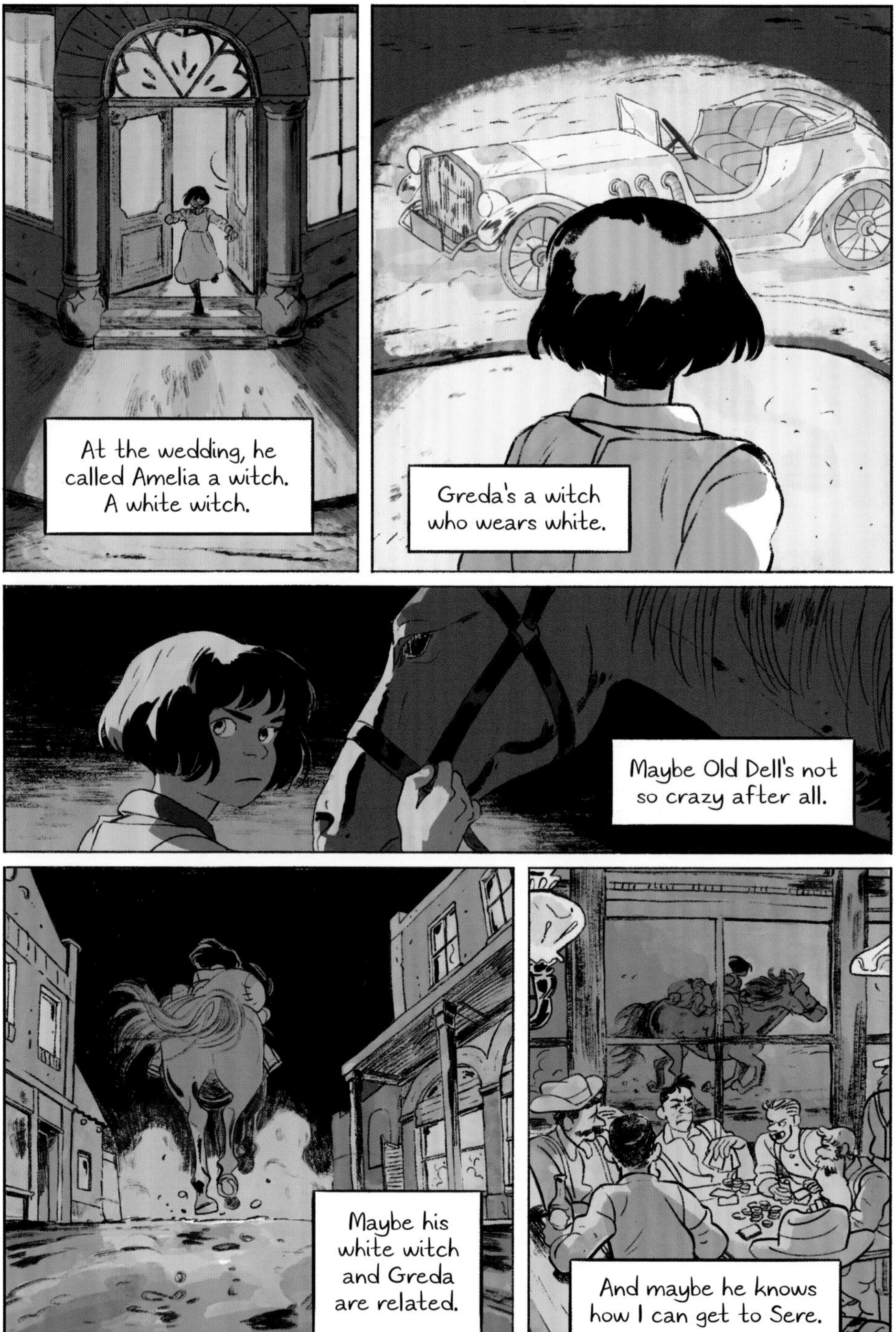
At the wedding, he called Amelia a witch. A white witch.
Greda's a witch who wears white.
Maybe Old Dell's not so crazy after all.
Maybe his white witch and Greda are related.
And maybe he knows how I can get to Sere.

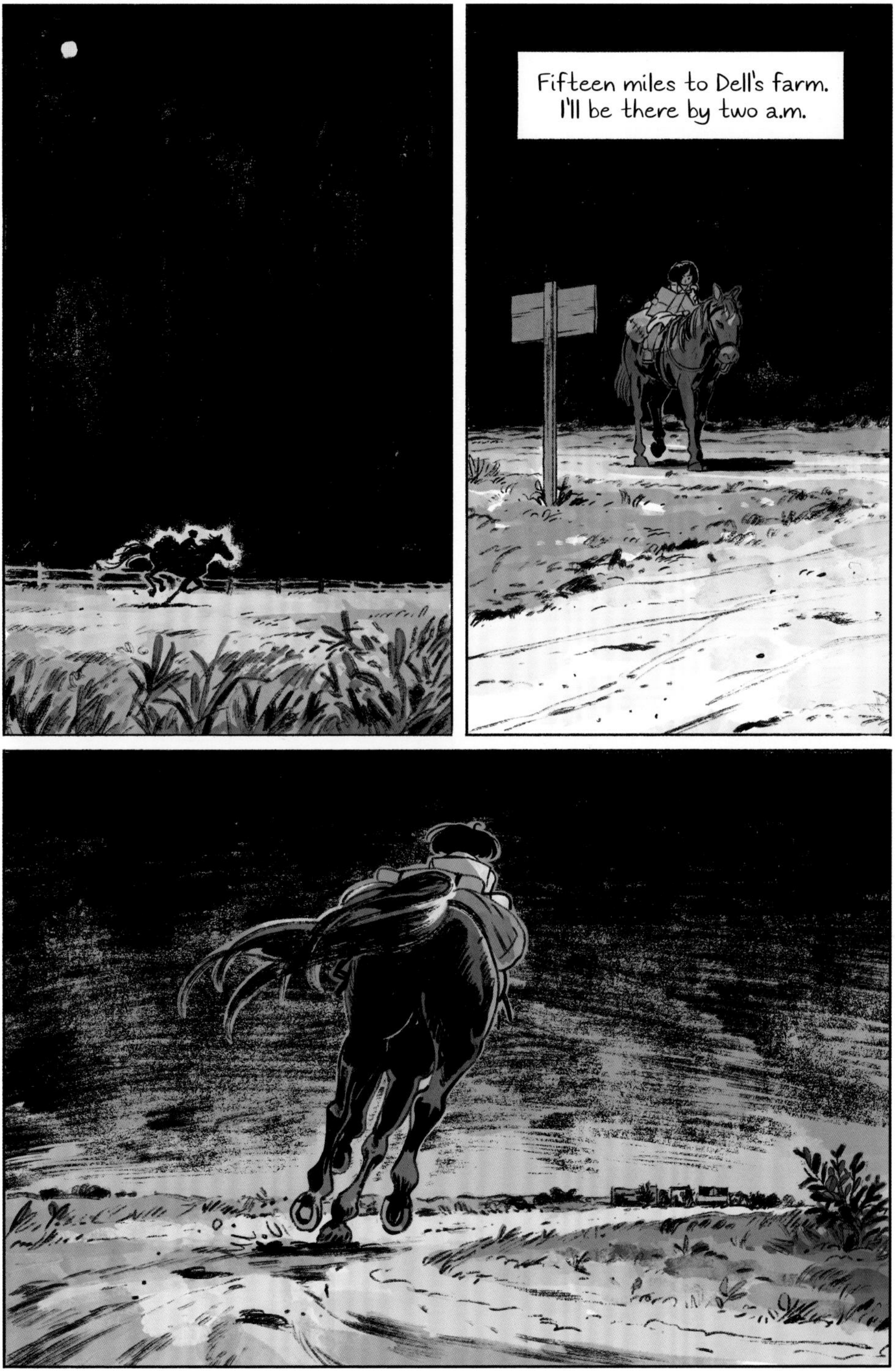
Fifteen miles to Dell's farm.
I'll be there by two a.m.

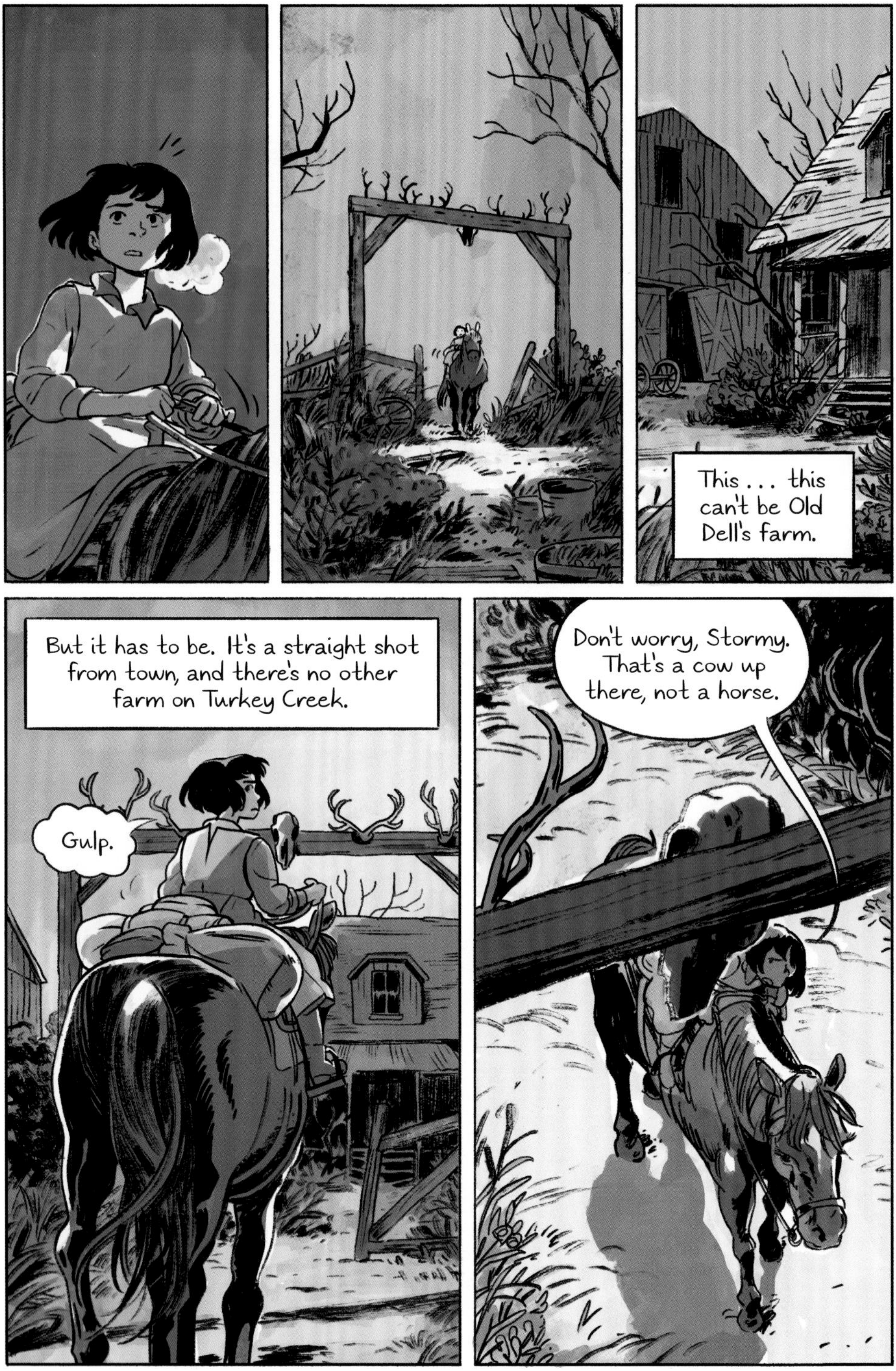
This . . . this can't be Old Dell's farm.
But it has to be. It's a straight shot from town, and there's no other farm on Turkey Creek.
Gulp.
Don't worry, Stormy. That's a cow up there, not a horse.

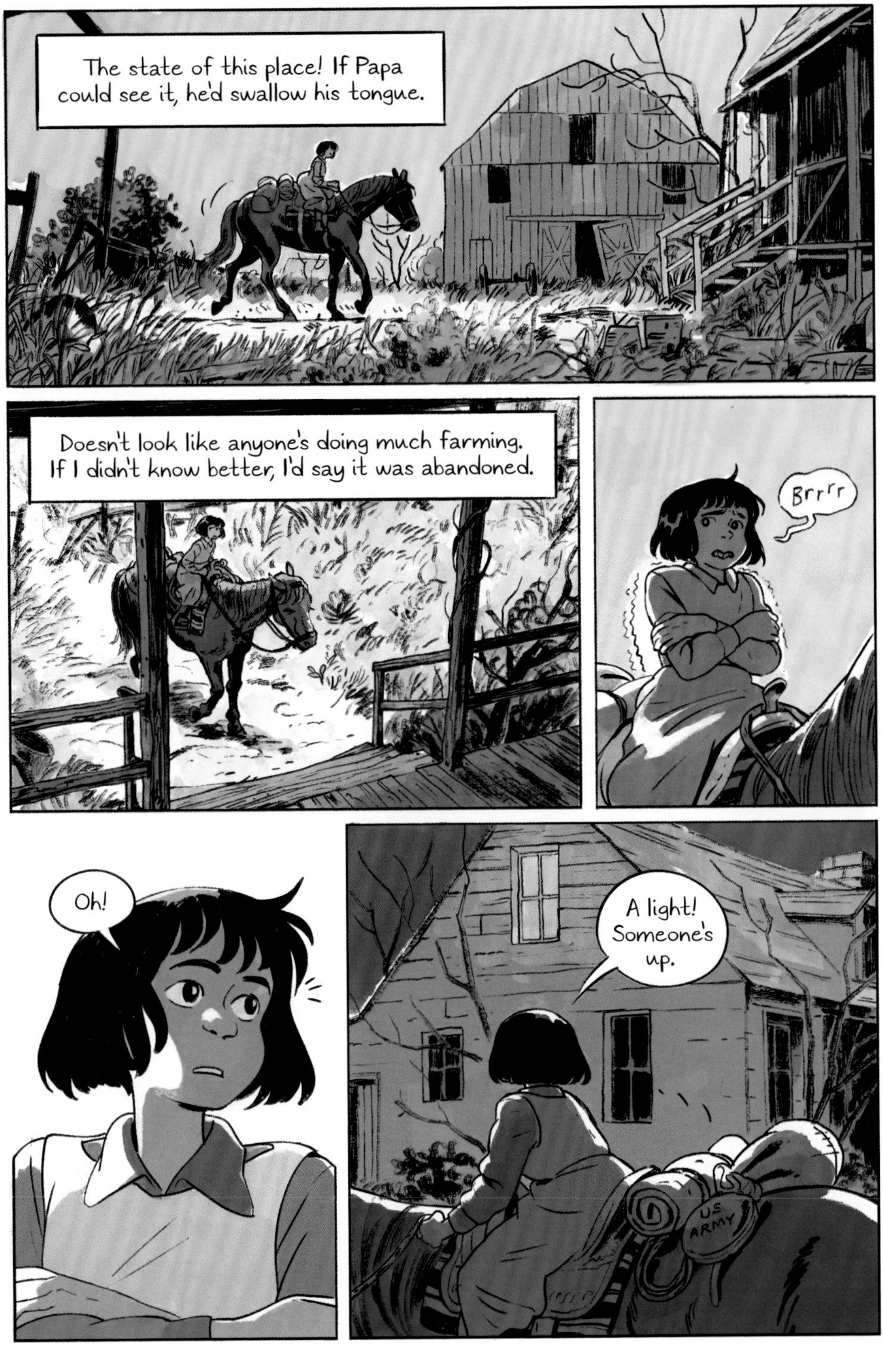

The state of this place! If Papa could see it, he'd swallow his tongue.
Doesn't look like anyone's doing much farming. If I didn't know better, I'd say it was abandoned.
Brrrr
Oh!
A light! Someone's up.
US ARMY

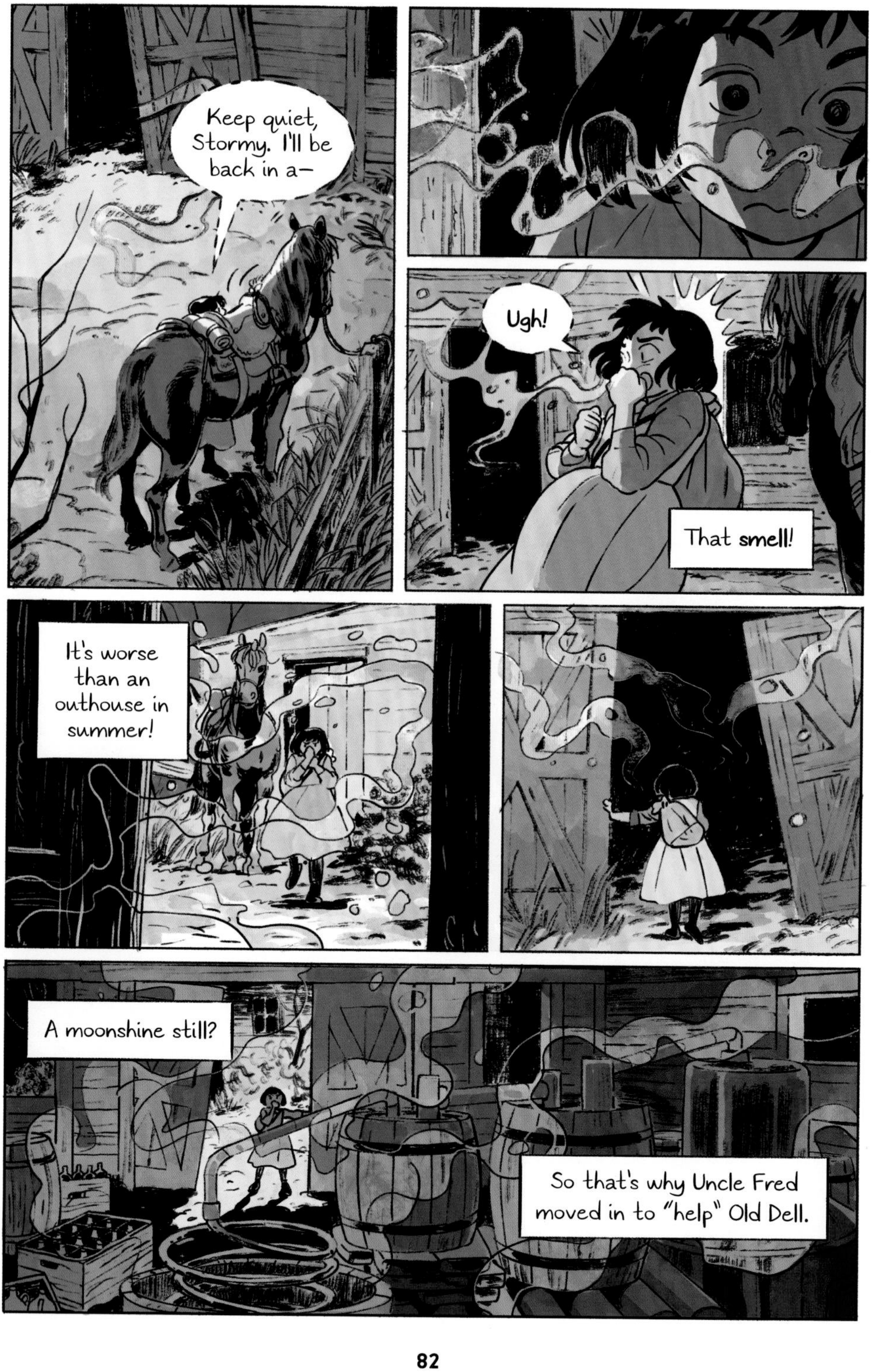
Keep quiet, Stormy. I'll be back in a–
Ugh!
That smell!
It's worse than an outhouse in summer!
A moonshine still?
So that's why Uncle Fred moved in to "help" Old Dell.

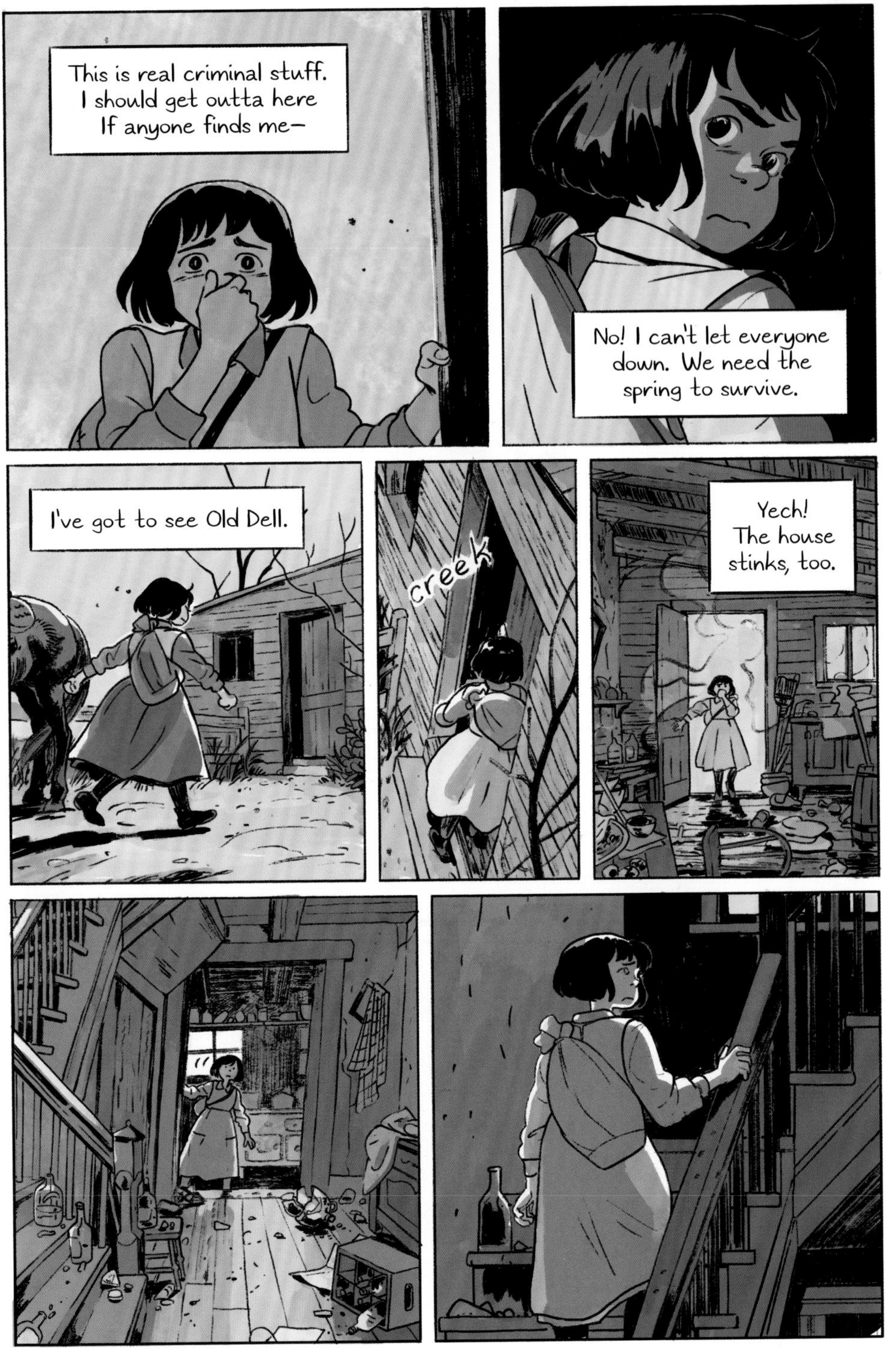
This is real criminal stuff. I should get outta here If anyone finds me—
No! I can't let everyone down. We need the spring to survive.
I've got to see Old Dell.
creek
Yech! The house stinks, too.

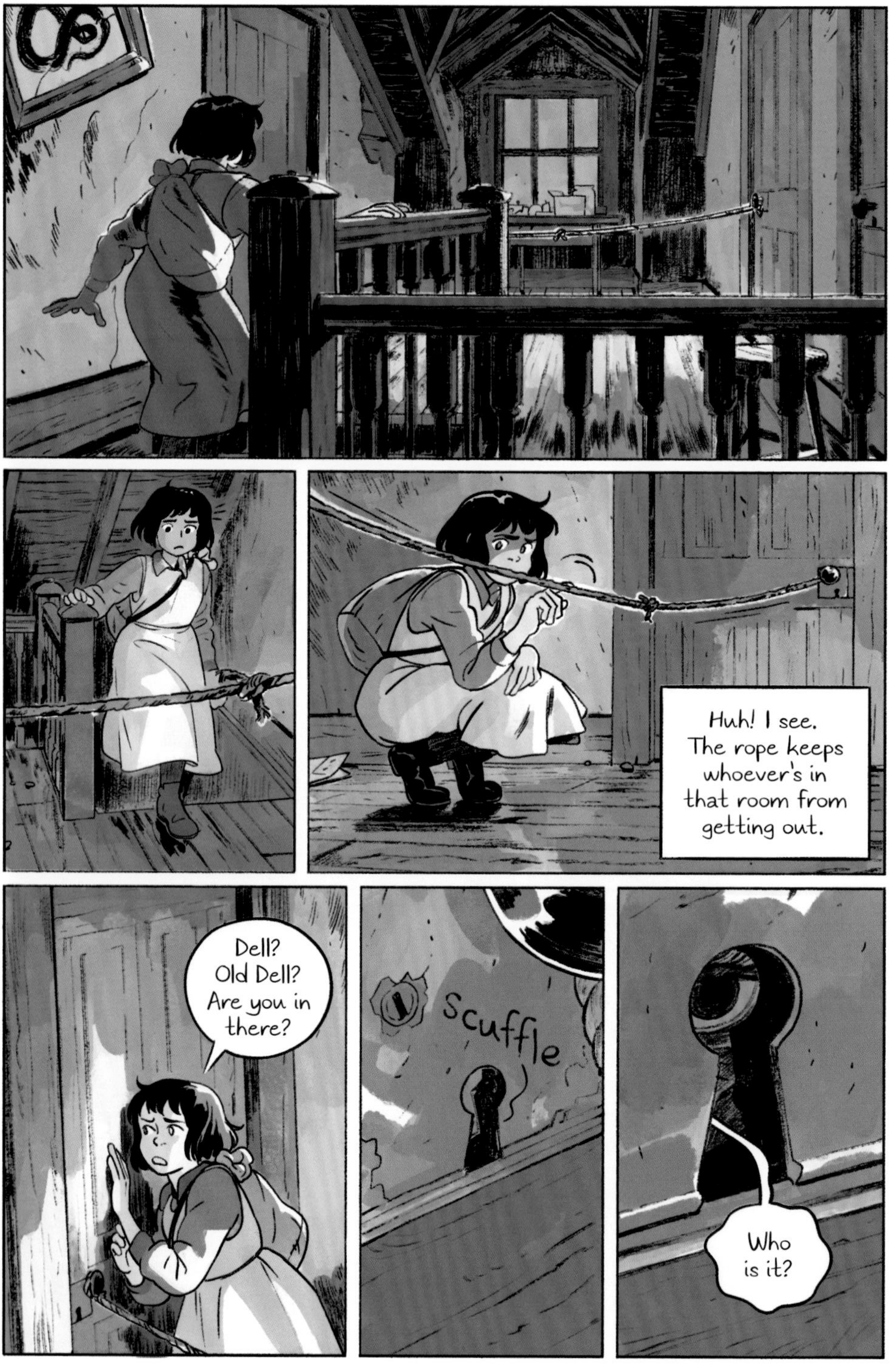
Huh! I see. The rope keeps whoever's in that room from getting out.
Dell? Old Dell? Are you in there?
Scuffle
Who is it?

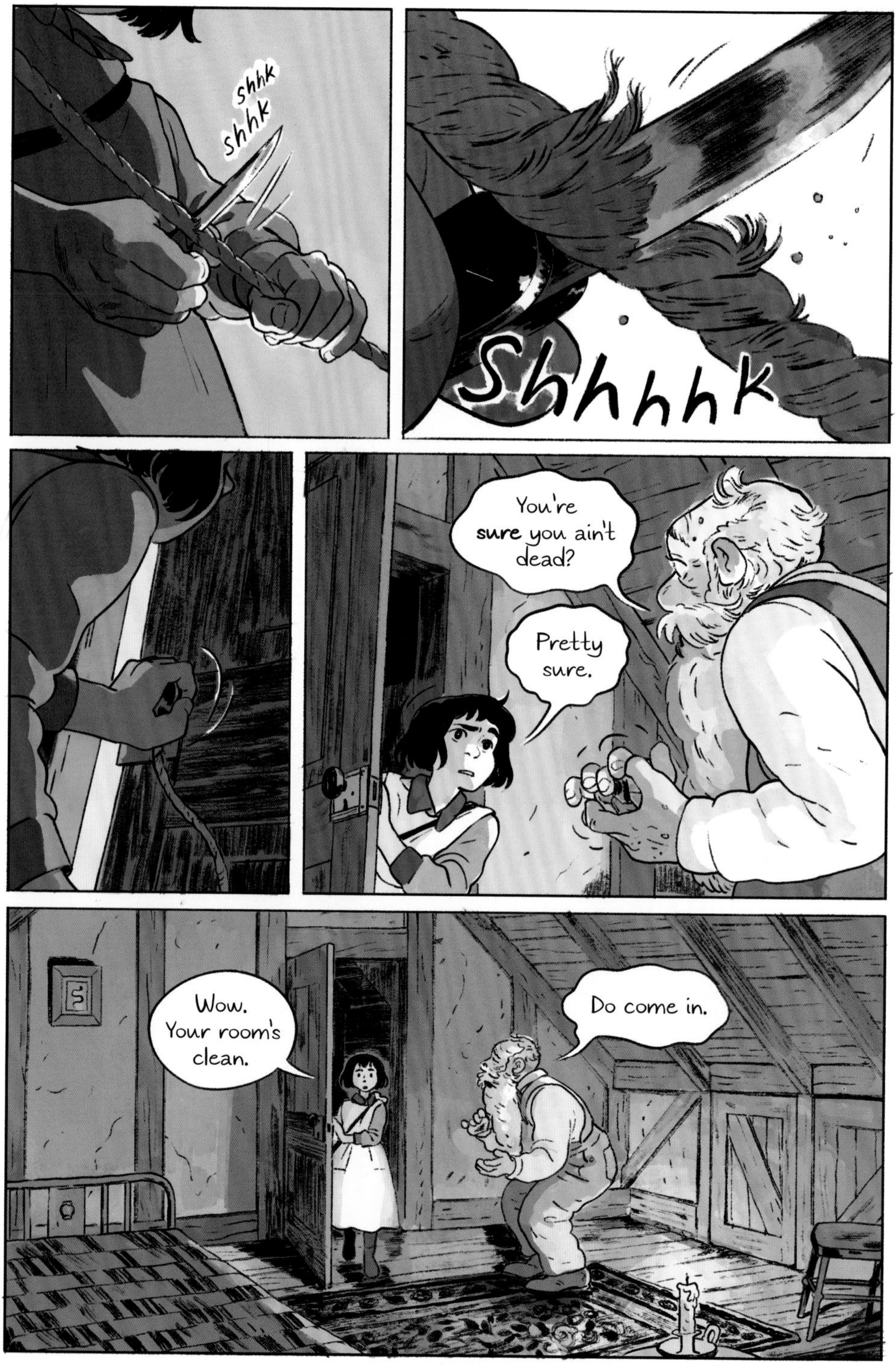
shhk
shhk
Shhhhk
You're **sure** you ain't dead?
Pretty sure.
Wow. Your room's clean.
Do come in.

Chapter Six

The Lady of Sere

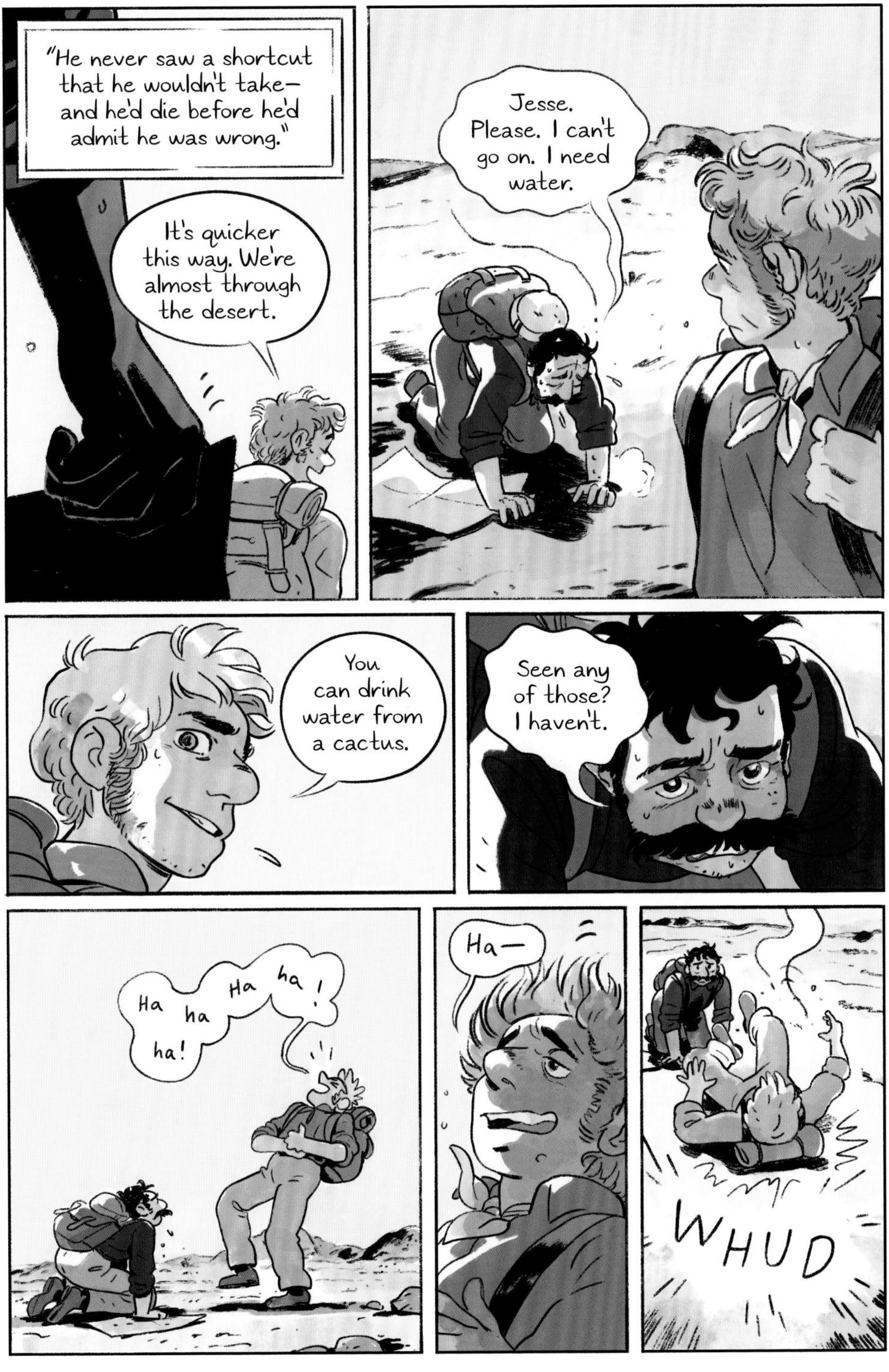
"He never saw a shortcut that he wouldn't take—and he'd die before he'd admit he was wrong."
It's quicker this way. We're almost through the desert.
Jesse. Please. I can't go on. I need water.
You can drink water from a cactus.
Seen any of those? I haven't.
Ha ha ha! Ha ha!
Ha—
WHUD

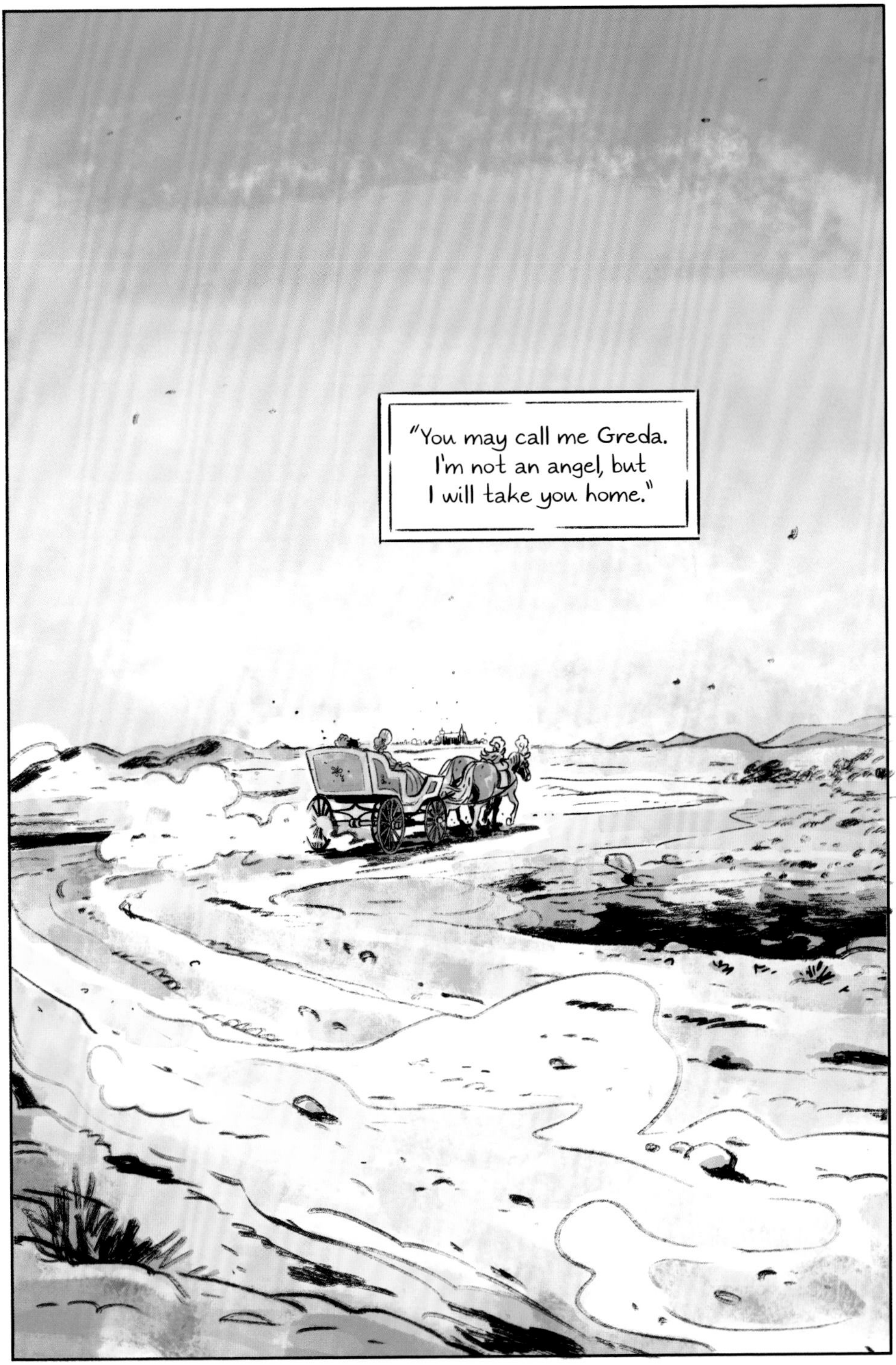
"You may call me Greda.
I'm not an angel, but
I will take you home."

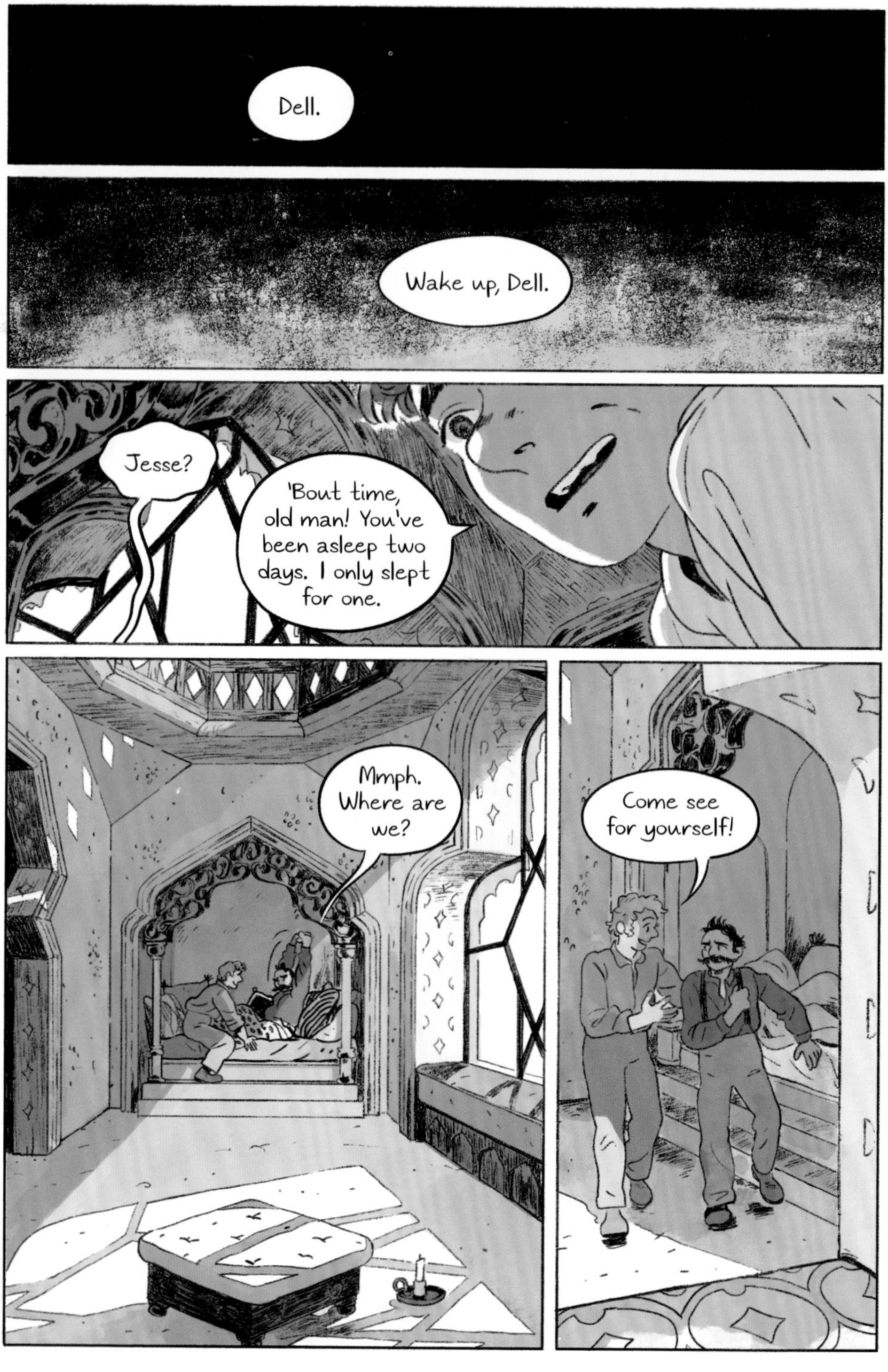
Dell.
Wake up, Dell.
Jesse?
'Bout time, old man! You've been asleep two days. I only slept for one.
Mmph. Where are we?
Come see for yourself!

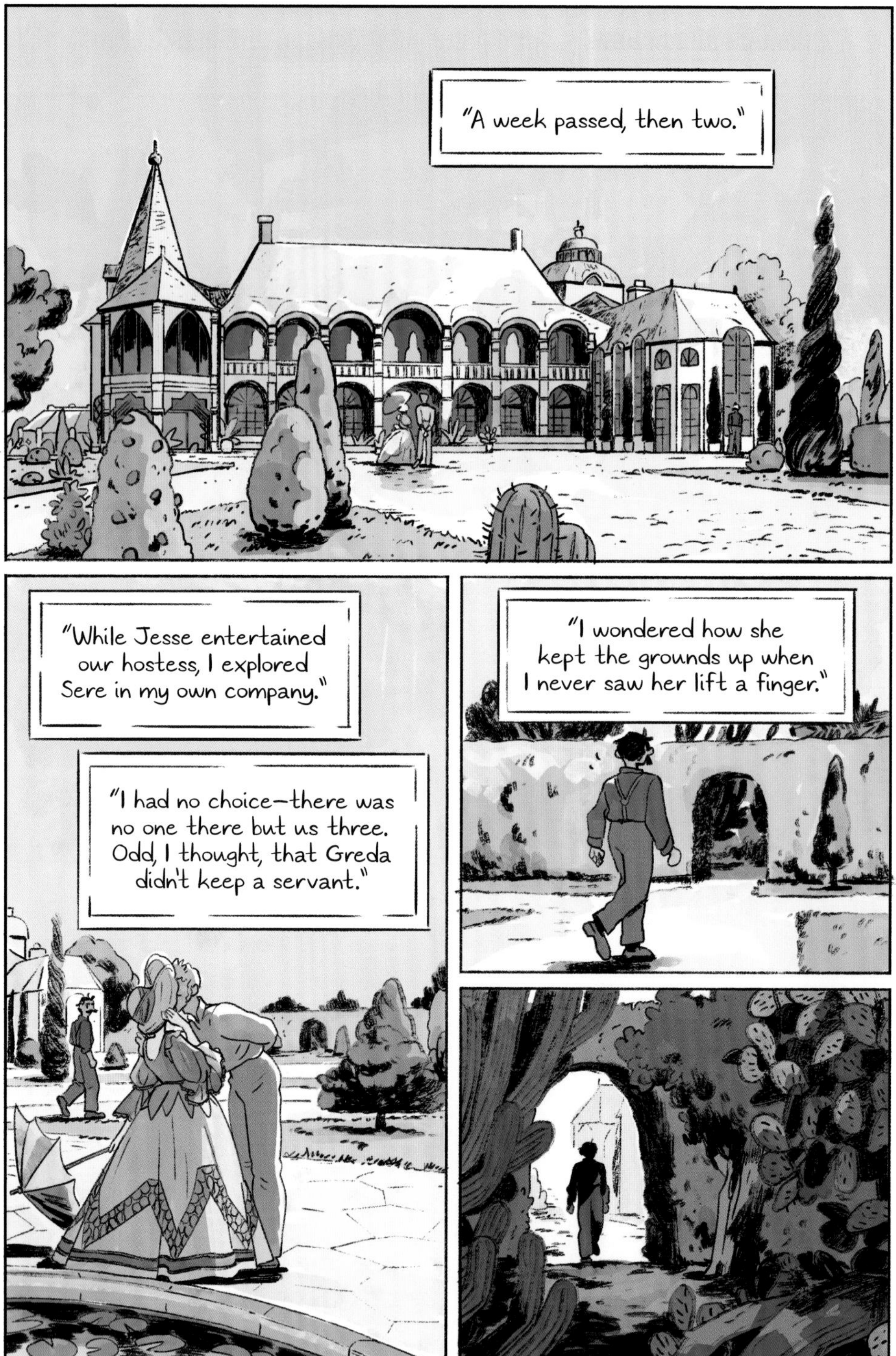
"A week passed, then two."
"While Jesse entertained our hostess, I explored Sere in my own company."
"I had no choice—there was no one there but us three. Odd, I thought, that Greda didn't keep a servant."
"I wondered how she kept the grounds up when I never saw her lift a finger."

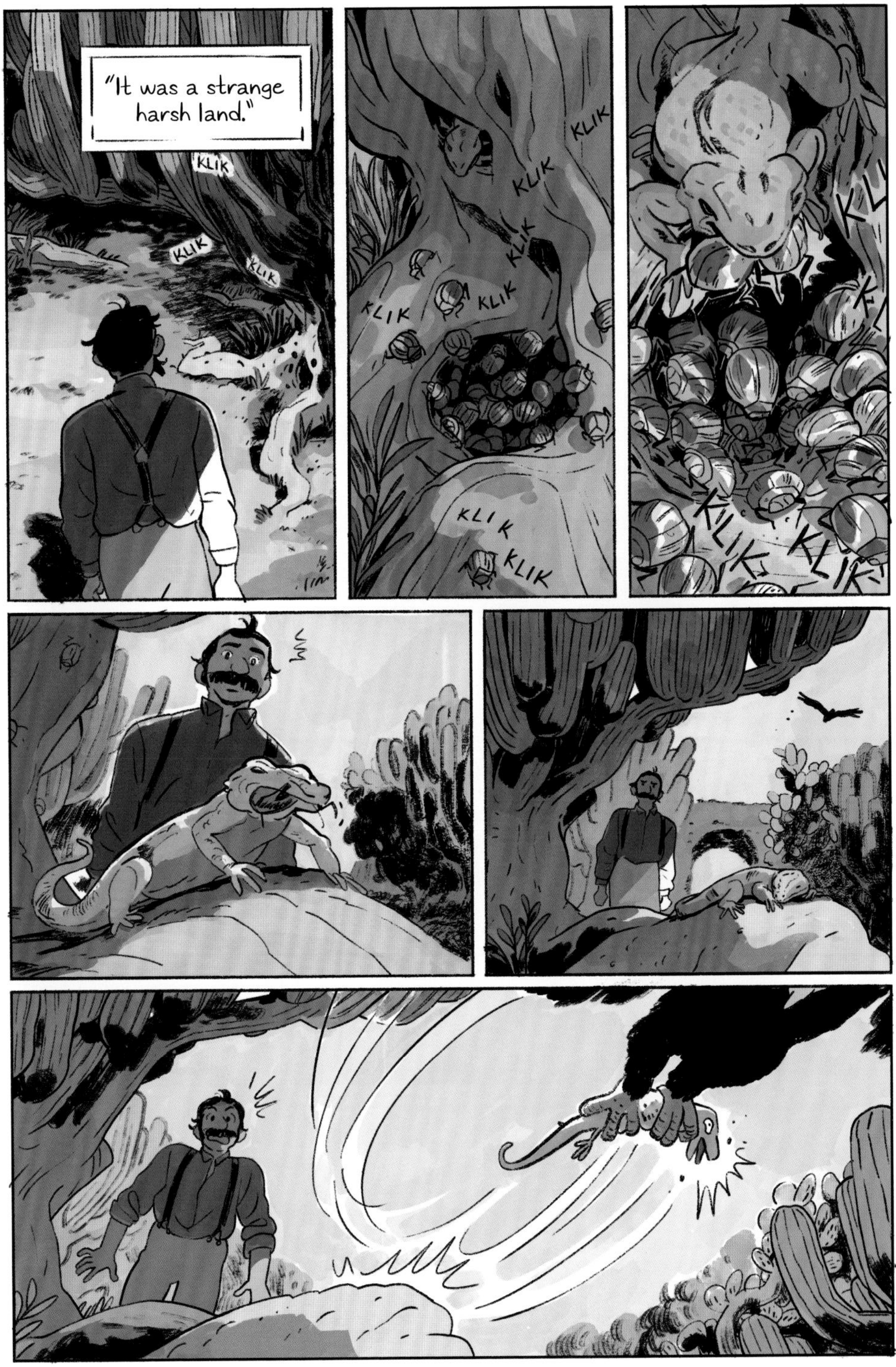
"It was a strange harsh land."
KLIK
KLIK
KLIK
KLIK
KLIK
KLIK
KLIK
KLIK
KLIK
KLIK
KLIK
KLIK
KLIK

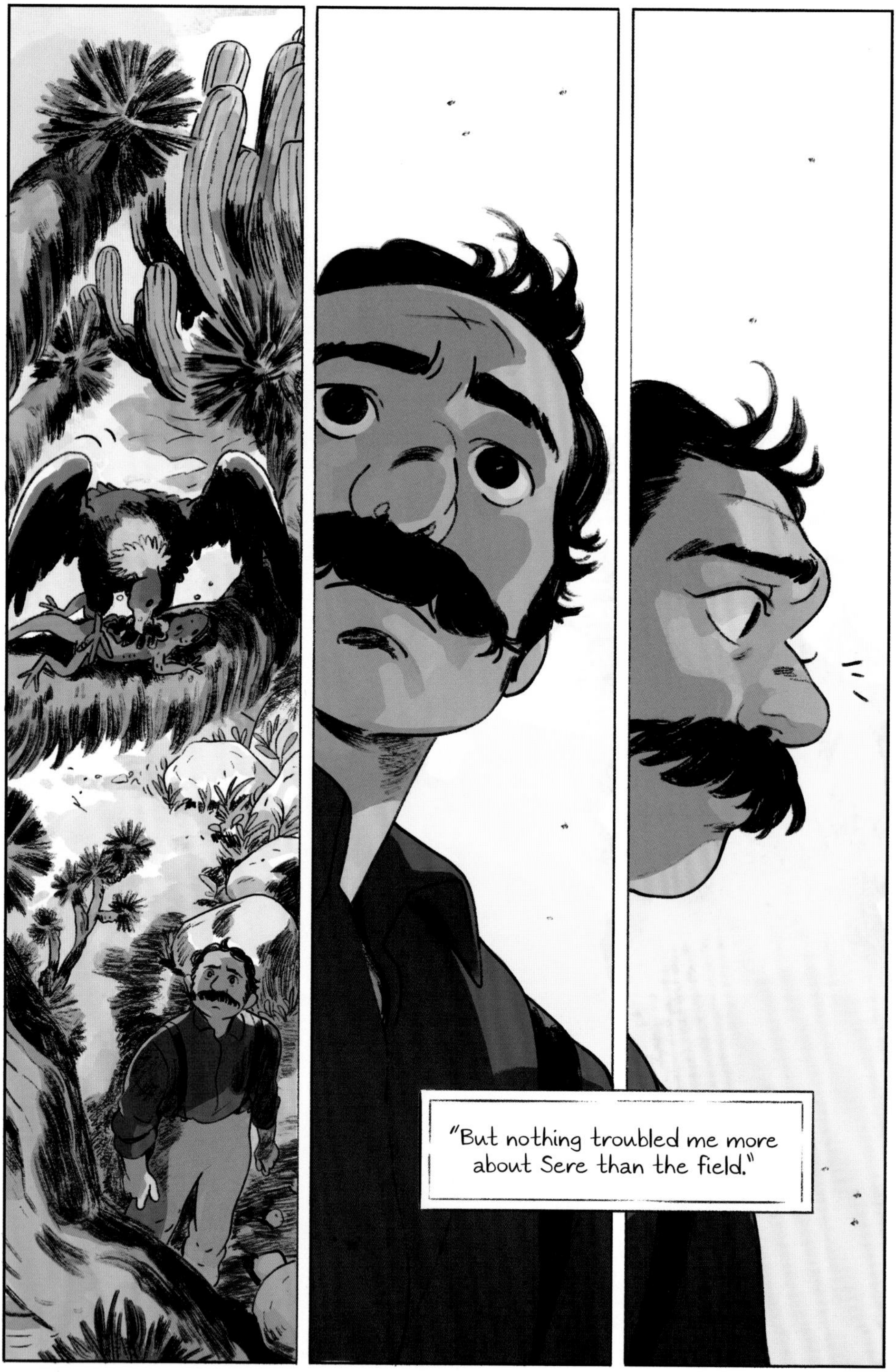
"But nothing troubled me more about Sere than the field."

"The moment I stepped foot there, the wind rushed toward me like a cry."

R-RRRRRRRUUUUUUUUU

RRUUUNNNNN

"It said, Run."

RRRUUUU

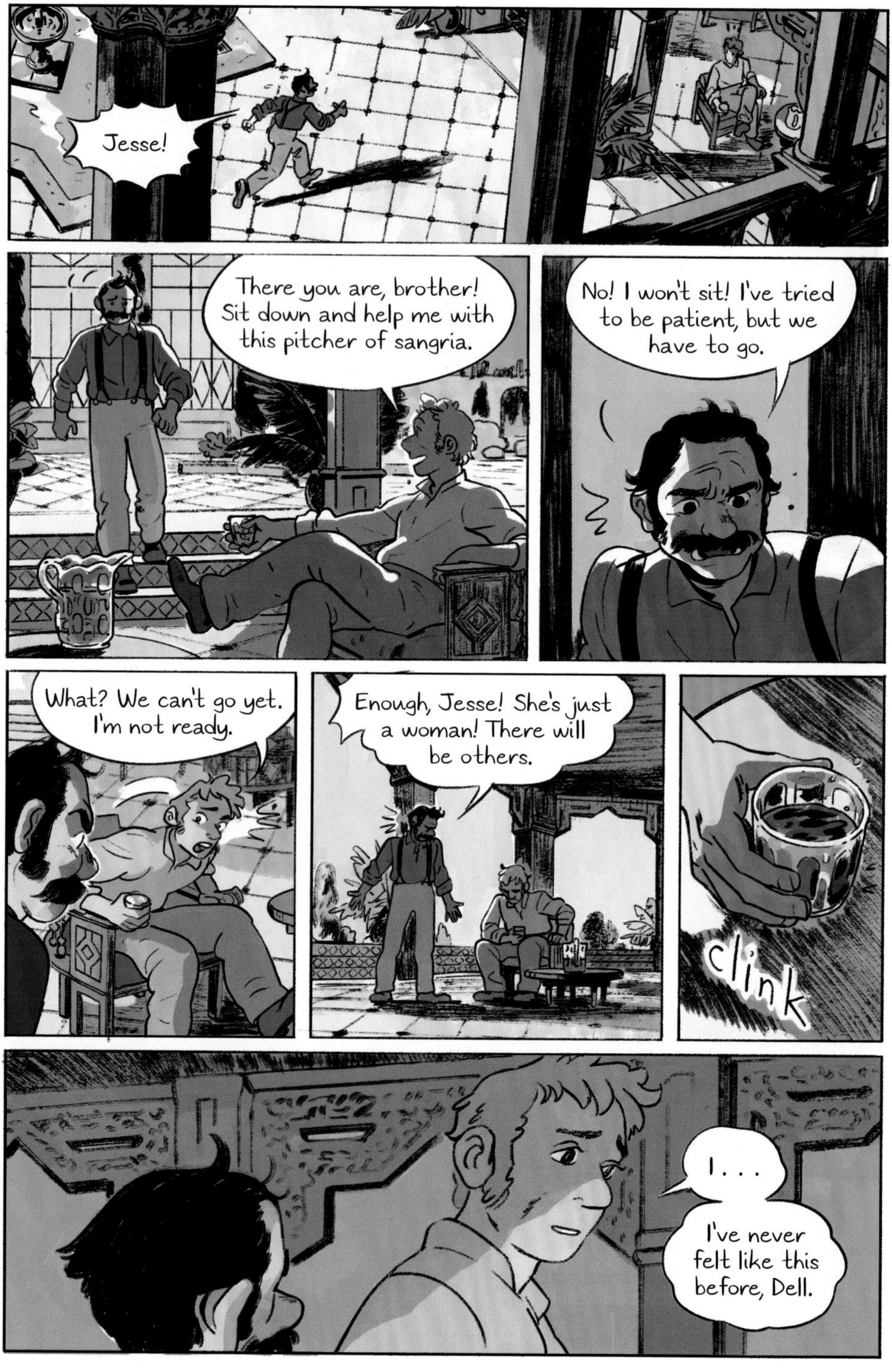
Jesse!
There you are, brother! Sit down and help me with this pitcher of sangria.
No! I won't sit! I've tried to be patient, but we have to go.
What? We can't go yet. I'm not ready.
Enough, Jesse! She's just a woman! There will be others.
clink
I . . .
I've never felt like this before, Dell.

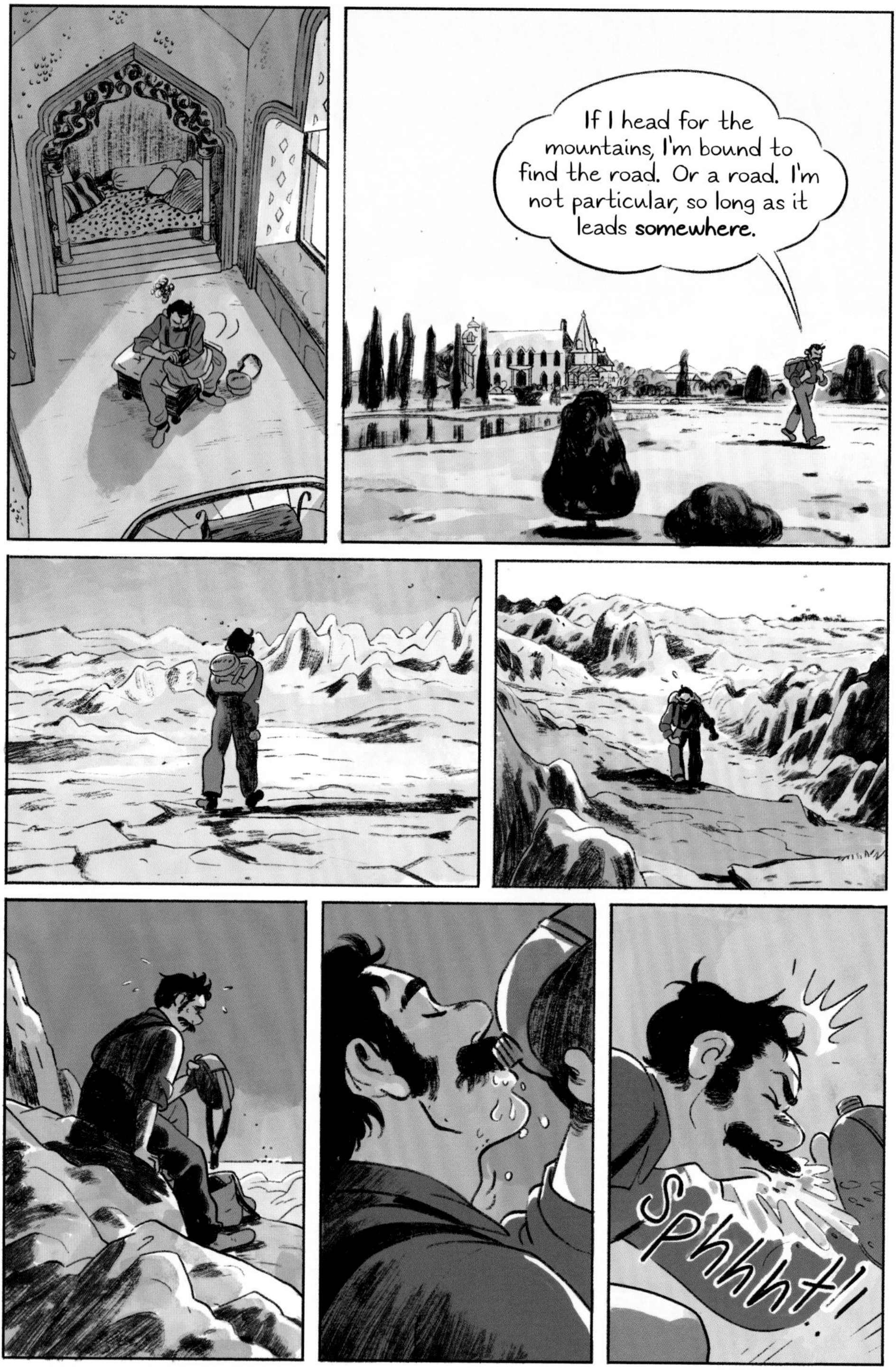
If I head for the mountains, I'm bound to find the road. Or a road. I'm not particular, so long as it leads **somewhere.**
Sphhht!

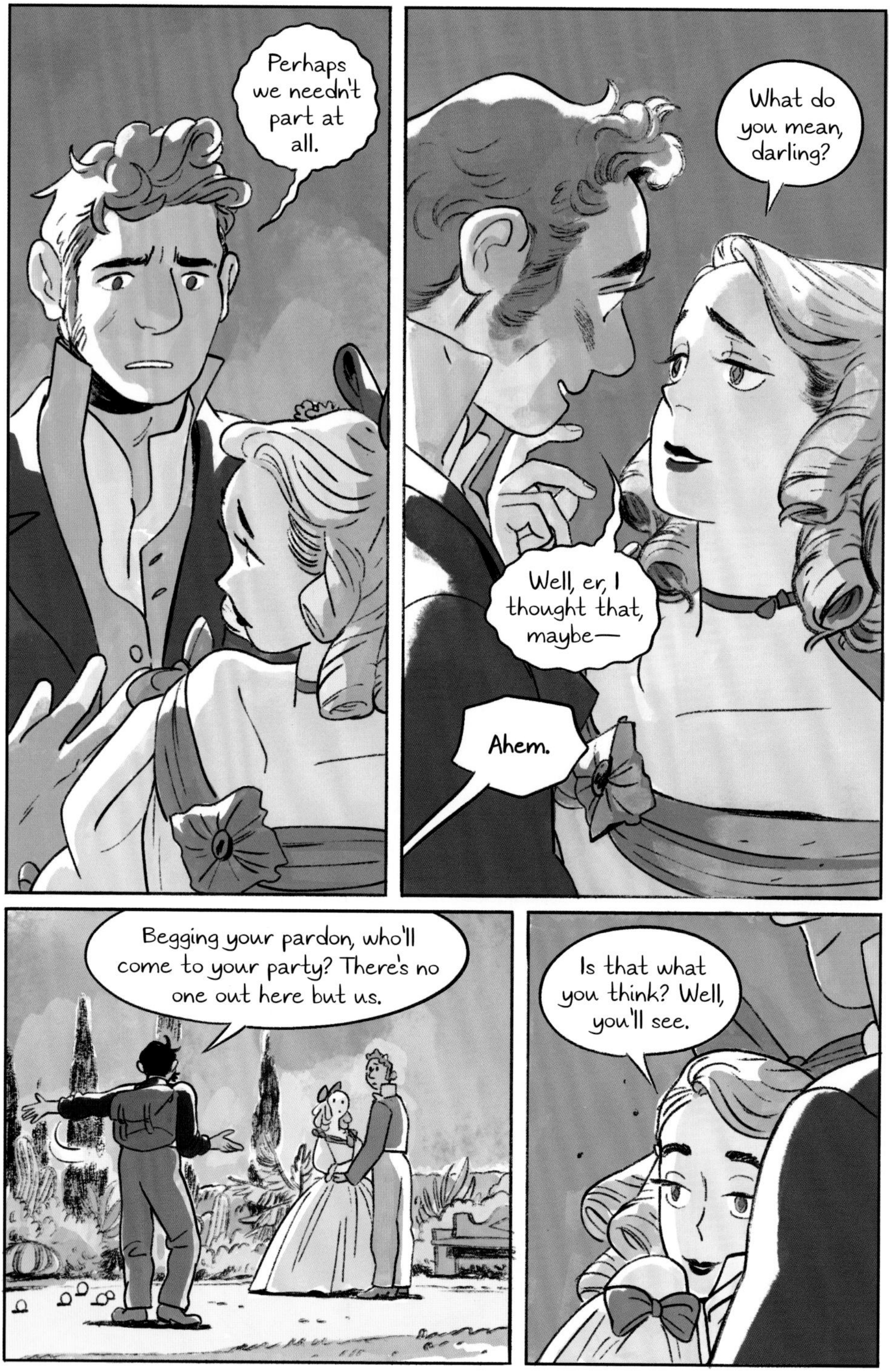
Perhaps we needn't part at all.
What do you mean, darling?
Well, er, I thought that, maybe—
Ahem.
Begging your pardon, who'll come to your party? There's no one out here but us.
Is that what you think? Well, you'll see.

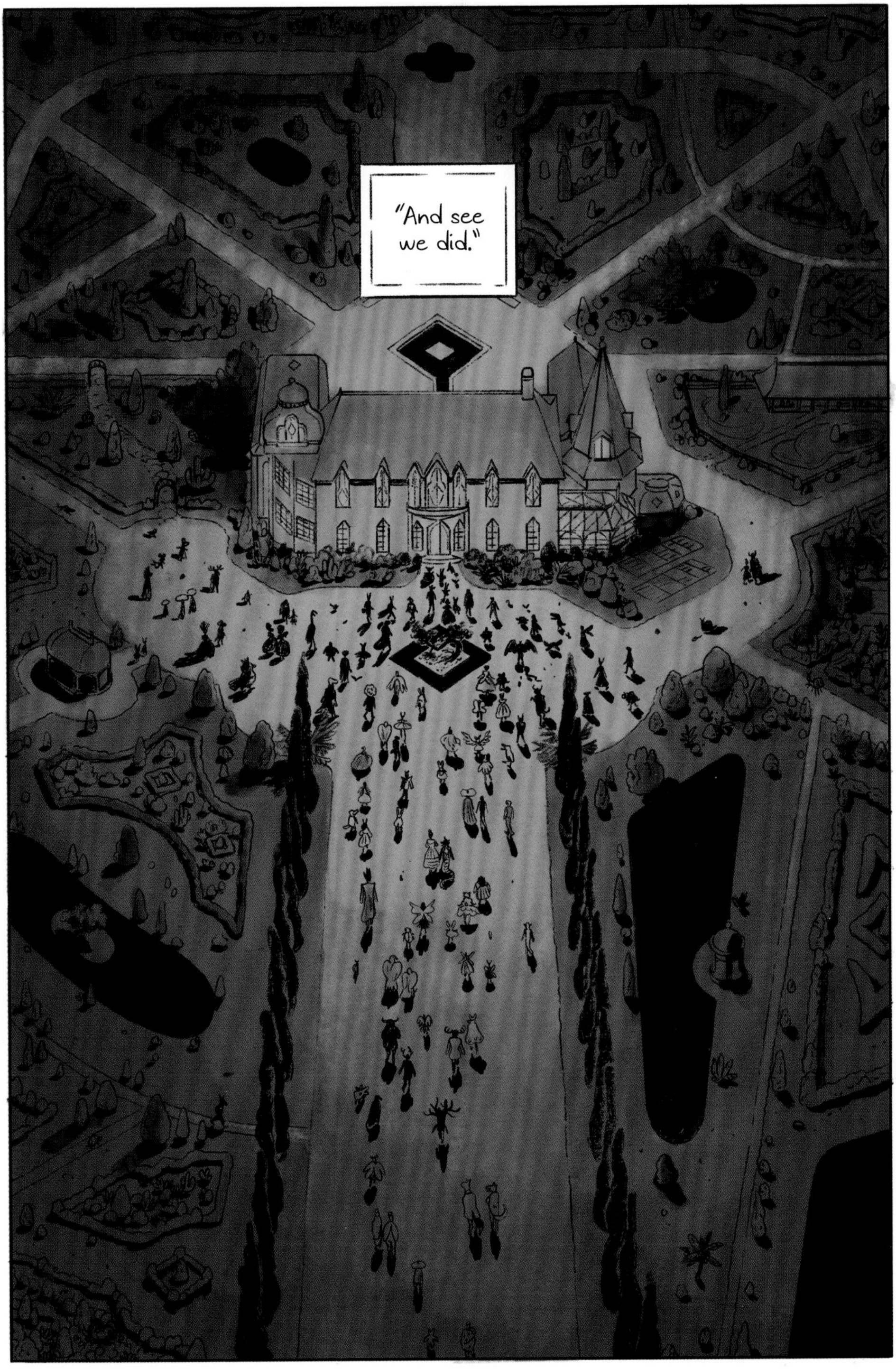
"And see we did."

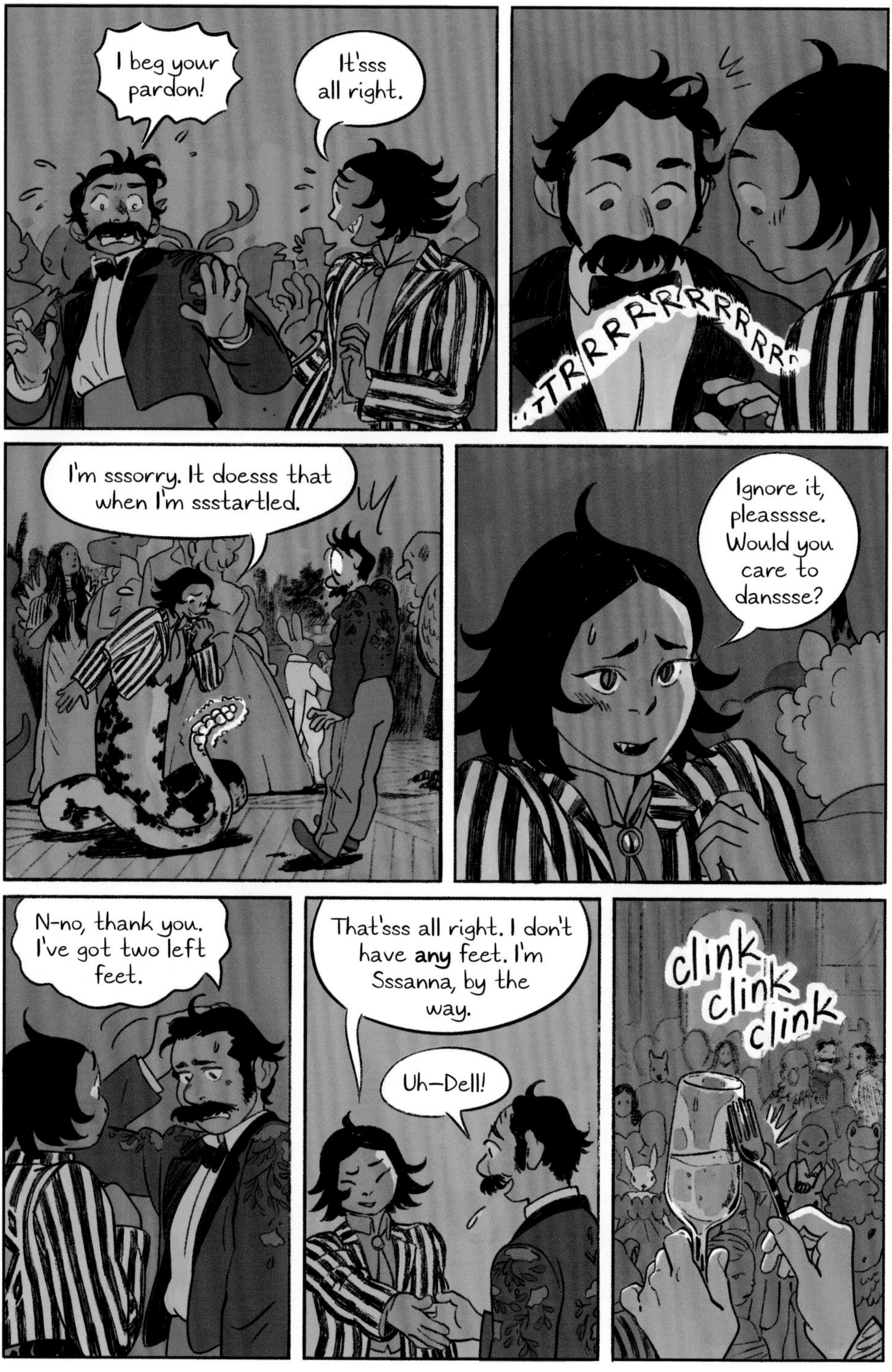

I beg your pardon!
It'sss all right.
TRRRRRRRRRRRR
I'm sssorry. It doesss that when I'm ssstartled.
Ignore it, pleasssse. Would you care to danssse?
N-no, thank you. I've got two left feet.
That'sss all right. I don't have **any** feet. I'm Sssanna, by the way.
Uh—Dell!
clink clink clink

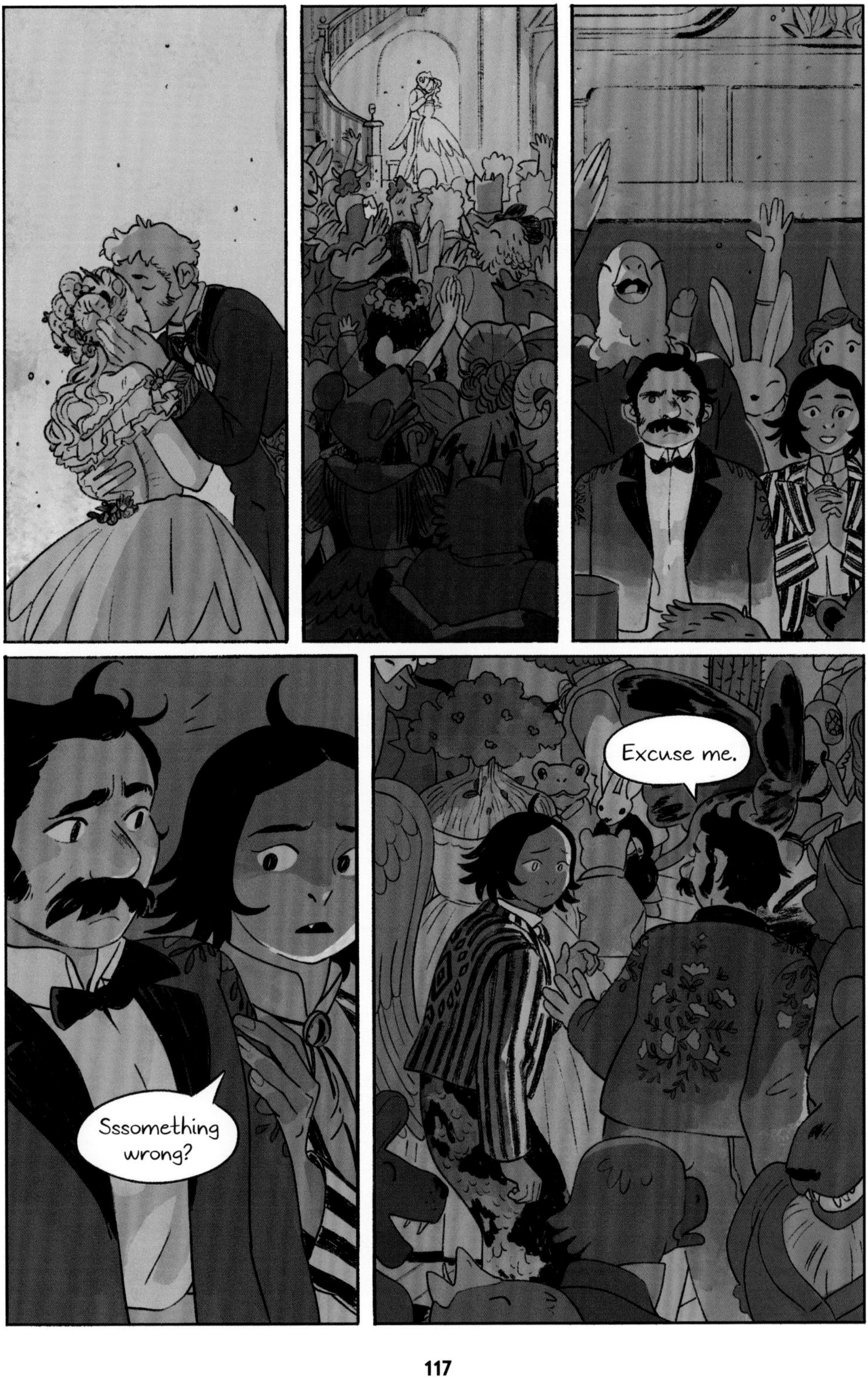
Sssomething wrong?
Excuse me.

"My head was spinning. I stood in the yard and looked up at the moon."

"The moon—another lady in white who quickens men's blood and drives them mad."

"I felt sick with betrayal. I'd followed Jesse, and he'd abandoned me."

"Then, suddenly, I understood. I wasn't angry with Jesse, or even Greda."

"Jesse was a fickle navigator, but without him . . ."

"I was repulsed by my own cowardice."

"Without him, the path and the consequences were mine alone."

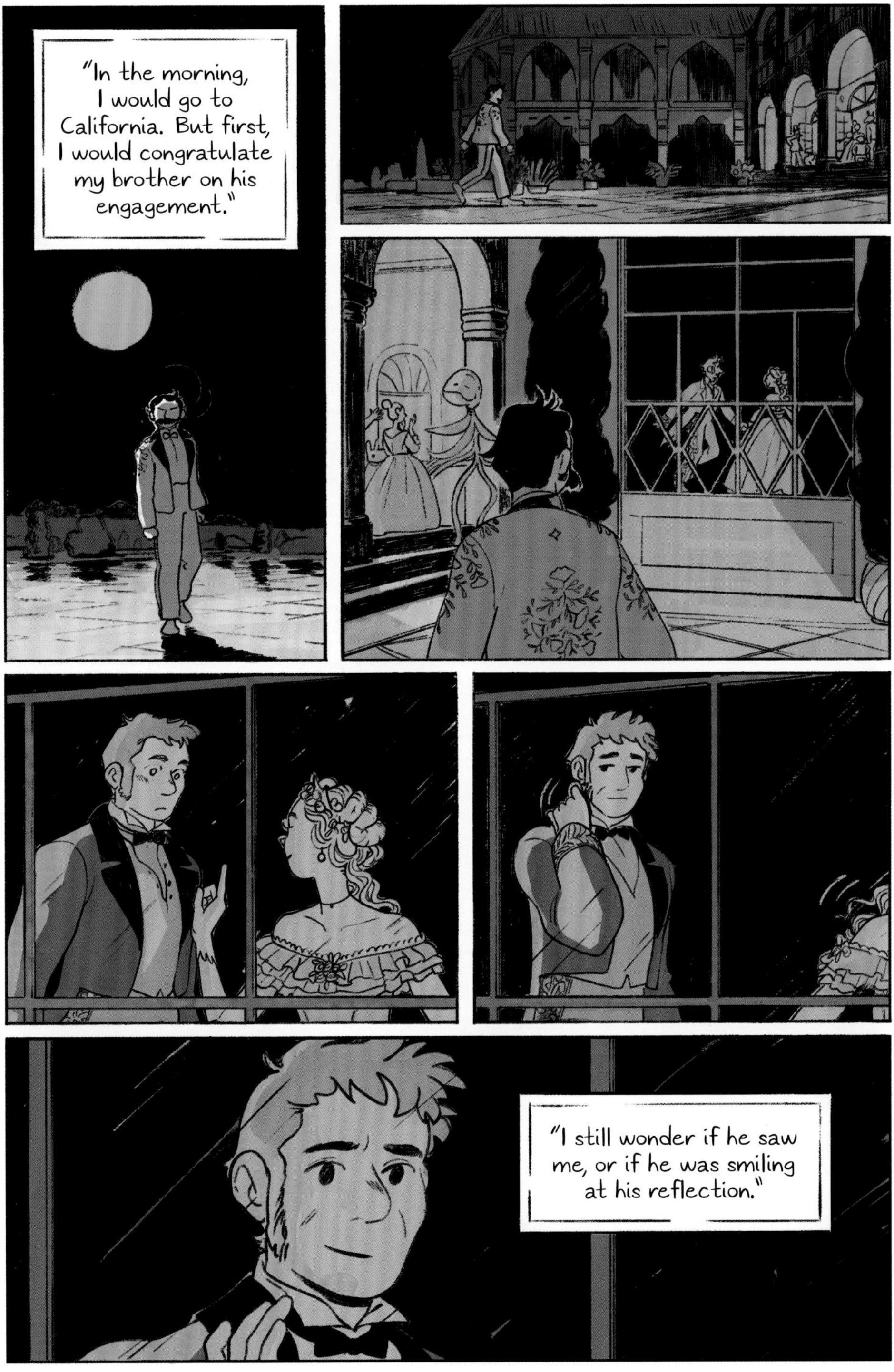
"In the morning, I would go to California. But first, I would congratulate my brother on his engagement."
"I still wonder if he saw me, or if he was smiling at his reflection."

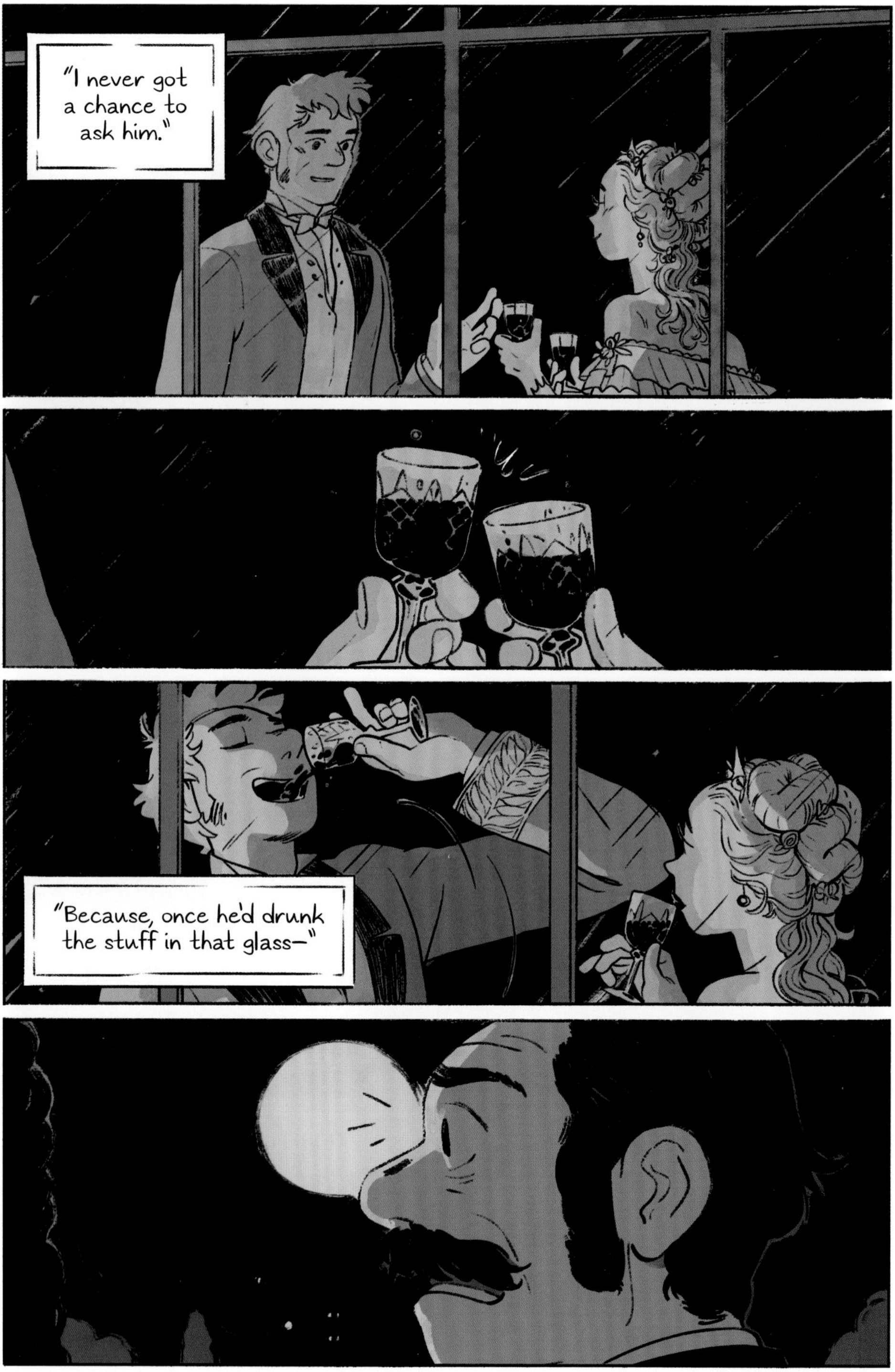
"I never got a chance to ask him."
"Because, once he'd drunk the stuff in that glass—"

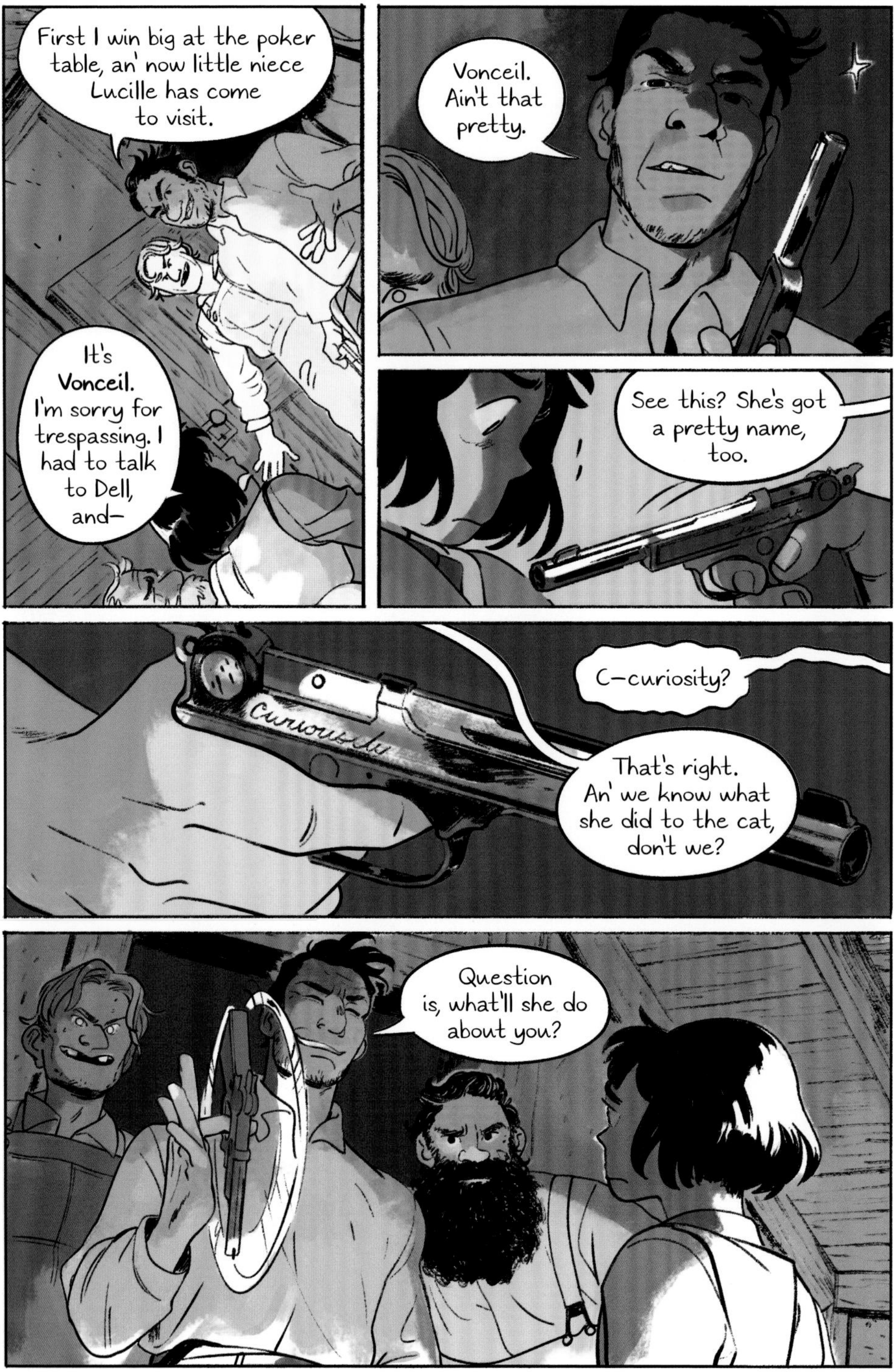
First I win big at the poker table, an' now little niece Lucille has come to visit.
It's **Vonceil.** I'm sorry for trespassing. I had to talk to Dell, and–
Vonceil. Ain't that pretty.
See this? She's got a pretty name, too.
Curiosity
C–curiosity?
That's right. An' we know what she did to the cat, don't we?
Question is, what'll she do about you?

Chapter Seven

Scavengers

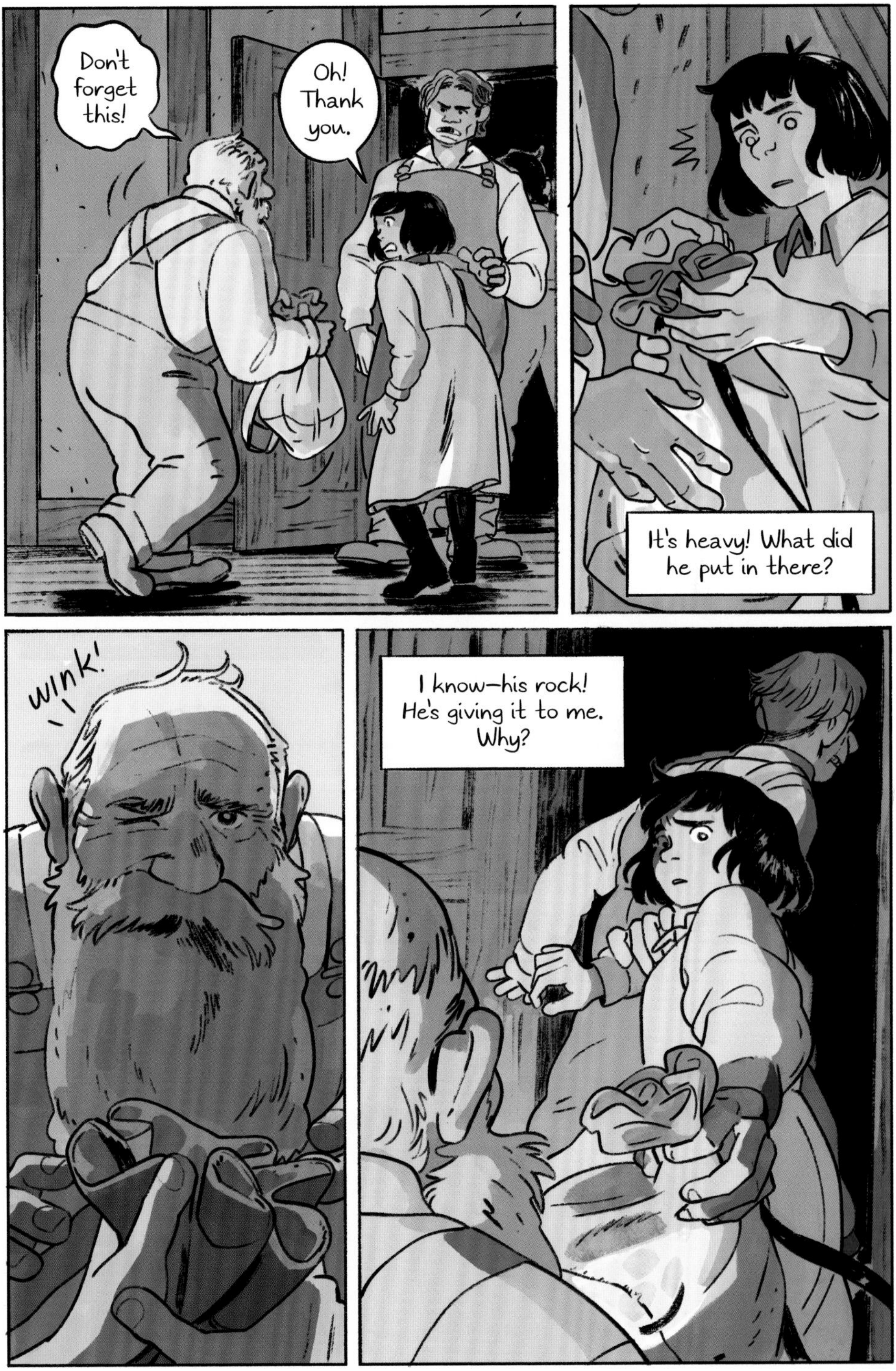
Don't forget this!
Oh! Thank you.
It's heavy! What did he put in there?
WINK!
I know—his rock! He's giving it to me. Why?

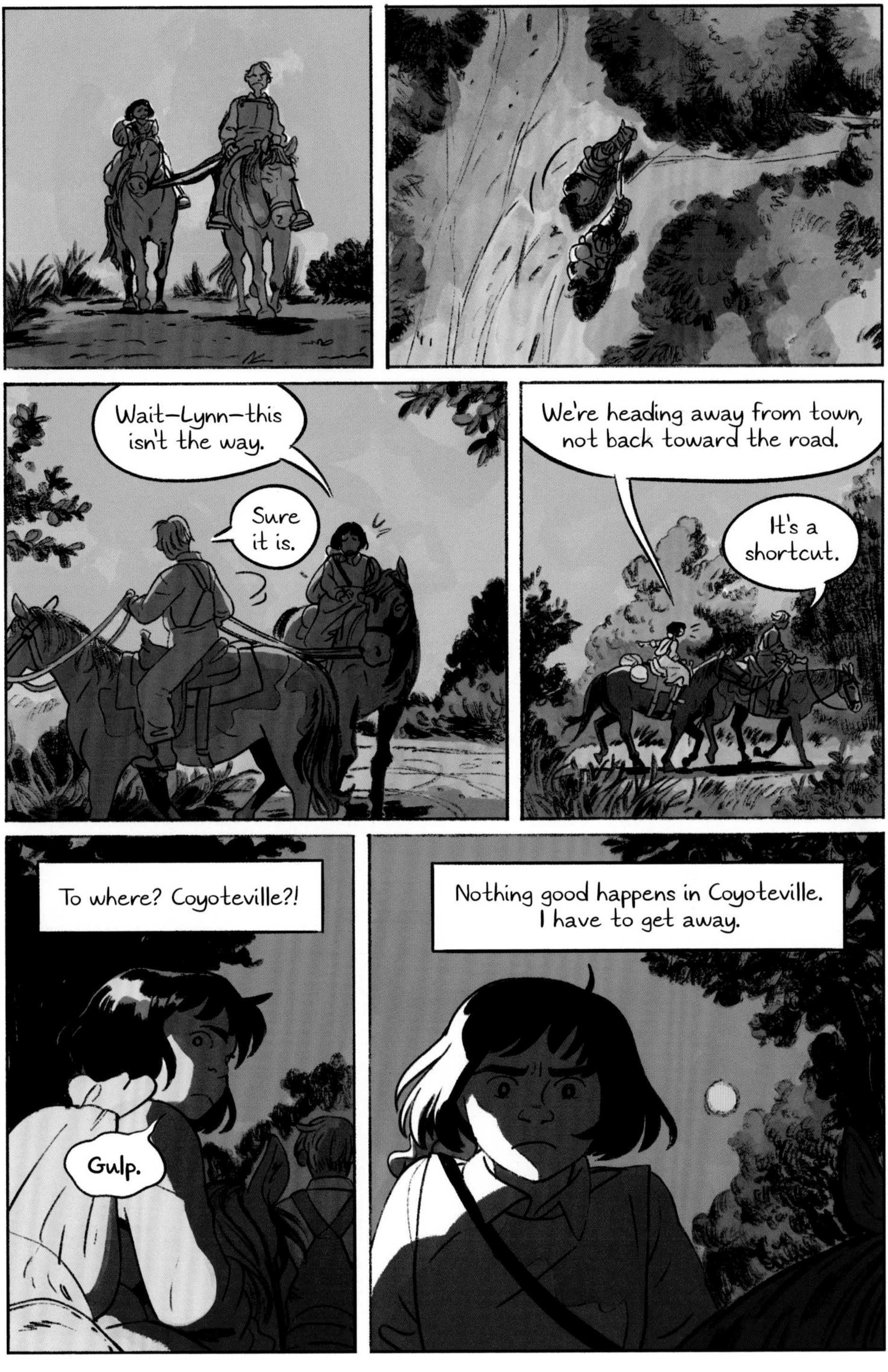
Wait–Lynn–this isn't the way.
Sure it is.
We're heading away from town, not back toward the road.
It's a shortcut.
To where? Coyoteville?!
Gulp.
Nothing good happens in Coyoteville. I have to get away.

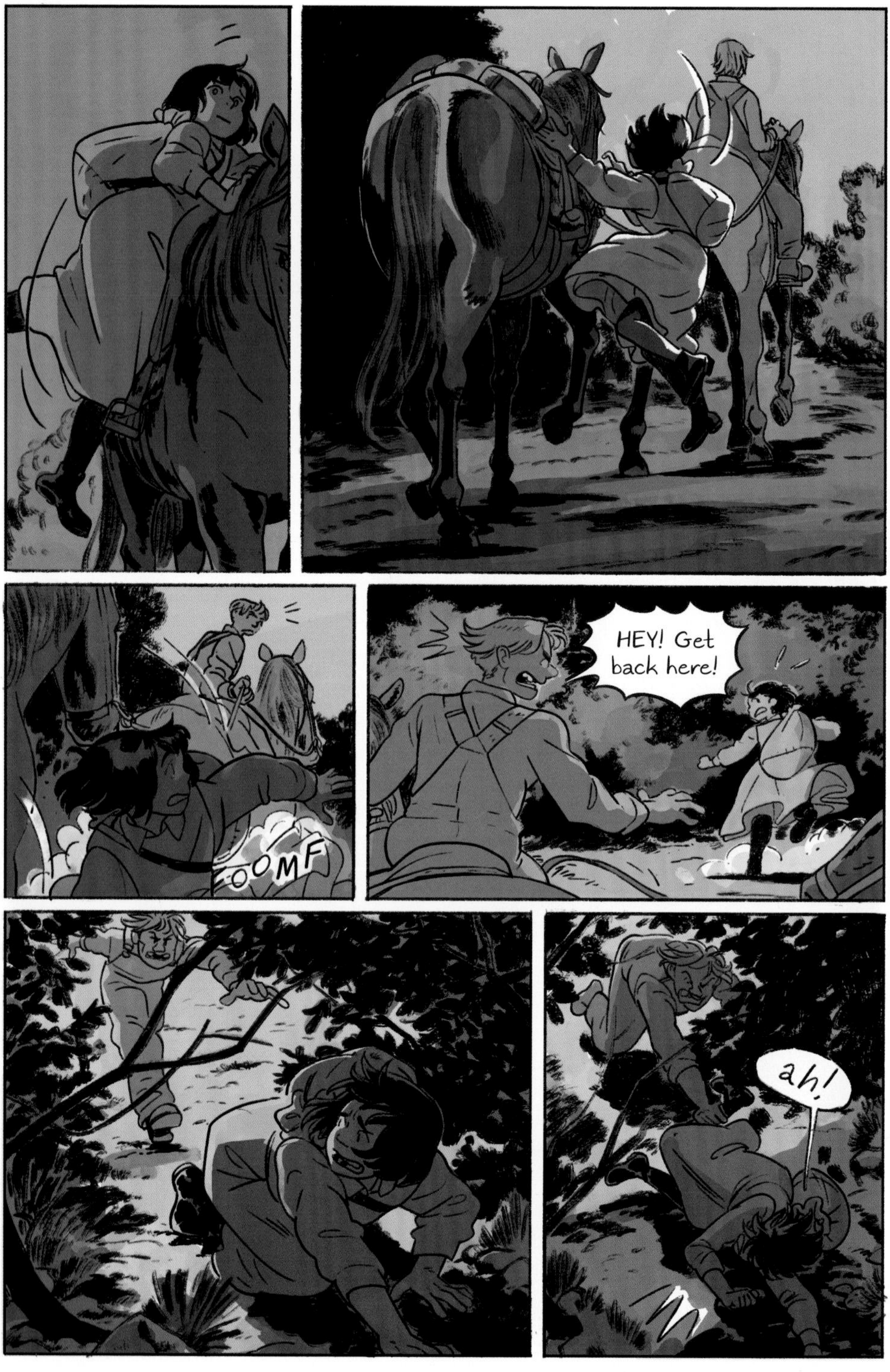
OOMF
HEY! Get back here!
ah!

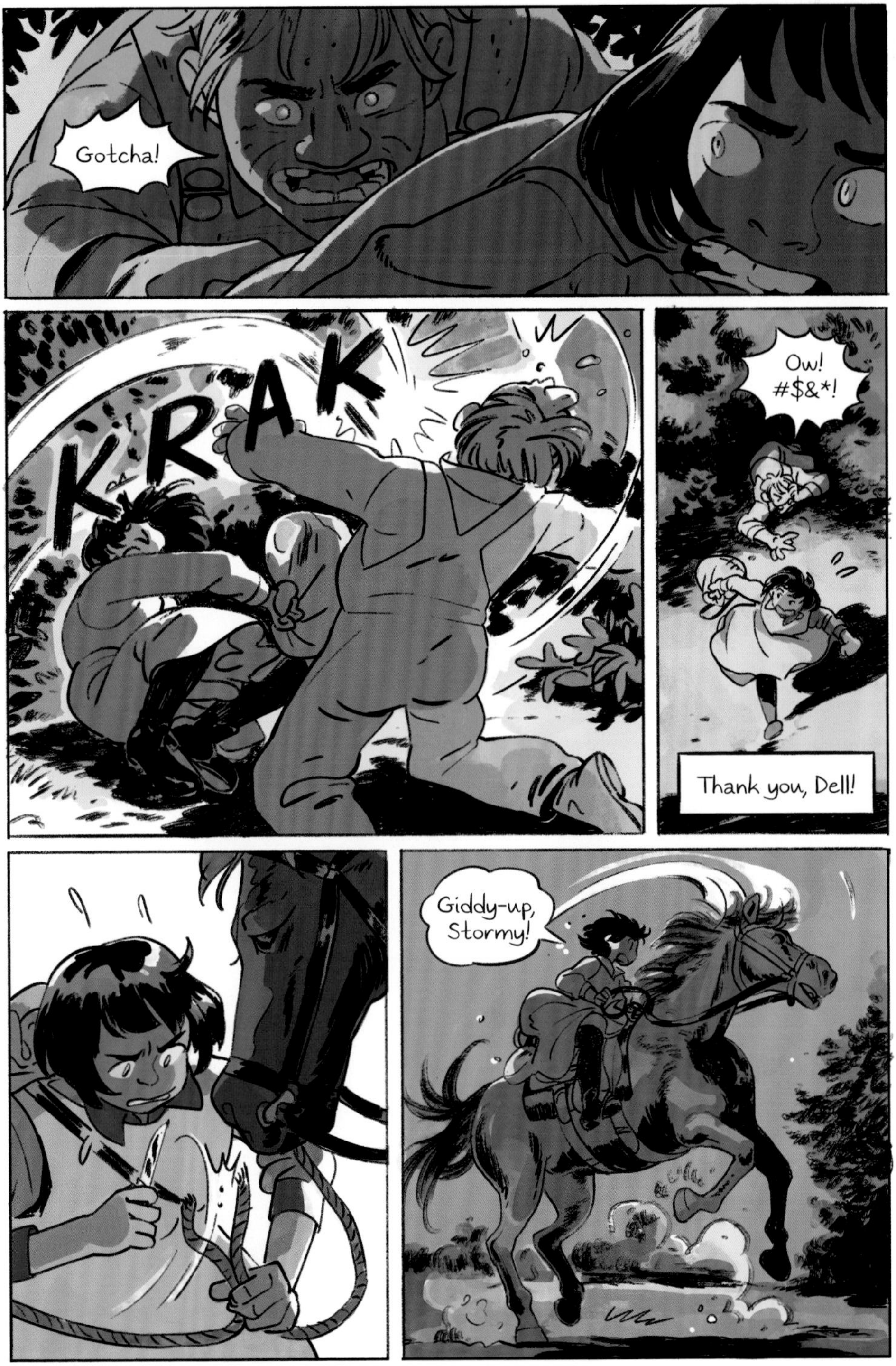
Gotcha!
KRAK
Ow! #$&*!
Thank you, Dell!
Giddy-up, Stormy!

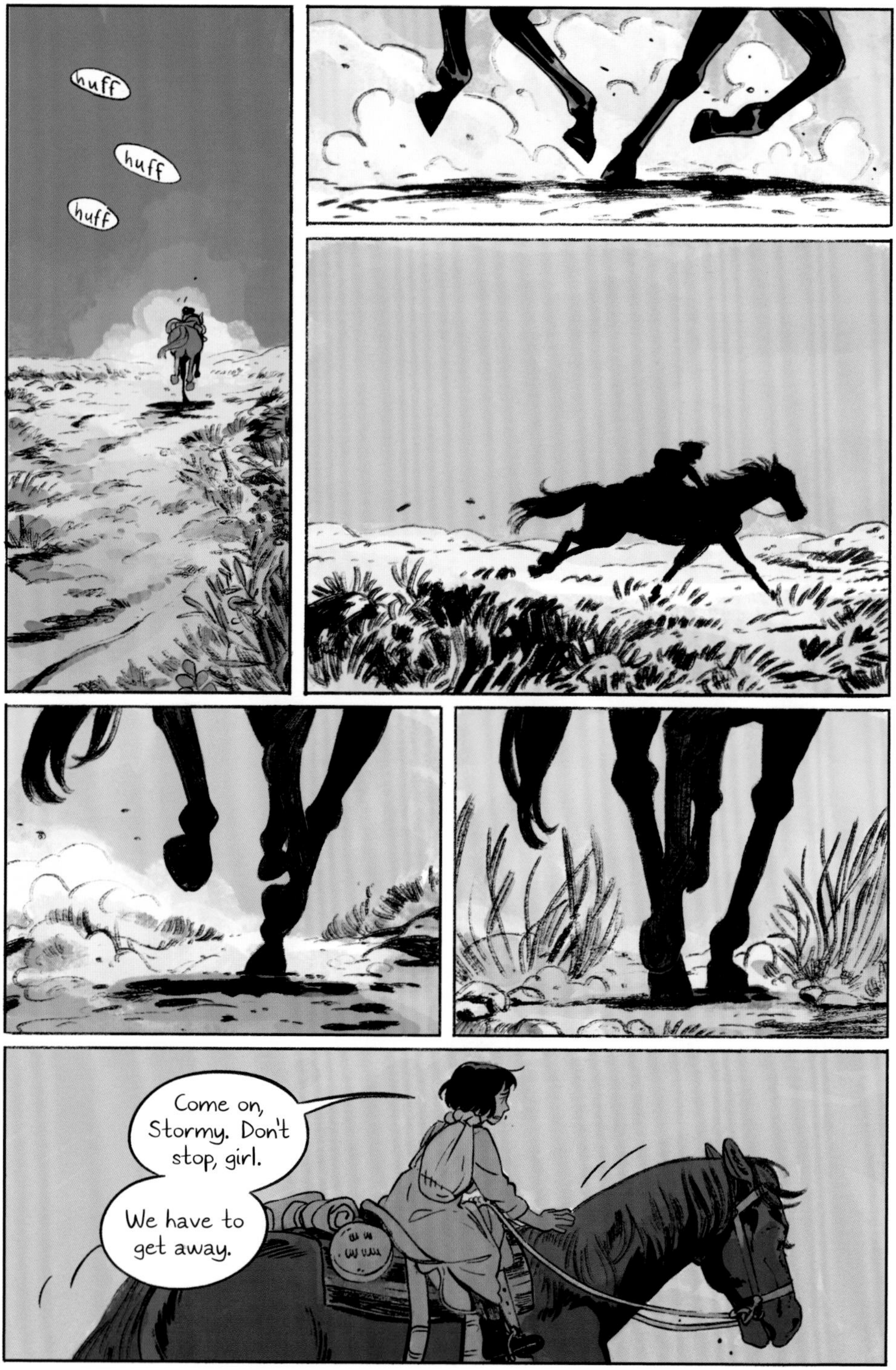
huff
huff
huff
Come on, Stormy. Don't stop, girl.
We have to get away.

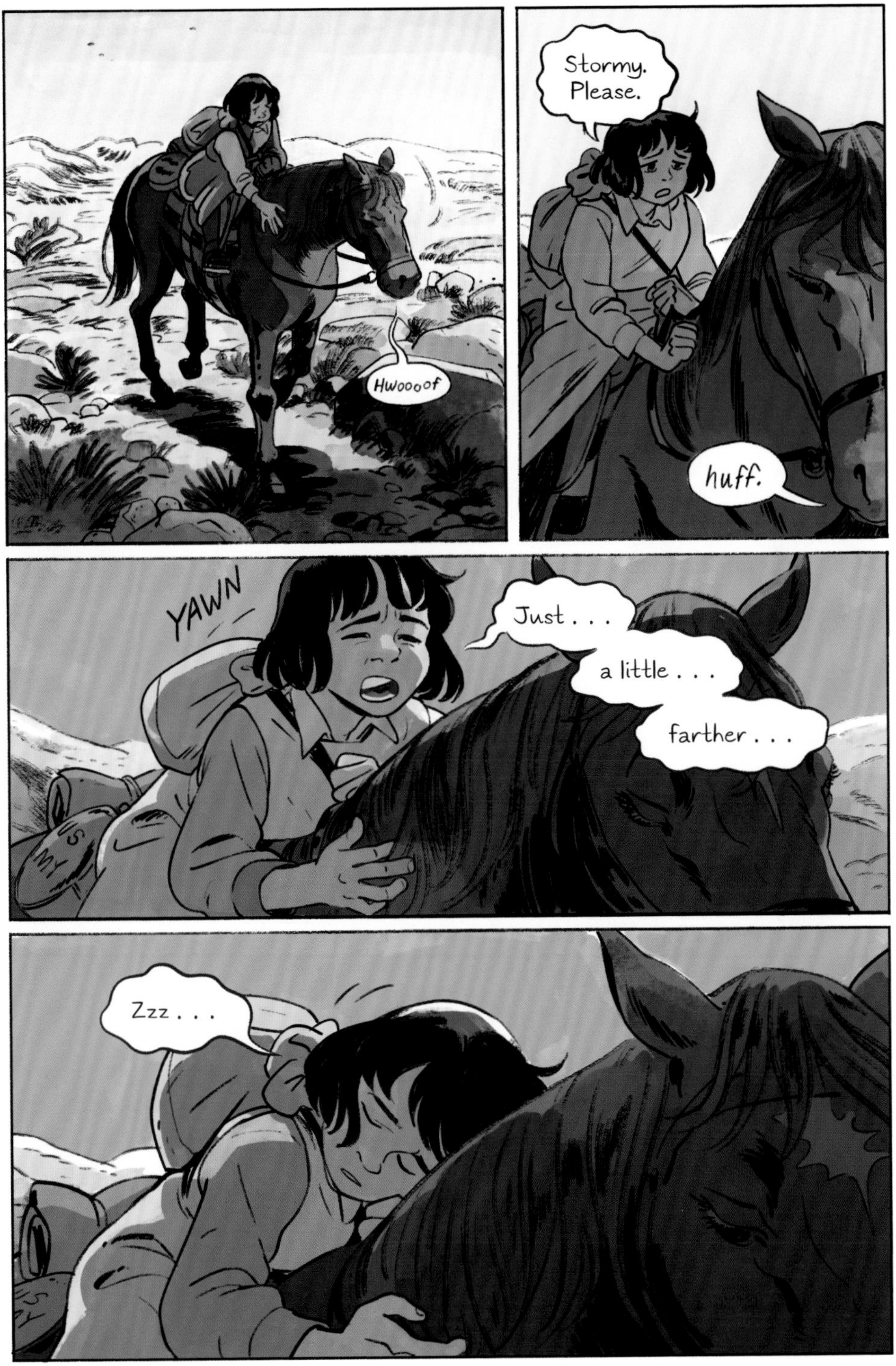
Hwoooof
Stormy. Please.
huff.
YAWN
Just . . .
a little . . .
farther . . .
Zzz . . .

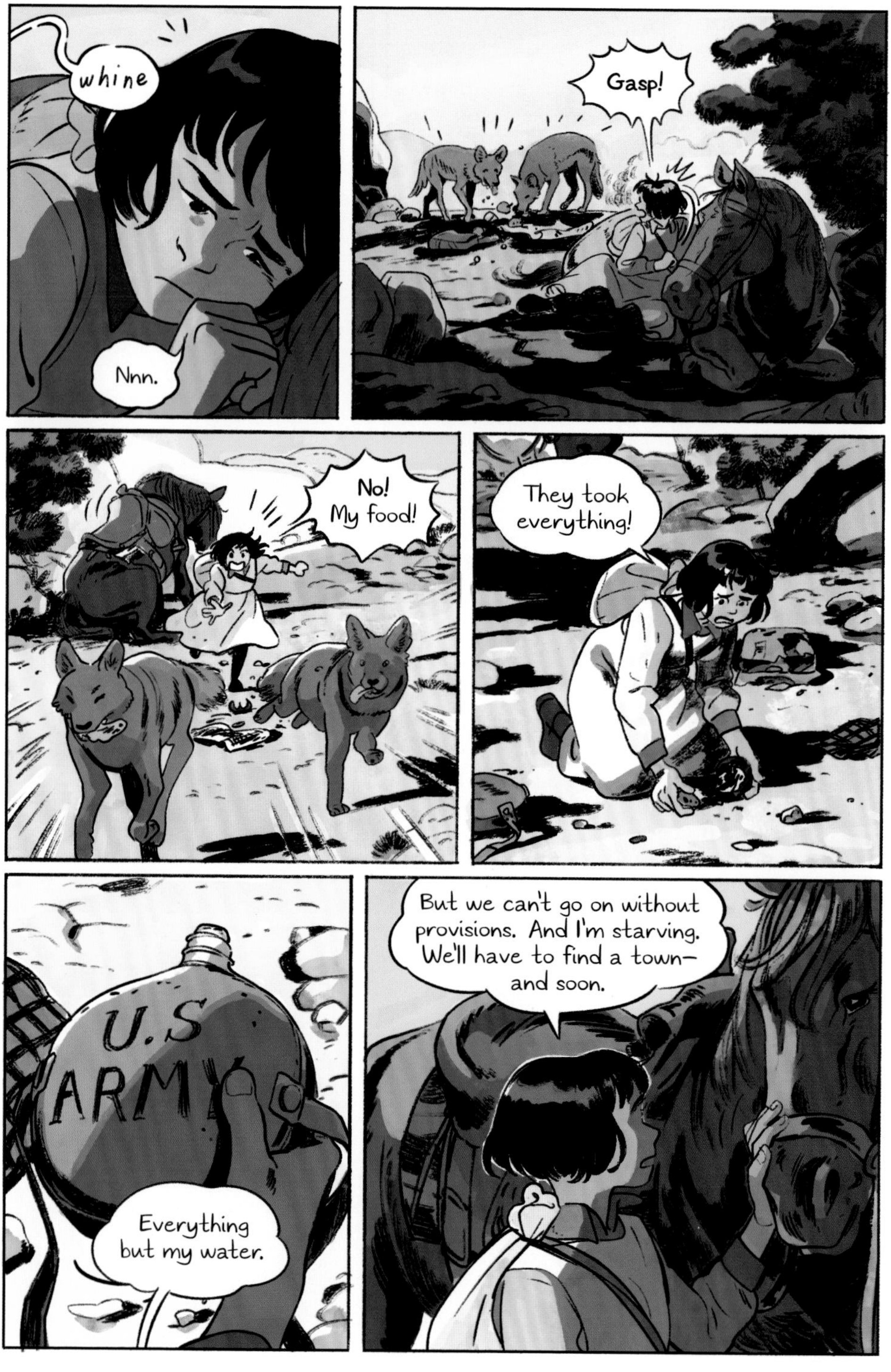
whine
Nnn.
Gasp!
No! My food!
They took everything!
Everything but my water.
U.S ARMY
But we can't go on without provisions. And I'm starving. We'll have to find a town— and soon.

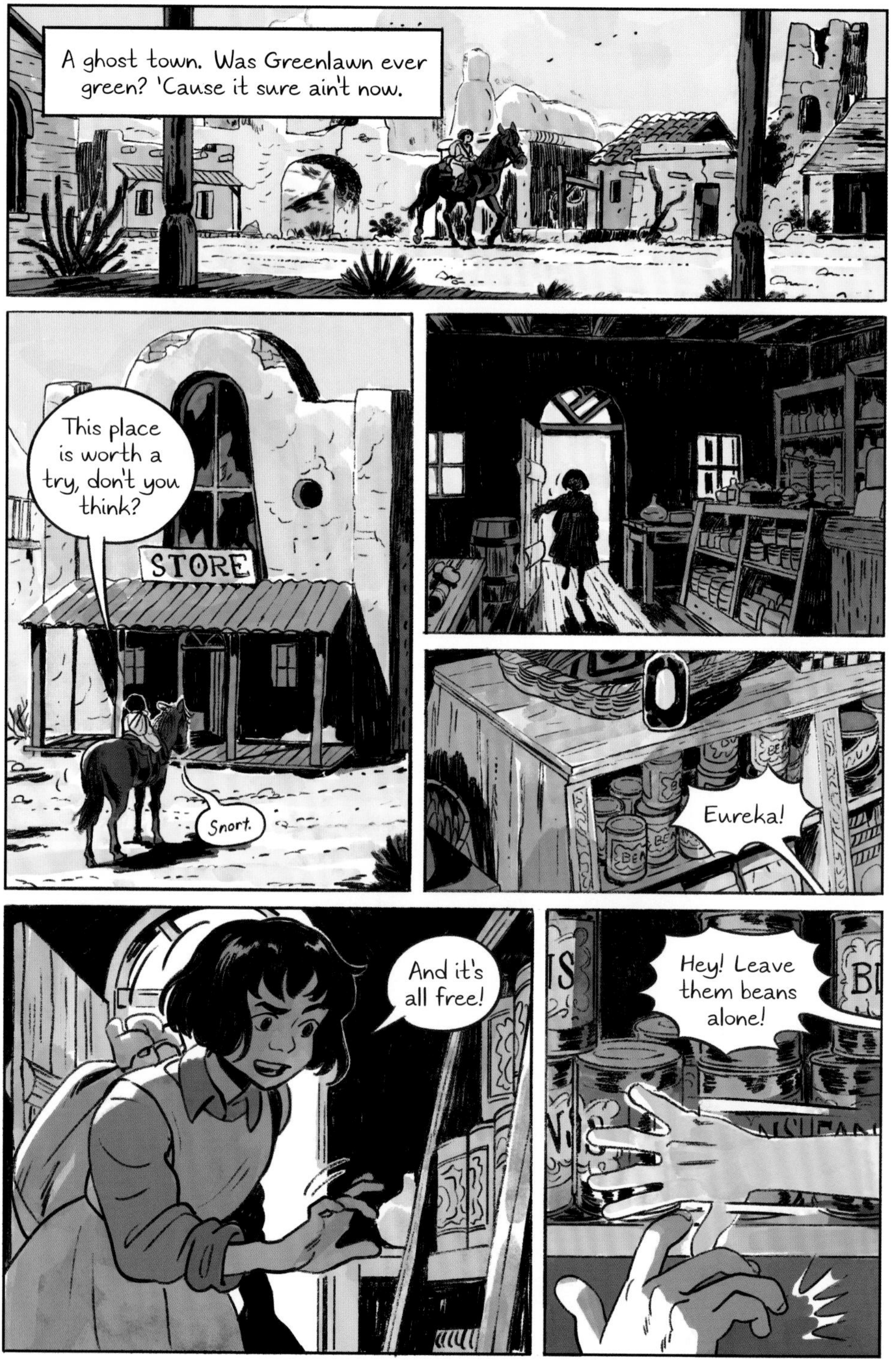
A ghost town. Was Greenlawn ever green? 'Cause it sure ain't now.
This place is worth a try, don't you think?
STORE
Snort.
Eureka!
And it's all free!
Hey! Leave them beans alone!

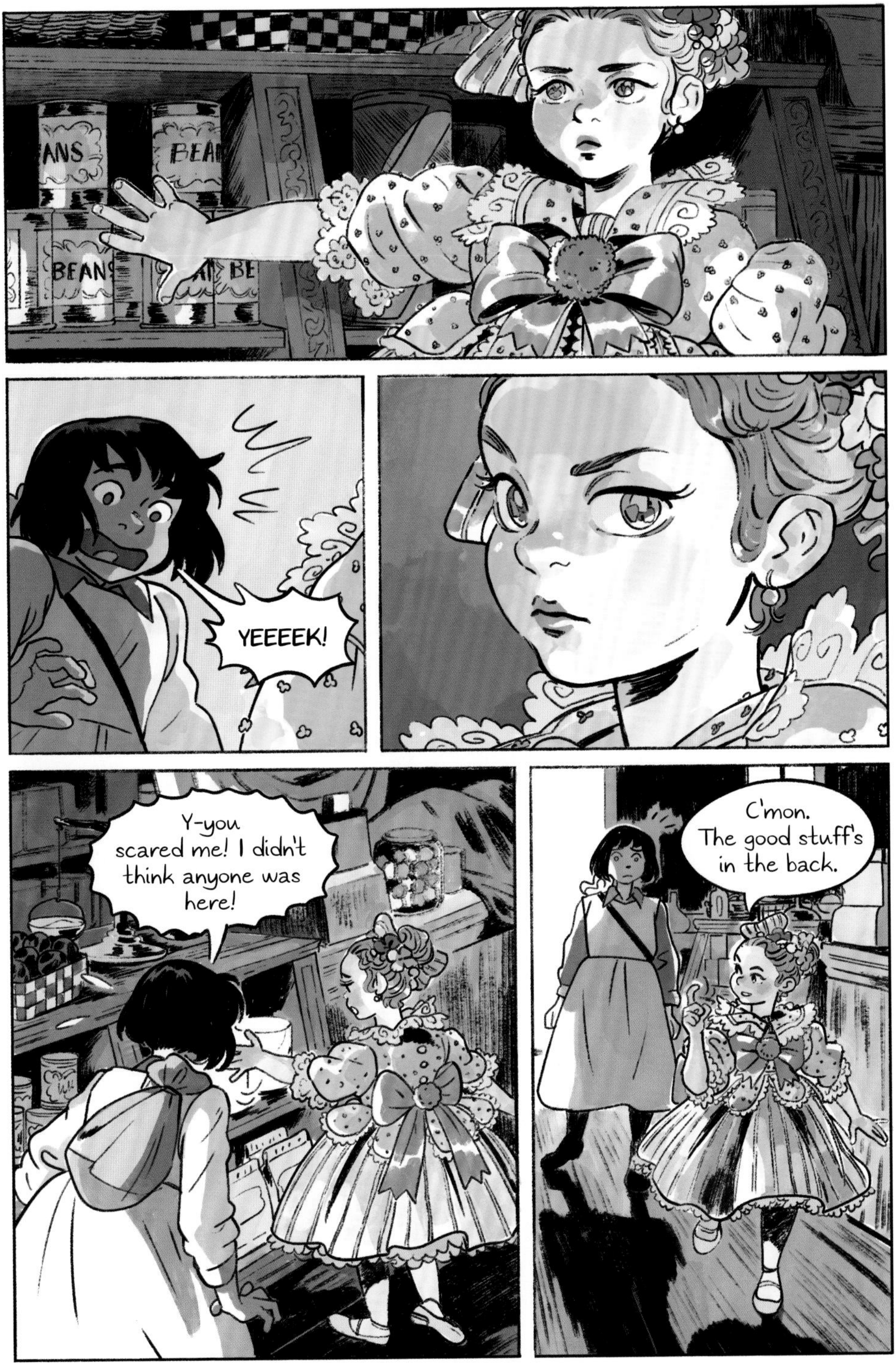
BEANS
BEANS
YEEEEK!
Y-you scared me! I didn't think anyone was here!
C'mon. The good stuff's in the back.

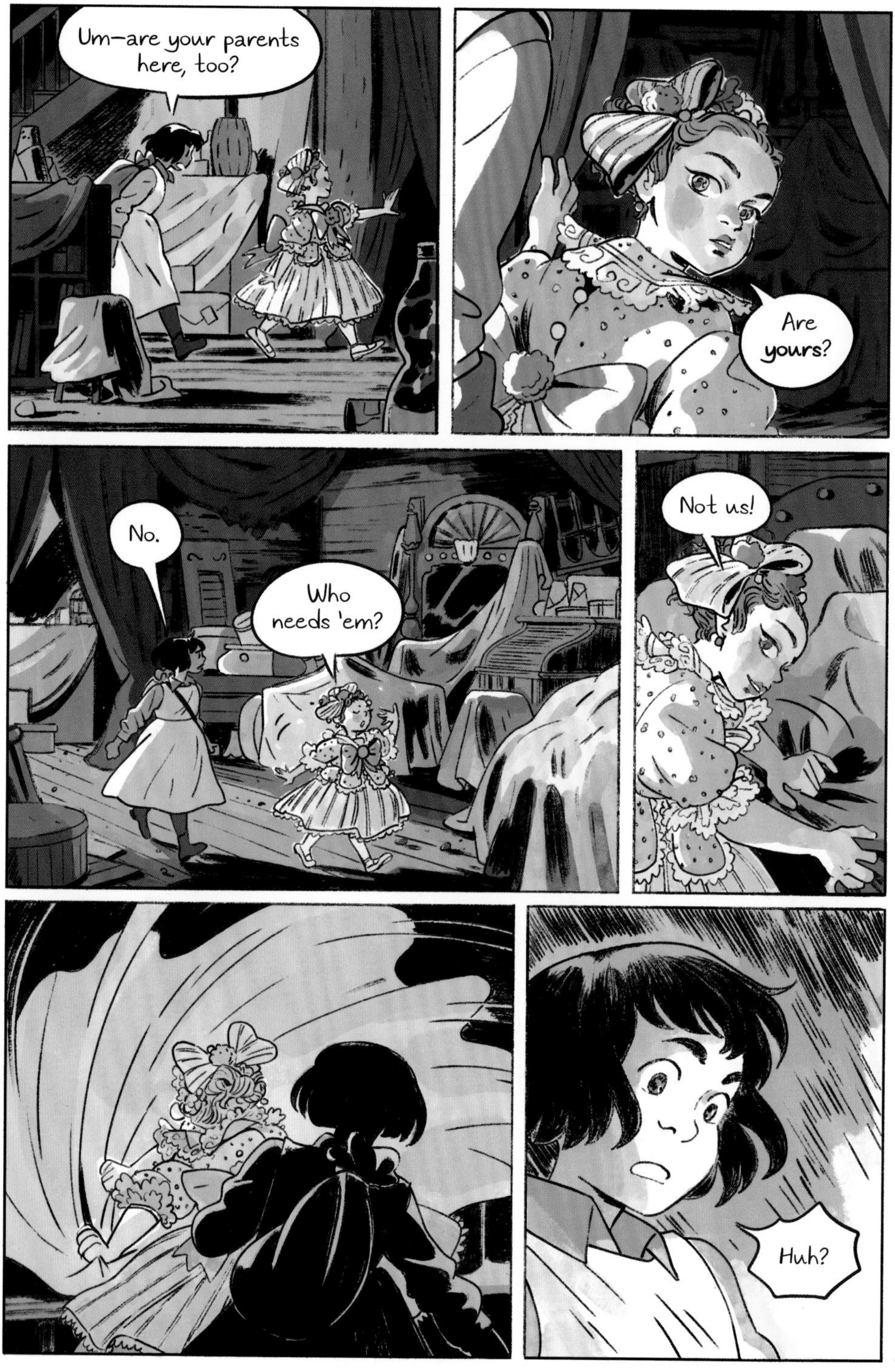
Um—are your parents here, too?
Are yours?
No.
Who needs 'em?
Not us!
Huh?

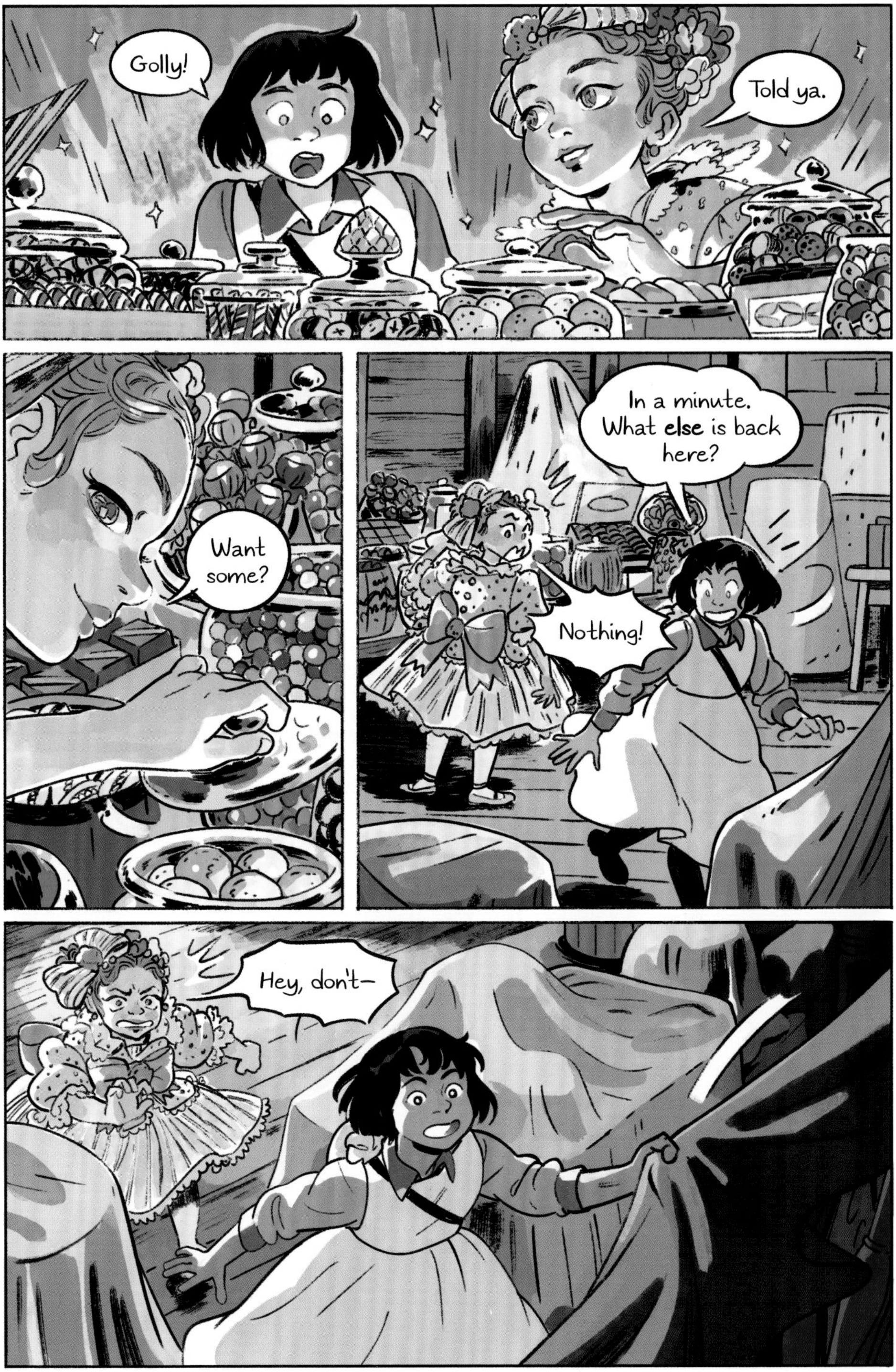
Golly!
Told ya.
Want some?
In a minute. What else is back here?
Nothing!
Hey, don't—

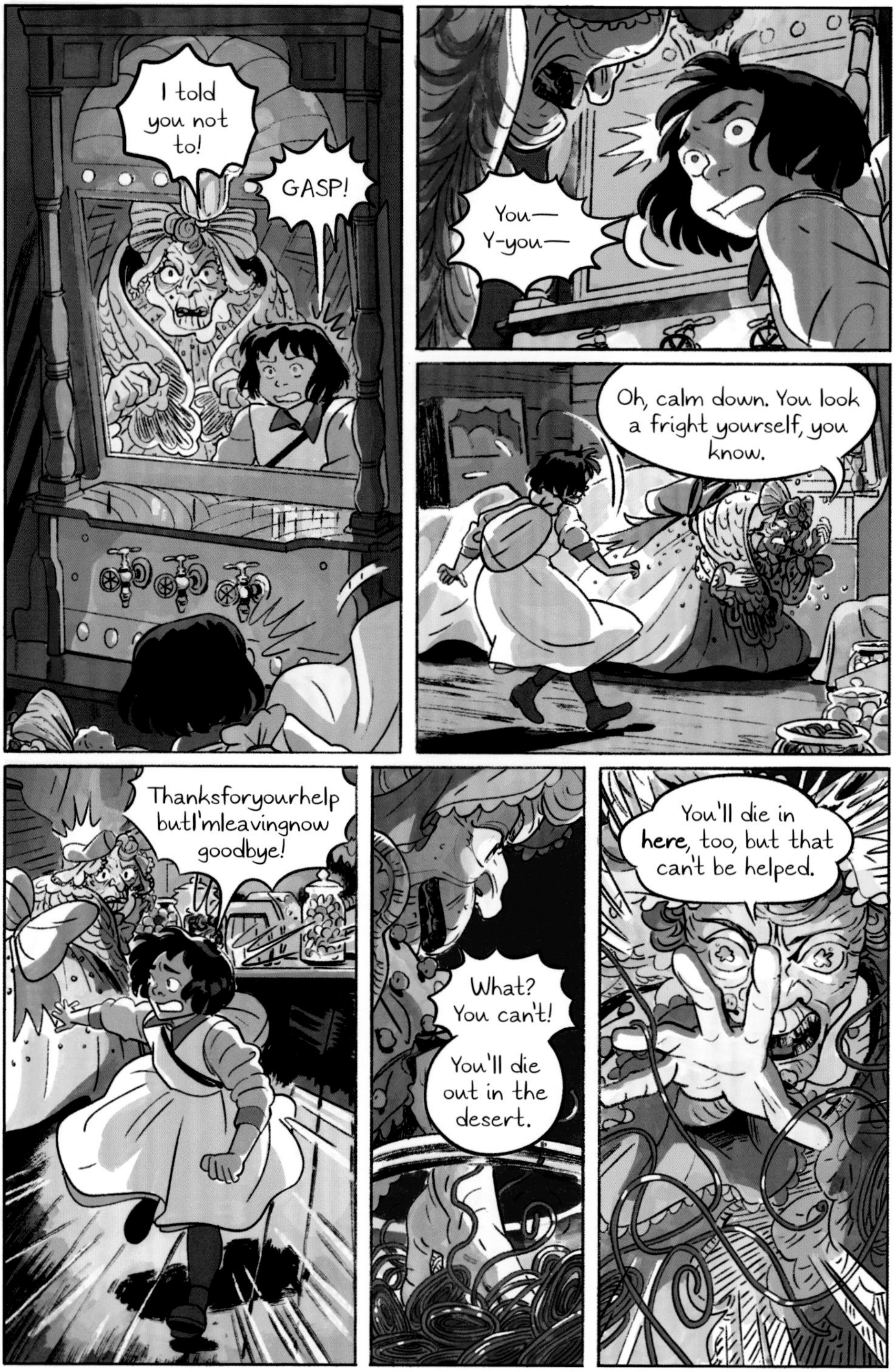
I told you not to!
GASP!
You—
Y-you—
Oh, calm down. You look a fright yourself, you know.
Thanksforyourhelp butI'mleavingnow goodbye!
What? You can't!
You'll die out in the desert.
You'll die in **here**, too, but that can't be helped.

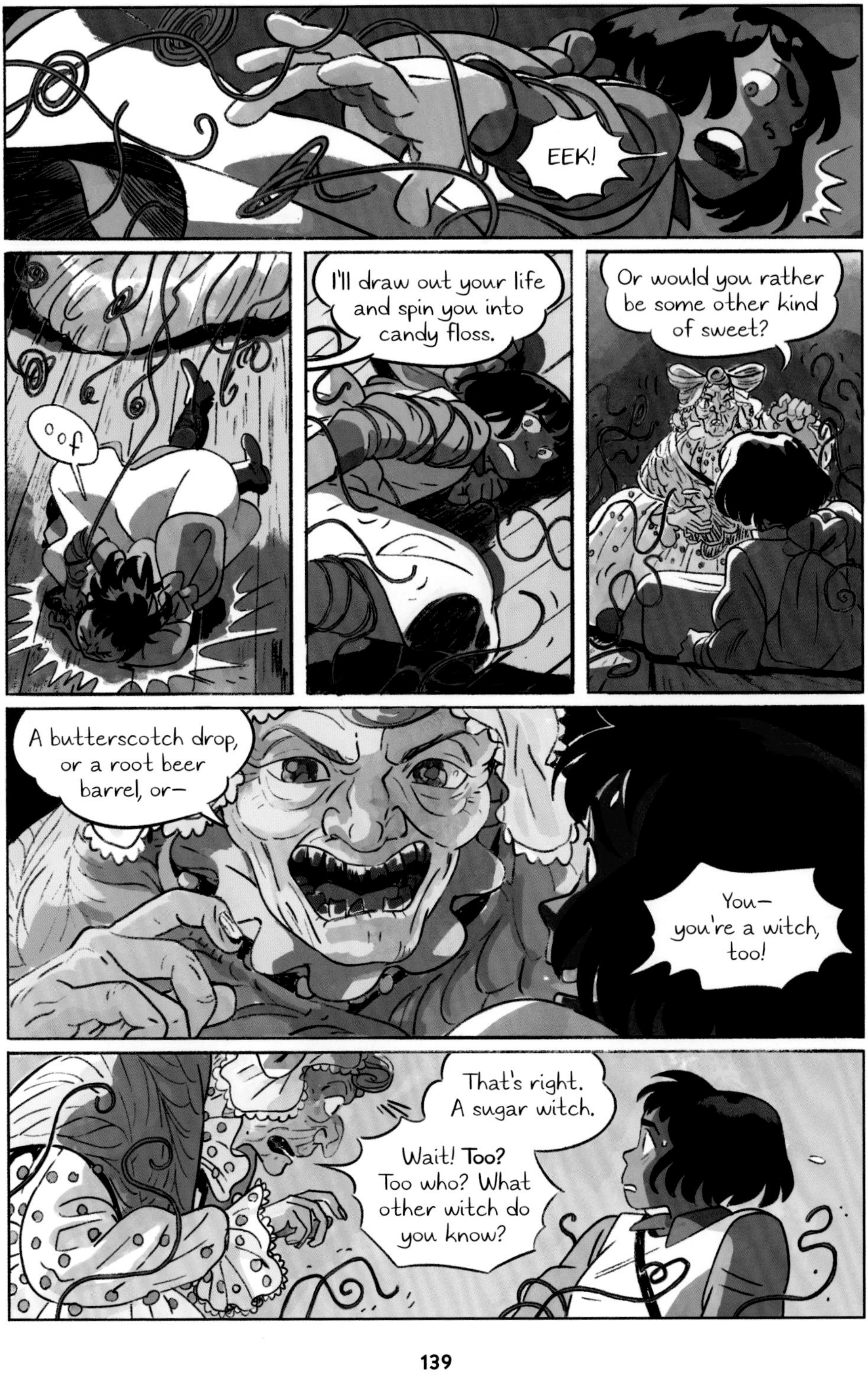
EEK!
oof
I'll draw out your life and spin you into candy floss.
Or would you rather be some other kind of sweet?
A butterscotch drop, or a root beer barrel, or—
You— you're a witch, too!
That's right. A sugar witch.
Wait! **Too?** Too who? What other witch do you know?

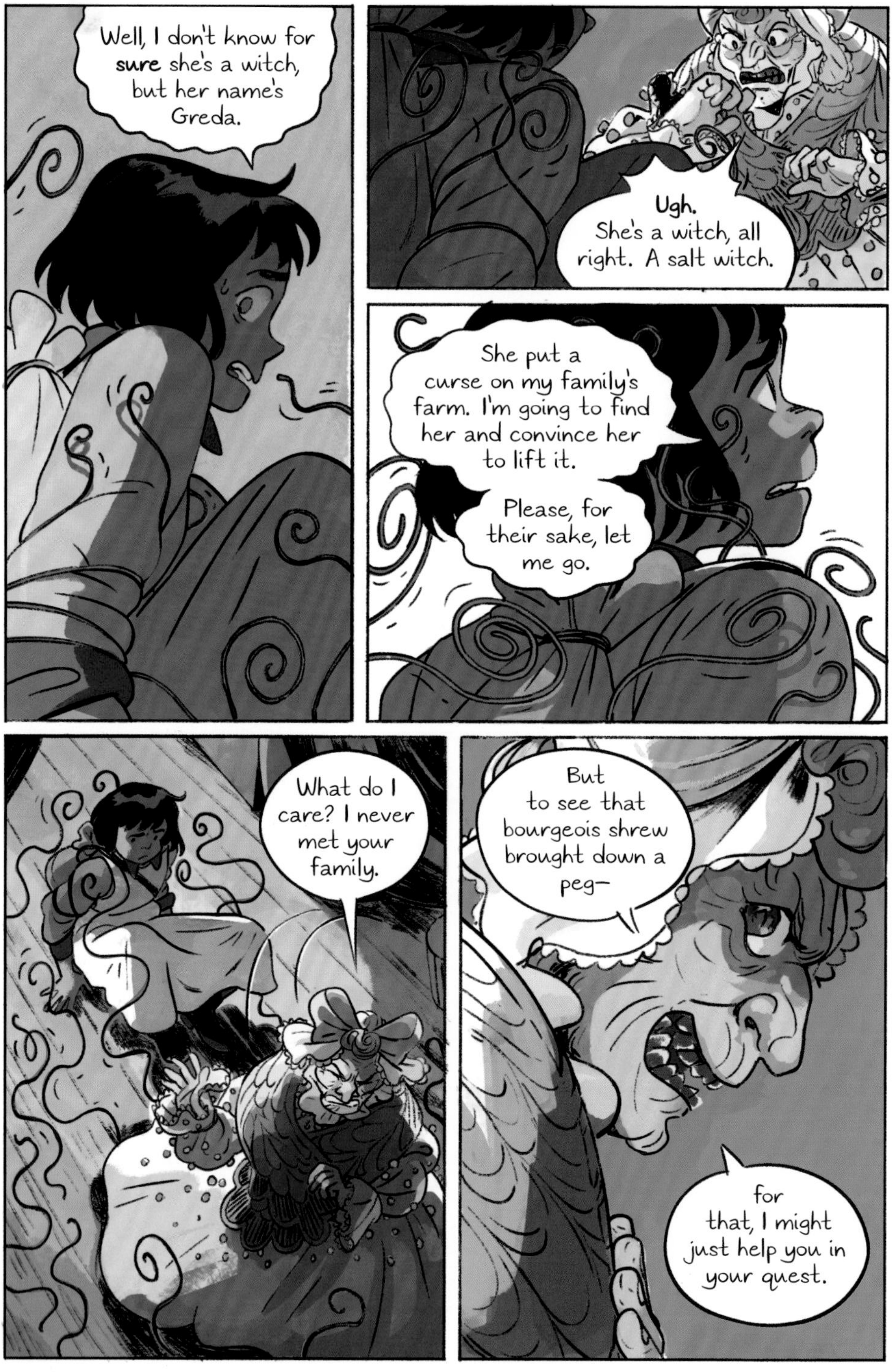
Well, I don't know for **sure** she's a witch, but her name's Greda.
Ugh. She's a witch, all right. A salt witch.
She put a curse on my family's farm. I'm going to find her and convince her to lift it.
Please, for their sake, let me go.
What do I care? I never met your family.
But to see that bourgeois shrew brought down a peg—
for that, I might just help you in your quest.

Chapter Eight

Rock Candy

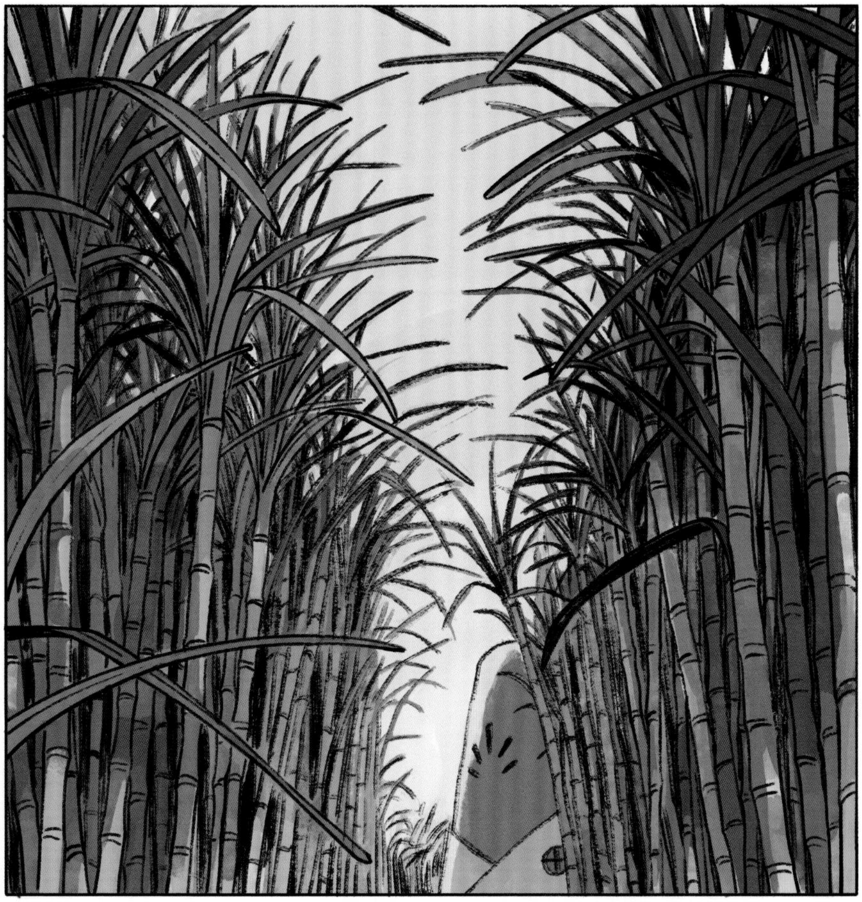

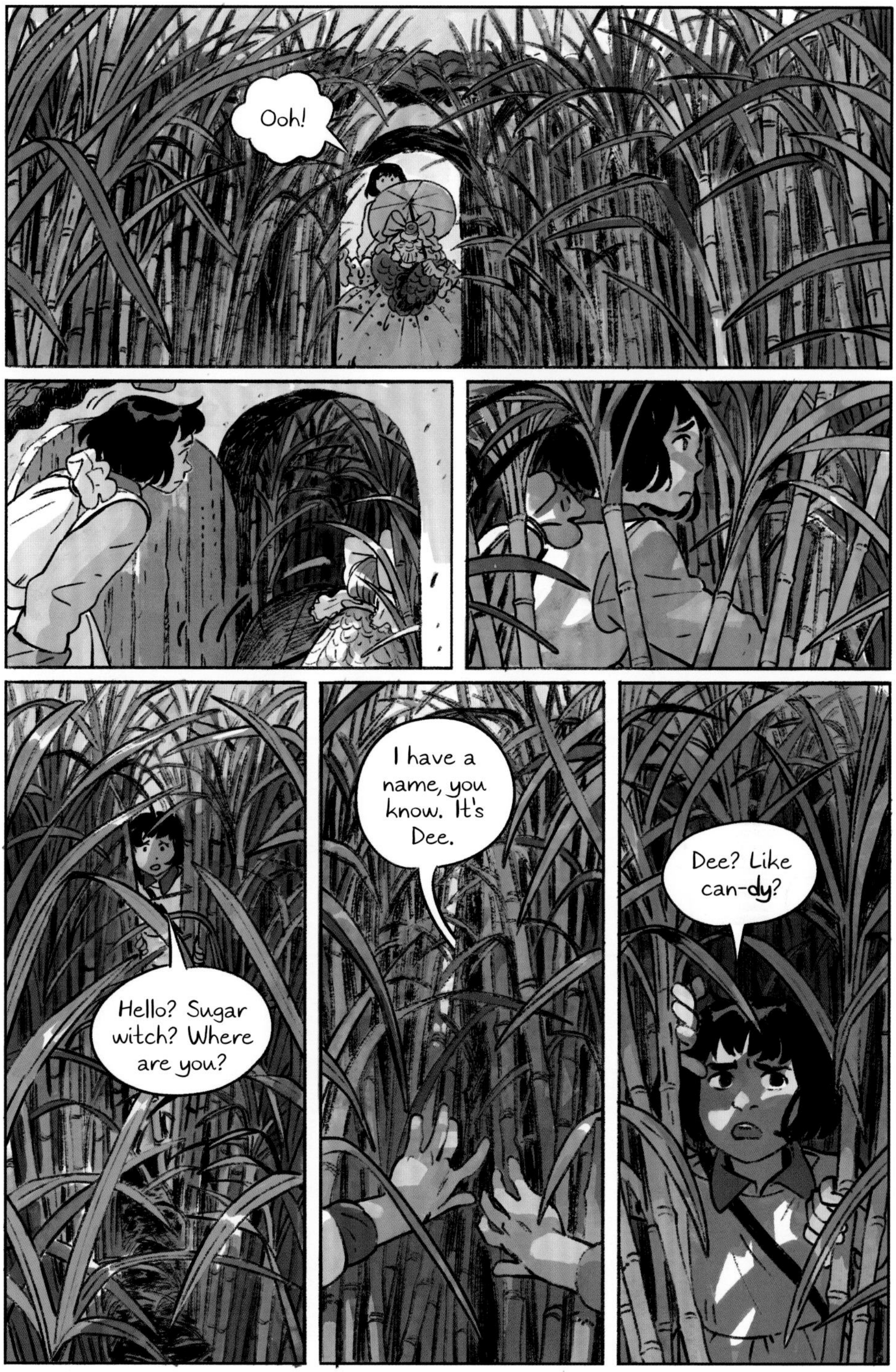
Ooh!
Hello? Sugar witch? Where are you?
I have a name, you know. It's Dee.
Dee? Like can-dy?

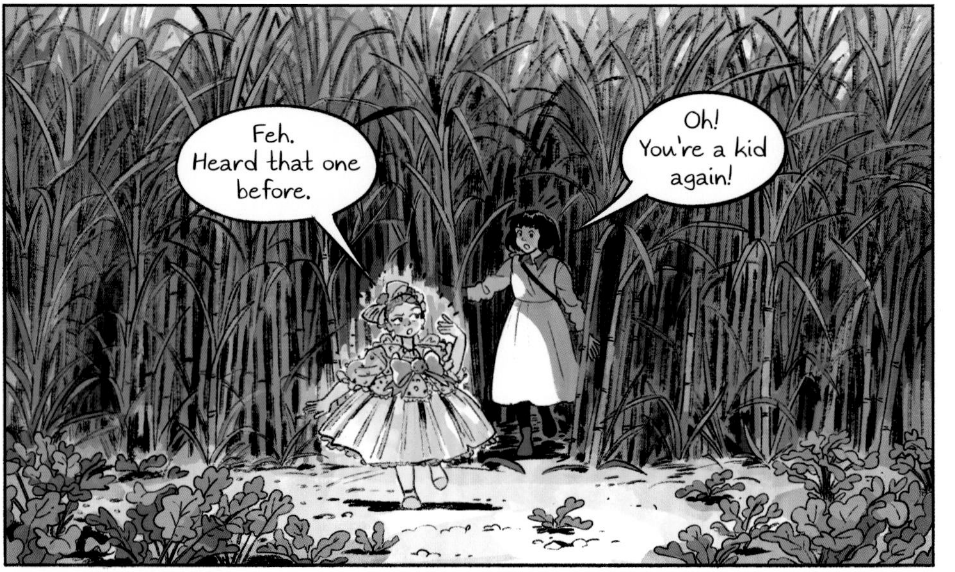
Feh. Heard that one before.
Oh! You're a kid again!

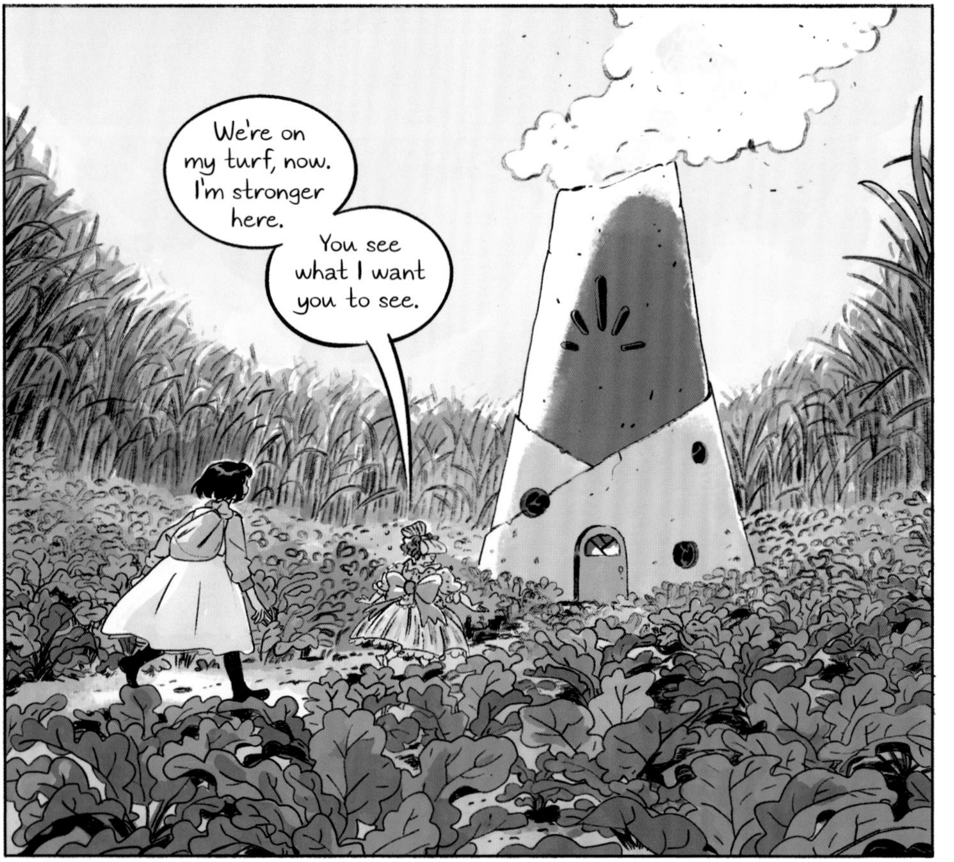
We're on my turf, now. I'm stronger here.
You see what I want you to see.

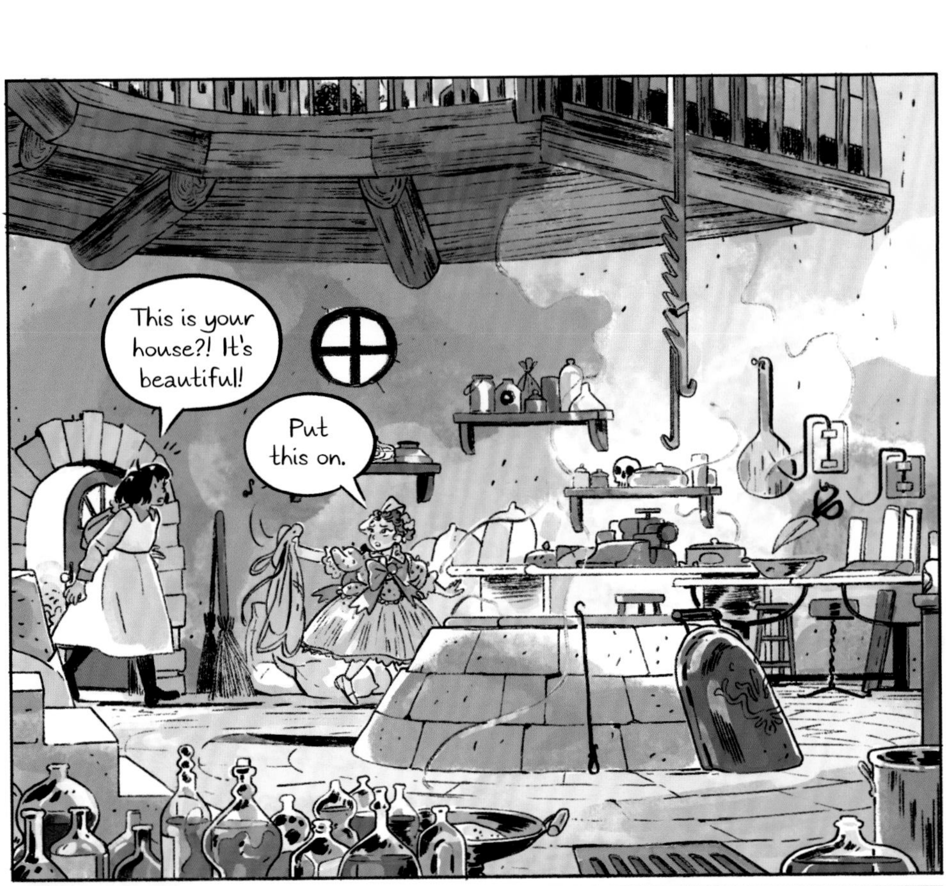
This is your house?! It's beautiful!
Put this on.

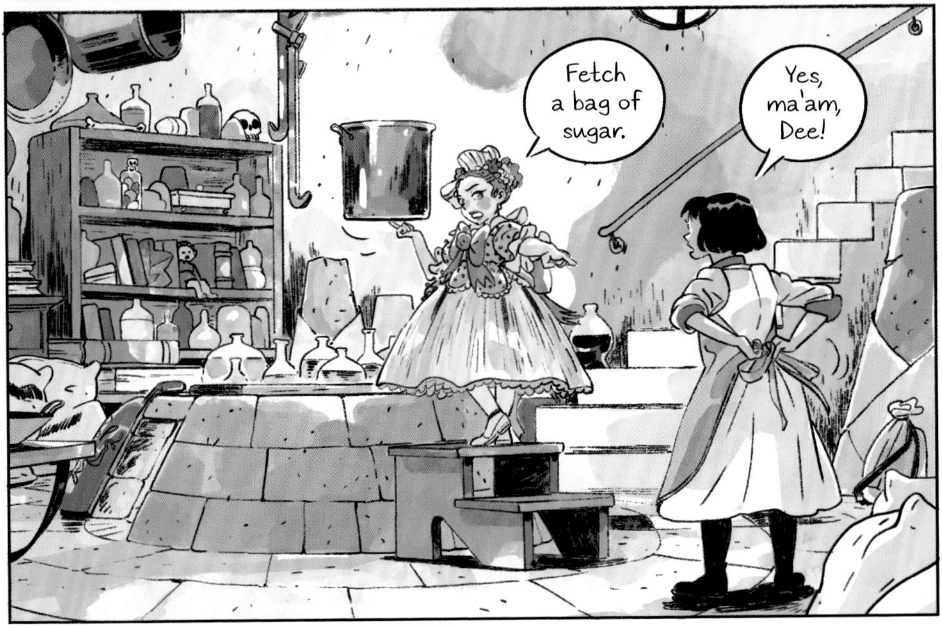
Fetch a bag of sugar.
Yes, ma'am, Dee!

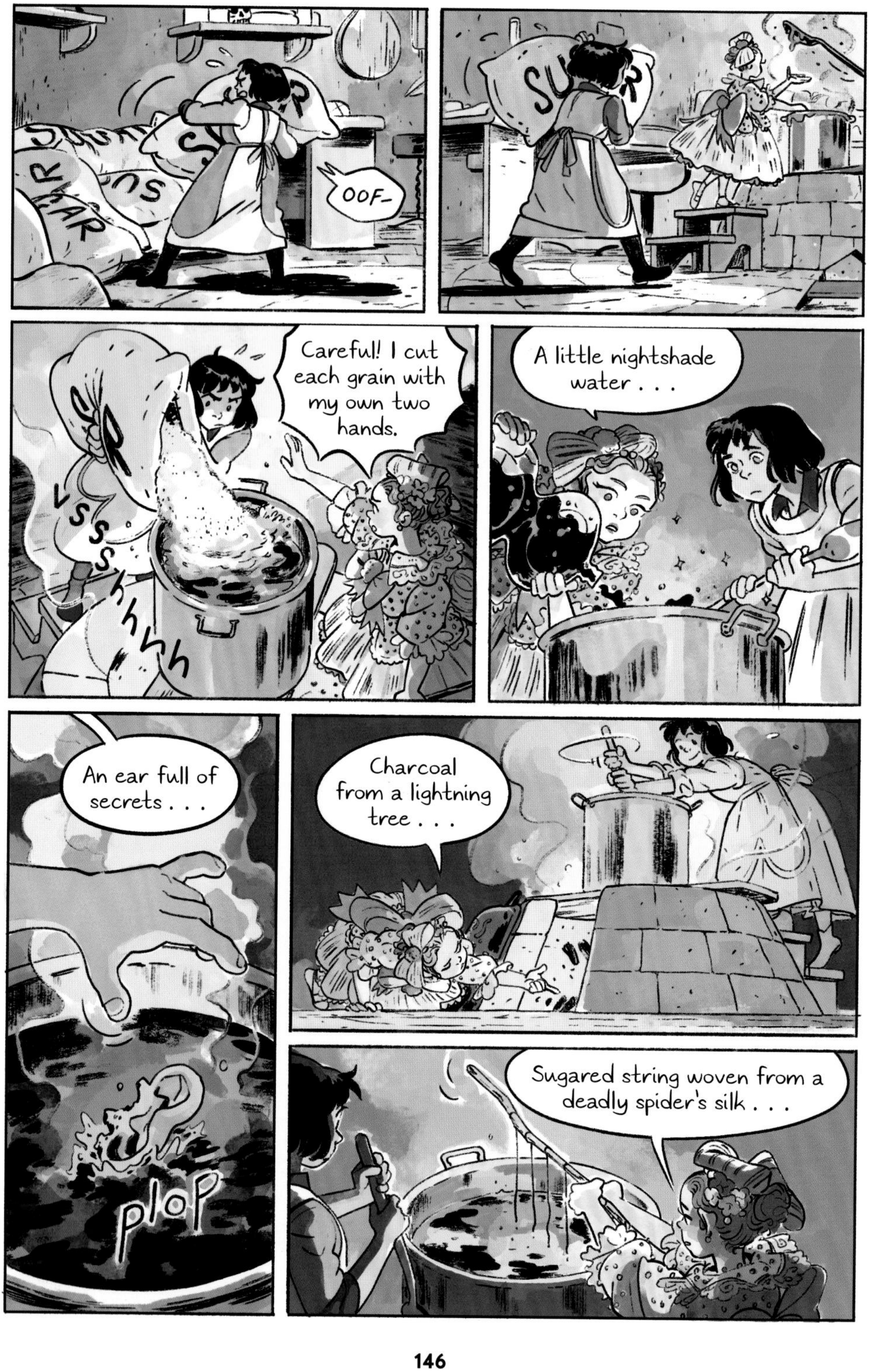

SUGAR
SUGAR
SUGAR
OOF—
SUGAR
Careful! I cut each grain with my own two hands.
VSSShhhh
A little nightshade water . . .
An ear full of secrets . . .
plop
Charcoal from a lightning tree . . .
Sugared string woven from a deadly spider's silk . . .

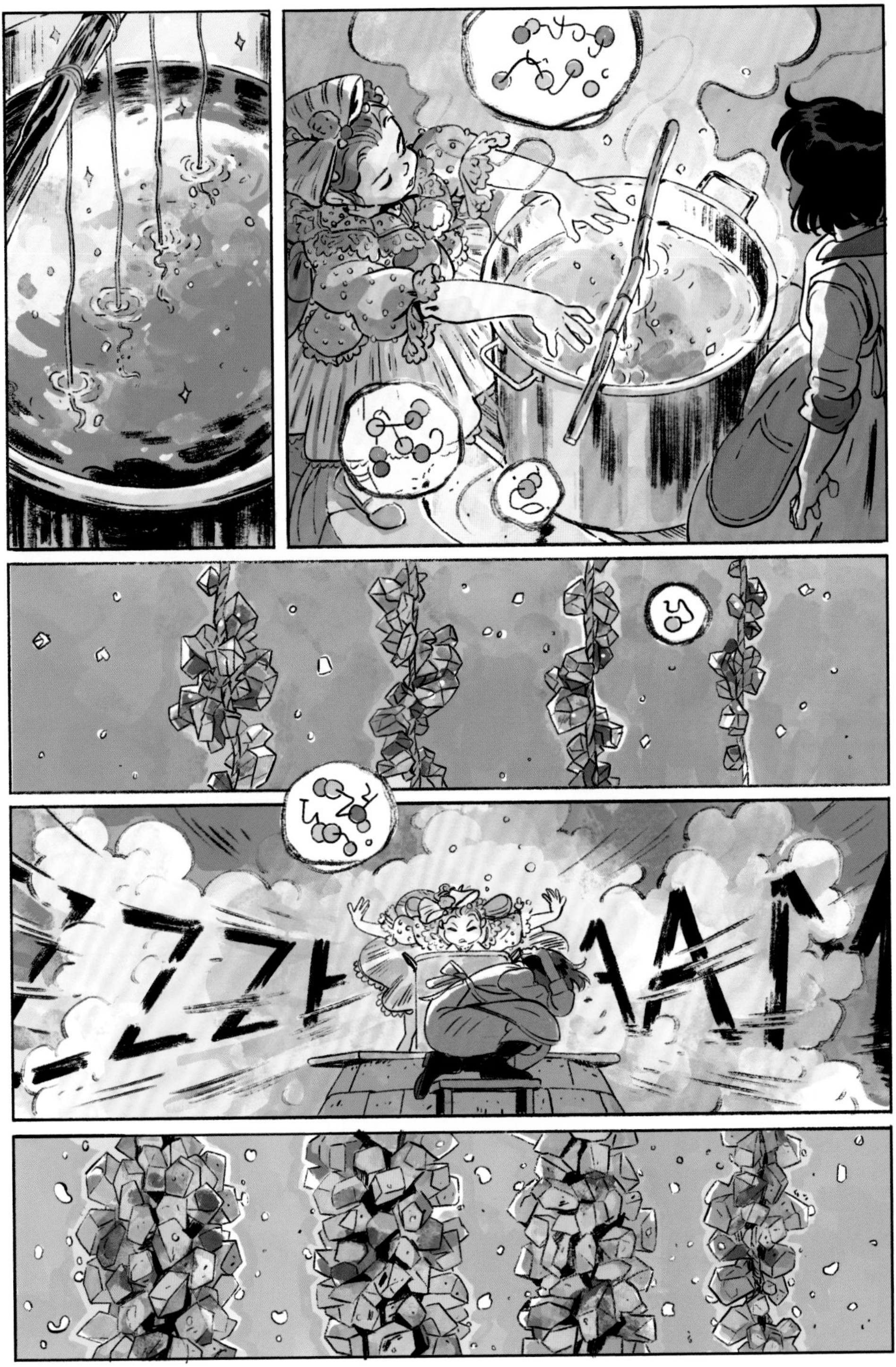

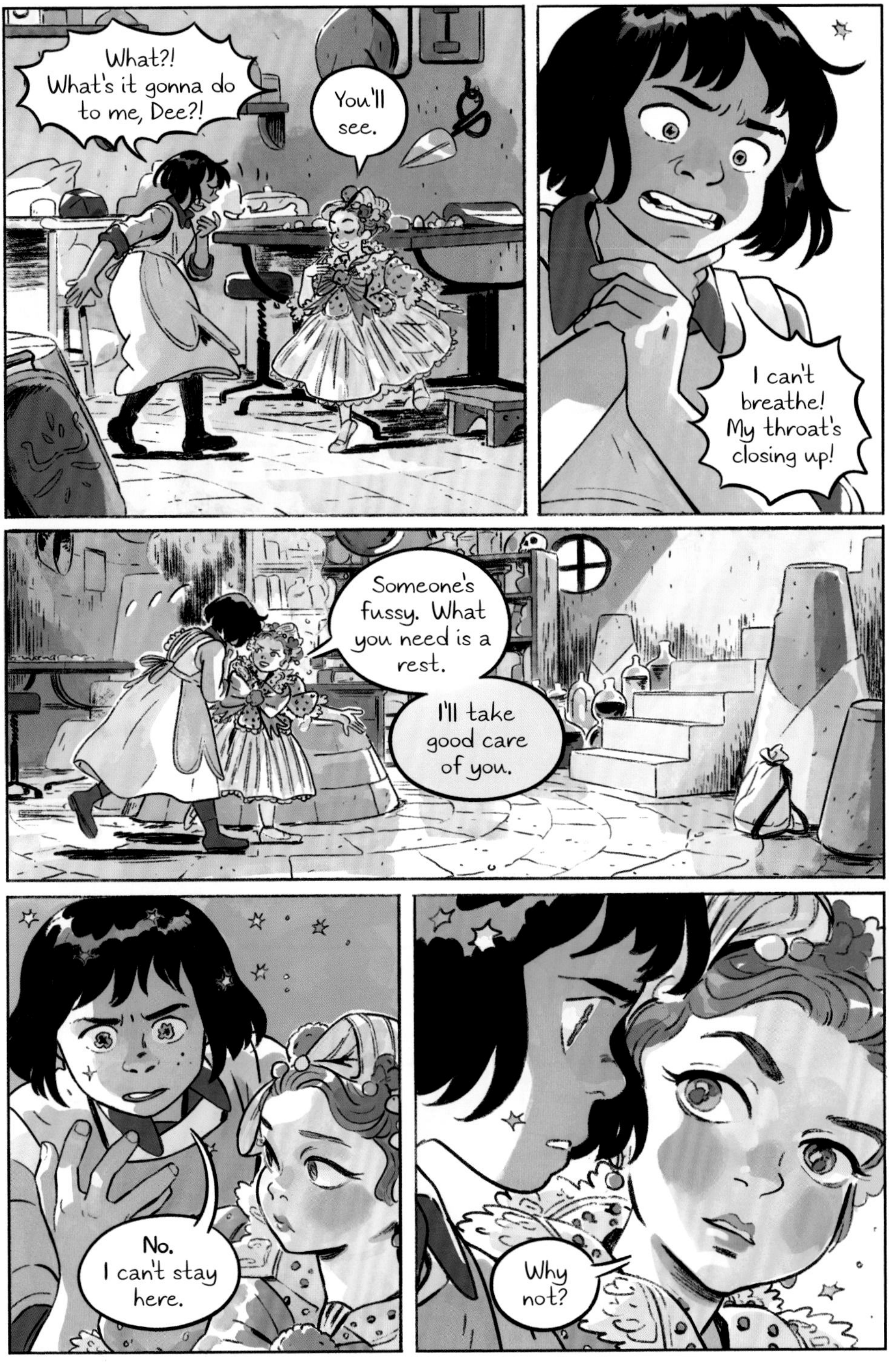
What?! What's it gonna do to me, Dee?!
You'll see.
I can't breathe! My throat's closing up!
Someone's fussy. What you need is a rest.
I'll take good care of you.
No. I can't stay here.
Why not?

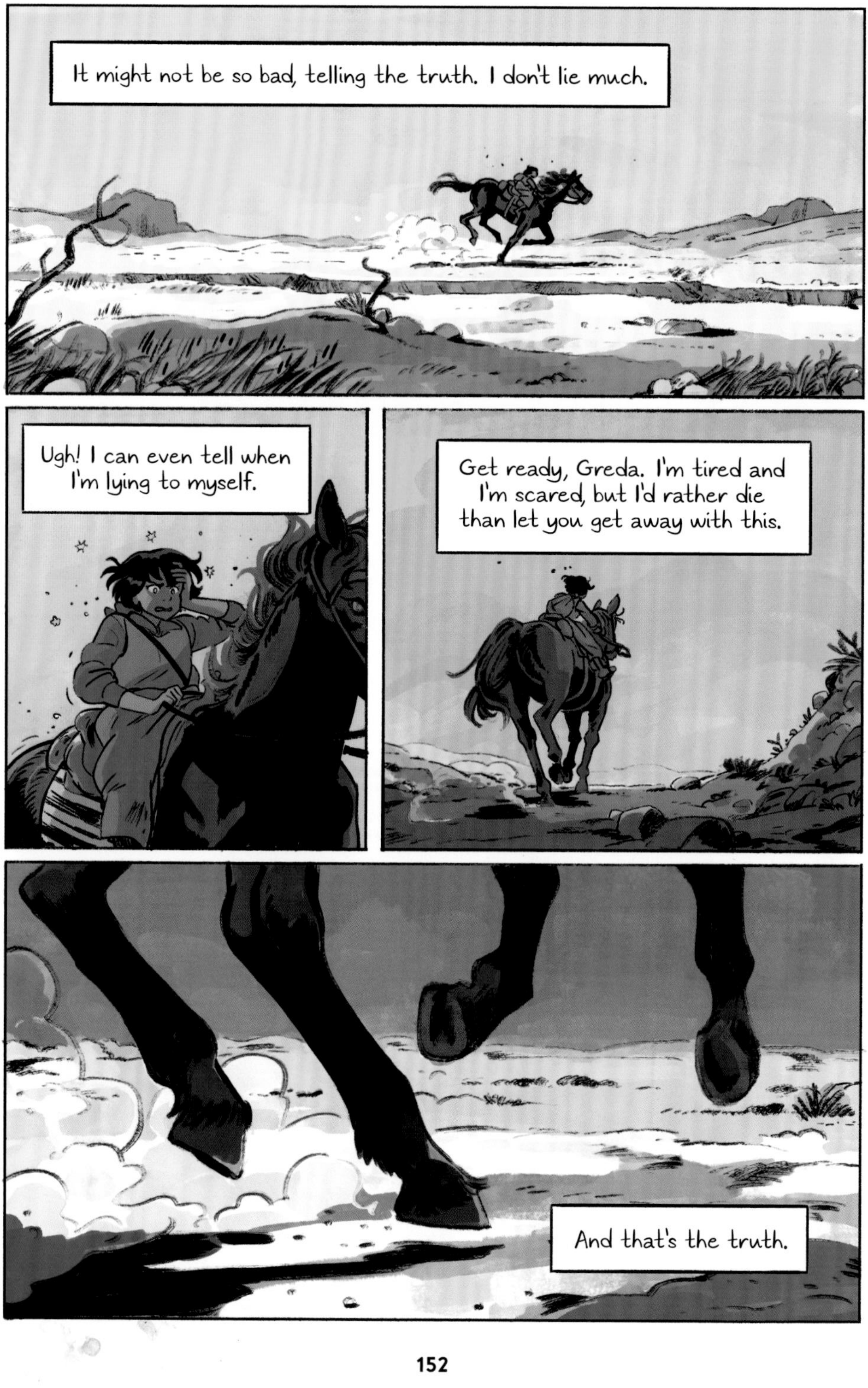
It might not be so bad, telling the truth. I don't lie much.
Ugh! I can even tell when I'm lying to myself.
Get ready, Greda. I'm tired and I'm scared, but I'd rather die than let you get away with this.
And that's the truth.

Chapter Nine

Hospitality

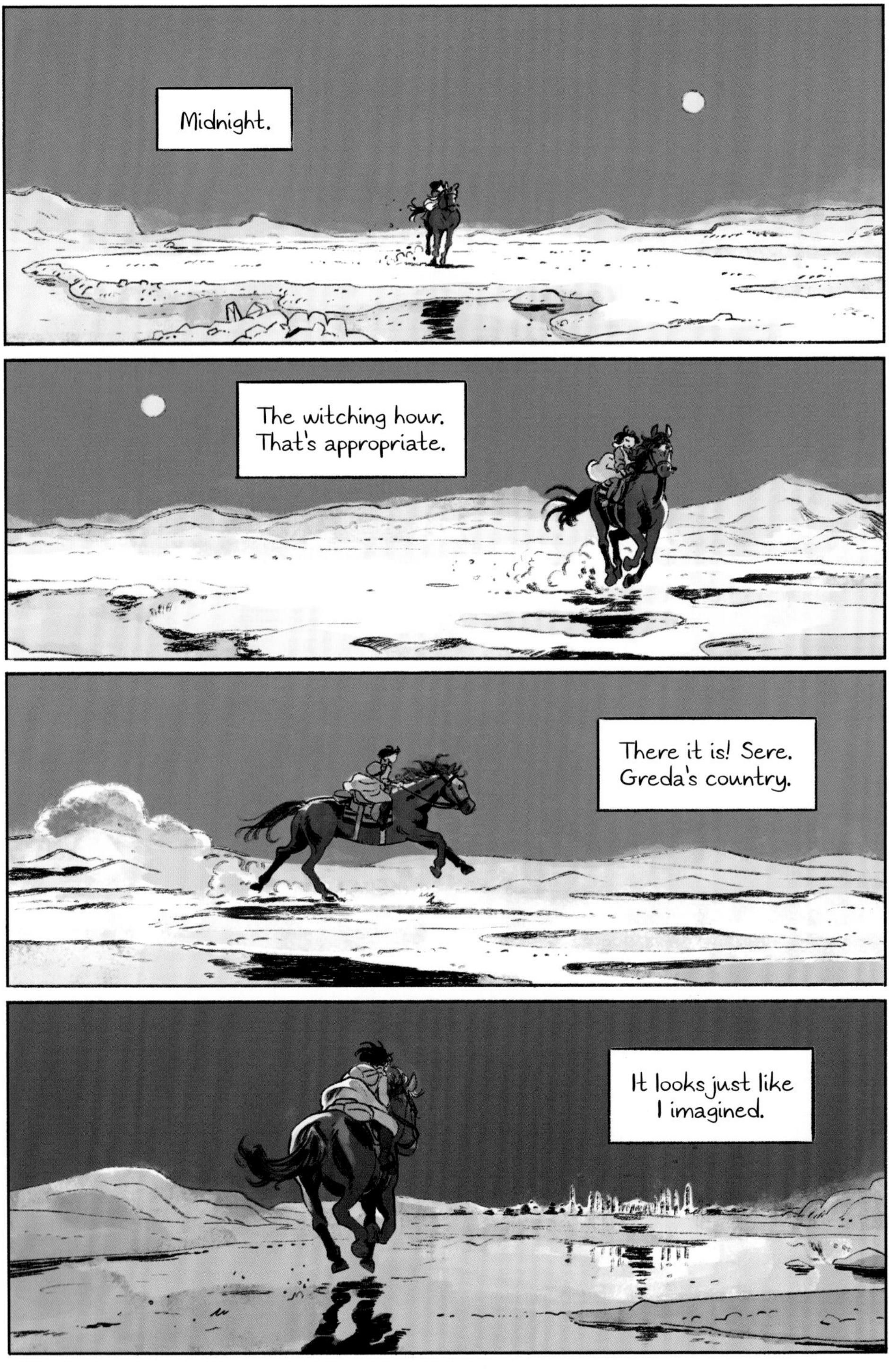
Midnight.
The witching hour. That's appropriate.
There it is! Sere. Greda's country.
It looks just like I imagined.

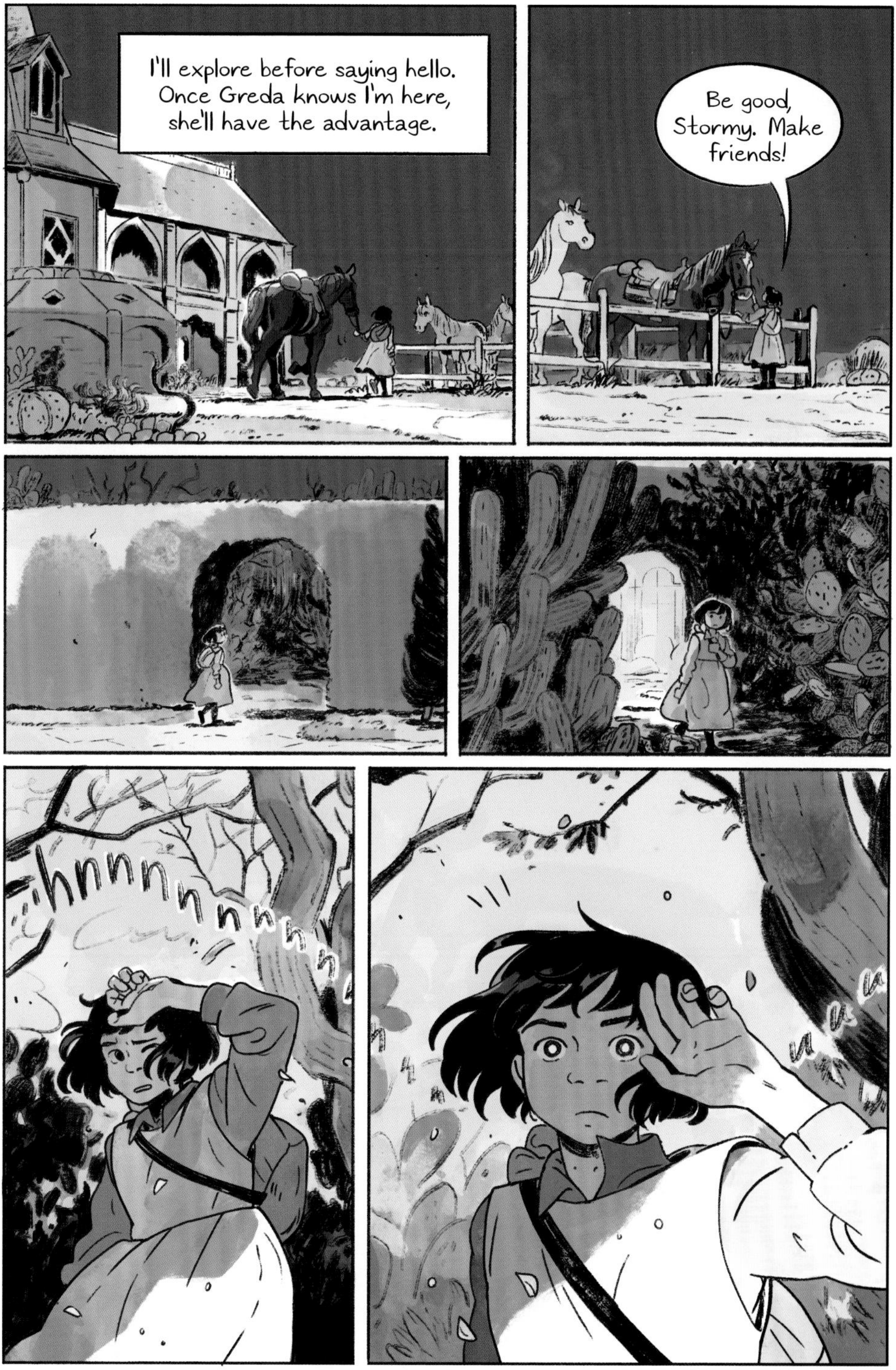
I'll explore before saying hello. Once Greda knows I'm here, she'll have the advantage.
Be good, Stormy. Make friends!
hnnnnnnnnn

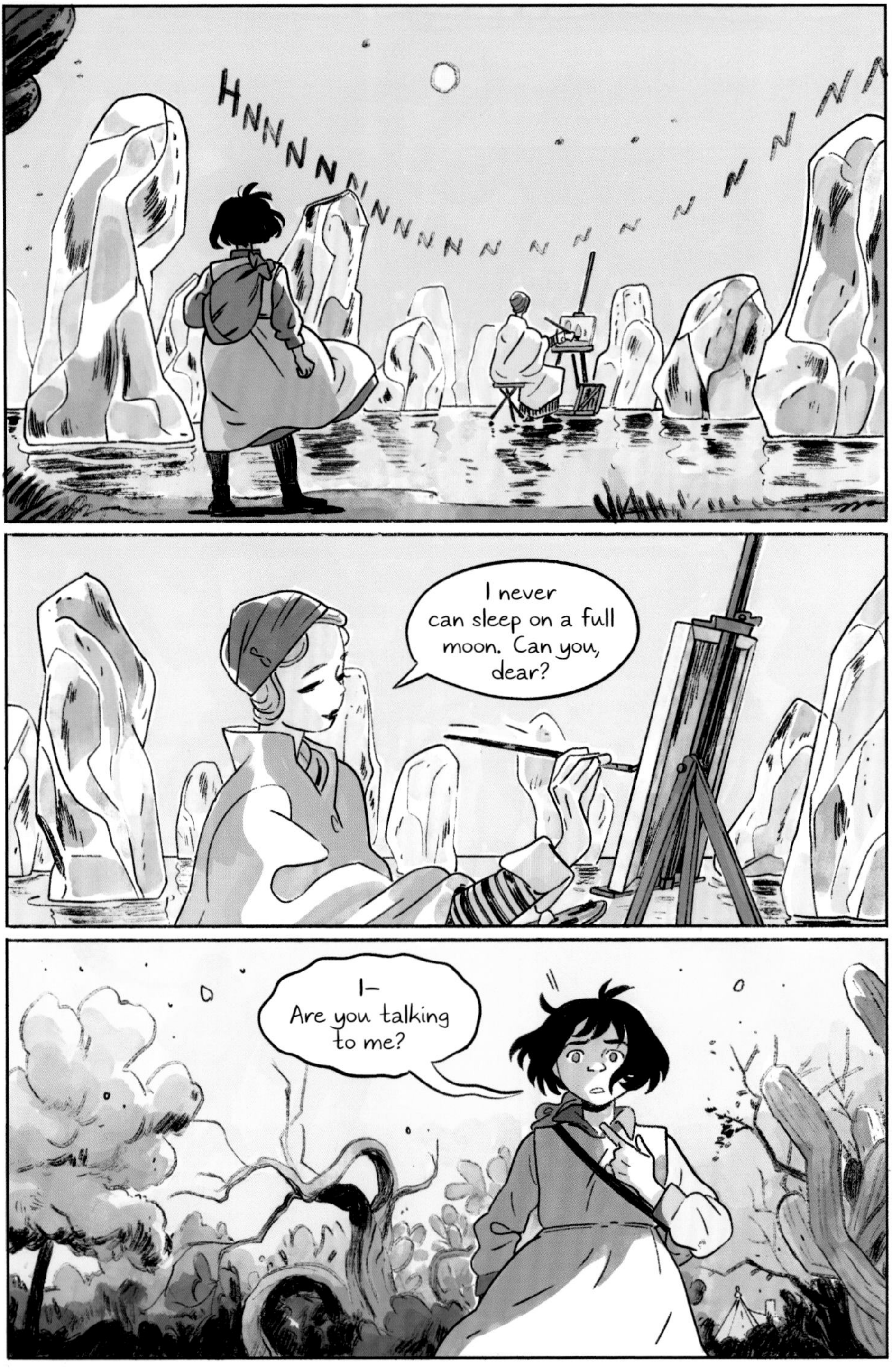
HNNNNNNNNNNNNNNNNNNNNN
I never can sleep on a full moon. Can you, dear?
I– Are you talking to me?

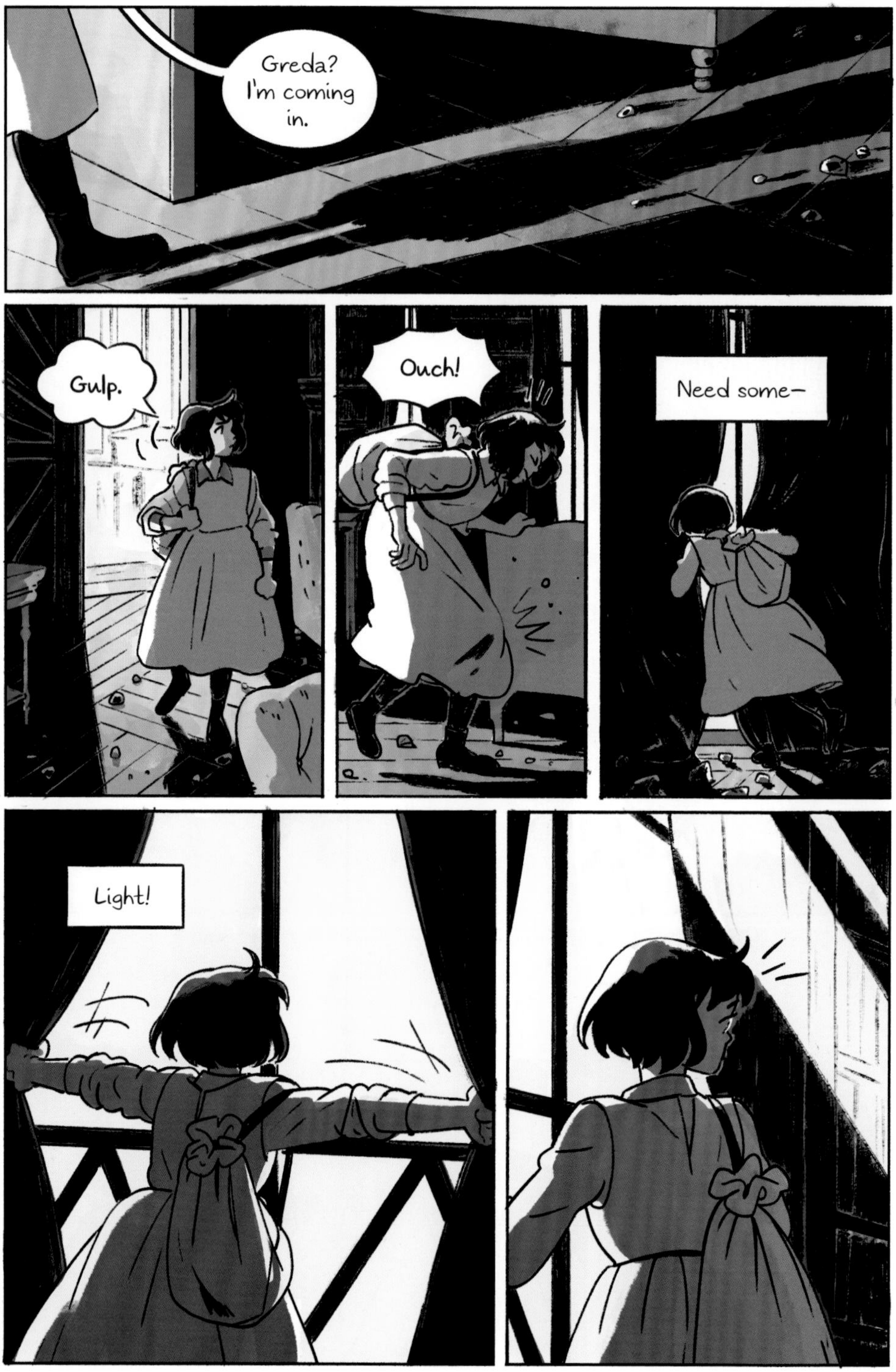
Greda? I'm coming in.
Gulp.
Ouch!
Need some–
Light!

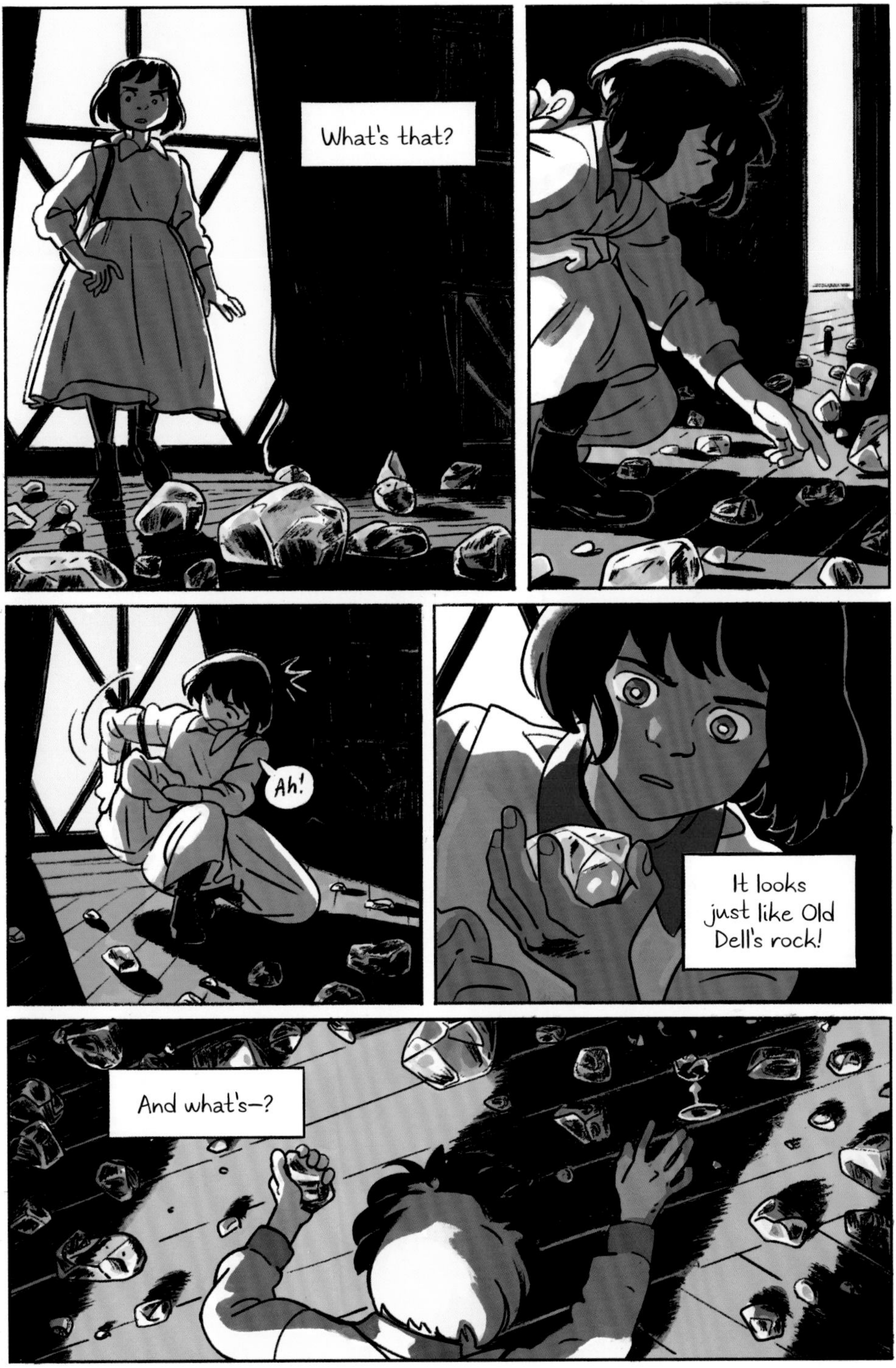
What's that?
Ah!
It looks just like Old Dell's rock!
And what's—?

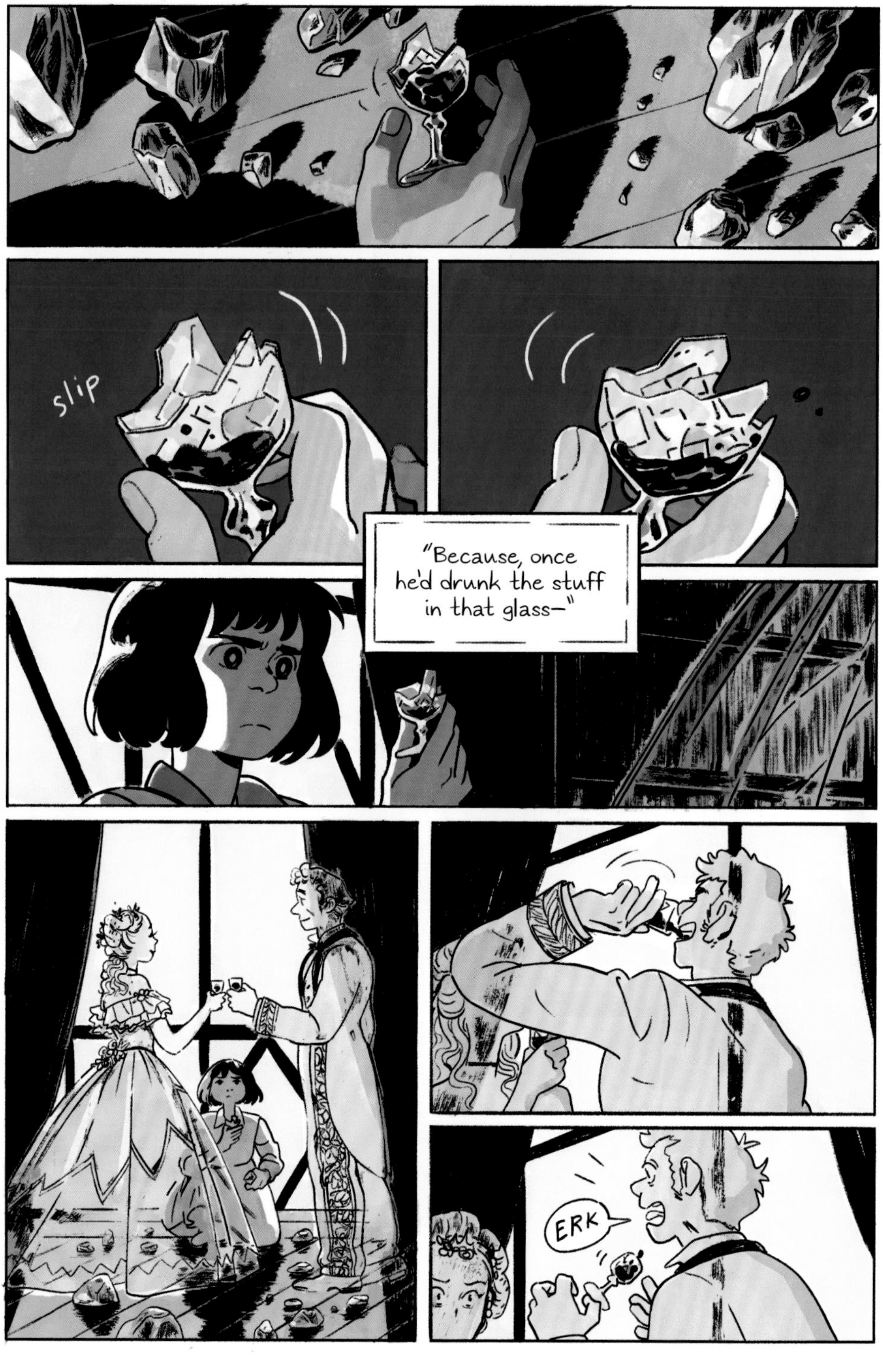
slip
"Because, once he'd drunk the stuff in that glass—"
ERK

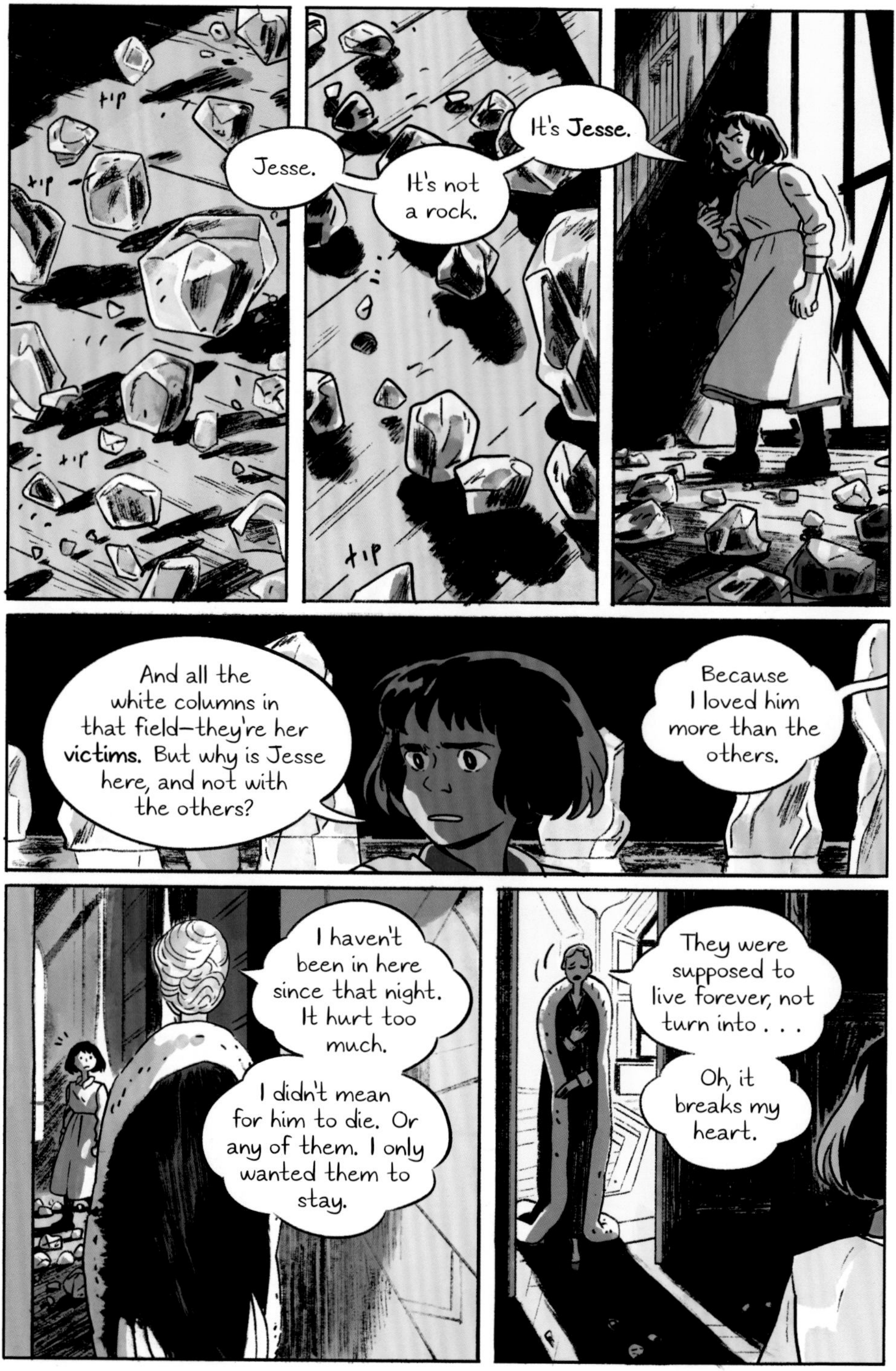
tip
tip
tip
Jesse.
It's not a rock.
tip
It's **Jesse.**
And all the white columns in that field—they're her **victims.** But why is Jesse here, and not with the others?
Because I loved him more than the others.
I haven't been in here since that night. It hurt too much.
I didn't mean for him to die. Or any of them. I only wanted them to stay.
They were supposed to live forever, not turn into . . .
Oh, it breaks my heart.

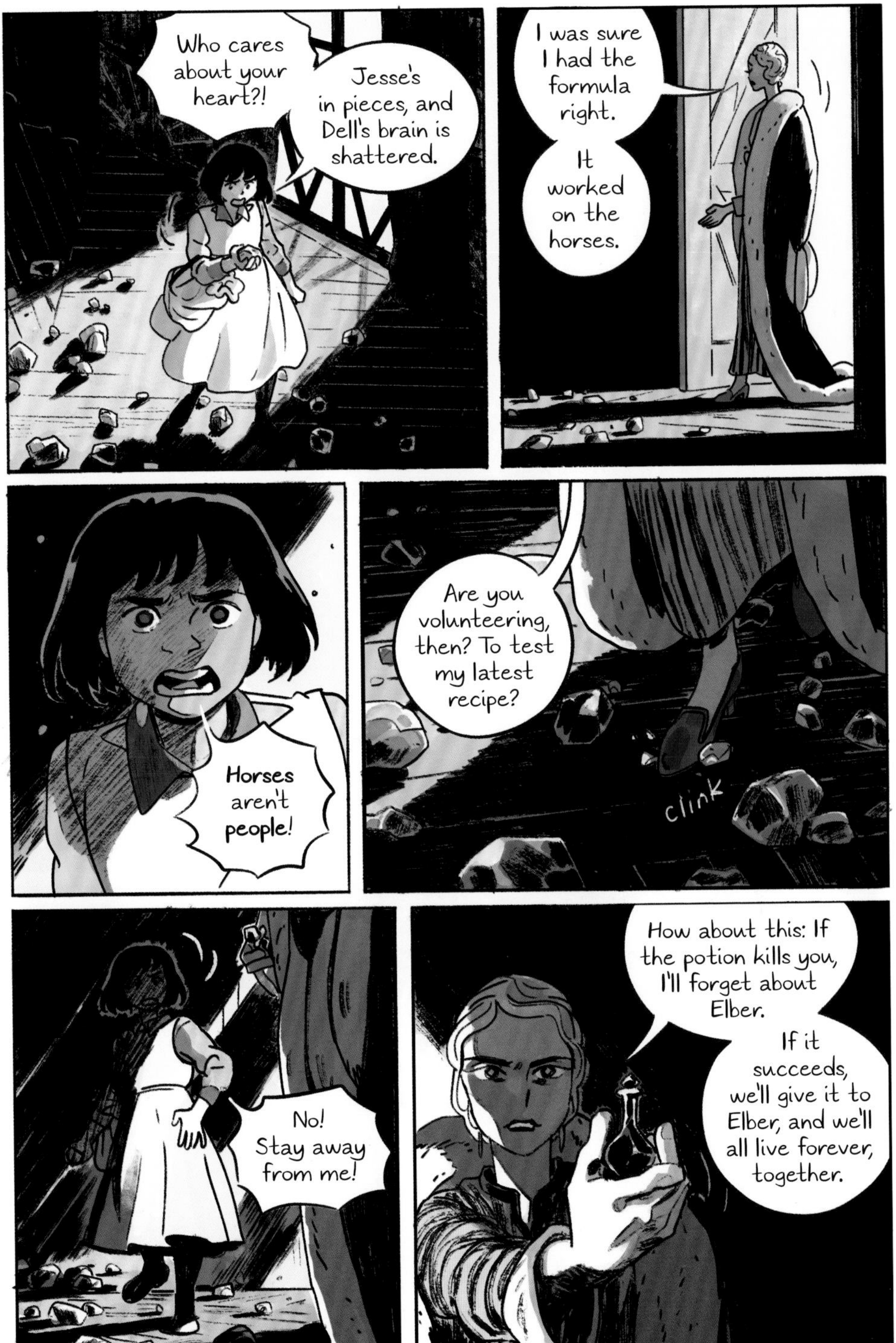
Who cares about your heart?!
Jesse's in pieces, and Dell's brain is shattered.
I was sure I had the formula right.
It worked on the horses.
Horses aren't people!
Are you volunteering, then? To test my latest recipe?
clink
No! Stay away from me!
How about this: If the potion kills you, I'll forget about Elber.
If it succeeds, we'll give it to Elber, and we'll all live forever, together.

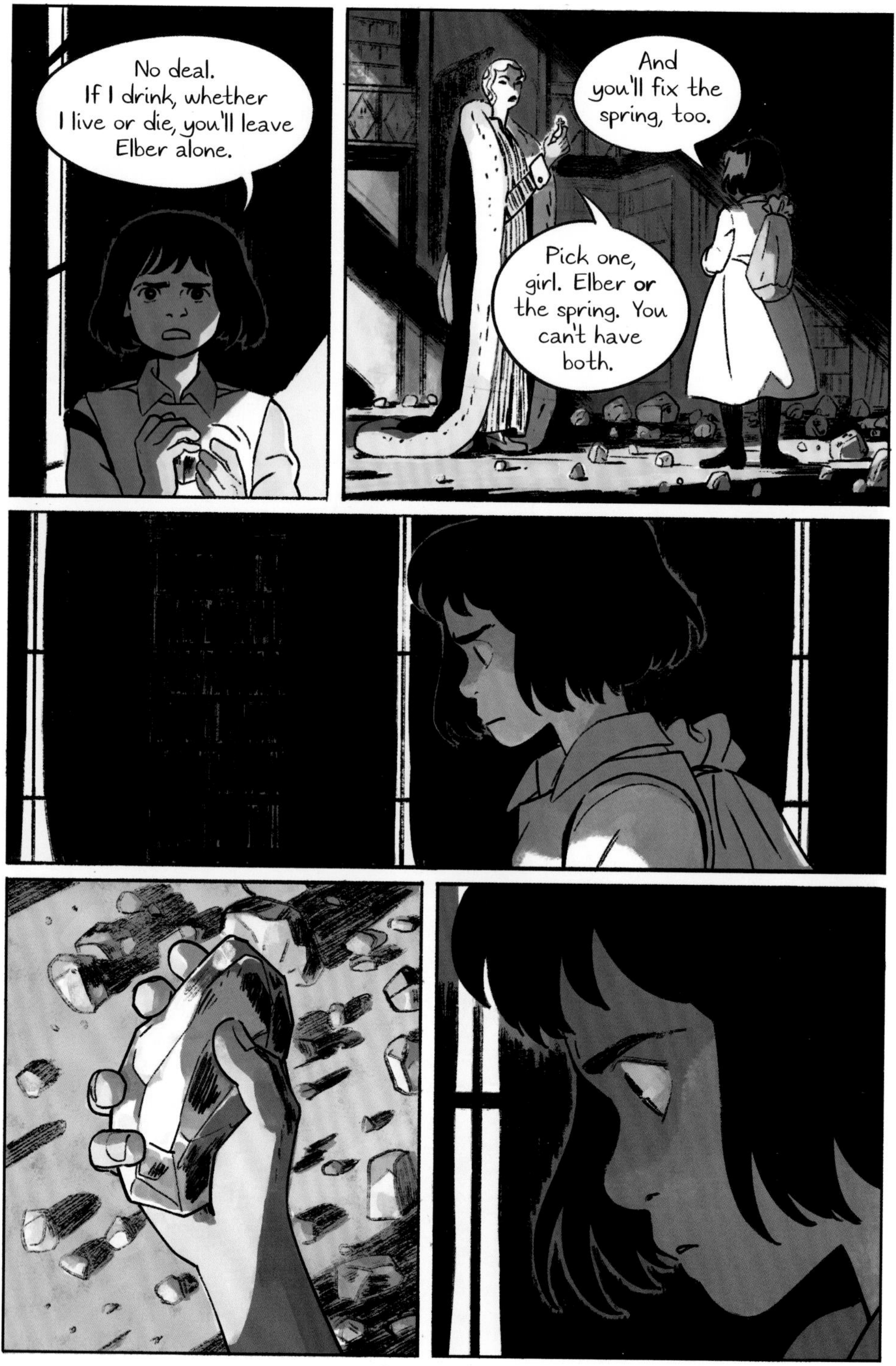
No deal. If I drink, whether I live or die, you'll leave Elber alone.
And you'll fix the spring, too.
Pick one, girl. Elber or the spring. You can't have both.

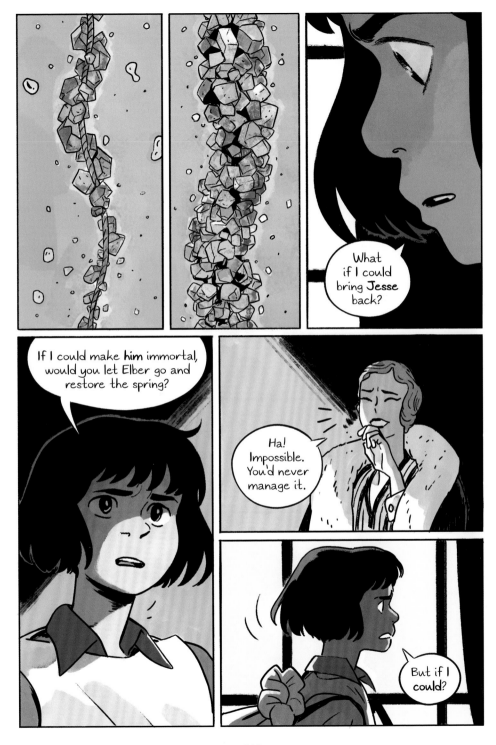

What if I could bring **Jesse** back?

If I could make **him** immortal, would you let Elber go and restore the spring?

Ha! Impossible. You'd never manage it.

But if I **could**?

169

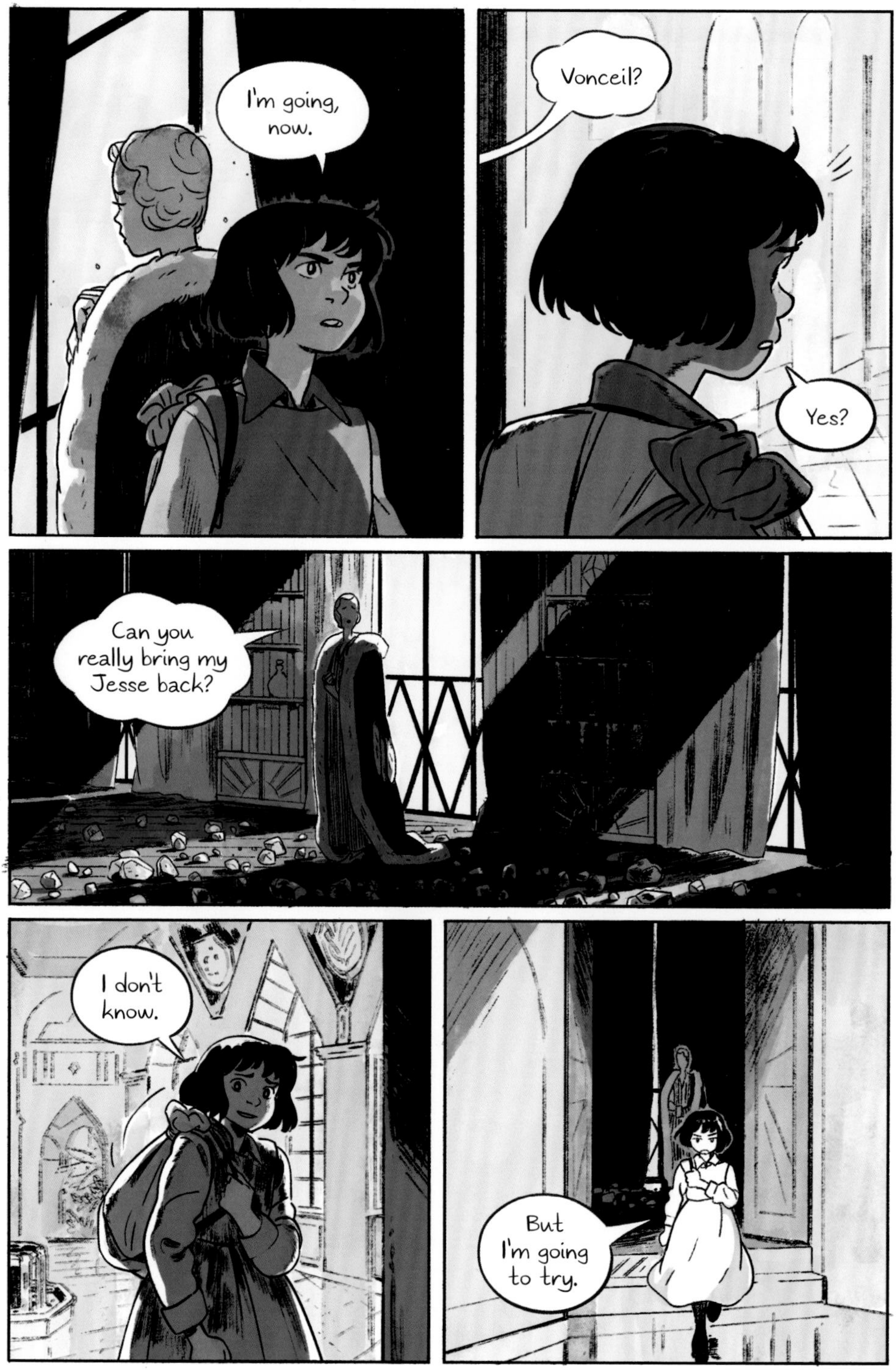
I'm going, now.
Vonceil?
Yes?
Can you really bring my Jesse back?
I don't know.
But I'm going to try.

Chapter Ten

The Magic of Tears

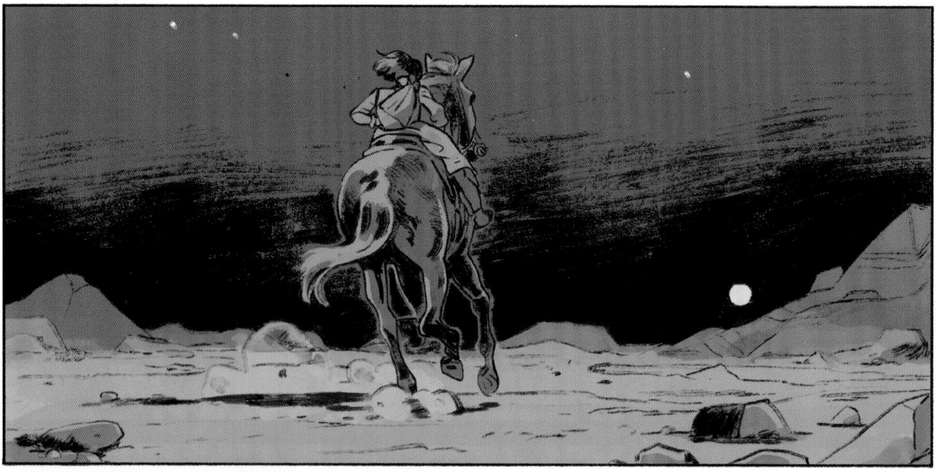
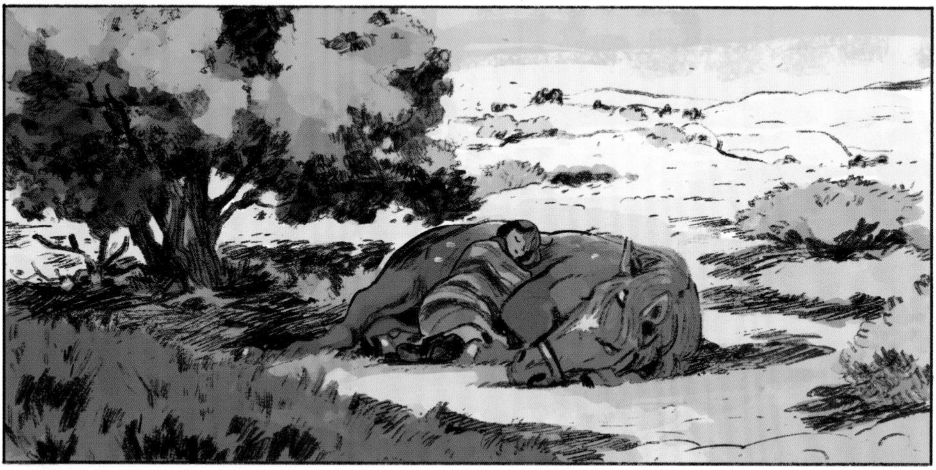
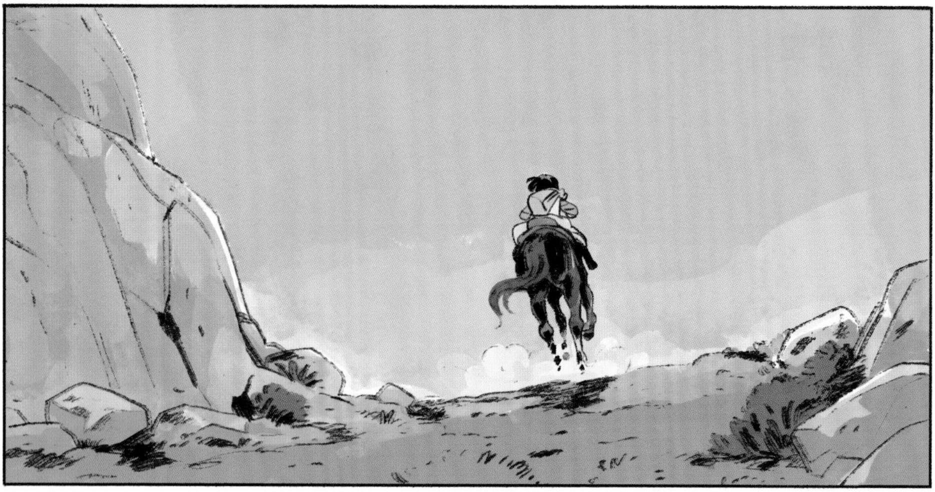

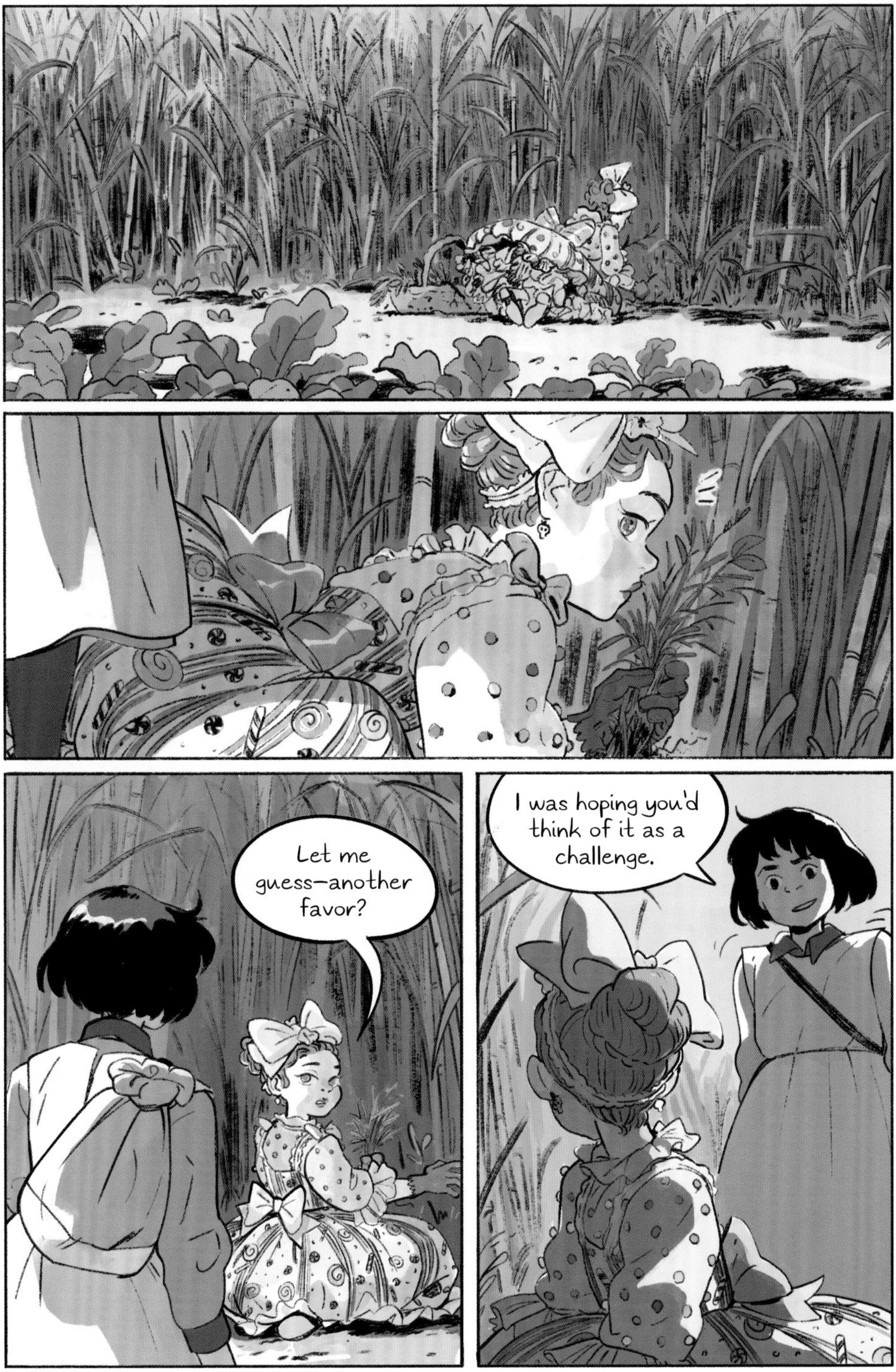
Let me guess—another favor?
I was hoping you'd think of it as a challenge.

177

178

180

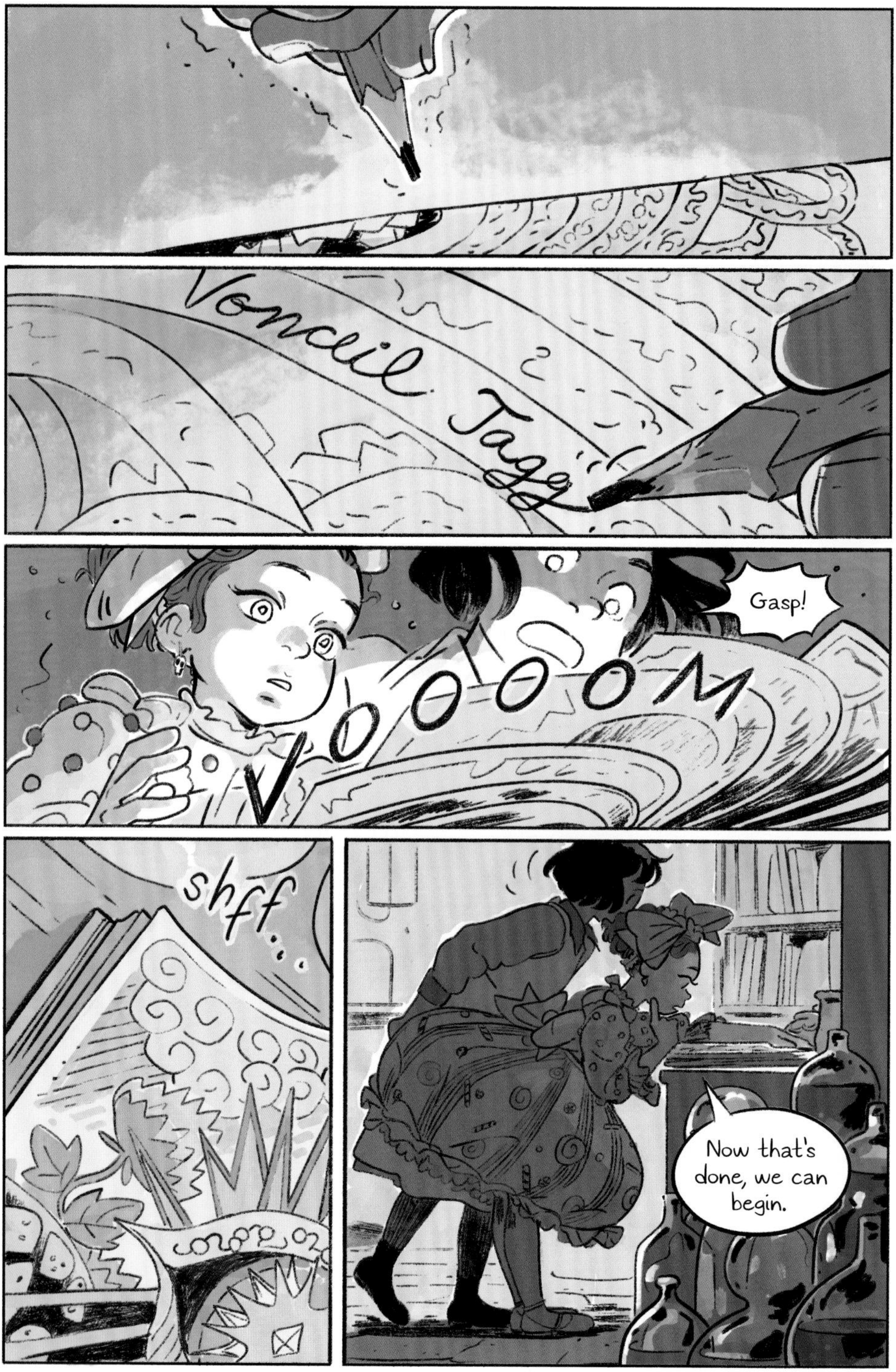
Voncil Jagg
Gasp!
VOOOOOM
shff...
Now that's done, we can begin.

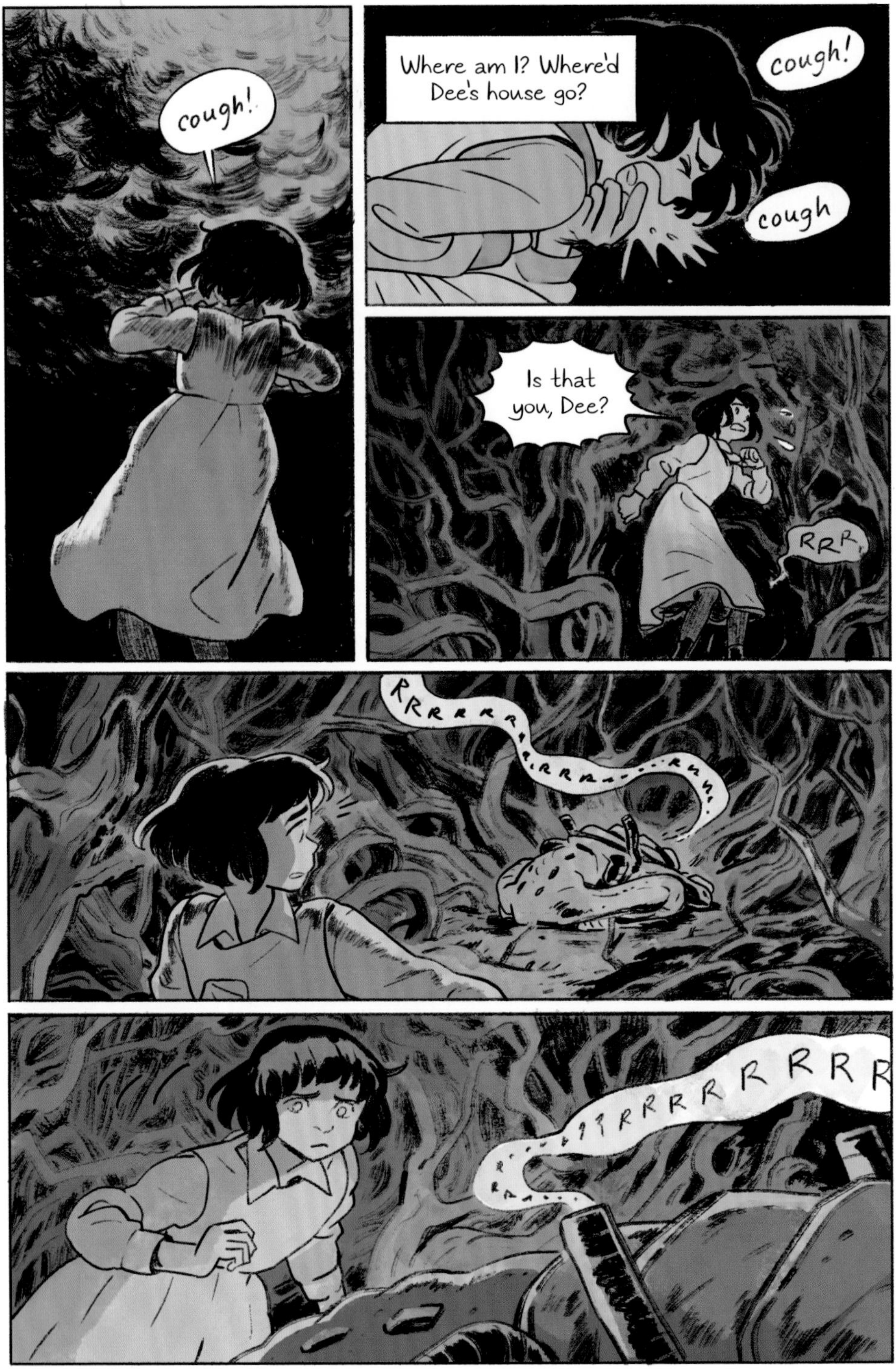
cough!
Where am I? Where'd Dee's house go?
cough!
cough
Is that you, Dee?
RRR
Rrrrrrrrrrrrr...rrr
RRRRRRRRRR

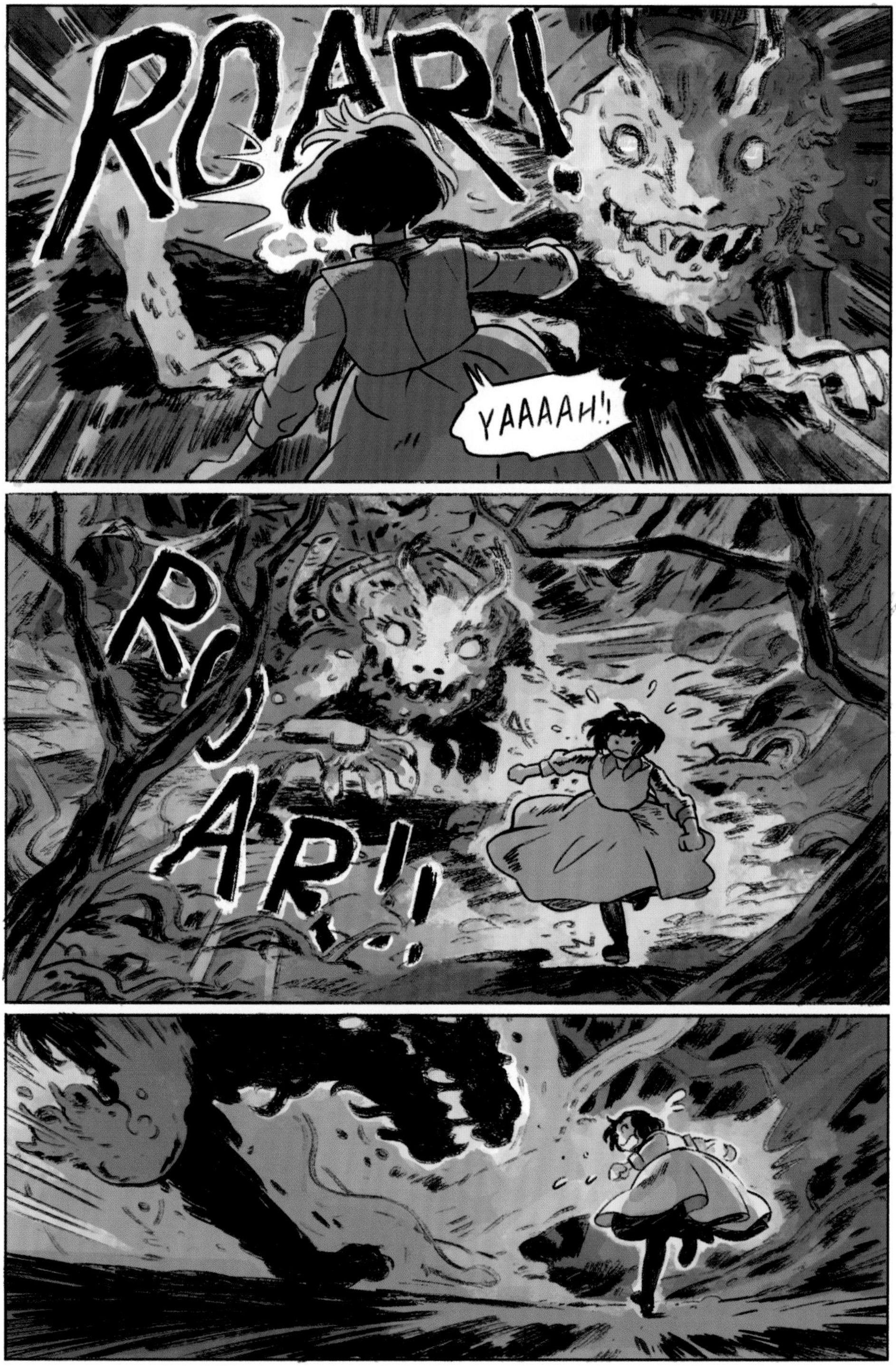
ROAR!
YAAAAH!!
RUAR!!

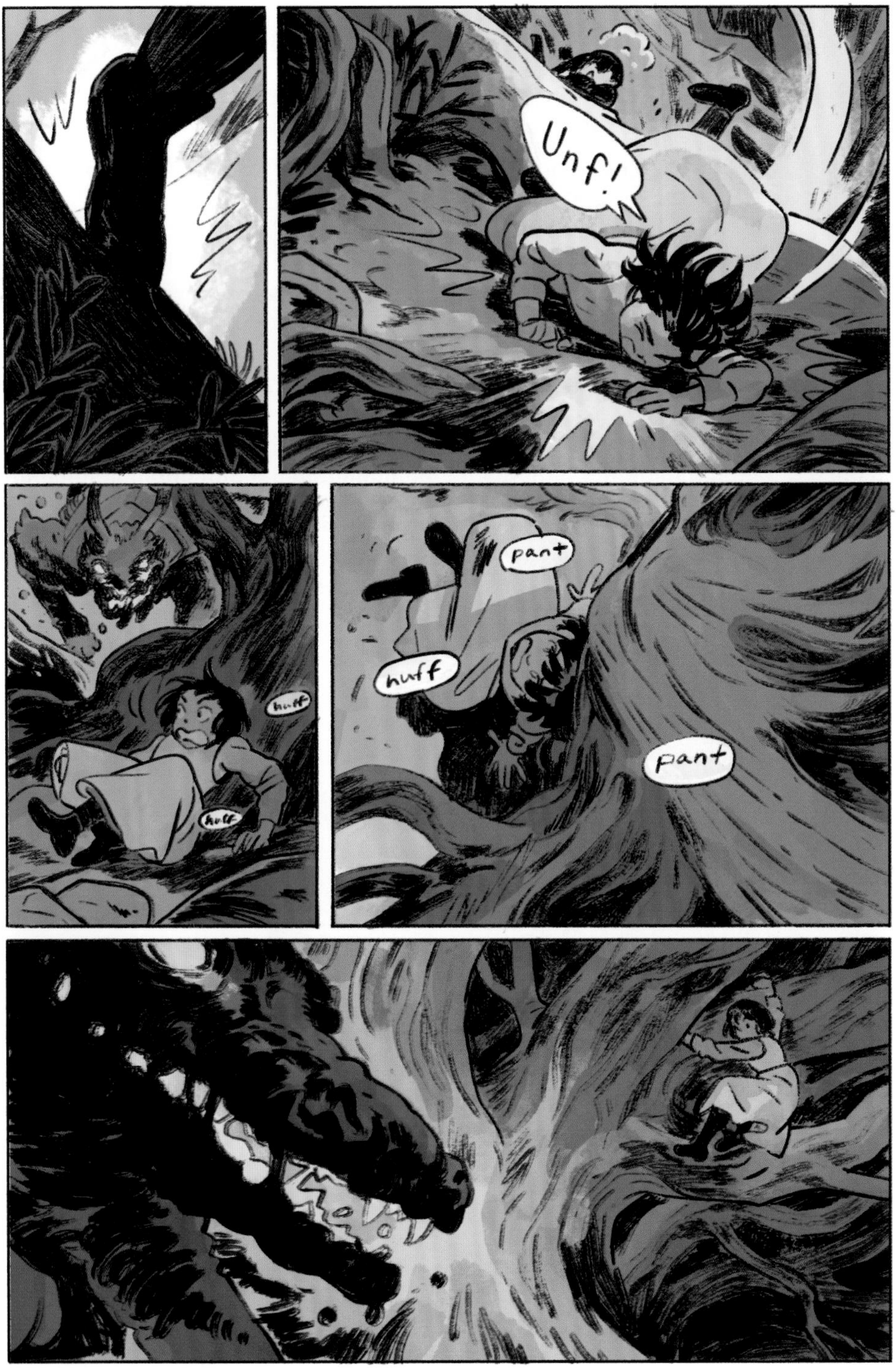
Unf!
pant
huff
huff
huff
pant

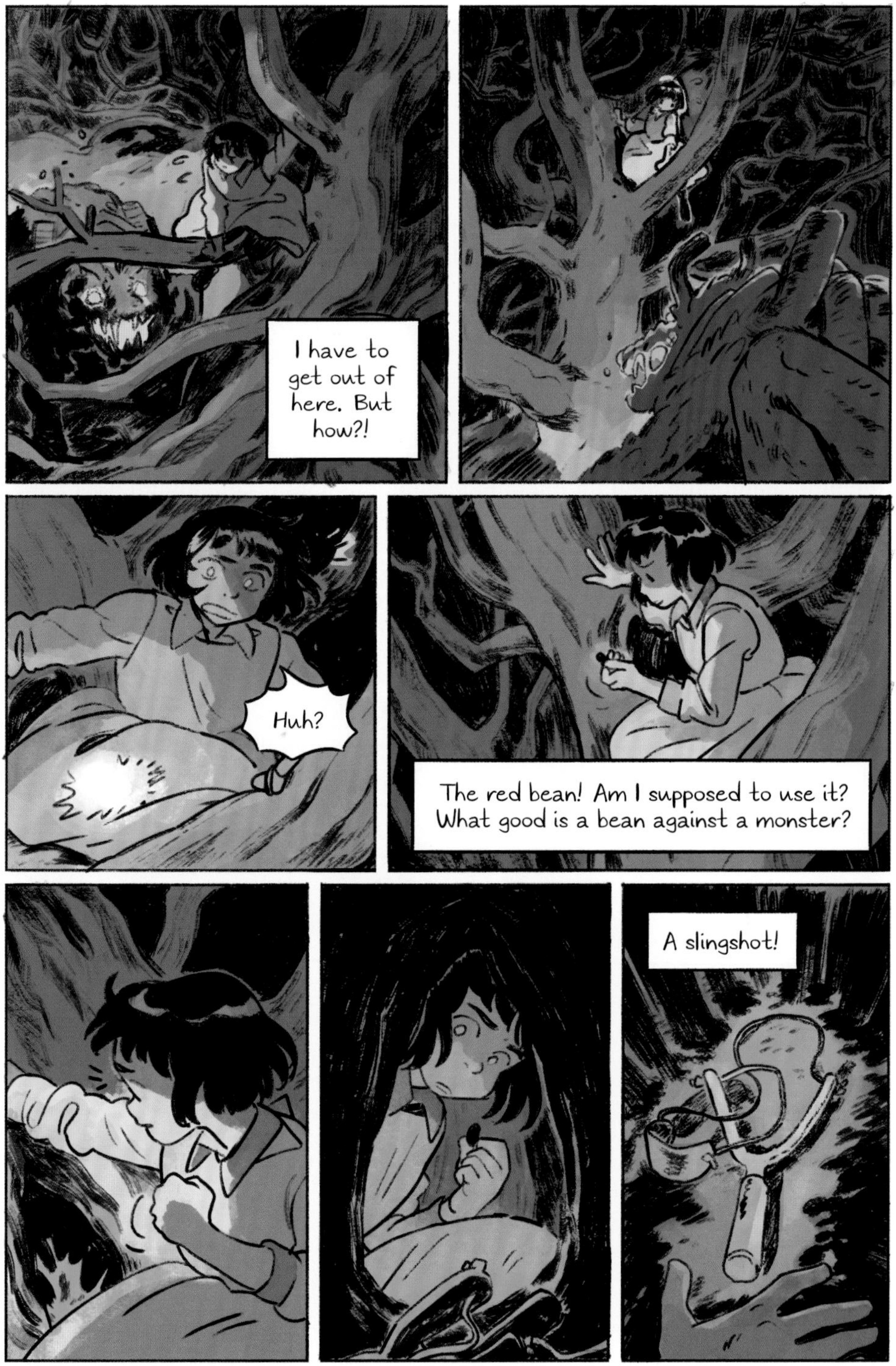
I have to get out of here. But how?!
Huh?
The red bean! Am I supposed to use it? What good is a bean against a monster?
A slingshot!

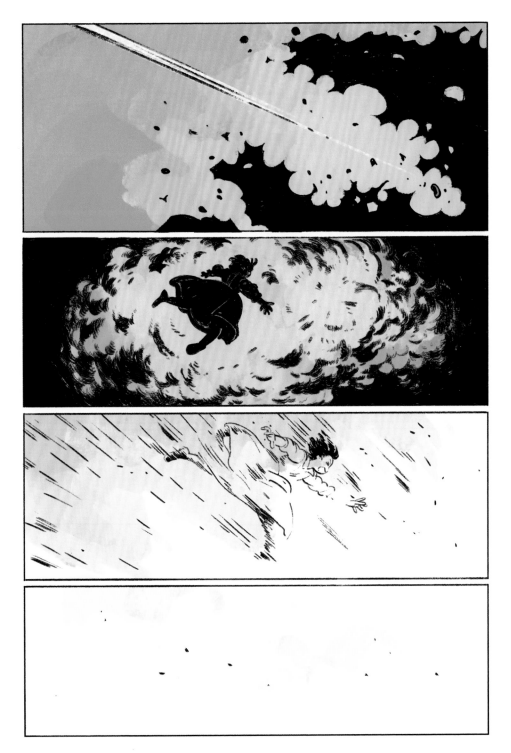

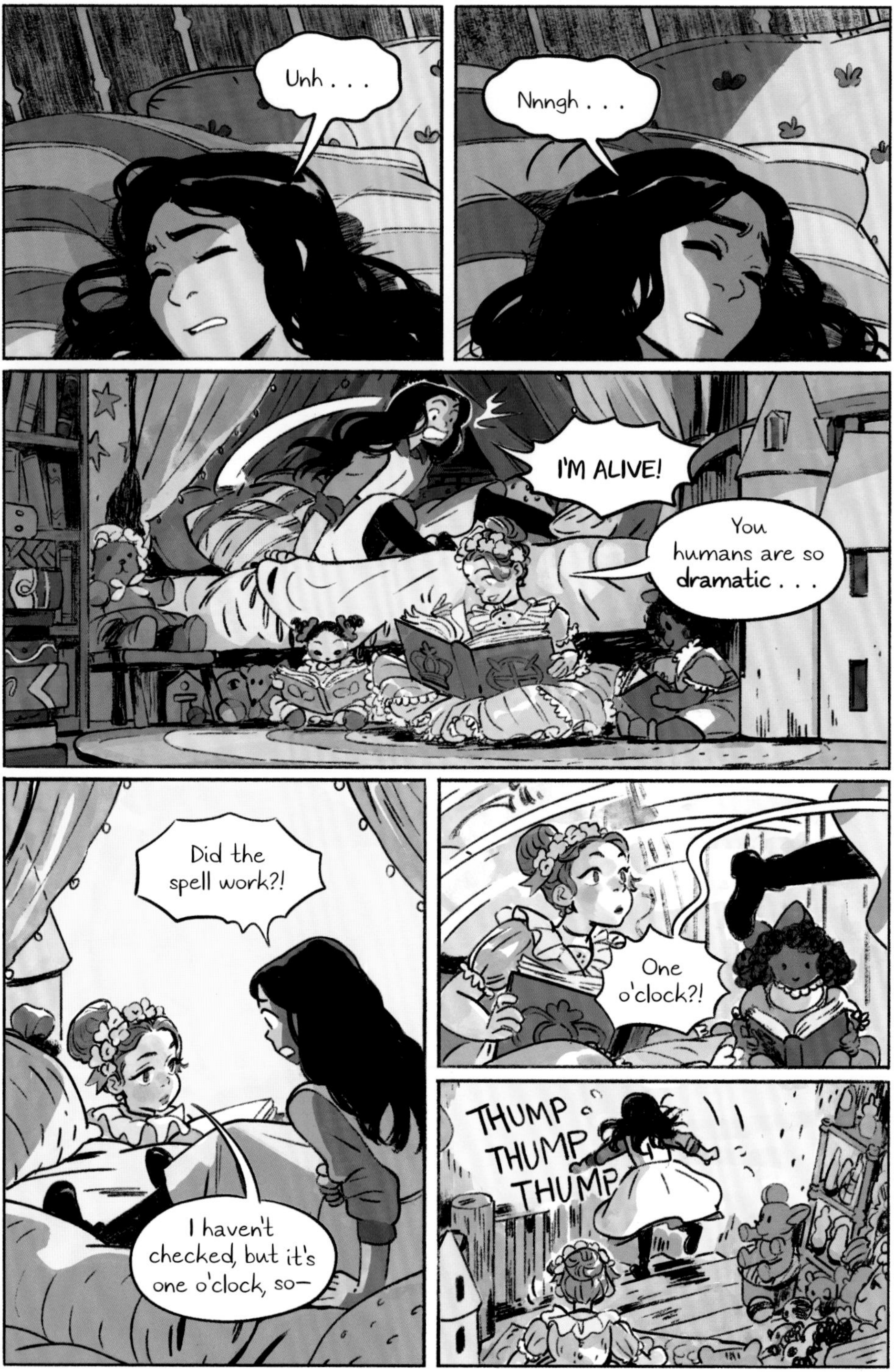
Unh . . .
Nnngh . . .
I'M ALIVE!
You humans are so dramatic . . .
Did the spell work?!
I haven't checked, but it's one o'clock, so—
One o'clock?!
THUMP THUMP THUMP

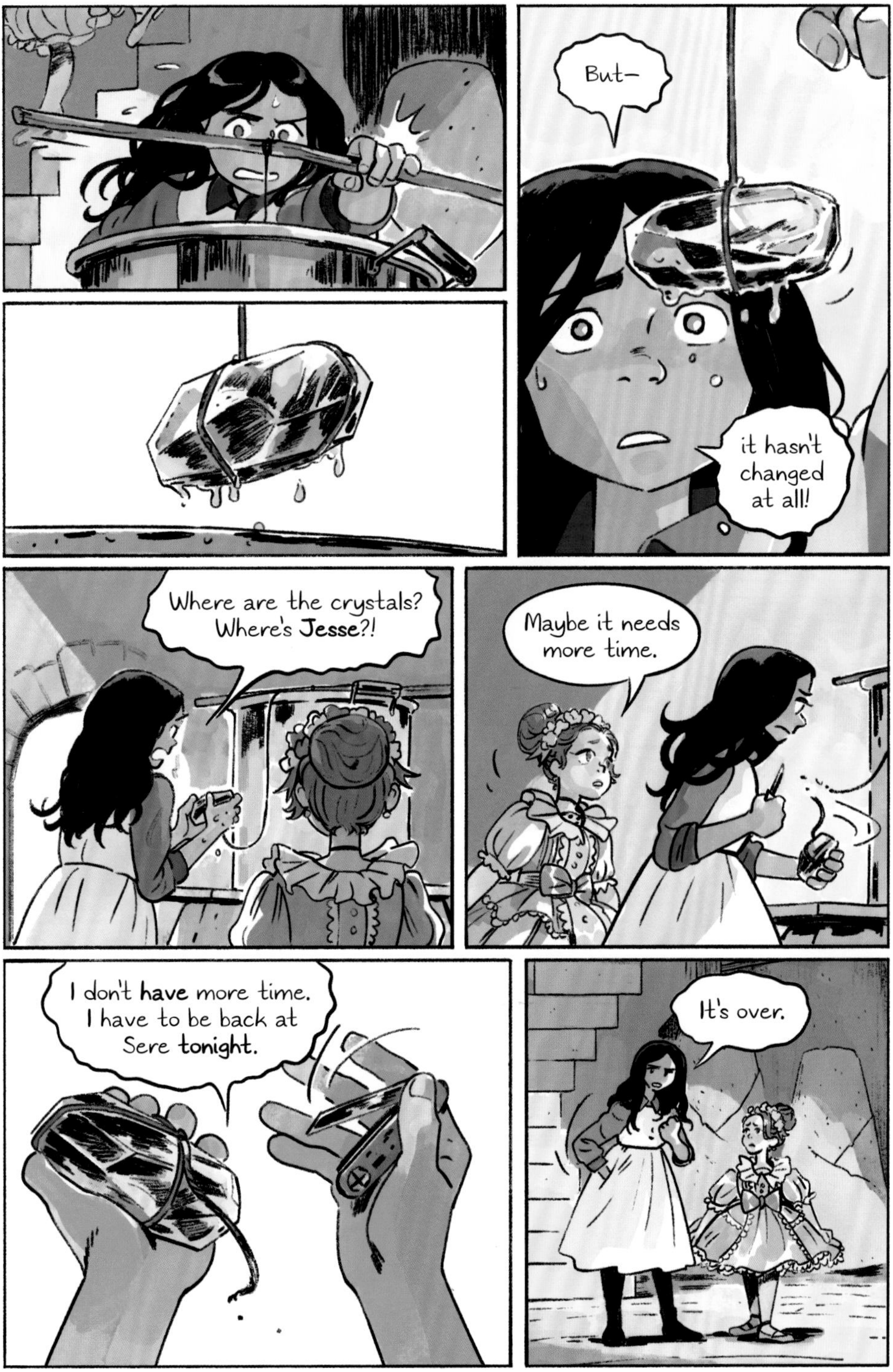

But–
it hasn't changed at all!
Where are the crystals? Where's **Jesse**?!
Maybe it needs more time.
I don't **have** more time. I have to be back at Sere **tonight**.
It's over.

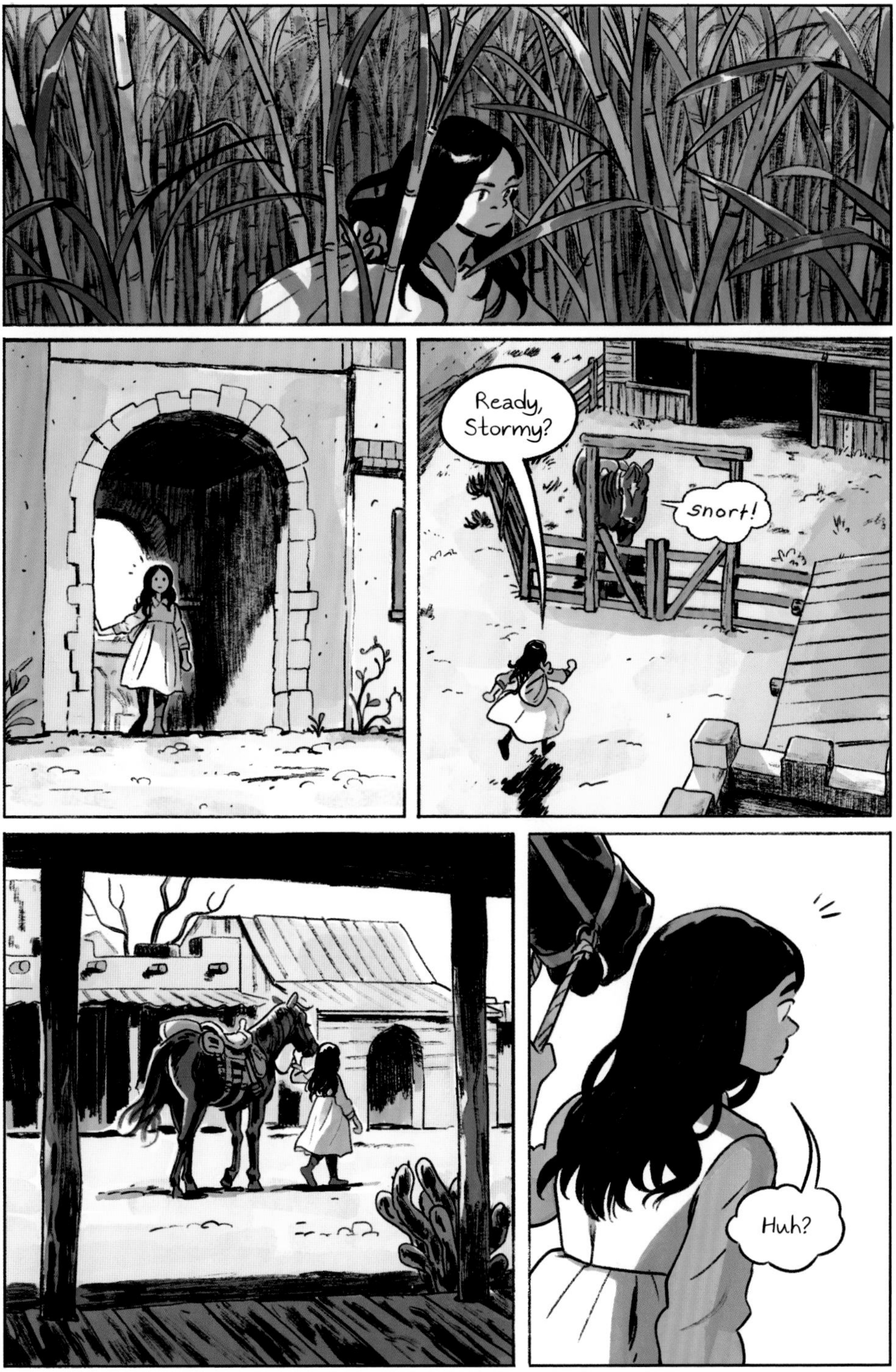
Ready, Stormy?
snort!
Huh?

200

Chapter Eleven

An Uninvited Guest

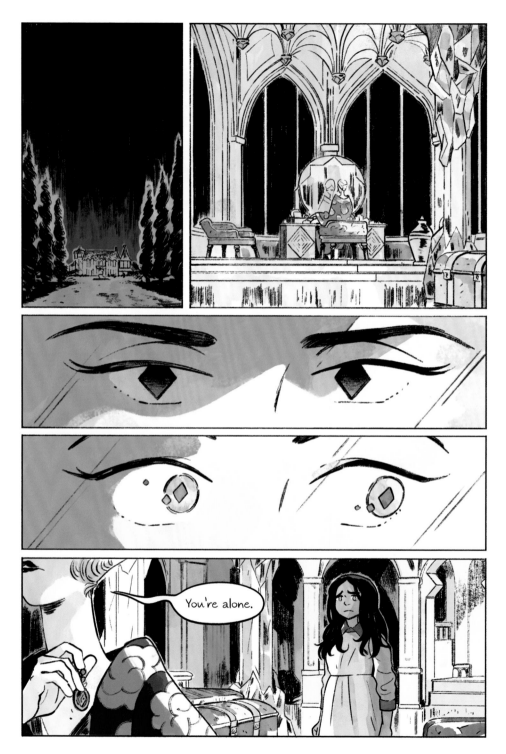

You're alone.

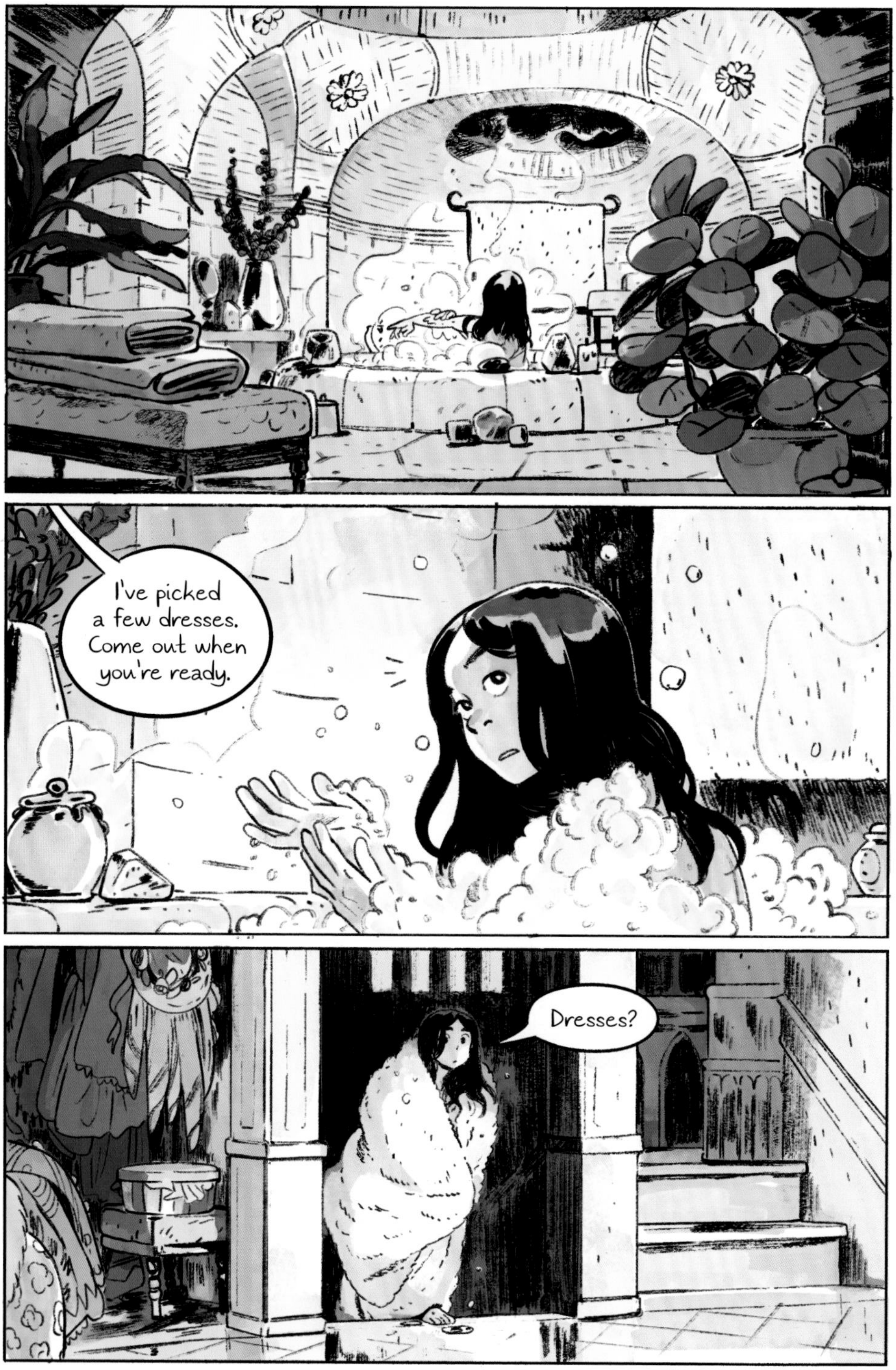
I've picked a few dresses. Come out when you're ready.
Dresses?

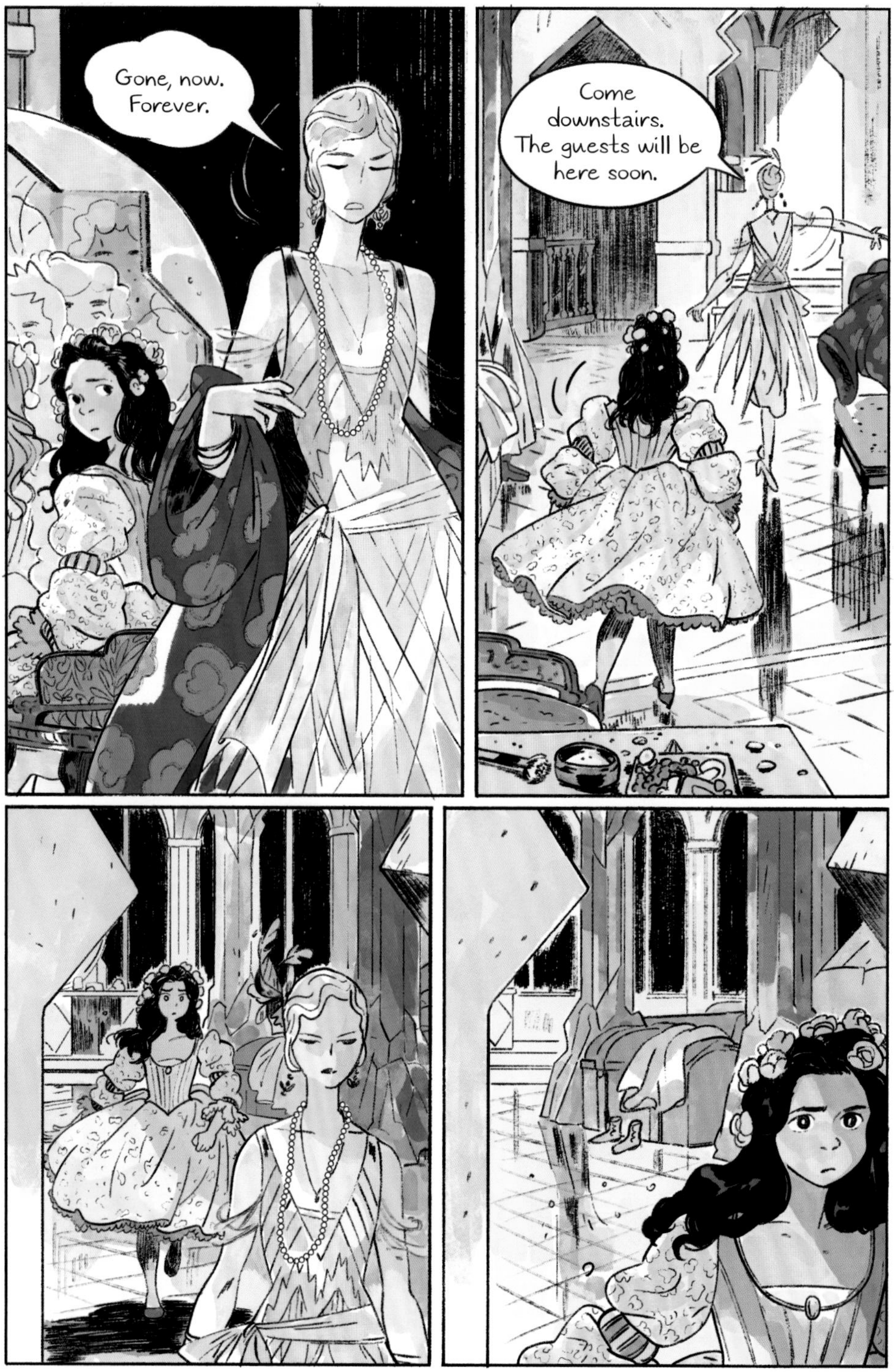
Gone, now.
Forever.
Come
downstairs.
The guests will be
here soon.

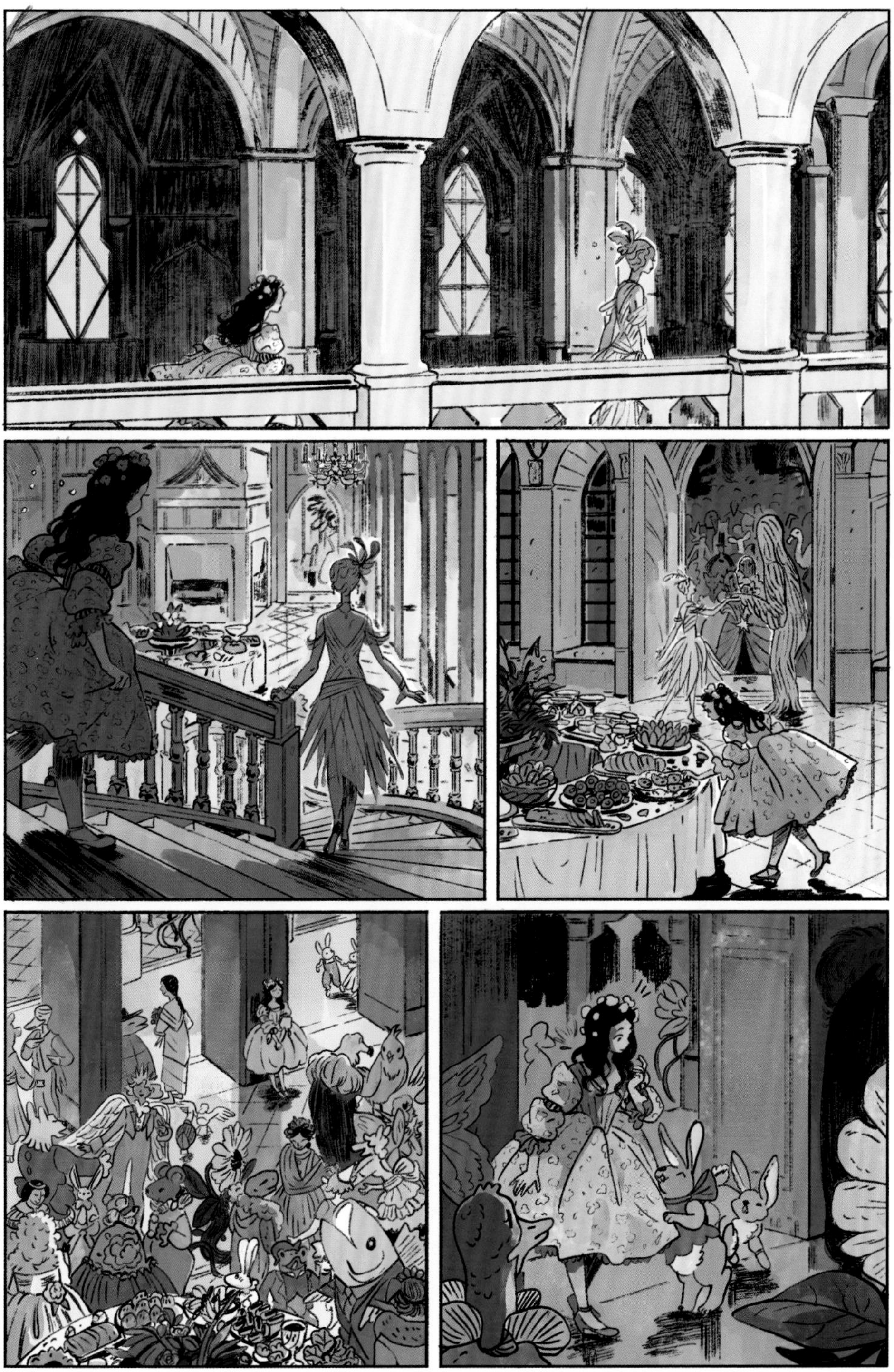

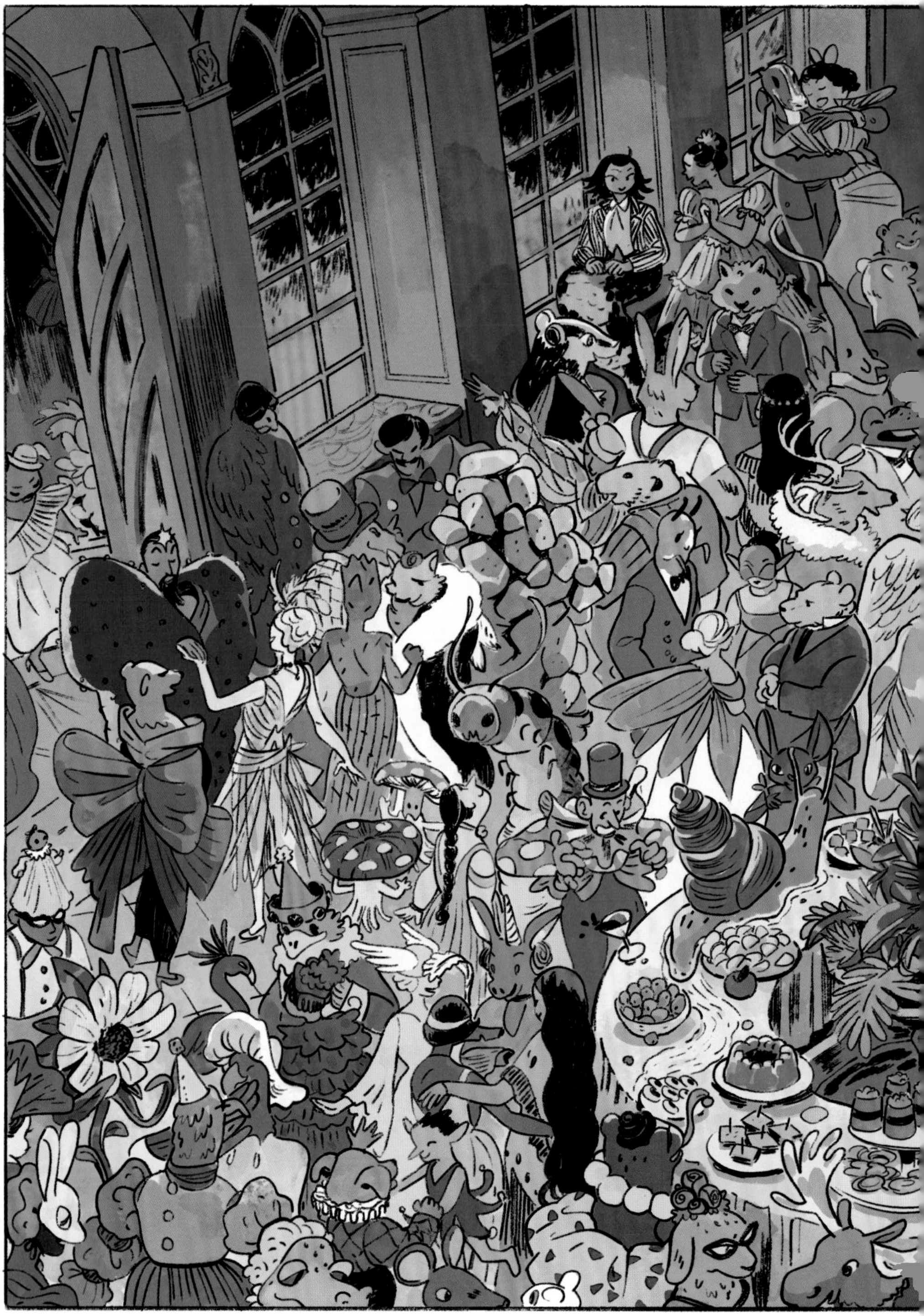

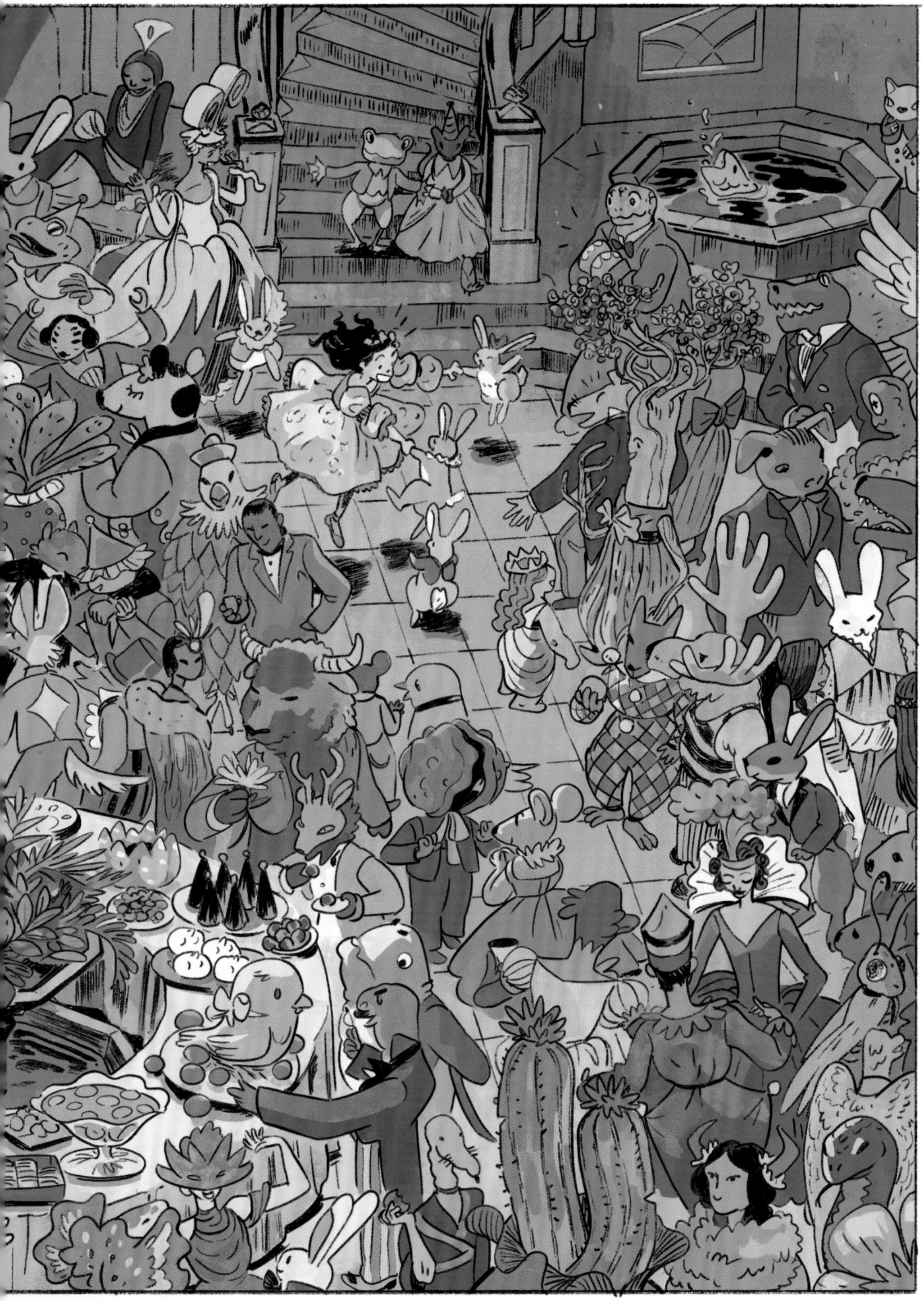

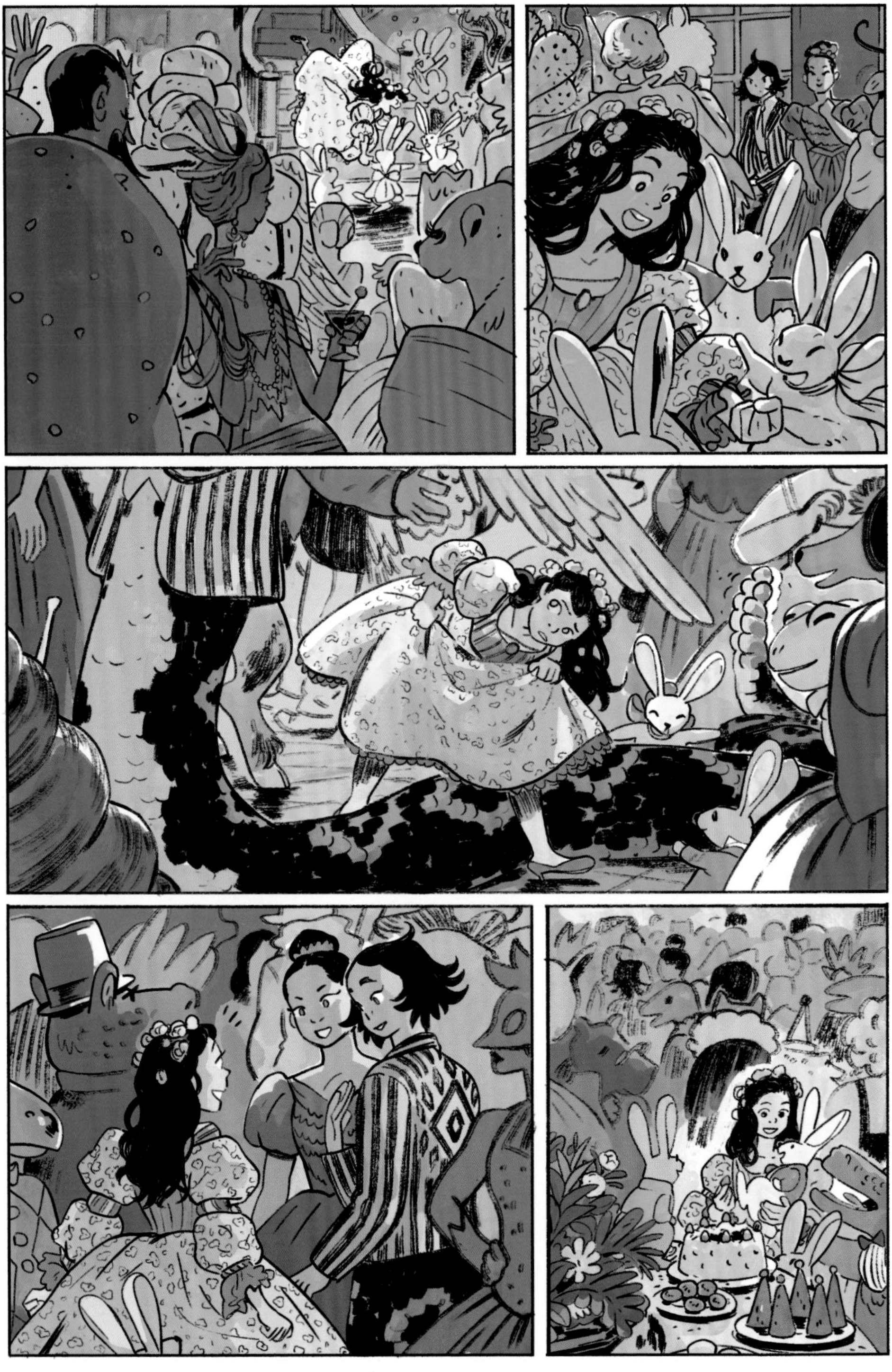

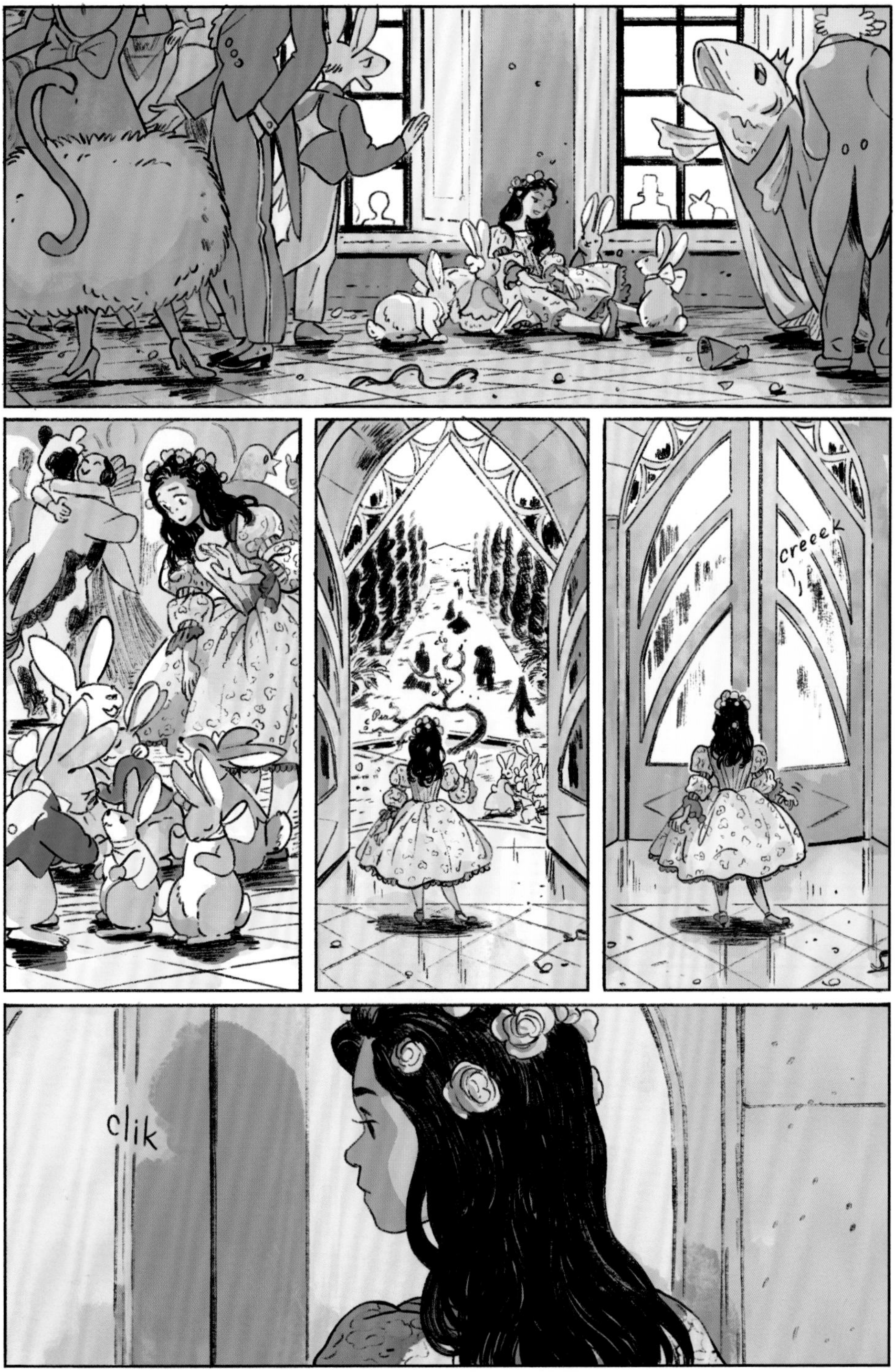
Creeek
clik

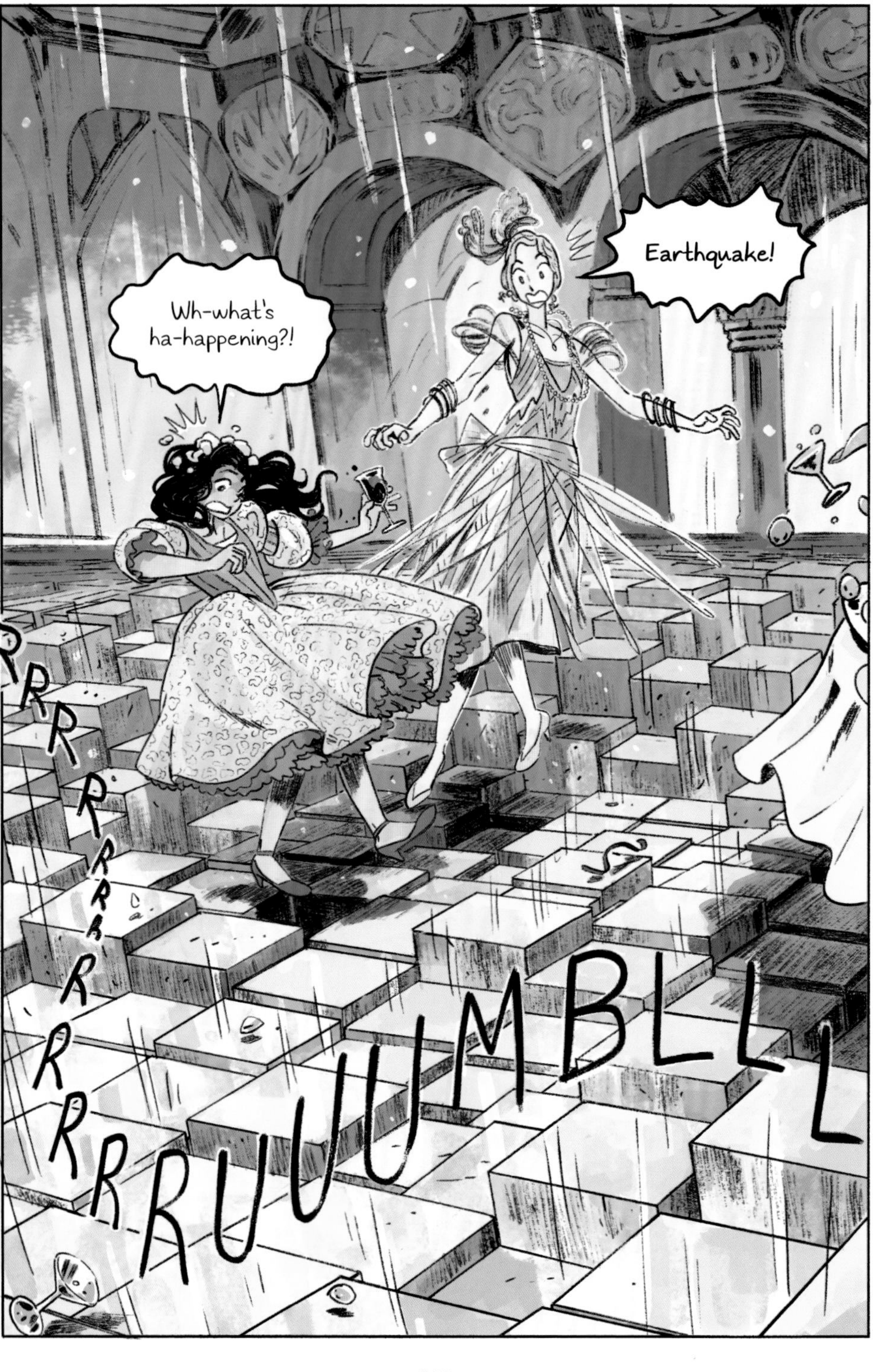
Wh-what's ha-happening?!
Earthquake!
RRRRRRRRRRRRRUUUMBLLL

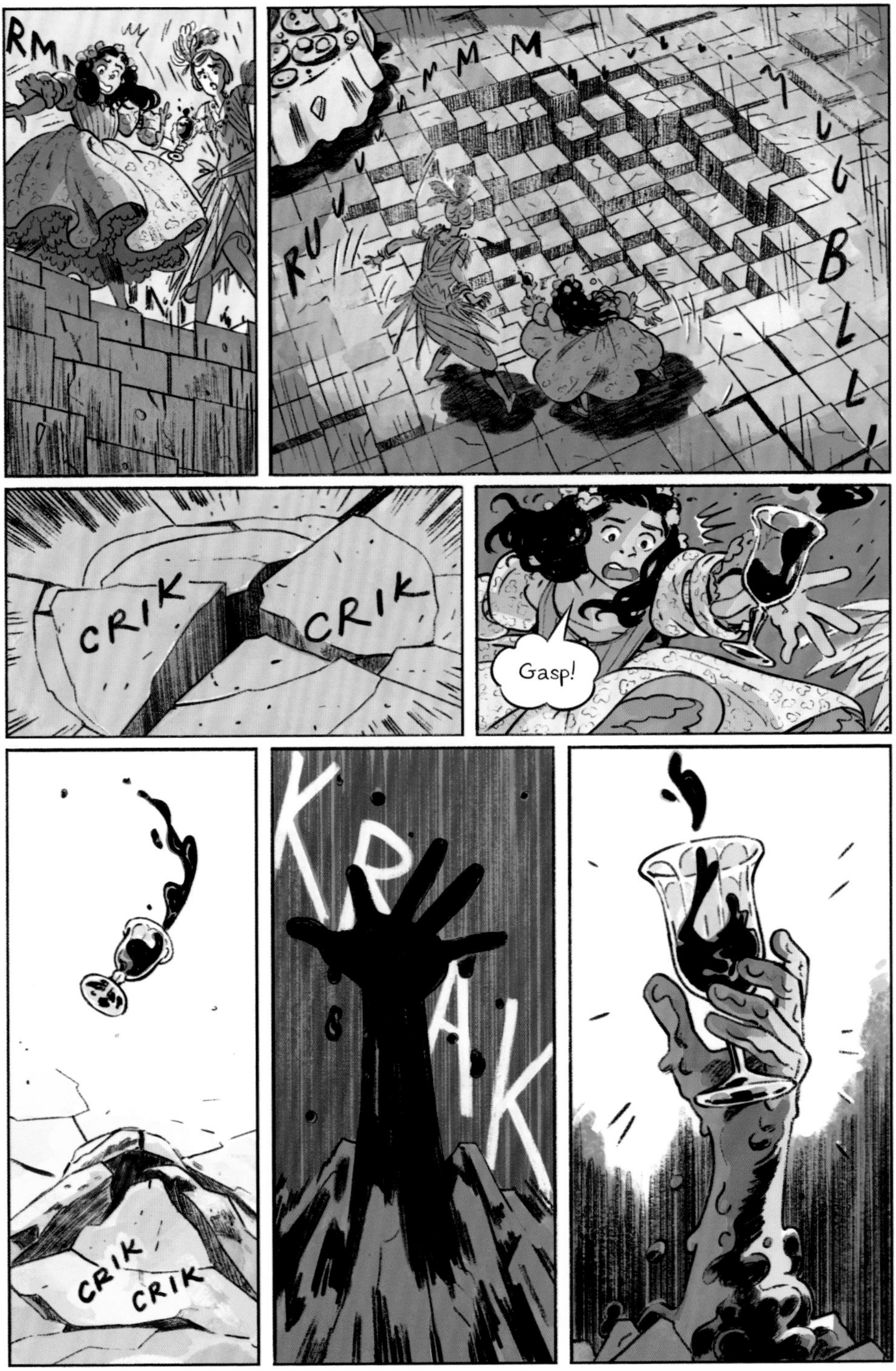
RM
RUUUNMMM
UUBLLL
CRIK
CRIK
Gasp!
CRIK
CRIK
KRAK

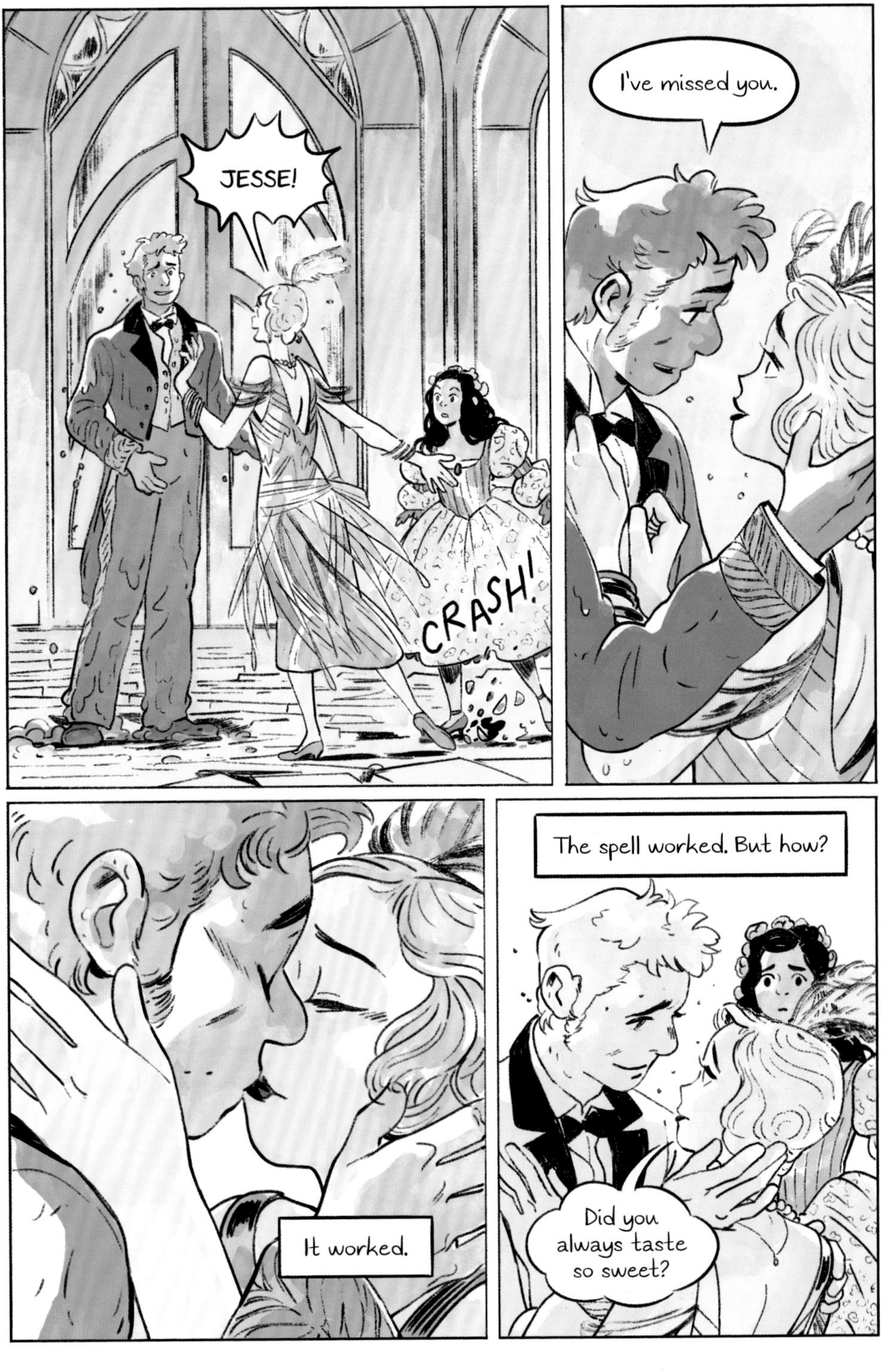
JESSE!
CRASH!
I've missed you.
It worked.
The spell worked. But how?
Did you always taste so sweet?

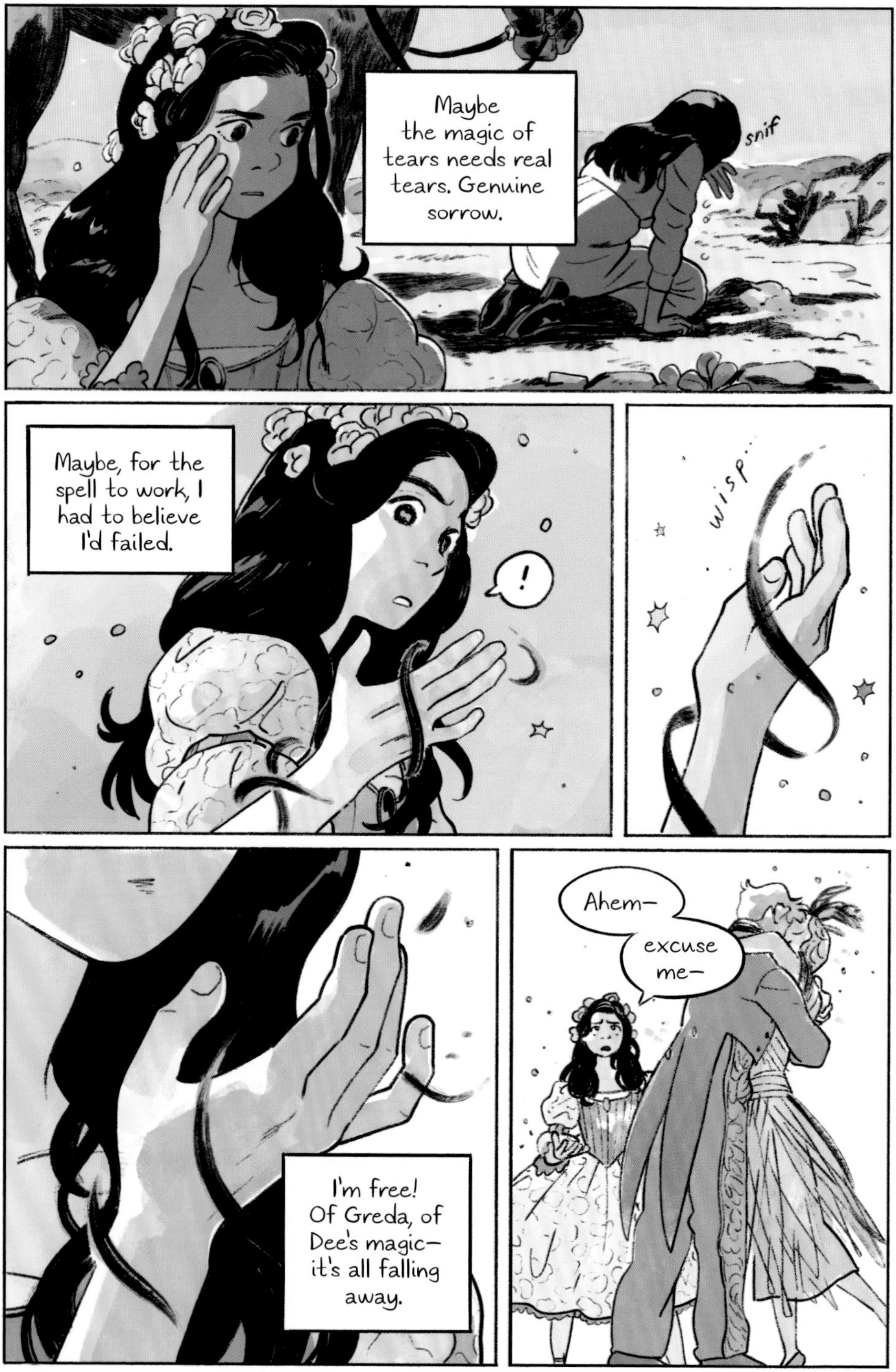
Maybe the magic of tears needs real tears. Genuine sorrow.
snif
Maybe, for the spell to work, I had to believe I'd failed.
!
wisp...
I'm free! Of Greda, of Dee's magic— it's all falling away.
Ahem—
excuse me—

Chapter Twelve

About Time

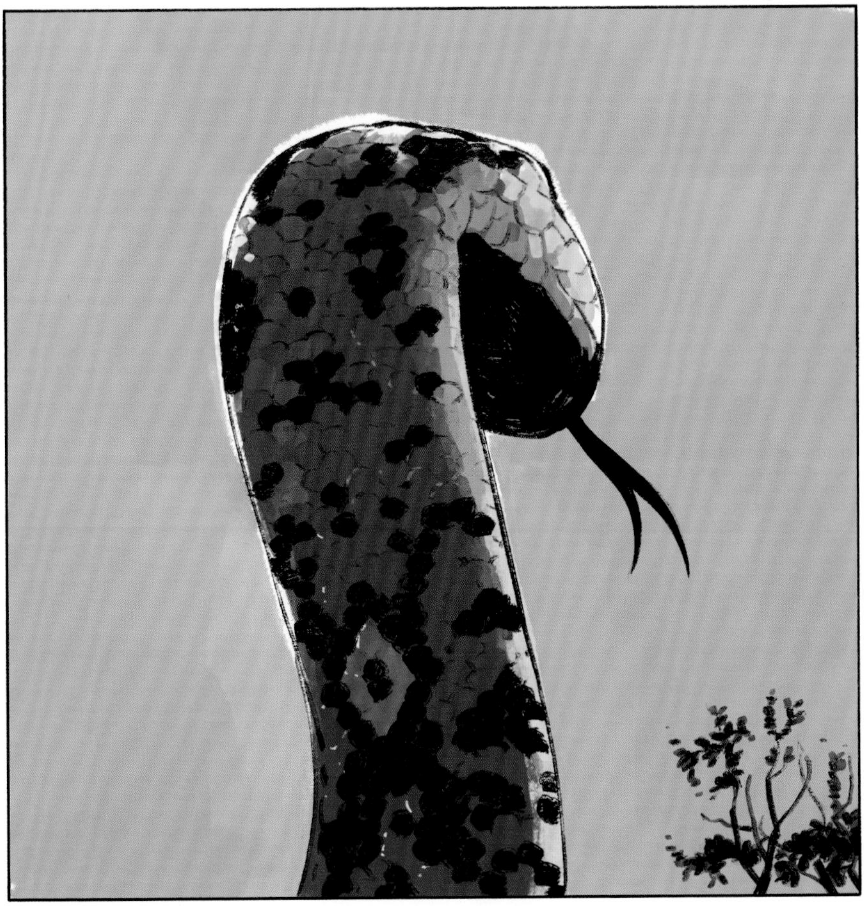

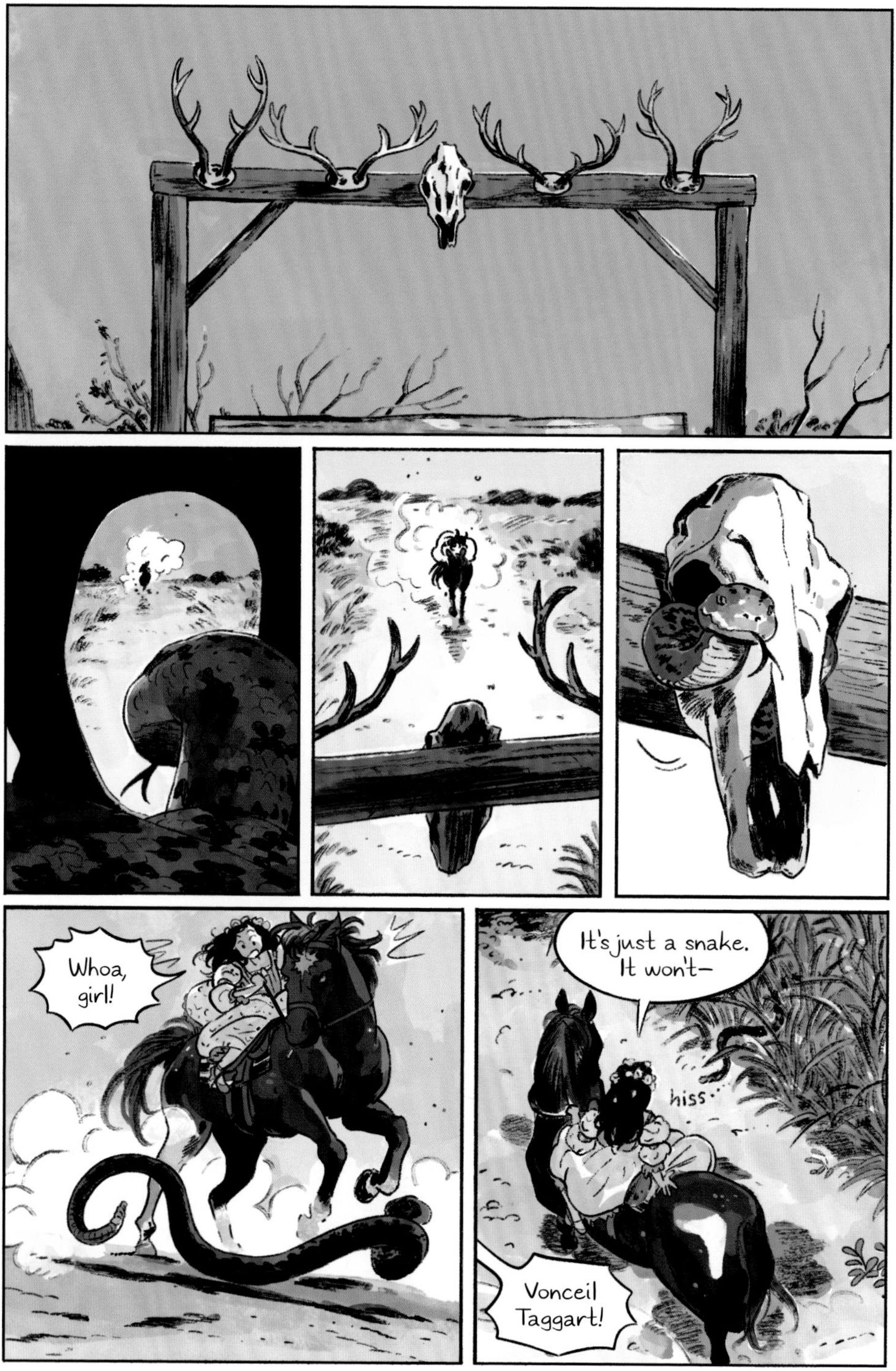
Whoa,
girl!
It's just a snake.
It won't—
hiss
Vonceil
Taggart!

Epilogue

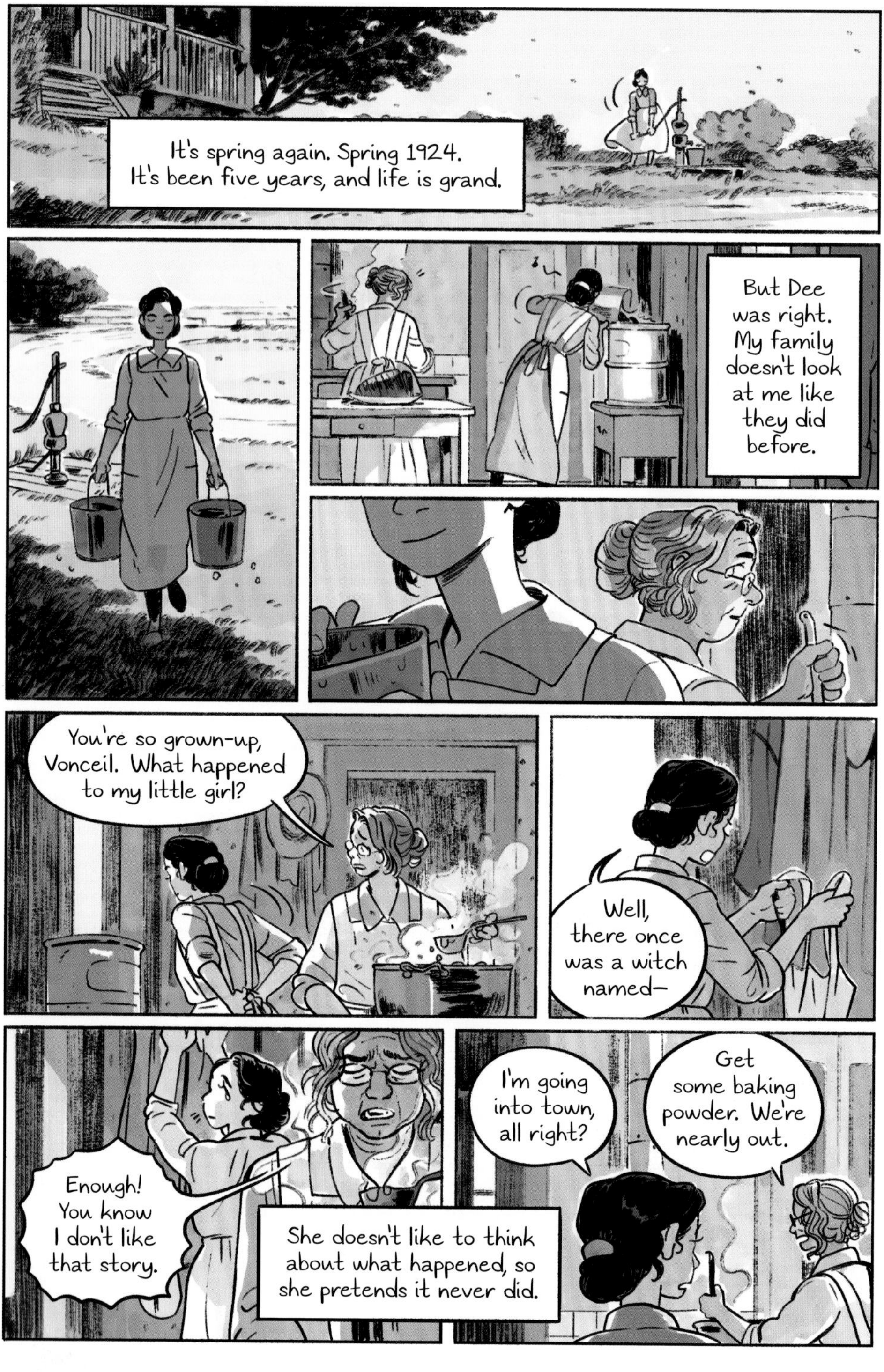
It's spring again. Spring 1924.
It's been five years, and life is grand.
But Dee was right. My family doesn't look at me like they did before.
You're so grown-up, Vonceil. What happened to my little girl?
Well, there once was a witch named—
Enough! You know I don't like that story.
She doesn't like to think about what happened, so she pretends it never did.
I'm going into town, all right?
Get some baking powder. We're nearly out.

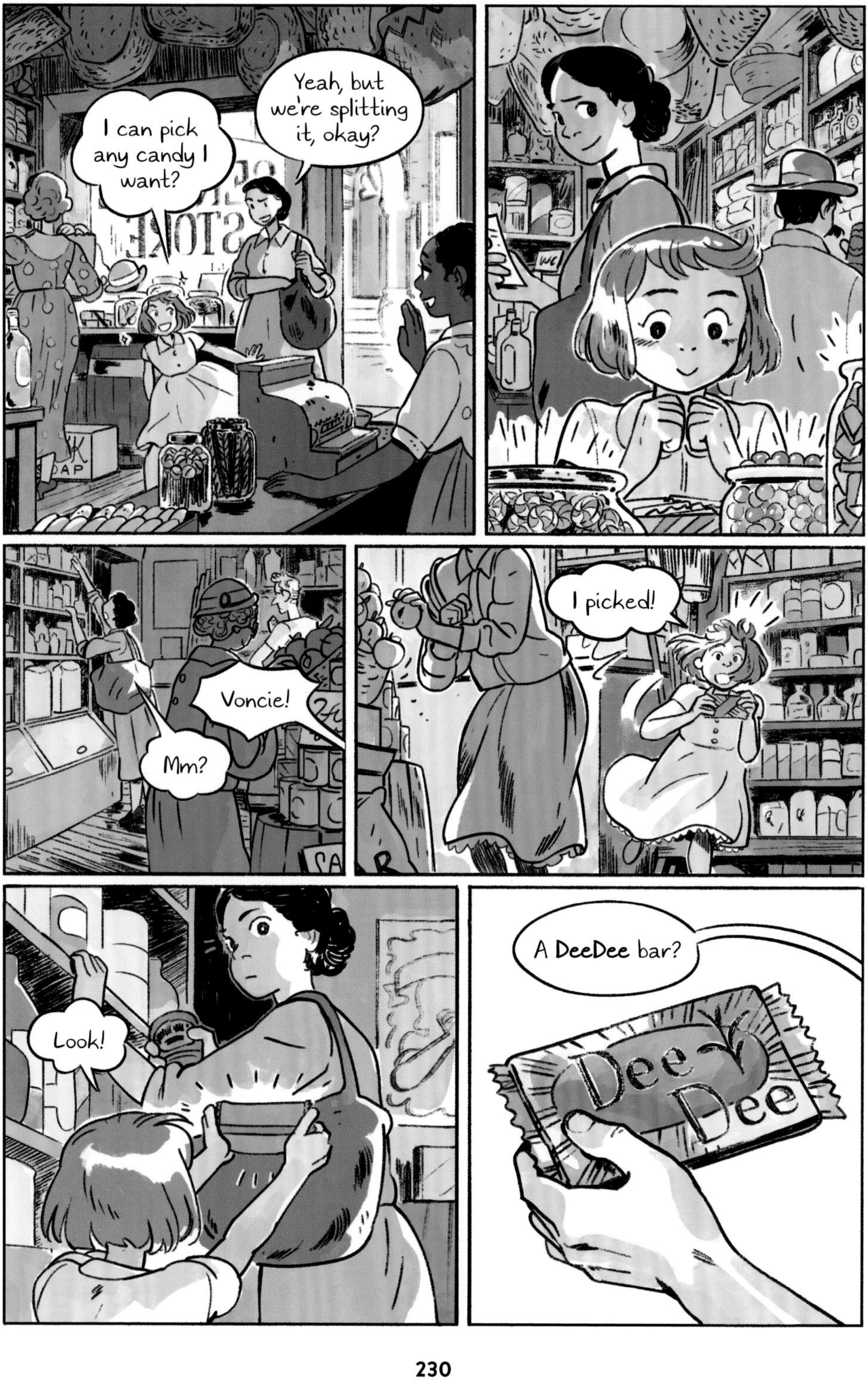
I can pick any candy I want?
Yeah, but we're splitting it, okay?
Voncie!
Mm?
I picked!
Look!
A DeeDee bar?
Dee Dee

The second bean—the spark of life—Dee wanted it for her.

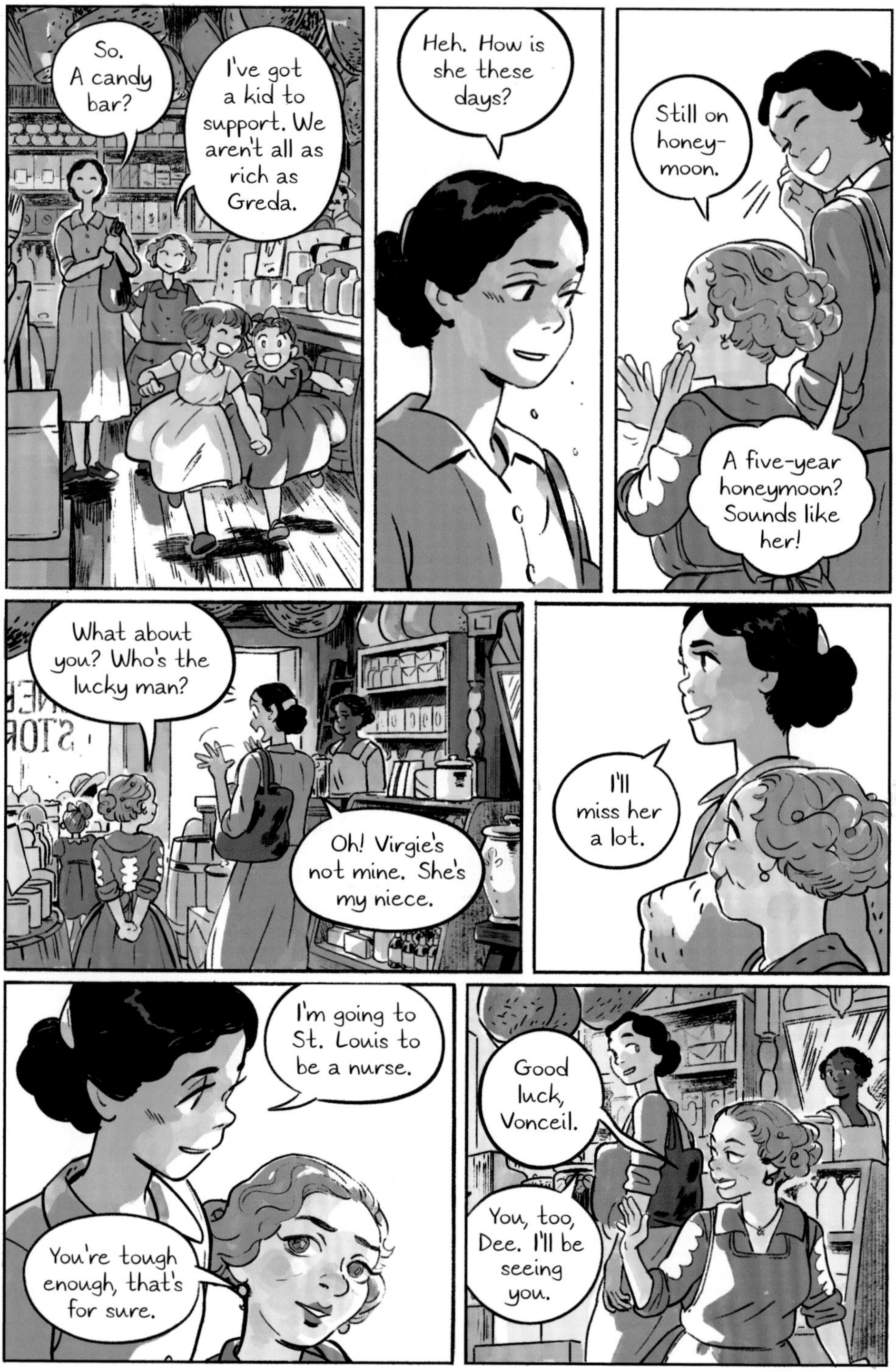
So. A candy bar?
I've got a kid to support. We aren't all as rich as Greda.
Heh. How is she these days?
Still on honey-moon.
A five-year honeymoon? Sounds like her!
What about you? Who's the lucky man?
Oh! Virgie's not mine. She's my niece.
I'll miss her a lot.
I'm going to St. Louis to be a nurse.
You're tough enough, that's for sure.
Good luck, Vonceil.
You, too, Dee. I'll be seeing you.

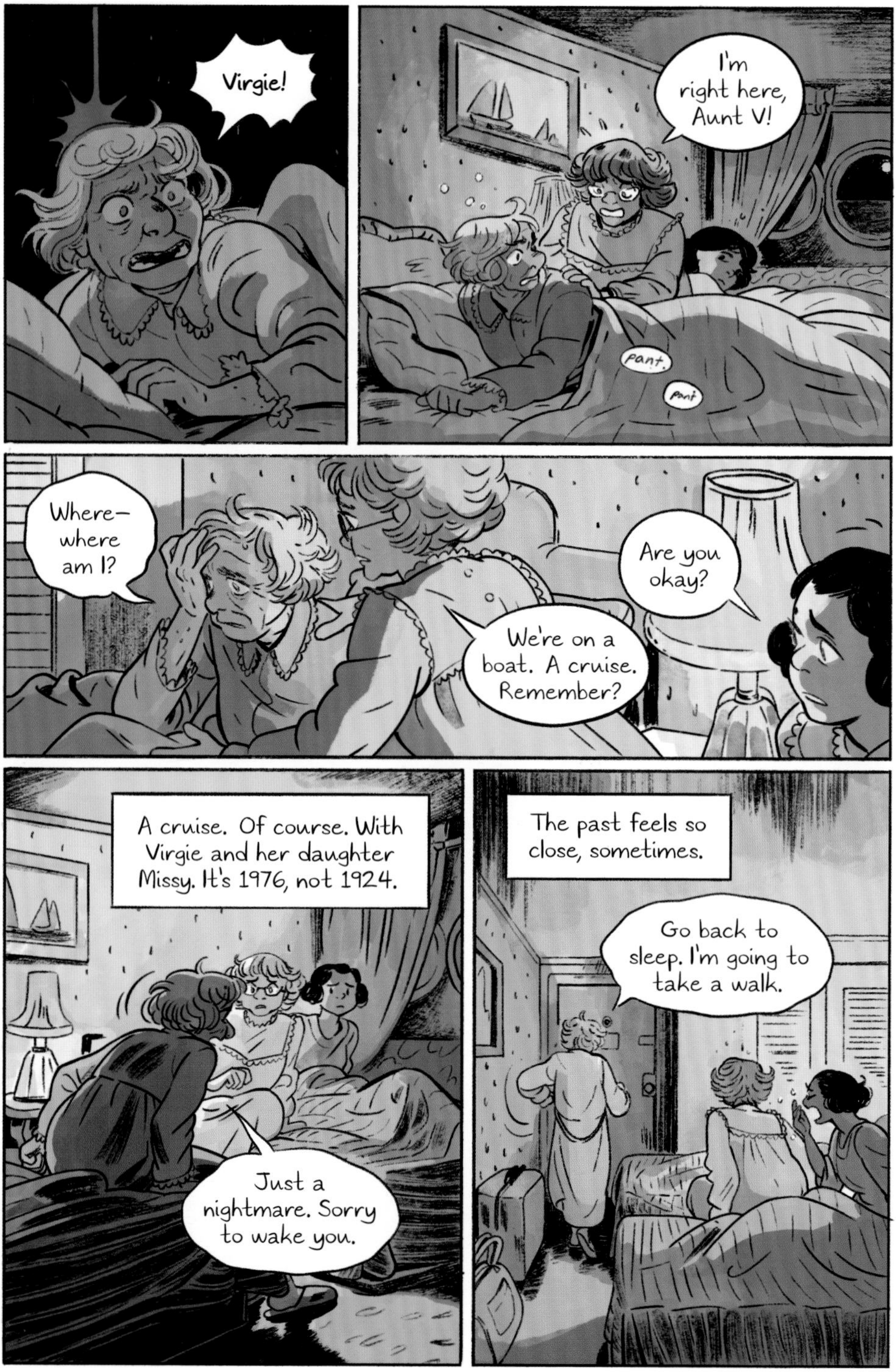
Virgie!
I'm right here, Aunt V!
pant
pant
Where— where am I?
We're on a boat. A cruise. Remember?
Are you okay?
A cruise. Of course. With Virgie and her daughter Missy. It's 1976, not 1924.
Just a nightmare. Sorry to wake you.
The past feels so close, sometimes.
Go back to sleep. I'm going to take a walk.

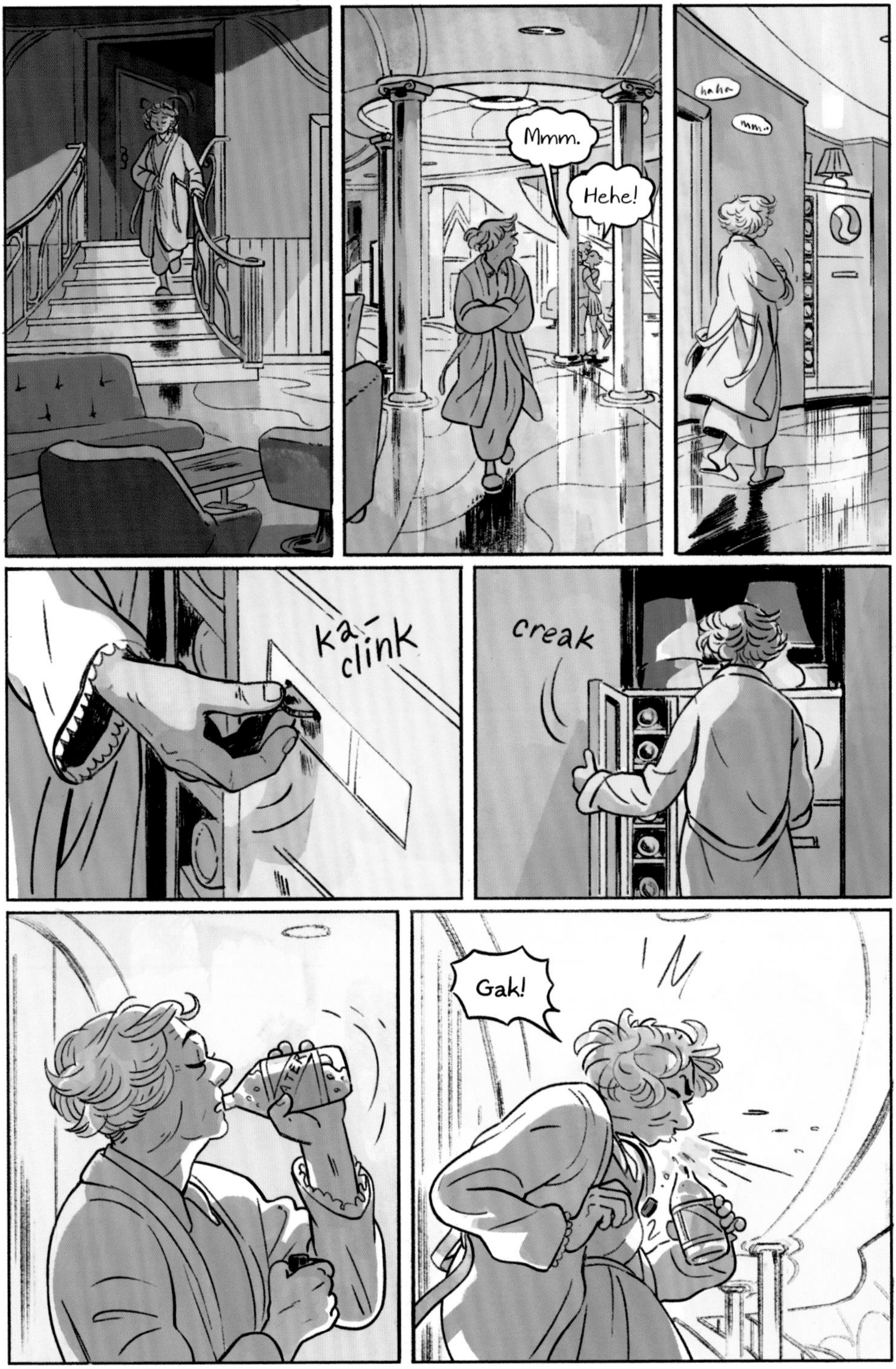
Mmm.
Hehe!
haha
mm..
ka-clink
creak
Gak!

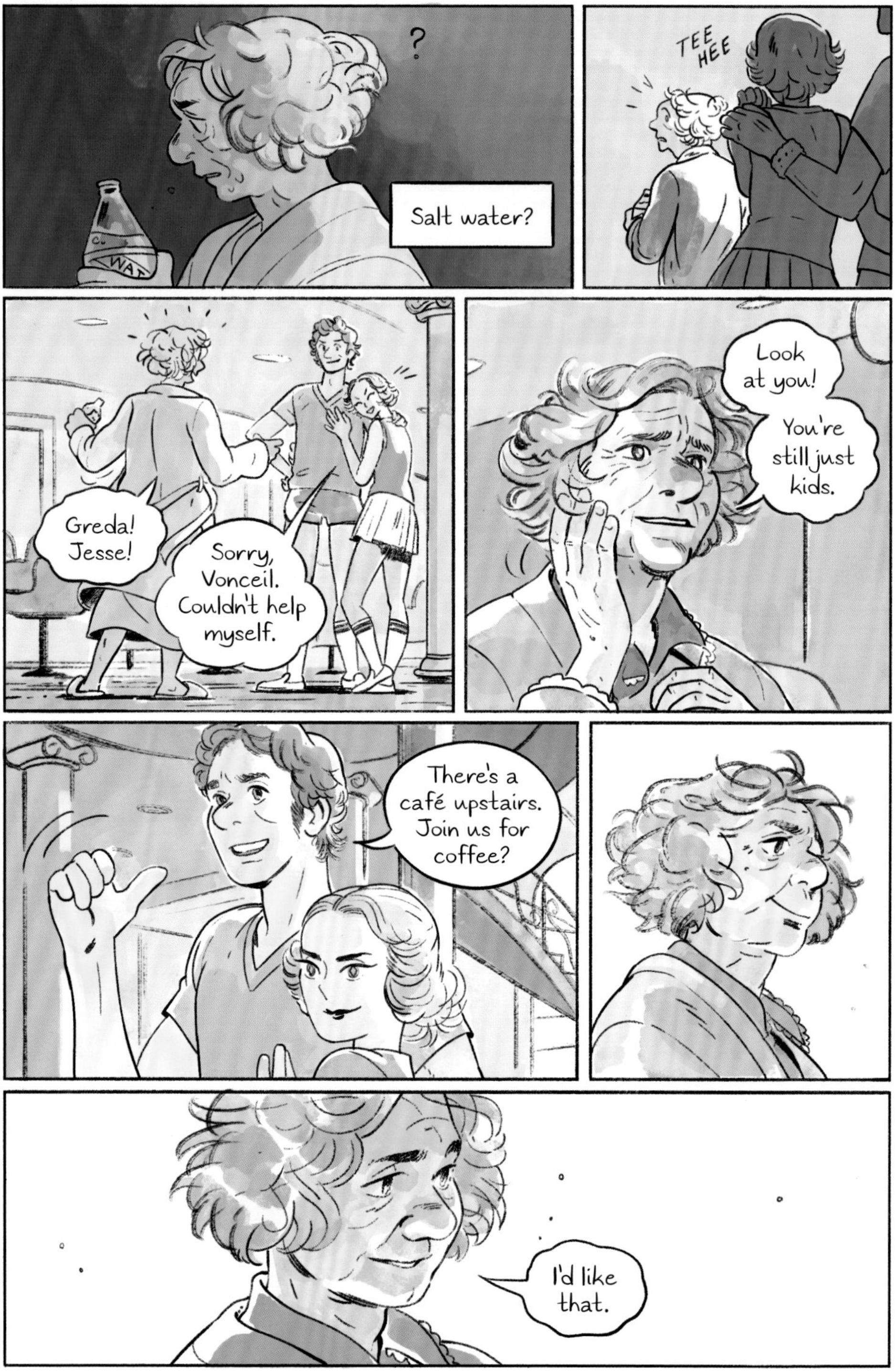
?
Salt water?
TEE HEE
Greda! Jesse!
Sorry, Vonceil. Couldn't help myself.
Look at you!
You're still just kids.
There's a café upstairs. Join us for coffee?
I'd like that.

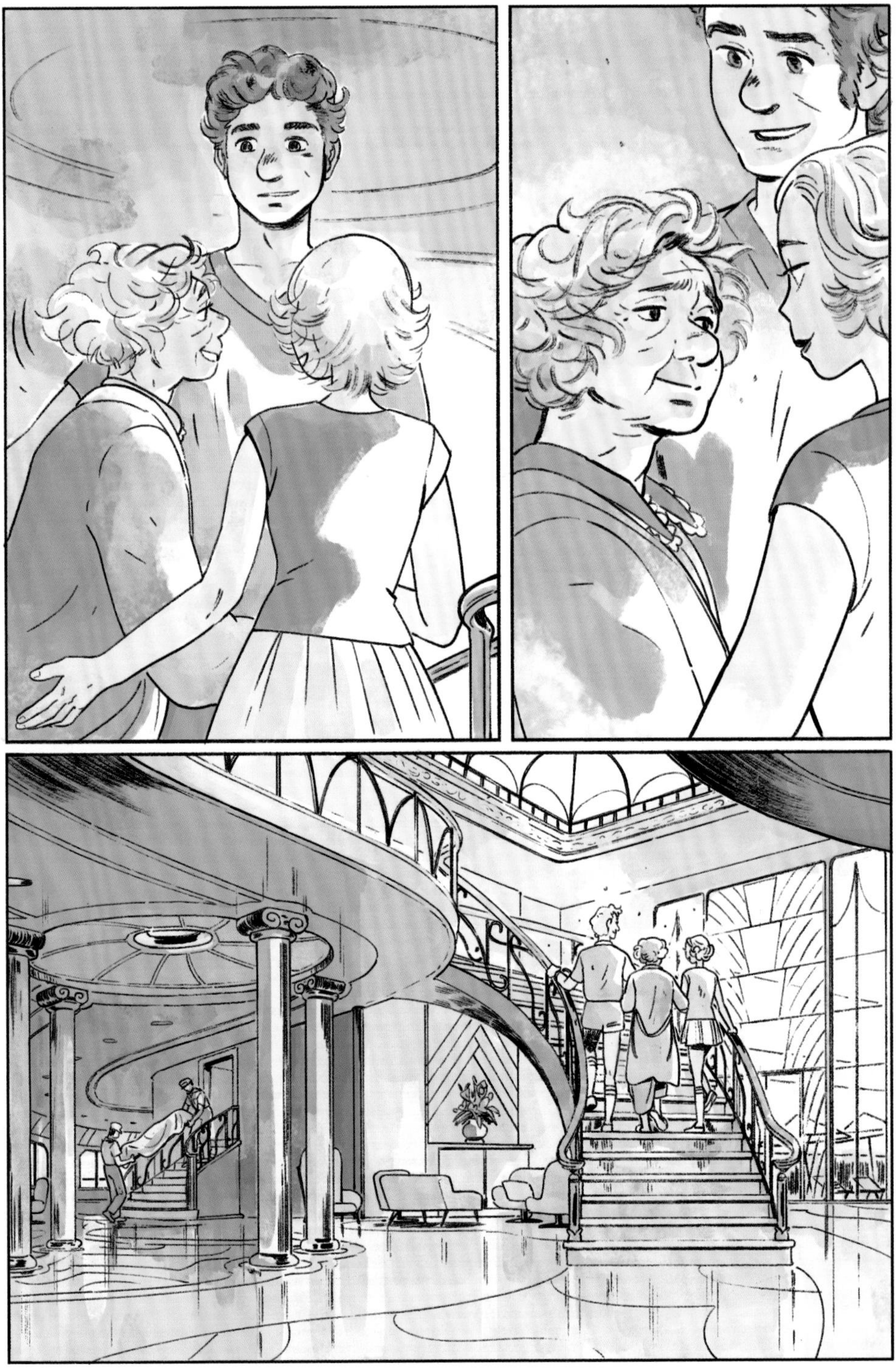

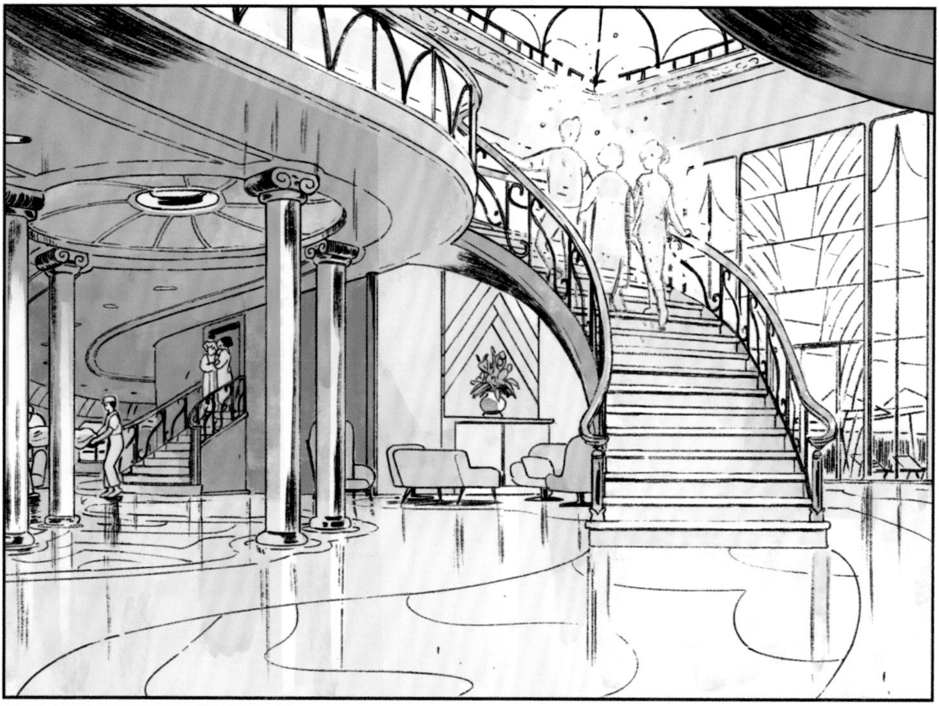

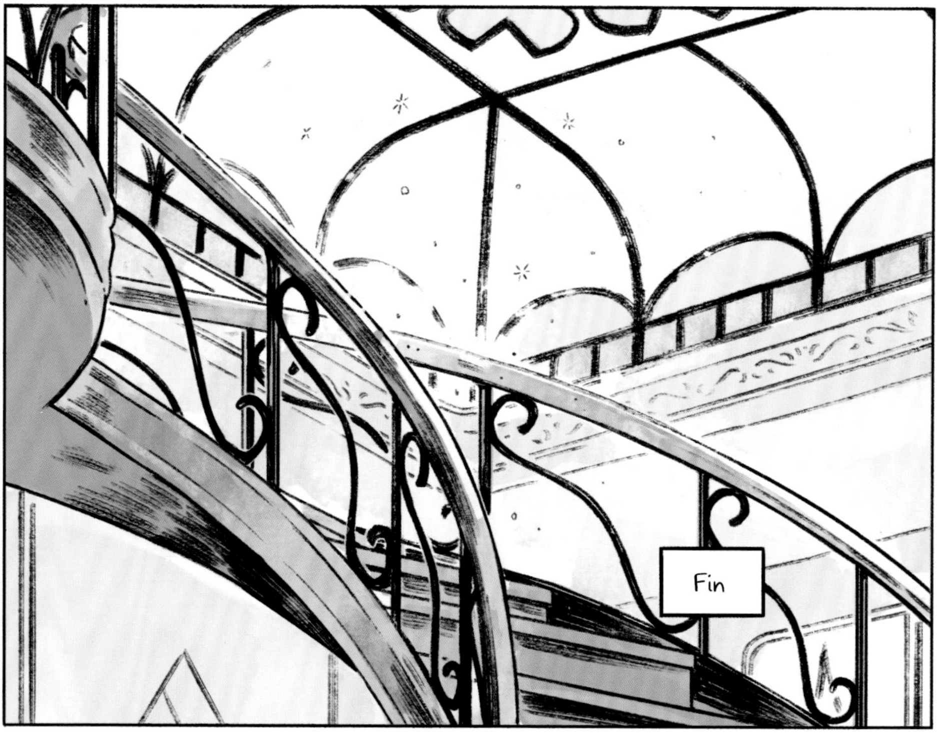
Fin